LORNA DOONE

Lorna Doone

BY

R. D. BLACKMORE

ADAPTED BY
HENRY I. CHRIST

Head of English Department
Andrew Jackson High School
Queens, New York

AND

JEROME CARLIN

Reading Counselor
George Westinghouse Vocational High School
Brooklyn, New York

J. J. LITTLE & IVES CO., INC. • NEW YORK

Contents

CONTENTS

LORNA DOONE

Chapter One

John Introduces Himself

If anybody cares to read a simple tale told simply, I John Ridd, farmer of Exmoor in the southwest of England, have seen and had a share in some exciting events in this neighborhood. I will try to set them down in order.

My father, John Ridd the elder, was well to do, owner of the best and largest of the three farms into which our township is divided. Being a great admirer of learning and well able to write his name, he sent me, his only son, to be schooled at Tiverton in Devon county. Here, by the time I was twelve years old, I had risen into the upper school.

On the 29th of November, 1673, the very day when I was twelve years old, we came out of school at five o'clock as was usual. After fun and chatter, several of us were leaning against the iron bars of a gate, looking out on the road. Though there was plenty of room for all of us, a certain boy leaning up against me would not allow my elbow room and struck me in the stomach. I resented this so much that I struck him in the face without stopping to think. Upon this he put his head down and butted me so violently in the middle of my jacket that he knocked the wind out of me.

Before I came to myself again, the boys had decided that we should move to the "Ironing Box," as the triangle of lawn was called where our fights were usually held. But suddenly a horse and rider leading a pony appeared on the road.

"Please," said the red-faced rider, "can you tell me where John Ridd is?"

"Here he is," answered a sharp little chap, and the boys pointed to me.

"Oh, John Fry," I cried as I recognized our hired man, "what's the use of coming now? The holidays don't begin for two weeks yet. To think of your not knowing that!"

"I know that, Master John. I guess every one of us knows that, even if we don't go to school as you do."

He checked himself suddenly, and frightened me. I knew John Fry's way so well.

"And Father—oh, how is Father?" I pushed the boys right and left as I said it. "John, is Father up in town? He always used to come for me, and let nobody else do it."

"Your father is at the crooked post on the other side of the meadow. He couldn't leave his work."

John looked at the horse's ears as he said it. Being familiar with John Fry's ways, I knew that it was a lie. And my heart fell, like a lump of lead. I leaned back on the gate and longed no more to fight anybody. But the boys would not let me out of it.

"Take coward's blow, Jack Ridd," cried half a dozen little boys, shoving my opponent Bob Snell forward to do it.

I looked up to John Fry. "Shall I fight, John? I wish you hadn't come."

"I think you had better fight, John Ridd," he answered in a whisper through the gate. "There's a lot of fighting ahead of you. It's best to begin now."

I felt a certain responsibility to maintain, in the presence of John Fry, the manliness of the Ridd family and the honor of Exmoor. I wondered how Bob Snell felt. It's very likely he thought nothing of it, for he often got into fights. But I felt my heart go up and down, as the boys came round to strip me. I dreaded being beaten. I blew hot upon my knuckles.

"Come now, shake hands," cried a big boy, jumping with sheer joy at the sight. "Shake hands, you little devils. Be good sports."

Bob took me by the hand, gazed at me disdainfully, and then struck me painfully on the face before I could get my hands up. I replied with all the strength I could master, and the battle began in a serious style. We paid no heed to anything else, being in the midst of swinging. All I know is that I went to my corner at the end of the round with hard lumps in my chest.

"Finish him off, Bob," cried a big boy who had eaten some of my candy that afternoon. "Finish him off, neck and crop. He deserves it for standing up to a man like you."

But I was not to be finished off even though nothing held except my legs. I fought the next round more carefully, recalling some of the things I'd been taught. During this round John Fry was prowling about, asking the boys what they thought of it and whether I was likely to be killed. However, finding that I had already fought about sixty battles, he slid up to me and whispered, "Don't come back to Exmoor if you lose!"

With that it was all up with me. A simmering buzzed in my brain. At once I set both fists again. Either Bob Snell should kill me, or I would conquer Bob Snell. So I went in again with my courage up and Bob came smiling for victory, and I hated him for smiling. He let go at me with his left hand, and I gave him my right between his eyes. I feared him not and spared him not. My breath came again, and my heart stood cool. I knew that I would die rather than shame my birthplace. What happened I'm not sure of. But when the fight was over, I helped put Bob Snell to bed.

Chapter Two

The War-Path of the Doones

From Tiverton to my home town of Oare is a very long and unpleasant journey. On the way John Fry refused to say any more about his coming for me and told me what I feared were lies about Father's good health, but I hoped for the best, as all boys will, especially after a victory.

We dined at Dulverton upon the rarest and choicest food I
ever did taste. Even now, at my time of life, it gives me appetite
to think of it. When we had eaten, I went to wash at the pump,
being a lover of soap and water. While I was running the water
over all my head, shoulders, and arms, a lady's maid came out.
I was bashful, but she spoke to me with an Italian accent, "Good
little boy, come here to me. How far is it to Wash. . . . Wash—"

"To Watchett, likely you mean, madam. Oh, a very long way,
and the roads are as soft as the road to Oare. That is where I live
—at Oare," I told her proudly.

"Ah, I shall remember. Perhaps some day I shall come to visit
you. But now, make the pump flow, my dear, and give me some
water."

I pumped very heartily. When the water suited her, she filled
the glass and wanted to kiss me. But I was very shy; so I ducked
under the pump-handle and she knocked her chin on the knob
of it. At this several of the stable keepers came out and asked
whether they would do as well! Disdaining to reply, she left
with dignity to return to her mistress.

Travelers going to Watchett and those going to Oare must ride
out of town together until they reach the fork. So it happened
that on our way from Dulverton to Oare John Fry and I came
upon a great coach and six horses trudging very slowly. In the
front seat of the coach, which was half-way open, sat the foreign
lady who had met me at the pump and tried to kiss me. By her
side was a little girl, dark-haired and very wonderful. Bashful
as I was, I could not look at her for two glances, nor did she look
at me once, being such a little child and busy watching the
hedges.

In the rear of the coach sat a handsome lady with a lively little
boy at her side. The young lad took a liking to my pony and
called his mother's attention to both of us. I took off my cap to
her and she put up her hand and kissed it to me. But then the
lady's maid, who had been busy with little Mistress Dark-Eyes,
looked around and saw me. I was about to wave to her at a
distance, but she looked at me as though she never wanted to

see me again, evidently considering me responsible for her embarrassment at the pump. I was so startled that I dug my pony with the muscles of my legs. My mount being fresh from the stable started off suddenly, so that I could do no more than tip my cap to the beautiful lady. We saw no more of them after that.

The fog came down on the moors as thick as I had ever seen it, and there was no sound to guide us. Soon it was too dark to see even the stubby trees that stood here and there. John Fry was bowing forward with sleep upon his saddle until I could no longer see the frizzle of wet upon his beard.

"Mercy of God! Where are we now?" said John Fry, waking suddenly. "Listen!"

We drew our horses up and listened through the thickness of the air, and with our hands laid to our ears. At first there was nothing to hear except the panting of the horses and the trickle of the drops from our clothing. Then there came a very low and mournful noise. Three times it came and went again.

"Hold your tongue, lad," John said sharply. "We're near the Doone road now. If they are abroad tonight, we'll have to crawl along, boy."

I knew at once what he meant—those bloody Doones of Bagworthy, the awe of all Devon and Somerset counties, outlaws, traitors, murderers.

"But, John," I whispered warily, moving close to him, "dear John, you don't think they will see us in such a fog as this?"

"God never made fog they can't see through," he whispered in answer, fearfully. "Go easy, lad, if you wish ever to see your mother again."

I was inclined, in the manner of boys, to make a run of the danger and cross the Doone road at full speed, to rush for it and be done with it. But even then I wondered why he talked of my mother so, and said not a word of Father. We rode very carefully, listening all the while. We were coming near the crest of a small hill when I heard something and caught John's arm. It was the sound of horses' feet knocking up through splashy ground, then a grunting of weary men.

"Goodness' sake, John, slip off the pony and let her go where she will."

As John Fry whispered, so I did, for he was off his horse by this time. The two animals were too tired to go far and began to crop the grass, sniffing louder than they should have. I crept to John's side very softly with the bridle on my arm.

"Let go the bridle; let go, lad! Pray that they take them for forest-ponies, or they'll send a bullet through us."

I saw what he meant and let the bridle go, for now the mist was rolling off. We were against the sky-line to the dark procession below us. Then just as the first horseman passed, scarcely twenty yards below us, a puff of wind came up the glen rolling the fog before us.

I could keep still no longer, but wriggled away from John's arm until I was only twenty feet above the heads of the riders. They were heavy men, large of stature, reckless how they carried their guns or rode their horses. Plunder was heaped behind their saddles. I counted more than thirty pass. Some had carcasses of sheep swinging with their skins on. Others had deer. One had a child flung across his saddle-bow. She hung head downward, whether dead or alive I knew not. They had seized her, no doubt, for the sake of the dress which shone as if with gold and jewels.

It touched me so to see that child that in my foolish rage I stood up and shouted to them, raving madly. Two of the men turned around. One aimed his gun at me, but the other said it was an elf and urged him to save his powder. Little they knew that the elf before them would some day destroy their castle. And little I knew that the little girl they carried would some day be the most important person in my life.

John Fry now came up to me cross and stiff.

"Small thanks to you, John, that my new wife isn't a widow. It would serve you right if I threw you down into the Doone road."

And that was all he had to say instead of thanking God! But I said nothing. The horses were glad to see us and anxious to be away.

My father never came to meet us, although the dogs made such a noise he should have heard us. I looked at the gateposts in the dark, because they were tall, like Father, and then at the door of the harness-room where he used to smoke his pipe and sing. Then I thought he had guests perhaps.

Woe is me! How I knew the truth about Father I cannot tell. By and by, the sound of women's weeping came down to me. Although they were my dearest loves, I could not bear to look at them.

Chapter Three

A Rash Visit

My dear father had been killed by the Doones of Bagworthy, while riding home from Porlock market on Saturday evening. With him were six brother-farmers. The robbers had no grudge against him, for he had never opposed them. The seven farmers were jogging along, singing hymns to keep their courage up, when suddenly a horseman stopped in the starlight in front of them. By dress and arms they knew him a Doone, as well as by his size and stature.

Father had always thought that any man should strike a blow for his own possessions. So, while his companions took off their hats, he set his stick above his head and rode at the Doone robber. With a trick of his horse the wild outlaw escaped the sudden rush although he must have been amazed that any dared resist him. As if despising this defense, the robber advanced to plunder the other farmers. Father, trying to turn his horse around to help them, was surrounded by a dozen men. Neverthe-

less he struck furiously, and since he was powerful and strong
they had no easy job with him. With the play of his wrist he
struck three or four over their heads until the rest drew their
horses away. But a man beyond the range of Father's stick was
crouching with a long gun set to his shoulder. He caught poor
Father against the sky, and I cannot tell the rest of it. His horse
came home bloody, and Father was found in the morning dead
on the moor. Whether this was an honest fight let God judge
between the Doones and me.

Thus, Mother found herself a widow and her children father-
less. There were only three of us children, none of us old enough
to be useful yet. I was the eldest; next came sister Annie, two
years younger, and then little Eliza.

Now before I got home and found my sad loss, Mother had
done a strange thing, which made all the neighbors say she
must be mad. Monday morning, while her husband still lay un-
buried, she put on a hood and cloak and set off on foot for the
Doone-gate without telling anyone. In the early afternoon she
came to the hollow and barren entrance, where in truth there
was no gate, only darkness to go through. When she requested
the guards who stood there to take her to their master, they
placed a cloth over her eyes and led her in by the hand.

At the end of a rough road they uncovered her eyes and she
could scarcely believe what she saw. She stood at the head of a
deep green valley carved from the mountains in a perfect oval,
with sheer rock standing round it eighty or a hundred feet high.
By her side a little river glided out from underground and fell
into the valley. Further down on either bank were square stone
houses. Deep in the quiet valley there, away from noise and
violence, any man would have considered them homes of sim-
plicity and innocence. Yet every house there was the home of
murder!

Two men led my mother down a steep stairway to the captain's
house. There they left her at the door, trembling yet determined
to speak her mind. Now, after all, what right had she, a common
farmer's widow, to object to the Doones, who were of such high

birth? But she remembered her husband, how good he was, and
the tears were in her eyes.

A tall old man, Sir Ensor Doone, came out. With his white
locks moving upon his coat he stopped and looked down at my
mother. She could not help but curtsy to him under the fixed
gaze of his black eyes.

"Good woman, you are not a Doone? Who has brought you
here?"

In the depth of her grief Mother cried out, "Traitors! Cut-
throats! Cowards! Give me back my husband!" She could not say
more because her heart was filled with grief.

"Madam," said Sir Ensor Doone—for he was born a gentleman,
although a very bad one—"I beg your pardon. If we have your
husband prisoner, he shall go free without ransom."

"Sir," said my mother, "please let me cry a bit."

He stood away and seemed to know that they had killed her
husband. Having felt grief himself, he waited for her to begin
again.

"I would not," said Mother sobbing, "accuse any one unfairly,
Sir Ensor Doone, but I have lost the very best husband God ever
gave to a woman." Here Mother burst out crying again.

"This matter shall be seen to at once," the old man answered,
moved a little. "Madam, if any wrong has been done, trust the
honor of a Doone. Come inside and rest while I inquire. What
was your good husband's name?"

"John Ridd, sir, and there was not a finer or better man in
Somerset or Devon. He was coming home from Porlock market
with a new dress for me. . . . Oh, how good he was to me!"

"Madam, this is a serious matter," Sir Ensor Doone said gra-
ciously and with concern. "My boys are a little wild, I know.
Yet I cannot think that they would willingly harm any one. But
you do seem wronged. Send Counselor to me," he shouted from
the door of his house, and down the valley went the call, "Send
Counselor to Captain."

Counselor Doone came in, a square-built man of enormous
strength, with a long gray beard and great shaggy eyebrows.

"Counselor," said Sir Ensor Doone, "here is a lady who charges the Doones with having unjustly slain her husband."

"Murdered him! Murdered him!" cried my Mother, "if ever there was a murder. Oh sir, oh sir! you know it."

"What was his name?" asked the Counselor.

"John Ridd, a worthy man and a peaceful one, who didn't meddle with us. If any of our boys have been rough, they shall answer for it dearly. Yet I can scarcely believe it. Counselor, you are our record. Tell us the truth."

"Few words will be enough for this," he answered. "Four or five of our best behaved and most peaceful gentlemen rode into Porlock. They bought some household articles and rode home. When they drew bridle to rest, a robber of great size and strength rode into their midst to kill or terrify them. John Ridd, for it was he, had struck three of our men senseless when our brave and noble Carver beat him down with a mighty blow and saved the lives of our brethren. Despite all this we hoped Ridd's wound might not be serious or fatal."

At this tale of lies Mother was too amazed to do more than look at him. She turned suddenly on Sir Ensor and thought she caught a smile on his lips and a sense of quiet enjoyment.

"All the Doones are gentlemen," declared the old man gravely. "We are always glad to explain, madam, any mistake which the country people may make about us. We will not charge your poor husband with robbery. We will forgive him. Perhaps at that time of night he could not tell right from wrong or good from evil."

At this, Mother's head went round so she scarcely knew where she was. She knew that right was with her but she could see no way to prove it. She dried her tears in haste and went into the cold air. On the way home, when they had blindfolded her, someone thrust a heavy leather bag into her hand.

"Captain sends you this," he whispered. "Take it to the little ones."

But Mother let it fall in a heap and prayed so pitifully even the Doones felt sorry for her.

Chapter Four

The Doones of Bagworthy

Good folks who dwell in a lawful place may judge our land harshly unless the whole truth is set before them. Let me explain how and why it was the robbers came to such power in the midst of us. We would rather not have had it so, but is came upon us gently in the following manner.

In the year 1640, when England was rushing toward civil war, great estates in the north of England were suddenly taken away from their proprietors by order of the King. The owner of one such estate was Sir Ensor Doone, a gentleman of brisk intellect. Some say in the bitterness of that wrong he slew a noble of the Court whom he suspected of having had a hand in the loss of the estate. Others say that he defied King Charles the First himself in a manner beyond forgiveness. One thing at any rate is sure. Sir Ensor was made a criminal outlaw.

He asked assistance of many people, for in his days of good fortune he had been generous to all who asked help. But now all these gave him advice but nothing else, making him more bitter than ever.

In great despair he came to our part of the country where none knew him. Here in this rugged and desolate place he discovered a place which seemed almost to have been created for him, being easily defended and difficult to enter. For a while some of the farmers nearby brought him little presents—bacon, cider, mutton, or deer. But when the Doone family had been there awhile and still refused because of their noble blood, to plow the fertile valley, the farmers stopped offering food. It was then that the young Doones, who were growing up, began to take the things they would not ask for.

Perhaps their den might soon have been stormed if honest people had only agreed to do so when first these high-born robbers started plundering. But having respect for the Doones' high birth and pity for their misfortunes, the farmers at first did nothing more than grumble gently or even joke about it. After awhile they found the matter no cause for laughter, as violence and murder were added to robbery. Every woman clutched her child and every man turned pale at the very name of *Doone*—for the sons and grandsons of Sir Ensor were proud, wild, and brutal. They had so fortified themselves and so grown in numbers that nothing less than a troop of soldiers could have dared to enter their premises.

Among the Doones every one was a mighty man, straight and tall, able to lift at least four hundred pounds. If son or grandson of Sir Ensor Doone failed at the age of twenty, while standing on his naked feet, to touch with his forehead the top of Sir Ensor's door, and to fill the doorway with his shoulders, he was put out of the valley in disgrace. That doorway was over six feet high and nearly two feet wide! Yet no more than two of their following had ever failed of that test. Of course, I think nothing of that standard, for at twenty I was much larger, though even then not at my full strength. Still, the Doones were far beyond the average size of our neighborhood. In addition, they were excellent marksmen with a gun. Even a boy among them could put a bullet through a rabbit's head at eighty yards.

These were the murderers of my father. We buried him quietly. Annie was not allowed to come because she cried so terribly. Even little Eliza realized what it is to lose a father. As for me, about the rest of that winter I remember very little, being only a young boy then, but I resolved to practice firing with Father's great Spanish gun. As I became more and more skilled, I often looked off in the direction of the Doone Valley.

Chapter Five

Hard It Is to Climb

About our farm there are trees, bright green grass, and orchards full of contentment. A man can scarcely see our brook, though he hears it everywhere. About two miles below our farm the Lynn stream runs into the Bagworthy and makes a real river. There are plenty of fish all down this way. The further you go the larger they get having deeper grounds to feed in. Sometimes when Mother didn't need me in the summer, I came down here with Annie and caught a basketful of minnows and trout. Yet I had never been to that part of Bagworthy stream which runs through the Doone valley.

When I was turned fourteen years old, I resolved to set out to catch some fish. Since it was Valentine's Day and still cold, I didn't tell Annie but slipped away without anyone's seeing me. I took off my shoes and stockings and put them into a bag around my neck. Then I took a three-pronged fork firmly bound to a rod with cord, and a piece of canvas with a lump of bread inside it. I waded into the pebbly, icy water, trying to think how warm it was. For more than a mile down the stream I left scarcely a stone unturned looking for the small fishes we call loaches. When I had traveled unsuccessfully about two miles, I found a good stream flowing into our brook.

Now the rest of my life hung upon that moment. It seemed a sad business to go back now and tell Annie there were no loaches. Yet it was frightening to go where no man dared go, up the Bagworthy stream. However, after I had stopped to eat, my spirits rose and I resolved I'd not be a coward. So I put the bag round my neck again and started up the Bagworthy stream, toward the Doone Valley.

Here, although I found it dark and overgrown, I had great success with loaches, trouts, and minnows. Now if you have ever been fishing, you will not wonder that I was led on, forgetting all about danger. In answer to my shouts there was never any sound at all, except a rocky echo, or a scared bird hustling away.

Now the day was falling fast and the leafless trees seemed giants to me. Every moment the cold of the water got worse and worse until I nearly cried with it. Finally I came to an opening in the bushes where a great black pool lay in front of me, whitened with foam. Though I was a good swimmer, I had no desire to go over head and ears into this great pool, for I was weary and cold and wet. And the look of this black pit would have been enough to stop one from diving into it even on a hot summer's day with sunshine on the water—if the sun ever shone there. As it was I drew back, shuddering at the peculiar motion of the water around whose deep black center spun whirling white foam.

Soon I saw the reason, for skirting the edges I came to an amazing sight. I stood at the foot of a long slide of water, rushing smoothly down for a hundred yards or more, fenced in on either side by a straight shining cliff. There was no siderail, nor any place to walk upon, only the channel two yards wide and the surrounding crags shutting out the evening.

Though the look of this place scared me very greatly, I said to myself, "John Ridd, these trees and pools and lonesome rocks are making a coward of you." But there was nearly as much trouble going backward as forward, for the journey back was roundabout. Then, too, I had a great desire to know what was at the top of that water. So I started up.

I let my feet into the dip and rush of the torrent, but my legs were knocked from under me in a moment and I had no time to cry out. Just as I thought all was over, my fork, praise God, stuck fast in the rock and I was washed up upon it. With this aid I gathered my legs back slowly, and thus I won a footing. Then I said to myself, "John Ridd, the sooner you get yourself out by the way you came, the better it will be for you." But to my great dismay I saw that I had no choice now but to climb somehow up that hill of water, or else be washed down into the whirlpool and drowned.

Having said the Lord's Prayer, I grasped the fork and steadied me with my left hand. With a sigh of despair I began my course up the fearful torrent. To me it seemed at least a half mile of sliding water above me, but in truth it was little more than an eighth as I found out later. It would have been a hard climb, even without the slippery slime on the bottom and the force of the river over it. Nevertheless my terror left me, now that I was face to face with the danger, and I set myself to do my best.

The water was only six to nine inches deep, and here and there I found a resting place, to hold on by the cliff and pant awhile. Gradually as I went on, a warmth of courage breathed into me, to think that perhaps no other had dared to try that pass before. I wondered what Mother would say to it.

How I went carefully, step by step, keeping my arms in front of me and never daring to straighten my knees is more than I can tell clearly or even like to think of. Only I must admit that the greatest peril of all was just where I saw no danger, where I came upon a patch of black weed not far from the summit.

Here I fell and might have broken my kneecap. The torrent got hold of my other leg while I was rubbing the bruised one. Then a cramp disabled me, so that for awhile I could only roar till my mouth was full of water and my body was sliding. But the fright of that brought me to again, and my elbow caught in a rockhole.

Now being in dreadful fear, because I was so near the top and hope was beating within me, I labored hard with both hands, going like a mill, and grunting at each motion. At last, the rush of forked water, where it first came over the lips of the fall, drove me into the middle. I stuck there with my toes on the slippery weed and the world was green and whirling before my eyes,

while I dared not look behind me. The thought of death lost
its horror, for then my legs would ache no more and my heart
would suffer no pain from my gasping breath. But it seemed a
pity, after fighting so long, to give in. Once more I fought toward the light. Suddenly I felt fresh air and fell into it headlong.

Chapter Six

John Meets Lorna

When I came to myself again, my hands were full of young grass
and a little girl kneeling at my side was rubbing my forehead
tenderly.

"Oh, I am so glad," she whispered softly, as I opened my eyes
and looked at her; "now you will try to be better, won't you?"

I had never heard so sweet a sound as her voice, nor seen anything so beautiful as the long black hair and large dark eyes
intent upon me, full of pity and wonder. I sat upright and was
much afraid to speak to her because of my country accent. But
she clapped her hands and danced around me as if I were a
great toy.

"What is your name?" she said. "And how did you come here,
and what are these wet things in the bag?"

"You had better let them alone," I said; "they are fish for my
mother, but I will give you some, if you like."

"Dear me, how much you think of them! Why, they are only
fish. But how your feet are bleeding! Oh, I must tie them up for
you. And no shoes nor stockings! Is your mother very poor,
poor boy?"

"No," I said indignantly; "we are rich enough to buy all this
great meadow. And here are my shoes and stockings."

"Why, they are quite as wet as your feet."

"I don't think much of that. I never saw anyone like you before. My name is John Ridd. What is your name?"

"Lorna Doone," she answered in a low voice, as if ashamed of it, "I thought you must have known it."

Then I stood up and touched her hand and tried to make her look at me, but she only turned away the more. Though she was young and surely free of any blame, the mention of her name seemed to make her feel guilty. I could not help looking at her

tenderly. Finally her blushes turned into tears and her tears to long, low sobs.

"Don't cry," I pleaded; "I am sure you have never done any harm. I will give you all my fish, Lorna, and catch some more for Mother. But don't be angry with me."

She looked at me so piteously that what did I do but kiss her. Then I felt my cheeks go burning red and I was sorry. For though she was not a haughty child, yet by birth she was far above me. I was a farmer's boy and she was a lady born. In spite of her being such a little girl, eight years old or so, she realized how I felt. She turned to the stream in a bashful manner and began to watch the water.

I was a bit hurt by her actions; so I took up all my things to go, making a great fuss to let her know I was leaving. But she did not call me back at all. Since I knew that to try to go down the way I came was certain death, I turned round and called back to her, "Lorna."

"Oh, I thought you were gone," she answered. "Why did you ever come here? Do you know what they would do to us if they found you here with me?"

"Beat us, I suppose, or me at least. They could never beat you."

"No, they would kill us both outright, and bury us here by the water."

"But why?"

"Because you have found the way up here by yourself and they never could believe it. Now, please go; oh, please go. They will kill us both in a moment. I like you very much and I will call you John Ridd, if you like; but please go! And some time you can come back to tell me how you are."

"But I tell you, Lorna, I like you very much, too, nearly as much as Annie and a great deal more than Lizzie. I must come back again tomorrow, and so must you. And I will bring you lots of things—apples, a thrush I caught with only one leg broken, and our dog has just had puppies . . ."

"Oh dear, they won't let me have a dog. There is not a dog in the valley. They say they are such noisy things. Hush!"

A shout came down the valley. My heart trembled. Lorna's face was changed from pleasant play to terror. She shrank to me and looked up so meekly that I at once made up my mind to save her, or to die with her. I longed for my gun.

"Come with me down the waterfall. I can carry you, and Mother will take care of you."

"No, no," she cried. "I will tell you what to do. They are only looking for me. Do you see that hole over there?"

She pointed to a little crack in the rock about fifty yards from us. In the fading twilight I could just see it.

"Yes, I see it, but they will see me crossing the grass to get there."

"Look! Look!" She could hardly speak. "There is a way out from the top of it. They would kill me if they knew I told it. Oh, here they come. I can see them."

The little girl turned white and she cried, "Oh dear! Oh dear!" And she began to sob aloud, being so young. But I drew her behind some shrubs. Here they could not see either of us from the upper valley. Luckily I had picked up my fish and my three-pronged fork.

Crouching there I saw a dozen fierce men come down on the other side of the water. They had no firearms. "Queen, queen!" they were shouting here and there. "Where has our little queen gone?"

"They always call me 'queen' and I am supposed to be queen by and by," Lorna whispered to me. "Oh, they are crossing by the timber there and then they are sure to see us."

"Wait," said I; "I have an idea what to do. I must get into the water and you must go to sleep."

"But how bitter cold it will be for you." However, there was no time to lose.

"Now mind you, never come again," she whispered over her shoulder, "even though I'll be here sometimes—oh, here they are!"

Hardly daring to peep I crept into the water and lay down bodily in it, with my head between two blocks of stone. The dusk was deepening between the hills, and a white mist lay on the river. All this time the Doones were shouting and swearing so that my heart quaked. But for Lorna's sake I knew I had to be brave and hide myself. She was lying beneath a rock thirty or forty yards from me, pretending to be asleep.

Soon one of the great rough men came round a corner upon her. He stopped and gazed awhile at her beauty and innocence.

Then he caught her up in his arms and kissed her. If I had brought my gun, I would have tried to shoot him.

"Here's our queen. Here's the captain's daughter," he shouted to his comrades, "fast asleep!" He set her upon his great square shoulder and marched away. This way of her going annoyed me. I leaped upright in the water and might have been spied by some of them but for their haste to get back to the feasting and drinking which were always going on in that valley.

Going up that darkened glen, little Lorna turned and waved a hand to me, and I waved back in the thick of the mist and the willows. I crept into a bush for warmth and rubbed my shivering legs on bark. Then as daylight disappeared I knew that now, if ever, was the time to get away. I managed to crawl to the crack in the cliff that Lorna had shown me.

In the dusk I had trouble finding the opening but finally succeeded. Once inside, however, I slipped and almost fell into a black pit of water. In my peril I heard a robin singing, and gathering comfort from his song I climbed safely through, hearing in the distance the cold greedy waves lapping against the hollow depths of darkness.

I can assure you that I scrambled to the mouth of that pit as though the devil were after me. Though already very large for my age, I had lost none of the nimbleness of boyhood and managed to climb down the side of the rocks out of the Doone valley. How I found my way home through the Bagworthy forest is more than I can remember.

When I got home, all were eating supper. Nobody could get from me where I had been all day, though all had been very much worried. I merely smiled knowingly and let their curiosity grow. To tell the truth, I was sorry for my boyish folly and vowed never to go back into that accursed valley. But I didn't keep that vow!

Chapter Seven

A Brave Rescue and a Rough Ride

One November evening when I was about fifteen and growing in strength very rapidly, my sister Annie and I had an adventure. A great deal of rain had fallen so that even the ducks in the court made a terrible quacking. The old white drake, the father of all, was marooned in the middle of the raging stream near our house, unable to leave the piece of wood he was perched on.

For a moment I could not help laughing, as he gave me a sorrowful look and a loud quack to second it. Annie was crying and wringing her hands, and I was about to rush into the water, although I did not like the look of it. Suddenly a man on horseback came round the corner.

"Ho, there," he cried; "get back, boy. The flood will carry you down like a straw. I will do it for you and no trouble."

With that he leaned forward and spoke to his beautiful strawberry mare. She arched up her neck, as though disliking the job, yet attempting it for him. She entered the flood, with her dainty forelegs sloped in front of her and her delicate ears pricked forward. By the pressure of his knees he kept her straight in the turbulent stream. She looked back and wondered at him, as the forces of the torrent grew stronger, but he urged her on—and on she went. Then as the rush of the water swept her away, she struck with her forefeet down the stream. Her rider leaned from his saddle in a manner which I never could have thought possible, and caught up the old drake with his left hand. In a moment all were carried downstream.

They landed safely some thirty or forty yards lower. The rider did not speak to us until he had explained to his mare.

"Sweetheart, I knew you could leap it," he said, as he patted her cheek, being on the ground by this time. The horse nudged up to him. "I had good reason, Winnie, for making you go through it." She answered him kindly with her soft eyes and sniffed at him very lovingly, and they understood each other.

"Well, young 'uns, what are you staring at?" He gave pretty Annie a chuck on the chin and looked at me.

"Your mare," said I, standing stoutly up, being a tall boy now, "I never saw such a beauty, sir. Will you let me have a ride on her?"

"Do you think you could ride her, lad? She will have no burden but mine. You could never ride her. I'd hate to kill you."

"Ride her!" I cried with the bravest scorn, for she looked so kind and gentle. "There never has been an Exmoor horse I couldn't tackle in half an hour. Only I never ride upon saddle. Take the saddle off her."

He looked at me, with a dry little whistle, and thrust his hands into his pockets, grinning. "Well, the ground is soft to fall upon after the rain. Come into the yard. I am your mother's cousin, Tom Faggus is my name, as everybody knows, and this is my young mare, Winnie."

What a fool I must have been not to know it at once! Tom Faggus, the great highwayman, and his famous strawberry mare! Already her fame was nearly as great as her master's. My longing to ride her grew tenfold, but I was afraid, too.

"Is she able to leap, sir? There is good take-off on this side of the brook."

"Good tumble-off, you mean, my boy. Well, there can be little harm to you. I am related to your family and know the thickness of your skulls."

A crowd of farm hands were running up now, and Tom felt the honor of the mare was at stake. He spoke very softly to the horse. "Not too hard, my dear. Let him gently down on the haystack. That'll be enough."

I was on her in a moment. She started at first so easily that I

egan to be overconfident. Then her master gave a shrill clear
whistle, and I knew I was in for it.

First she reared upright in the air, and then down on her fore-
eet. Finding me still sticking to her, she flew away with me
aster than ever I went before or after. She drove full-head at
he wall—"Oh, John, slip off," screamed Annie—then the mare
urned like lightning, grinding my left knee against the stones.
If you kill me, you shall die with me," I cried into her ears.

Next she took the court-yard gate at a leap, knocking my words
etween my teeth, and then over a hedge, while I lay on her
eck and wished I had never been born. All I knew of the speed
ve made was the frightful flash of her shoulders, and her mane
ke trees in a tempest. I felt the earth under us rushing away,
nd the air left far behind us, and my breath came and went,
nd I prayed to God.

All this while I clung to her crest and shoulders and was proud
f holding on so long, though sure of being beaten. At length in
er fury at feeling me still, she leaped the wide water-trough
ideways across, to and fro, till no breath was left in me. The
azel boughs scratched me and my back ached. Just when I
hought I could endure no more, there came a shrill whistle. The
are stopped as if with a bullet, then set off smoothly and si-
ntly back. I sat up again, but my strength was gone. Off I
umbled from her back into a haystack.

"Well done, lad," Mr. Faggus said, good-naturedly, only to be
terrupted by Mother, who had just come up.

"Foul shame to you, Tom Faggus," she cried wrathfully, "to
isk my boy's life as though it were worth no more than yours!"
s she scolded him, she checked to see whether I had been hurt.

"Look at his jacket, Mother!" cried Annie.

"What do I care for his clothes? Take heed and mind your
wn business," and Mother gave Annie a slap which sent her
winging up against Mr. Faggus. He caught her and kissed and
rotected her, and she looked at him with great tears in her soft
lue eyes. Mother was even more angry with Mr. Faggus be-

cause she had beaten Annie. And she scolded the men for letting
me ride the mare.

But Tom cleverly praised me for my spirit and compared me
to my father in fearlessness, thus causing Mother to forgive him.
Tom became a frequent visitor to our house after that day and a
great favorite with all of us.

Chapter Eight

Uncle Reuben Huckaback's Visit

One Christmas time some years later, my mother's uncle, Reuben
Huckaback, set out to visit us. Except for us he had no other
relatives but his little grand-daughter, Ruth Huckaback. It had
been settled between us that we should expect him soon after
noon on the last day of December. Since the Doones were lazy
and fond of bed, the country people would travel in the morning
before the Doones were up and about. However, this time the
Doones had never gone to bed, for they had stayed up all night
in search of mischief. That morning my uncle met them on the
way.

Dinner time came, but still Uncle Ben, as we called him, had
not arrived. Much worried, I set out with my gun to look for
him. The fog hung close around me. The moor was lonesome
and desolate. My gun was loaded and ready. I was nervous
though I knew myself to be a match in strength for any two
average men in our neighborhood—except for those in the Doone
Valley. The soft white mist came thicker around me as the evening fell. Far from finding Uncle Ben I was lost myself. The
mist kept rolling around me, and everything disappeared from
sight.

Suddenly a noise came to me as of many horses galloping at

distance and in my fright I set my gun. For a moment I stood like a root, without power to move hand or foot. But the noise died away.

I walked on a bit further to the crossroads by the black pool and heard through the patter of my own feet a low moaning.

"Lord have mercy upon me," came a voice wheezing and coughing; "even if I did cheat Sam Hicks last week, he deserved it. Oh Lord, where am I going?"

I made toward the sound in the fog.

"Help, good friend; God has sent you, not to rob me, for that has been done already."

"Uncle Ben!" I cried in amazement, "Uncle Ben, you—in this difficulty! Don't you recognize me, your nephew John Ridd?"

Not to make a long story of it, I cut the bonds and set him on a little horse which had been grazing near by. He had been robbed by the Doones, and mistreated by them for two or three hours. After some difficulty I got him home.

When he was finally well again, he stormed furiously about the robbery. "I was robbed in this township. It's a scandal. The township should make good my loss." When we explained that we were practically helpless before the power of the Doones, he declared, "John, guide me tomorrow to a place where I may observe these scoundrel Doones. I will revenge myself upon them some day."

I agreed and at once thought of Lorna Doone, the little maid of so many years back. Had she ever thought of me? I wondered awhile over that question.

We set out and in time reached Bagworthy forest, the blackest and loneliest place I know. Even now in winter time, with most of the shade gone, it hung around us like a cloak. There was no path of any kind. Though the air of gloom and loneliness was uncomfortable, it gave us courage, for we knew that the robbers were not in the habit of passing there. The going was very difficult, so much so that I had to leave my gun behind.

At last we reached the top and looked forth over the valley. Now for the first time I was amazed at the appearance of the

Doones' stronghold and understood its nature. For when I had
last been here seven years before, I was but a boy and had noted
no details. Rimmed with sheer black rock lay a bright green
valley. There were two clefts in the rocks, one the chasm by
which I had entered as a boy, and the other the Doone-gate by
which the robbers entered and left.

Uncle Ben spoke to me, but I didn't hear him. I was gazing
at the little opening in the cliff through which I had made my
exit, and thinking of my adventures that day. Suddenly I saw
a little figure come, and pause, and pass into it. My heart came
to my ribs and my face was flushed. Though seven years had
gone and she must have forgotten me, I felt that I was face to
face with fate, and that fate was Lorna Doone.

Chapter Nine

John Meets Lorna Again

On the way back Uncle Ben cross-examined me, for he had noted
my confusion and eager gaze at something unseen by him in the
valley. He had learned that I had been in the Doone valley several years before and might be induced to venture there again.
But I told him nothing as to how I had got in or what I had seen.

After he had left for his home in Dulverton next day, I began
to yearn for adventure, particularly a lonely visit to Doone Valley by way of the perilous passage discovered in my boyhood.
I was now twenty-one years old and shy about my great size and
tremendous strength. Many a time I longed to be no bigger than
John Fry, whom now I could lift with my left hand.

So it happened that once again on a St. Valentine's day I set
out for the Doone Valley. The winter had been a very mild one,
so that every bush was touched with spring. I reached the spot

without mishap. As I looked around I heard a voice singing and there by the side of the stream was Lorna Doone coming to me. When she caught sight of me, she turned to flee, not knowing me, but I cried out, "Lorna Doone!"

She knew me at once from my manner and my ways, and a smile broke through her trembling. "Oh indeed," she cried, with a pretense of anger, "who are you, sir, and how do you know my name?"

"I am John Ridd," I answered, "the boy who gave you those little fish when you were only a tiny thing, seven years ago today."

"Yes, the poor boy who was frightened so, and obliged to hide here in the water."

"And do you remember how kind you were, and saved my life by your quickness, and went away riding upon a huge man's shoulder, as if you had never seen me, and yet looked back through the willow trees?"

"Oh, yes, I remember everything, because it was so rare to see anyone except the Doones. But you seem not to remember, sir, how dangerous this place is."

As she looked at me I could not answer her, but was overcome with thinking, and feeling, and confusion.

"I think, Master Ridd, you cannot know," she continued, with her eyes turned away from me, "what the dangers of this place are, and the nature of the people."

"Yes, I know enough of that, and I am frightened greatly— except when I look at you."

She was clearly concerned for my safety, so I decided I'd better go and have no more to say to her until the next time I came.

"Mistress Lorna, I will depart"—mark you, I thought *depart* a powerful word!—"in fear of causing uneasiness. Try to think of me now and then, and I will bring you some new-laid eggs next time."

"I thank you heartily," said Lorna, "but you need not come to see me. You can put them in my little hiding-place, where I go daily to read and be away from the Doones."

"Oh, show me where it is. Three times a day I'll come and stop . . ."

"No, Master Ridd, I'd never show you because of the danger— but it so happens that you have found the way already." And she smiled at me.

I was so taken with her that on the way home I was angry with every man in the world who would dare to think of marrying her!

Chapter Ten

Two Interviews

The following week I could do little more than dream and dream and rove about. I cared not for the people around me and took no delight in food. That I had fallen head-over-heels in love with Lorna Doone I had no doubt. I dared not tell anyone because the Doones had killed my father.

In desperation I consulted Mother Melldrum, who had the reputation of being a witch. Although it was near the end of March, the wind blew wild and piercing as I approached her house on foot. I had decided not to take a horse for fear she should put a spell upon him. The sun was low on the hills by the time I neared her dwelling. The shadows of rocks fell far and deep. In patches underneath the crags a few wild goats were browsing. Taking one thing with another and feeling all the lonesomeness of the place, I was inclined to go back and come again some other time. But I hated to run away from anything.

As I debated, a woman in the distance lifted up her staff to me. As she came nearer, I was glad to sit down on a rock because my knees were shaking so. But when she came close enough so that

I could see her clearly, I found something kindly in her countenance.

"Give me your hand, John Ridd, and tell me why you have
come to me. Have no fear of me. I have no gift to harm anyone
and even if I did, I wouldn't hurt you."

Seeing how she looked at me, I lost my fear and began to like
her. I gave some excuse for coming.

"How simple you are! Now tell me, for you cannot lie to me:
what has brought you to me?"

Being so ashamed and bashful I had been half-inclined to tell
a lie, but now I could not. "I have come to know," I said, looking
at a rock the while to keep my voice from shaking, "when I may
go to see Lorna Doone."

I could say no more, though my mind was charged with fifty
questions.

She spoke sadly to me, "John Ridd, if you have any value for
your body or soul, or your father's name, have nothing to do with
any Doone."

She gazed at me earnestly and raised her voice in saying it so
that the whole valley echoed mournfully, "Doone."

My heart refused to accept this. If it were God's will for me
to see Lorna no more, let a sign come out of the rocks and I
would try to believe it, but no sign came. I left hurriedly, seeking no more such advice.

When the weather changed in earnest and the frost was gone,
I could not keep from thinking of Lorna. Without waiting longer
I decided to set forth once again to find her. I had to dress in
the barn, for I had told no one of Lorna, not even dear Annie. I
had tried many a time, but had never been able to.

This time I longed to take my gun and was half resolved to
do so, but when I remembered the steepness and slippery nature
of the waterslide, there seemed little chance of keeping the powder dry. Therefore I was armed with nothing but a good stout
holly staff, seasoned well for many a winter in our kitchen chimney. When I got to the Doone glade, the stream was rushing

down in strength, a rain having fallen the night before. However, I reached the head with more difficulty than danger and sat in a place which comforted my back and legs.

Then I grew so happy at being on dry land again that I fell asleep. However, my sleep was broken by a shadow cast over me. Between me and the sunlight Lorna was standing.

"Master Ridd, are you mad?" she said, and took my hand to move me.

"Not mad, but half asleep," I answered, pretending not to notice her, so that she might keep hold of me.

"Come away, come away, if you care for life. The patrol will be here soon. Be quick, Master Ridd, let me hide you."

"I will not stir a step," said I, though in great fright, "unless you call me 'John.'"

"Well, John, then—Master John Ridd, be quick, if you have any to care for you."

Without another word she led me, though with many frightened glances towards the upper valley, to and into her little hiding-place. Inside this cavern of stone the plainest thing of all to see, at any rate by daylight, was the stairway cut from rock and leading up the mountain by means of which I had escaped as a boy. On the left was a narrow crack in the wall, very difficult to see, having a sweep of gray ivy over it. A man coming into the cavern, with eyes dazed by sunlight from the brightness of the outer air, would never even see this narrow crevice.

Lorna raised the ivy for me, but I had difficulty passing through the crack on account of my huge size. However, I got through at last and broke into the pleasant room, the lone retreat of Lorna.

The chamber was of uncut rock, about twenty feet across and gay with fern and moss and lichen. Overhead there was no ceiling but the sky itself. The floor was made of soft, low grass, mixed with moss and primroses. While I was gazing at these things, Lorna turned upon me lightly and said, "Where are the new-laid eggs, Master Ridd, or has the hen stopped laying?"

"Here are some," I answered; "I would have brought you twice as many, but I feared to crush them on the climb, Miss Lorna."

I laid out two dozen upon the moss of the rock ledge. Lorna looked with growing wonder, as I added one after another. To my amazement she burst into a flood of tears!

"What have I done?" I asked, scarce daring even to look at her.

"You have been too kind, and I am not used to kindness."

I was embarrassed at her words and weeping; so I refrained from speaking. Her eyes were soft with trouble. Needing some-one to listen to her story, and liking me—though she didn't love me yet—she told the following tale.

Chapter Eleven

Lorna Tells Her Story

"I cannot go through all my thoughts to make them clear to you," she began. "I am very confused and if I look for help to those around me, I meet with laughter or anger.

"There are but two who ever listen and try to help me. One of them is my grandfather, Sir Ensor Doone, and the other is a man of wisdom whom we call the Counselor. Grandfather seems to know what is right and what is wrong, but not to want to think of it. The Counselor, on the other hand, treats my questions playfully, as if I were a favorite, but not to be taken too seriously.

"I have no remembrance now of father or of mother, although they say that my father was the eldest son of Sir Ensor Doone, and the bravest and best of them. And so they call me heiress to this realm of violence, and in joking sometimes call me their Princess or their Queen.

"Many people living here, as I am forced to do, would perhaps be very happy, and perhaps I ought to be so. We have a beautiful valley, sheltered from the cold of winter and the power of the summer sun. But all around me is violence and robbery, coarse delight and savage pain, reckless joke, and hopeless death. Is it any wonder that I cannot sink with these, that I cannot so forget my soul as to sink to the level of brutes? There is none to lead me forward, none to teach me right; young as I am, I live beneath an everlasting curse."

Here Lorna broke down for a while and cried—pitifully. Not knowing how to comfort her I kept quiet and tried to set her an example by looking cheerful.

"Master Ridd," she began again, "I am ashamed and annoyed at my own childish folly. It does not happen many times that I give way like this. Sometimes I am so full of anger at things they cannot hide from me that I dare not speak. You would be surprised that reckless men should care so much to keep things from me. They used to boast to my Aunt Sabina of their evil deeds and cruelty on purpose to enrage her, but to me they have never spoken a word of their wickedness. It even makes me smile sometimes to see how awkwardly one will come, seeking to tempt me to accept a gift from a shining packet, half concealed, of ornaments, rings, or jewels lately belonging to other people.

"Often I wonder at the odds of fortune, which made me, helpless and fond of peace and reading, the heiress of this wild domain. Though I shall not have much power of authority, yet the Counselor's son, Carver Doone, desires to marry me. We should not be so quiet here and safe from interruption if I had not begged one privilege, to keep this part of the valley to myself. Therefore, no one besides the sentries on guard ever comes here, except my grandfather, or Counselor, or Carver.

"By your face, Master Ridd, I see that you have heard of Carver Doone. For strength and courage and resourcefulness he is first among the Doones, as might be expected from the son of the Counselor. But he differs from his father in being very hot headed and savage.

"You must be tired of this story, but my life from day to day shows so little change. There is none of the young men I really care for. Neither is there any one among the old men whom I can revere or love, except my grandfather. Nor is there any whom I like to deal with, except my maidservant, whom I saved from starving. She is a young Cornish girl named Gwenny Carfax. For the kindness I did her, she took me for an angel. I brought her home with me and she made herself my sole attendant, without so much as asking me.

"Ah me! We are to be pitied greatly, rather than condemned, by people whose possessions we have taken. I have read that there are places on the earth where gentle peace and love and neighborliness prevail. There honest folk may go to work with the hope of coming home again, quite safe in the quiet evening, and finding all their children untouched and unharmed. I have never known such peace, and perhaps never shall. Be content now, John Ridd, and ask me no more, so that you will still be able to sleep as I found you, with untroubled dreams."

But I, John Ridd, being young and fond of high adventure, urged her to say more, hoping perhaps that she might need me one day when the worst came to the worst and feeling that meanwhile I should learn as much of her position as I could. Therefore she went on again.

"It is less than a year ago, although it seems ten years, that I truly learned the evil of our living, the scorn for the law, the outrage and the sorrow caused to others. Up to that time the men had tried to hide the roughness from me. My grandfather, Sir Ensor Doone, had given strict orders, as I discovered later, that in my presence all should seem to be kind and gentle. Nor was it very difficult to keep most of the mischief from me, for no Doone ever robs at home, nor do the men quarrel much except when gambling. And though Sir Ensor Doone is now so old and feeble, he still has his own way, and no one dares deny him.

"But now at the time I speak of, one evening of last summer, a horrible thing happened which took all my childhood play from me. I had been at the waterslide at this lower end of the valley, at a place where I was not likely to meet any of our people. As

I hastened along near dusk, ready to draw back and run from hare or rabbit or small field mouse, suddenly a man leaped out from behind a tree and seized hold of me. I tried to shriek, but my voice was still and I could hear only my heart.

" 'Now, Cousin Lorna, my good cousin,' he said with ease and calmness, 'please be quiet or else be the death of your very best cousin and trusty guardian, Alan Brandir of Loch Awe.'

" 'You, my guardian!' I said, for the idea was too funny, and funny things always strike me first.

" 'I have in truth that honor,' he answered with a sweeping bow, 'unless I am mistaken in calling you Miss Lorna Doone.'

" 'You have not mistaken me. My name is Lorna Doone.'

" 'Then I am your faithful guardian, Alan Brandir, son of a worthy nobleman of Scotland. Now will you confide in me?'

" 'Confide in you!' I cried, looking at him in amazement; 'why you are not older than I am!'

" 'Yes, I am, three years at least. I, your worshipful guardian, am almost nineteen years of age!'

"Upon hearing this I looked at him with wondering interest. He led me in a courteous manner to an open place beside the water where the light shone through the trees.

" 'Now, am I fair to your liking, Cousin?'

" 'Truly, I know not,' I answered; 'but you seem good natured and harmless. Do they trust you with a sword?'

"For I had been used to seeing men of great size and strength, and this young lad seemed nothing but a doll to me. Although he had scared me in the wood, now that I saw him in good light, lo! he was little larger than I, and so overdressed that I scarce could keep from laughing at him.

" 'I fear that my appearance is not ferocious,' and he gave a clank to his sword as he spoke, 'but I assure you, Cousin, that I am not without skill and strength. Now if the boldest and biggest robber in all this valley dared cross me, I would cleave him from head to foot before he could fly or cry.'

" 'Hush,' I said; 'talk not so loudly, or you may have to fly or cry yourself.'

"For he was quite forgetting now, in his bravery before me, where he stood and with whom he spoke. As I gazed on this slight fair youth, clearly of high birth and breeding, a chill of fear came over me, for he had no strength and would be nothing but a pincushion before the great swords of the Doones.

" 'Worshipful guardian,' I said, 'tell me how you came to be my guardian.'

"He proceeded to explain at great length the connections between his family and the Doones before they left Scotland. Somehow he felt that he had become my protector legally.

"Now come with your faithful guardian, child. I shall bear you safe to London. Your aunt, my mother, is longing to see you.'

"I turned aside and thought a little. Although he seemed so giddy of mind and gay in dress and manner, I could not doubt his honesy. I saw, beneath his jaunty air, true bravery. As I debated, a storm gathered in the distance. Yellow lightning spread behind a bulk of clouds, I thought of my grandfather and all the care I owed him.

" 'I cannot go with you, Alan Brandir. I thank you much for coming, sir, but be off at once by the way you came. Pray, how did you come?'

" 'Down the cliffs I came, and up them I must make my way back again. Give me just one flower for token. Trust me well, fair cousin, I will soon be here again.'

" 'Never!' cried a powerful voice, and Carver Doone had Alan Brandir as a spider holds a fly. The boy made a little shriek at first, with the sudden shock and terror, but then he set his face to fight for it. Very bravely he struggled to free one arm and grasp his sword, but as well might an infant buried alive attempt to lift his gravestone. Carver Doone, with his great arms wrapped around the slim gay body, smiled at the poor young face turned up to him. Then as a nurse bears off an unwilling child to bed, he lifted the youth from his feet and bore him away into the darkness.

"I was young then. I am older now, older by ten years in

thought, although it was less than a year ago. If that black deed were done now, I could follow and combat it, could throw weak arms on the murderer and try to be murdered also. I am now at home with violence and no dark death surprises me.

"But being as I was that night, the horror overcame me. The crash of thunder overhead, the last despairing look so frightened me that I could not gasp. My breath left me and I knew not where I was, or who, or what. I lay and trembled under the great trees and could neither moan nor run.

"Yet listening, as a coward does, through the wailing of the wind, I heard a sharp sound as of iron and a fall of heavy wood. No cowardly shriek came with it, nor cry for mercy, but I knew that Carver Doone had murdered Alan Brandir."

Here Lorna could tell no more, being overcome with weeping. Only through her tears she whispered that she had seen that giant Carver, a few days later, with some of the possessions of her poor dead cousin Alan.

I could not press her any further with questions, for she was now in such condition that I dared not. Her fear now was all for me, and how to get me safely away without misfortune. Though I longed to see if Carver could have done for me so easily, as it grew near dusk I was not pleased to be there. For it seemed a lawless place, and some of Lorna's fright stayed with me, as I talked it away from her.

Chapter Twelve

A Royal Invitation

After hearing that tale from Lorna I went home in low spirits, having added fear for her and misery about her to all my other ailments. And was it not quite certain now that she, being full cousin to a lord of Scotland, should have nothing to do with me, a mere farmer's son? I was vexed with my own hesitation, stupidity, or shyness, which had held me back from saying, before she told me her story, that I loved her. But the worst of all was that I had promised to stay away from the Doone Valley for at least a month, and thus cause Lorna no further anxiety.

While my month was running—or rather crawling, for never did a month go so slowly for me—I looked once every day in vain for any sign of Lorna. All the beauty of the spring was for other eyes. Even my appetite suffered.

One morning as I was rejoicing that in five days my month would be over and I would be free to seek Lorna, a man came riding up from the direction of Lynn stream. He stopped at our gate, stood up from his saddle, and holloed as if he were somebody. All the time he flourished a white object in the air.

"Service of the King," he said; "service of the King! Come here, you, at risk of fine and imprisonment."

Although not pleased with this I went to him, as became a loyal man, but I refused to hurry for him.

"Is there anywhere in this cursed county a cursed place called Plover Barrows Farm? For the last twenty miles at least they've been telling me it's just around the corner. Tell me that and I'll thwack you, even if you are three times my size!"

"Sir!" I replied, "you'll not have the trouble. This is Plover Barrows Farm and you are kindly welcome. But why do you think ill of us? We don't like to be cursed so."

"I think no ill," he said, "but I've been riding for ten days and getting the worst of everything!"

All this time he was riding across the straw of our farmyard, getting his weary legs out of the stirrups and almost afraid to stand on them yet. He was a coarse-grained, hard-faced man about forty years of age, of middle height and build. His dark-brown riding-suit was smeared with Exmoor mud.

"Hungry I am and sore of body, yet I cannot rest until I have seen and spoken to John Ridd. I hope he isn't far away."

"Have no fear, good sir," I answered; "you have seen and spoken to John Ridd. I am he."

"Take these in the name of the King," he declared, as he touched me with the white thing he had waved in the air before. I saw it was a parchment with writing on it.

"Read it, if you can read. Don't stare at me. Read it; read it!"

"If you please, sir, what is your name?" I asked.

"Jeremy Stickles is my name, lad, in the service of our King."

I read the parchment. It was a summons to appear at once before the Justices of the King to give them information they thought I possessed—about what I knew not. At once I was taken with such a giddiness in my head and noise in my ears that I was forced to lean upon a side of the hay-rack for support.

"My son, don't be afraid. We aren't going to skin you. Just tell all the truth."

No more would he say about the King's order, but settled himself comfortably in our house as if he intended to stay for weeks. At eating, drinking, and sleeping he proved himself a noble servant of His Majesty, the King.

The next day I asked him, "Now, Master Stickles, when must we start?" He was admiring a young turkey strutting about the yard.

"Well, have that turkey killed tonight, for his fatness makes my mouth water, and we will have him for dinner tomorrow. Then on Friday morning we will set out upon the road, upon His Majesty's business."

"Good sir," I asked with some trembling, so eager was I to see Lorna; "if His Majesty's business will keep till Friday, may it not keep until Monday? We have a litter of young pigs and one of them is ready for roasting."

"Now that I come to think of it, Friday is not a good day to start. I'll choose the young pig tomorrow at noon, and we'll celebrate by carving him on Friday. Then we'll set forth early on Saturday."

This was little better to me than if we had set forth at once, Sunday being the very first day I could enter Doone Valley, according to my promise. But though I tried every possible means with Master Jeremy Stickles, offering him the choice for dinner of every beast on the farm, he dared not put off our departure later than Saturday. Therefore my only chance now of seeing Lorna before I went lay in watching from the cliff and catching sight of her, or a signal from her. This I did in vain, until my eyes were weary.

We set out for London, a long and tiresome journey. When we got there, the only things that pleased me much were the River Thames, and the hall and church of Westminster. Whenever I wandered in the streets, what with the noise the people made, the number of the coaches, the running of the footmen, the swaggering of great courtiers, and the thrusting aside of everybody, many a time I longed to be back among the sheep again, for fear of losing my peacefulness of spirit.

Though we had seemed in haste to get to London, time passed and I knew not the reason for my coming. At last I was able to see the Lord Chief Justice.

"May it please Your Worship," I declared; "I am John Ridd of Oare brought to this London two months ago by a special messenger whose name is Jeremy Stickles, and then bound to be at hand and ready when called upon to give evidence in a matter unknown to me. Three times I have met our Lord, the King, but he has said nothing to me. Every day except Sunday I have walked up and down the great hall of Westminster expecting to be called upon; yet no one has called upon me. And now I desire to ask your worship whether I may go home again."

He began to question me. "Is there in your neighborhood a certain nest of robbers and outlaws whom all men fear to handle?"

"Yes, my lord. At least I believe some of them to be robbers; and all of them are outlaws."

"And what is your high sheriff about, that he does not hang them all? Or send them up for me to hang without more to-do about them?"

"I reckon that he is afraid, my lord;—it is not safe to meddle with them. They are of good birth and reckless, and their place is very strong."

"What is the name of this pestilent race, and how many of them are there?"

"They are the Doones of Bagworthy Forest, and we reckon there are about forty of them besides the women and children."

"Forty Doones, all forty thieves! and women and children! Thunder of God! How long have they been there, then?"

"They may have been there thirty years, my lord; and indeed they may have been there forty. They came longer back than I can remember."

"Now a few more things, John Ridd; and for the present I have done with you."

All my heart leaped up at this, to get away from London so.

"Is there any sound round your way of disloyalty to His Majesty, the King?"

"No, my lord; no sign whatever. We pray for him in church, but after that we have nothing to say."

"That is as it should be, John. And the less you say the better. But I have heard of treason even in Exmoor. Now, John, I have taken a liking to you, for no man ever told me the truth so directly. Keep away from the Doones. I had meant to use you as a spy, but I see you are too honest and simple. Say nothing of what I have told you!"

Here the Lord Justice gave me such a glare, that I was glad to get away. I made a low bow and went. But though he had dismissed me I was not yet quite free to go, inasmuch as I had not money enough to take me all the way home unless I went on foot. But Jeremy Stickles got five pounds for me and I set out for home.

Chapter Thirteen

John Has Hope of Lorna

How shall I tell you the things I felt, and the swelling of my heart within me, as I drew nearer to the place of all I loved and owned, to the haunt of every warm remembrance—to home. When I saw the first sheep on the moor with a great red J. R. on his side, I do assure you my spirit leaped, and I shouted out, "Jem, boy!" He knew me in spite of the stranger horse; and I leaned over and stroked his head, and swore he would never be mutton.

Then I saw my sister Annie. She nearly pulled me off my horse. "I knew you would come. Oh John! Oh John! I have waited here every Saturday night, and I saw you for the last mile or more, but I would not come round the corner for fear that I should cry, John, and then not cry when I got you. Now I may cry as much as I like and you need not try to stop me, John, because I am so happy. But you mustn't cry, yourself, John; what will Mother think of you? She will be so jealous of me."

What Mother thought I cannot tell; and indeed I doubt if she thought at all for more than half an hour, but only managed to hold me tight and cry, and thank God now and then. Even my little sister Eliza wept. Happier people could not be found than all of us that evening.

Much as I longed to know more about Lorna, I could not leave my mother and Annie on the following day, which happened to be a Sunday. In church the whole congregation, man, woman, and child, looked at me with awe for having been to London to meet the King. However, all this wore off in time.

For my part, though I may have been none the wiser because of my stay in London, at any rate I was a much better man in coming home again, for now I had learned the joy of quiet and the gratitude for good things around us. I felt much inclined to tell dear Mother all about Lorna, how I loved her and yet had no hope of winning her. Often I had longed to do this and have done with it. But the thought of my father's terrible death at the hands of the Doones prevented me.

As soon as I could, the next day I left the men on the farm and went to the crest of the broken highland from where I had agreed to watch for any mark or signal. And sure enough at last I saw what I feared that I had come too late to see, a white stone covered over with a cloth or mantle—the sign agreed upon between us that something had arisen to make Lorna want me. For a moment I stood sick at heart, dreading evil fortune: that I should be too late in the very thing of things on which my heart was set! Then after eyeing anxiously every nook and cranny to be sure that Lorna wasn't in sight, I set off headlong to make the round of the outer cliffs and come up my old entrance.

Nothing could stop me. It was not long, although to me it

seemed an age, before I stood in the crack of rock at the head of the slippery watercourse, and gazed into the quiet glen. At last a little figure came, looking very light and slender in the moving shadows. I rushed out at once.

I know not whether my own Lorna was afraid of how I looked, or what I might say to her, or of her own thoughts of me. All I know is that she looked frightened, when I hoped for gladness. Therefore I went slowly towards her.

"Mistress Lorna, I had hope that you were in need of me."

"Oh, yes; but that was long ago—two months ago, or more, sir." And saying this she looked away as if it all were over. But I was now so dazed and frightened that it took my breath away, and I could not answer, feeling sure that I was robbed, and someone else had won her. And I tried to turn away without another word and go.

But I could not help one stupid sob, yet vexed with myself for allowing it. It came too sharp for pride to stay it, and told a world of things. Lorna heard it and ran to me, with her bright eyes full of wonder, pity, and great kindness, as if amazed that I had more than a simple liking for her.

"Master Ridd, I did not mean," she whispered very softly, "I did not mean to vex you. Come away from this bright place. I am watched and spied on of late. Come beneath the shadows, John."

I would have leaped into the valley of the shadow of death to hear her call me "John." She stole across the silent grass, but I strode quickly after her. Fear was all beyond me now, except the fear of losing her. She led me to her own secret chamber that I described before. All that I could see was the maiden moving gently, and afraid to look at me.

"Darling, do you love me?" was all that I could say to her.

"Yes, I like you very much," she answered with her eyes away from me.

"But do you love me, Lorna? Do you love me more than all the world?"

"No, to be sure not. Now why should I?"

"In truth, I know not why you should. Only I hoped that you did, Lorna. Either love me not at all, or as I love you, for ever."

"John, I like you very much; and I would not grieve you. You are the bravest and the kindest and the simplest of all men—I mean of all people. I like you very much, Master Ridd, and I think of you almost every day."

"That will not do for me, Lorna. Not almost every day, but every instant of my life, I think of you. For you I would give up my home, my love of all the world beside, my duty to my dearest ones. For you I would give up my life and hope of life beyond it. Do you love me so?"

"Not by any means," said Lorna; "no, I like you very much, when you do not talk so wildly, and I like to think that even Carver would be nothing in your hands—but as to liking you like that, what should make it likely? Especially when I have made the signal and for some two months or more you have never even answered it! If you like me so ferociously, why do you leave me for other people to do just as they like with me?"

"To do as they like! Oh, Lorna, not to make you marry Carver?"

"No, Master Ridd, be not frightened so. It makes me fear to look at you."

"But you have not married Carver yet? Say quick! Why keep me waiting so?"

"Of course I have not, Master Ridd. Should I be here if I had, do you think, allowing you to like me so?"

"Did they want you to marry Carver? Tell me all the truth of it."

"Not yet, not yet. They are not half so impetuous as you are, John. I am only just seventeen, you know, and who is to think of marrying? But they wanted me to give my word and be formally engaged to him in the presence of my grandfather. It seems that something frightened them. There is a youth named Charleworth Doone; everyone calls him Charlie; a headstrong and gay young man, very gallant in his looks and manner; and my uncle, the Counselor, felt that Charlie looked at me too much, coming by my grandfather's cottage."

Here Lorna blushed so that I was frightened and began to hate this Charlie more, a great deal more, than even Carver Doone.

"He had better not," said I; "I will fling him over the cottage if he dare."

"Master Ridd, you are worse than Carver! I thought you were so kind-hearted. Well, they wanted me to promise that I would wed my eldest cousin, this same Carver Doone, who is twice as old as I am, being thirty-five and upwards. That was why I gave the signal I wished to see you, Master Ridd. They pointed out how much it was for the peace of all the family and for my own benefit, but I would not listen for a moment, though the Counselor was most eloquent and Carver smiled his pleasantest, which is a truly frightful thing. And now I am watched and spied and followed, and half my liberty seems to be taken from me. I could not be here speaking with you, even in my own nook and refuge, but for the aid and skill and courage of my little maid, Gwenny Carfax. She is now my chief reliance and through her alone I hope to baffle all my enemies, since others have forsaken me."

Tears of sorrow and reproach were lurking in her soft dark eyes until I told her that my seeming indifference was nothing but my enforced absence. Before she could say another word or guess what I was up to, I put on her finger a ring I had chosen for her in London.

"Oh, you crafty Master Ridd!" said Lorna, looking up at me. "I thought that you were much too simple ever to do this sort of thing. No wonder you can catch the fish, as when I first saw you!"

"Have I caught you, little fish? Or must all my life be spent in hopeless angling for you?"

"Neither one nor the other, John! You have not caught me yet altogether, though I like you dearly, John; and if you will only keep away I shall like you more and more. As for hopeless angling—it shall be hopeless for others until I tell you otherwise."

And then she drew my ring off her finger and held it out for me.

"John, I dare not take it now; else I should be cheating you. I will try to love you dearly, even as you deserve and wish. Keep it for me till then. Something tells me I shall earn it in a very little time. Perhaps you will be sorry then."

But I knew quite well, while my heart was burning within me, that Lorna Doone had now begun, and would go on, to love me.

Chapter Fourteen

Lorna Acknowledges Her Love for John

Although I was not to see her for two months—for safety's sake —I had the lightest heart in Exmoor, for *she* was safe. I knew that daily by a mode of signals, well-arranged between us now.

"I have nothing now to fear, John," she had said to me as we parted; "it is true that I am watched and spied upon, but Gwenny is too keen for them. While I have my grandfather to prevent all violence and little Gwenny to keep watch over me, and you above all others, John, ready at a moment if the worst comes to worst—this neglected Lorna Doone was never better off before. Therefore, do not squeeze my hand, John; I am safe without it and you do not know your own strength."

Upon the very day when eight weeks were up I went in search of Lorna, taking the pearl ring hopefully and all the new-laid eggs I could find, as well as a dozen and a half of small trout from our brook. But alas! I was utterly disappointed, for although I waited for hours, no Lorna ever appeared at all, nor even the faintest sign of her. Another thing occurred as well, which annoyed me more than it should have done. This was that my little offering of the trout and the new-laid eggs was carried

off in the coolest manner by that vile Carver Doone. Thinking
to keep them the fresher and nicer, I had laid them in a little bed
of reeds by the side of the water and placed some leaves over
them. When I had quite forgotten about them, I became aware
of a great man coming leisurely down the valley. He had a
broad-brimmed hat, a leather jacket, and what was worst of all
for me a gun. Having nothing to met him with but a staff and
desiring to avoid disturbance, I withdrew out of sight, keeping
the tree between us.

When he was within fifty yards of me, I could observe his
features, and though I am not a judge of men's faces, there was
something in his which turned me cold, as though with a kind of
horror. Not that it was an ugly face—for it seemed rather a
handsome one, full of strength and vigor and will; but there was
nothing playful in it, nothing which a friend could like. Yet he
might have seemed a good man, but for the cold, cruel look in
his steel-blue eyes.

There I waited, with my staff ready to fly at him if only he
would come where strength, not firearms, might decide it. However, he suspected nothing of my nearness, but walked his round
like a sentinel and turned at the brink of the water. Then as he
marched back again, along the edge of the stream, he spied my
little offering covered with leaves. I saw him stoop, lay bare the
fish and the eggs, I thought now he knew all about me, but to my
surprise he laughed.

"Ha, ha! Charlie, have I caught you setting bait for Lorna?"
And he calmly packed up my fish and eggs and went away laughing.

Though I was glad that he thought another Doone had left the
food, I was grieved and angered too, at his impudence. I started
forth from my rocky perch with the intention of pursuing him,
until my better sense stopped me, barely in time to escape his
eyes. For I said to myself, even supposing I could battle him
successfully unarmed, it would be foolish to have my secret entrance known. It was better to bear this trifling loss, than to risk
my love and perhaps be shot into the bargain.

Having waited until there was no chance of Lorna's appearing I hastened homeward very sadly. Nevertheless I went every evening for two weeks, hoping in vain to see her.

On one visit I was nearly shot and killed. I was waiting unguardedly in our usual place being now a little desperate. Suddently a bullet went by me with a whistle, passing through my hat and sweeping it away all folded up. It fluttered far down the stream before I had time to go after it, and with the help of both wind and water was fifty yards away in a moment.

I had just enough mind to shrink back very swiftly and remain quiet, for I knew what a narrow escape it had been as I heard the bullet sing mournfully down the chasm. As I peered through my little cranny, I saw a wreath of powder-smoke still floating, and in the midst of it Carver Doone came forth. He ran very swiftly toward me to see what he had shot.

I had difficulty in keeping my footing, from the slipperiness of the stone beneath me. My foe came to the edge of the fall, and there he stopped for a minute or two on the very spot where I had fallen senseless as a boy. I could hear him breathing hard and grunting, since he stood within a yard of me, and I kept my right fist ready for him if he should discover me.

Then at the foot of the waterslide my black hat suddenly appeared, tossing in white foam, and fluttering like a wounded raven. I was glad that I had decided to take that hat with me, for its appearance saved me.

"Have I killed you, old bird, at last?" my enemy cried in triumph. "It's the third time I have shot at you. No more of your cursed croaking now to wake me in the morning. Ha, ha! There are not many who get three chances from Carver Doone, and none *ever* go beyond it."

I laughed inwardly at this, as he strode away in triumph. For was not this his third chance for me without knowing it? Then I thought that perhaps the chance might some day be on the other side, because to tell the truth I was heartily tired of lurking and playing bo-peep so long. Here was a man of strength fit for me to encounter and such as I had never met, since all my latest opponents had been too easy for me.

I was up the very next morning before the October sunrise and away through the wild woodland towards the Bagworthy water. The bar of rock with the waterslide breaking steeply through it stood bold and bare and dark in shadow. I was overjoyed when I saw my Lorna coming down the valley, not knowing that I looked at her. At sight of me she came to meet me gladly.

"At last then, you are come, John. I thought you had forgotten me. I could not make you understand—they have kept me prisoner every evening, but come inside the cavern. You are in danger here." I knew that the crowning moment of my life was coming, that Lorna would admit her love for me.

"You know what I am come to ask," I whispered very softly.

"If you have come on purpose to ask anything, why do you delay so?" She turned away very bravely, but I saw that her lips were trembling.

"I delay so long because I fear, because my whole life hangs in a balance on a single word, because what I have near me now may never more be near me after." As I spoke in a low voice, Lorna trembled more and more, but she made no answer, nor looked up at me.

"I have loved you long," I continued; "when you were a little child, as a boy I worshiped you. Now that you are a maiden, I love you—more than tongue can tell, or heart hold in silence. I have waited long, and though I am so far below you I can wait no longer, but must have my answer."

"You have been very faithful, John," she murmured; "I suppose you have deserved my affection."

"That will not do for me," I said. "I must have all love or none. I must have your heart of hearts, as you have mine, Lorna."

While I spoke she glanced up shyly, to prolong my doubt for one moment. Then she flung both arms around my neck and answered.

"Darling, you have won it all. I shall never be my own again. I am yours for ever and ever."

I was overcome with happiness. I took her hand and slipped my little ring upon the wedding finger, and this time Lorna kept it.

She looked at it with fondness, but suddenly she wept.

"Darling, weep no more, but live in peace and happiness. With me to guard and cherish you, who shall dare to vex you?"

"It can never, never be," she murmured to herself alone. "Who am I to dream of it? Something in my heart tells me it can never, never be."

Chapter Fifteen

Lorna's Signals Cease

There was, however, no possibility of depressing me at such a time. That I a mere clumsy farmer without wealth or family should be loved by Lorna was a thought no fears could lessen. I hurried home with deep exulting, yet with some misgivings, too, for Lorna had made me promise to tell my mother everything. I felt, though, that if once I could get Mother to look at Lorna, she would love and glory in her, too.

When I returned, I was greeted by Lizzie. "Oh, John," she cried, "Mother is all upset and Annie is crying her eyes out. What do you think? You never would guess, though I have suspected it for ever so long."

"No need for me to guess," I replied, for I realized that Mother had at last discovered our Annie's love for Cousin Tom Faggus, the retired highwayman, now turned an honest country gentleman. Mother had scarcely approved of him even as a visitor.

As Lizzie and I entered the house, Annie rushed to me. "Oh,

John, speak one good word for me," and her tearful eyes looked up at me.

"Not one, but a hundred," I answered; "I am going to make your case so bright by comparison that Mother will forgive you in five minutes." I had already confided to Annie my love for Lorna.

"Oh John, you won't tell her about Lorna today!"

"Yes, today, and at once, Annie. I want to have it over, and be done with it."

"Oh, but think of her, dear. I am sure she could not bear it, after this great shock already."

"She will bear it all the better," said I. "The one will drive the other out. I know exactly how Mother is."

And after much weeping and hasty speech, Mother at last accepted both our loves, though she had hated the very name of Doone. Not that she had forgiven yet the rivals to her love—Tom Faggus, I mean, and Lorna—but she was beginning to think a little better of them through the enthusiasm of her own children.

As might be expected Mother began at once to think of some means of keeping me out of danger. She was full of plans for fetching Lorna in some wonderful manner out of the power of the Doones entirely and into her own hands where she was to remain for at least a year, learning all that Mother and Annie could teach her of farm life.

As to stealing my beloved from Doone Valley, the deed itself was not impossible, nor beyond my daring. But would she come, leaving her old grandfather? And even if she did consent to come, would it be possible to keep her without a regiment of soldiers? Would not the Doones at once ride forth to scour the country, burn our house, and murder us, carrying her back triumphantly? She acknowledged with a sigh that nothing else remained for me but to keep a careful watch upon Lorna from a safe distance, observe the policy of the Doones, and wait for a turn of fortune.

Suddenly without any warning all my Lorna's signals, which I

had watched for daily, ceased. At first I could hardly believe my
eyes and thought it must be a mistake. However, my heart grew
heavier as I found from day to day no token.

Three times I went and waited long at the bottom of the valley, but no light footstep came to meet me. Once I ventured
far up the valley, where I had never been before, even beyond
the place where Lorna had found and lost her brave young
cousin. Following up the river channel in the shelter of the evening fog, I came within a stone's throw of the outlying cottage.
This was a gloomy, low, square house, without any light in the
windows, roughly built of wood and stone. Knowing from some
words of Lorna's that this was Carver's dwelling, I was led by
curiosity and jealously to have a closer look at it.

I crept warily forward. The back of Carver's house was near
the stream. Seeing a loop-hole, I looked in, but all was quiet;
there was no one inside. I had feared to find Lorna kidnaped in
there. Then I took a careful survey of the dwelling—its door, its
windows, and its appearance.

Having impressed upon my mind all the bearings of the place,
I decided to go further up, but a bar of light from one of the
houses prevented me. Inside this building there was a gathering
of loud and merry outlaws, making as much noise as if they had
the law upon their side.

Before I left for home, nevertheless, I had resolved to pene-
trate Doone Valley from the upper end and learn all about Lorna.
Dangerous though the mission was, I knew that I had to make it.

Chapter Sixteen

A Very Desperate Venture

The enterprise I had resolved upon was so much more dangerous than anything I had yet attempted that I went and made my will at Porlock. I arranged to leave my clothes, hats, and personal things to Lorna, but I left the farm to my immediate family.

The journey was a great deal longer to go around the southern hills and enter by the Doone-gate than to cross the lower land and steal in by the waterslide. I dare not take a horse for fear of the Doones. Thus I came to the robbers' highway, walking carefully, scanning the skyline of every hill and searching the folds of every valley for any moving creature.

Although it was now well on towards dark, I could see the robbers' road before me. At present there was no one passing, so far as I could see, but I thought it safer to wait awhile, as twilight melted into night. Then I crept down and stood upon the Doone-track.

As the road approached the entrance, it became more straight and strong like a channel cut from rock. Not a tree or bush was left to shelter a man from bullets. All was stern and stiff and rugged, as I could not help seeing, even through the darkness.

I seemed to be particularly unlucky, for as I drew near the entrance lightly and carefully, the moon broke upon me, filling all the open spaces with light. I shrank back into the shadowy section on the right side of the road and gloomily waited till the moonlight should pass the entrance.

Across the three rocky archways that lined the Doone-gate hung a felled oak, black and thick and threatening. This, as I had heard before, could be let fall in a moment, so as to crush

twenty men and bar the approach of horses. Behind this tree the
rocky mouth was spanned with brushwood and piled timber,
where thirty men might lurk unseen and fire at any invader.
From that defense it would be impossible to dislodge them, because the rock fell sheer below them twenty feet or more, while
overhead it towered three hundred, and so jutted out that nothing could be thrown down upon them.

The cleverest of their devices and the most puzzling to an
enemy was that instead of one mouth only, there were three to
choose from, with nothing to tell which was the right one, all
being pretty much alike. The common rumor was that in times
of danger when any force was known to be on hand in the
neighborhood, they changed their entrance every day and di-
verted the other two, by means of sliding doors, to the chasms
and dark abysses.

Now I could see those three rough arches, jagged, black, and
terrible, and I knew that only one of them could lead me into
the valley. Having no means of judging which was the right way
of the three and knowing that the other two would lead to almost
certain death in the ruggedness and darkness, I declare that I
was half inclined to go away and forget my plan.

However, I knew one thing for certain—that the longer I
stayed debating the less would my relish for the enterprise be.
It struck me that in times of peace the middle way was the
likeliest, and so I plunged into the middle entrance, holding a
heavy staff before me. Presently I was in black darkness, groping
along the wall and feeling a deal more fear than I wished to feel,
especially when, upon looking back, I could no longer see the
light which I had left.

Suddenly I stumbled over something hard and sharp and very
cold. I almost cried out with pain. But when I arose, I felt it
and knew it to be a cannon. I was somewhat happier at this
since it was not likely they would plant this weapon except in
the real and true entrance. Therefore I went on again more carefully and soon found it to be lucky I had received that knock and
put on my guard, for otherwise I might have blundered upon the

sentries and been shot without more ado. As it was, I had barely
time to draw back as I turned a corner upon them, and if their
lantern had been in its place they could scarcely have failed to
see me.

There seemed to be only two of them, of the Doone size and
stature, but I would not have feared to encounter them both if
they had been unarmed as I was. It was plain, however, that
each had a long and heavy gun—not in his hands as it should
have been, but standing close beside him.

The two villains looked very happy. Each was smoking a long
clay pipe, and each would laugh from time to time. They were
playing a game and arguing occasionally over the score.

Suddenly Charlie, or Charleworth Doone, the younger and
taller man, reached forth his hand to seize the money which he
swore he had won that time. Upon this the other jerked his arm,
vowing that he had no right to it, whereupon Charlie flung at
his face the contents of the glass he was sipping, but he missed
him and hit the candle, which spluttered and went out. At this
one swore, and the other laughed, and before they had settled
what to do I was past them and round the corner.

Then, foolishly, I gave them the whoop of an owl, done so exactly and echoed so fearfully that one of them dropped the tinder
box with which he was going to light the candle, and the other
caught up his gun and cocked it, to judge by the sounds they
made. Too late I knew my madness, for if either of them had
fired, no doubt the whole village would have risen and rushed
upon me. However, as luck would have it, the deed proved to
my advantage, for I heard one say to the other—

"Curse it, Charlie, what was that? It scared me so, I have
dropped my tinder box and the flint is gone. Will the candle
catch from your pipe, my lad?"

"My pipe is out, Phelps, ever so long. Curse it, I am not afraid
of an owl, man. Give me the lantern and stay here."

"Go straight to Carver's, mind you. No dallying now under
Captain's window. Lorna will have nothing to say to you, and
Carver will punch your head into a new wick for your lantern."

"Will he, though? Two can play at that." And so after some rude jests and laughter I heard Charlie coming toward me with a not too sober footfall. He reeled a little, but I would not move from his way one inch after his talk of Lorna. I longed to grasp him and would have done so, had common sense permitted it. His coat brushed against my thumb. If he had turned or noticed it, he would have been a dead man in a moment, but his drunkenness saved him.

I let him stagger on unharmed, for it occurred to me that I could have no better guide, passing as he would exactly where I wished to be, under Lorna's window. As I followed him I had a fair view of the robbers' township. I knew that the first house belonged to Sir Ensor Doone, the Captain, for both Lorna and my mother had described it to me, and Charlie paused there a moment and whistled softly.

As I passed Sir Ensor's house, my heart leaped up, for I spied a window higher than the rest above the ground and with a faint light moving. My courage grew tenfold, since I knew by Charlie's actions that Lorna must be there, and not in Carver's accursed dwelling. Charlie went on to Carver's house to kindle his lantern.

My heart was in my mouth when I stood in the shade by Lorna's window and whispered her name gently. I dared not speak aloud, because I saw another watchman posted on the western cliff. And now this man, having no companion for drinking or gambling, spied me against the wall of the house and advanced to challenge me.

"Who are you there? Answer! One, two, three; and I fire at you!"

The nozzle of his gun was pointed right at me, as I could see with the moonlight striking on the barrel. He was not more than fifty yards off and he began to count. Being almost desperate about it I began to whistle, wondering how far I should get before I lost my windpipe. Luckily my lips fell into that strange tune I had heard from Charlie. My mouth would scarcely frame the notes, being parched with terror, but to my surprise the man fell back, dropped his gun, and saluted.

That tune was Carver Doone's passport, as I heard long afterwards, which Charleworth Doone had imitated. The sentinel took me for that vile Carver, who was likely enough to be prowling there. Perceiving the danger of intruding on Carver's privacy, he not only retired along the cliff, but withdrew himself to good distance.

Meanwhile he had done me the kindest service, for Lorna came to the window at once to see what the cause of the shout was, and drew back the curtain timidly.

"Oh, Lorna, don't you know me?" I whispered from the side, being afraid of startling her by appearing suddenly.

But she knew me not from my whisper and was shutting the window hastily, when I caught it back and showed myself.

"John!" she cried, yet with sense enough not to speak aloud; "oh, you must be mad, John."

"Without any news of my darling you knew I would come; of course, you did."

"Well, I thought, perhaps . . . Oh, John, you know we can never have one another. Everyone is against it. Why should I make you miserable? Try not to think of me any more."

"And will you try the same of me, Lorna?"

"Oh, yes, John—if you agree to it. At least I will try to try it."

"Then you won't try anything of the sort," I cried with great enthusiasm, for her tone was so nice and melancholy. "The only thing we will try to try is to belong to one another. And if we do our best, Lorna, God alone can prevent us."

As I spoke so boldly, something swelled in her throat and prevented her from answering.

"Now tell me," I said; "what does all this mean? Why are you cooped up here? Why have you given me no sign? Has your grandfather turned against you? Are you in any danger?"

"My poor grandfather is very ill. I fear that he will not live long. The Counselor and his son Carver are now the masters of the valley, and I dare not go out of this house. When I went forth to signal you, Carver tried to seize me, but I was too quick for him. Little Gwenny is not allowed to leave the valley now, so that I could send no message. I have been worried for fear you should think me false to you. If grandfather dies—oh, I cannot bear to think of it. But I must not keep you here."

"I will not stay long; you tremble so, and yet for that very reason how can I leave you?"

"You must—you must," she answered. "I shall die if they hurt you. Oh! quick! someone is coming. Keep back from the window!"

However, it was only Gwenny Carfax, Lorna's little handmaid. Lorna introduced her to me, and we were both favorably impressed with each other. Lorna was very nervous and said finally, "Oh go, go, good John; if you love me, go."

"How can I go without settling anything?" I asked very sensibly. "How shall I know of your danger now? Hit upon something. You are so quick."

"I have been thinking long of something," Lorna answered very rapidly. "Do you see that tree with the seven birds' nests against the cliffs there? Can you count them from above, do you think?"

"No doubt I can, or if I cannot it will not take me long to find a spot from where I can."

"Gwenny can climb like a cat. She has been up there in the summer watching the young birds day by day. Now of course the nests are empty. If you see only six birds' nests, I am in peril and want you. If you see only five, I have been carried off by Carver."

"Good heavens!" said I, at the mere idea, in a tone which frightened Lorna.

"Don't fear, John," she whispered sadly, and my blood grew cold at it. "If you can come within one day of that man's getting hold of me, you will find me quite unharmed. After that you will find me either dead or alive, but not Carver's."

I said, "God bless you, darling," and she said the same to me.
I stole below Carver's house in the shadow from the eastern cliff
and, knowing the village well by now slipt out of the valley. A
weight of care was off my mind, though much trouble hung there
still. One thing was quite certain—if Lorna could not have John
Ridd, no one else should have her. And my mother, who sat up
for me and with me long afterward, agreed that this was a comfort.

Chapter Seventeen

A Good Turn for Jeremy

Jeremy Stickles was back in our township upon some mysterious
errand for the King. That he was spying upon the Doones for
the government seemed clear to me, but he confided nothing to
me until he had had a close call. And this is how it came about.

I was in the forest one day cutting wood. I made certain to be
near a place where I could overlook the Doone Valley, for I
gazed often at the seven birds' nests which proved my Lorna's
safety. Whenever I wanted a change from chopping or binding,
I was up and away to the ridge of the hill, instead of standing
and doing nothing.

When it was time to go home to supper, I wiped my tools very
carefully for I hated to leave them dirty. The gentle tinkle of
the stream was louder than my doings. To this, no doubt, I owe
my life, which then, without my dreaming it, was in great peril.

For, just as I was twisting the very last knot, there came three
men outside the hedge, where the western light was yellow. By
it I could see that all three of them carried guns. They were not
walking carelessly, but following along as though stalking some
enemy. For a moment it struck me cold to think that it was I

they were looking for. With the swiftness of terror I concluded that my visits to the Doone Valley were known and now my life was forfeit.

It was a lucky thing for me that I had heard their clothes catch in the brambles, and that I stood in a dark spot. I had no time to fly, but with a sort of instinct threw myself flat in among the thick fern and held my breath and lay still as a log. When the three came to the gap in the hedge, where I had been in and out so often, they stood up and looked over.

It is all very well for a man to boast that, in all his life, he has never been frightened, and believes that he never could be so, but the fright I was in now was horrible. All my bones seemed to creep inside me when I saw three faces in the gap, and, what was worse, three gun muzzles.

"Somebody's been at work here"—it was the deep voice of Carver Doone; "jump up, Charlie, and look about. We must have no witnesses."

"Give me a hand behind," said Charlie, the same handsome young Doone I had seen in the Doone-gate that night. "This bank is too devilish steep for me."

"Nonsense, man!" cried Marwood de Whichehalse who to my amazement was a third of the number, for he was the son of a respected neighbor. "Nonsense. It was only a peasant cutting wood, and of course he's gone home long ago. There's not even a rabbit here."

At that I drew my breath again, and thanked God I had gotten my coat on.

"Marwood is right," said Charlie. "There is nobody here now, captain."

"There is a big young fellow upon this farm," Carver Doone muttered sulkily, "with whom I have an account to settle if I ever come across him. He hates us because we shot his father. And he has been in London lately, for some traitorous job, no doubt."

"Oh, you mean that fool, John Ridd," answered Marwood, who had unsuccessfully courted my sister Annie; "he's a very simple clodhopper. There's no treachery in him, for he hasn't the head for it. All he cares about is wrestling. He's as strong as a bull and with no more brains."

"A bullet for that bull," said Carver, and I could see the grin on his scornful face; "a bullet for ballast to his brain the first time I come across him. Well, come on. No lingering or our man will get away. If he gives us the slip, both of you shall answer it."

Though they walked on, I was not safe from danger yet, for they might come back and see me unless I crept into the uncut

thicket. But in truth the words of Carver Doone had filled me with such anger and the presence of Marwood so excited my curiosity that I followed them as gently as a rabbit goes. I saw them enter a heavily wooded section by the side of the track which Jeremy Stickles followed every evening when he left our house upon business. And then I knew who it was they had come on purpose to murder.

How might I prevent the crime they were bound upon? To follow the armed men down the hill would have been certain death to me, because there was no cover there. My only chance to stop the mischief was to go round the hill as fast as I could while keeping out of sight and to stop the King's messenger from traveling any further, if only I could catch him there.

This is exactly what I did, and a terrible run I had for it, fearing at every step to hear the echo of shots in the valley. I crossed Bagworthy stream, not far below Doone Valley, and climbed the hill with my heart panting very heavily. Why Jeremy chose to ride this way, instead of the more direct one, was more than I could account for. But I had nothing to do with that. All I wanted was to save his life, and this I did by about a minute.

"Jeremy, Jeremy," was all I could say as I went up to him, and seized the horse's bridle.

"Spoken just in time, John Ridd!" cried Jeremy Stickles, who had been pointing his pistol at me. "I might have known you by your size. What are you doing here?"

"Come to save your life. For heaven's sake, go no further. There are three men in the thicket there, with long guns, waiting for you."

"Ha! I have been watched of late. That is why I pointed the pistol at you, John. Back around this corner and get your breath and tell me about it."

Jeremy Stickles was a man of courage and presence of mind, but he trembled greatly when he heard what I had to tell him.

"We will let them cool their heels, John Ridd," said Jeremy, after thinking a little. "I cannot fetch my musketeers in time to seize the fellows. And three desperate Doones, well-armed, are too many for you and me. One result this attempt will have. It will make us attack them sooner than we had intended."

He took me aside the next day and told me his business in our part of the country. As I had suspected, the Doones figured largely in his commission from the King.

Chapter Eighteen

John Meets Sir Ensor Doone

One day when the threat of frost was in the air and I was out on my farm, I saw a short figure approaching from a thickly-wooded hollow. To my great delight it proved to be Lorna's maid, Gwenny Carfax. She started a moment at seeing me, but then she laid both her hands upon mine.

"Young man," she said, "you must come with me. I was going all the way to fetch you. Old Ensor Doone, Lorna's grandfather, is dying, and he wants to see you."

"See me!" I cried. "What can Sir Ensor want with seeing me? Has Miss Lorna told him?"

"All about you and your doings? Yes she told him everything when she knew the old man was so near his end. He was so angry about your humble birth that we thought he'd come to life again to strike you."

It made me shiver to know that I must either go straight to the presence of Sir Ensor Doone or give up Lorna once for all, and rightly be despised of her. For the first time in my life I thought she had not acted fairly. Why not leave the dying man in peace, without bothering him about my affairs? But soon I saw again that in this matter she was right, that she could not receive the old man's blessing while she deceived him about herself and the life she had undertaken.

With great misgivings I followed Gwenny, who led me along very rapidly. We soon were at the top of the Doone valley. In the chilly dusk air it looked most untempting, especially owing to that state of mind under which I was laboring. As we crossed toward the Captain's house, we met a couple of great Doones lounging by the stream. Gwenny said something to them and although they stared very hard at me, they let me pass without hindrance. When Gwenny opened Sir Ensor's door, my heart thumped, quite as much with terror as with hope of Lorna's presence.

But in a moment the fear was gone, for Lorna was trembling in my arms and my courage rose to comfort her. She feared beyond all else that I was offended with her for telling her grandfather and bringing me into his presence. She left me a moment and returned, whispering, "Now be patient, dearest. Never mind what he says to you, nor attempt to answer him. Look at him gently and steadfastly."

She led me into a cold dark room, rough and very gloomy, although with two candles burning. What I noticed most was an old man, very stern and handsome, with death upon his countenance. He was not lying in his bed, but sat upright in a chair with a loose red cloak thrown over him. Upon this his white hair fell and his thin fingers lay in a ghastly fashion, without a sign or life or move. Only in his great black eyes, fixed upon me solemnly, all the power of his body dwelt, all the life of his soul was burning. I groaned that Lorna thought it good manners to leave us two together.

"Ah," said the old man, and his voice seemed to come from a cavern of skeletons, "are you that great John Ridd?"

"John Ridd is my name, sir," was all that I could answer.

"Son, have you sense enough to know what you have been doing?"

"Yes, I know right well," I answered, "that I have set my eyes far above my rank."

"Are you ignorant that Lorna Doone is born of one of the oldest families remaining in North Europe?"

"I was ignorant of that, your worship; yet I know of her high descent from the Doones of Bagworthy."

The old man's eyes, like fire, probed me.

"And do you know of your own low descent from the Ridds of Exmoor?"

"Sir," I answered, "the Ridds of Exmoor have been honest men twice as long as the Doones have been rogues."

He took this very quietly, when I expected fury.

"Now listen to me, boy or clown or honest fool, or whatever you are. You will pledge your word in Lorna's presence never to see her or seek her again, never even to think of her. Now call her, for I am weary."

He kept his great eyes fixed upon me with their icy fire, and although my heart rebelled at his words, I went in search of Lorna. I found her crying softly at a little window. I put my arm around her to comfort her, and so we entered Sir Ensor's room, together. Our appearance spoke for us all too plainly— that only death's command, not man's, would ever part us.

Old Sir Ensor looked much astonished. For forty years he had been obeyed and feared by all around him. I made him a bow and waited for him to begin.

"You two fools!" he said at last; "you two fools!"

"Please, sir," I answered softly, "maybe we are not such fools as we look. But if we are, we are well content, as long as we are two fools together."

"Why, John," said the old man with a smile in his eyes, "you are not altogether the clumsy farmer I took you for."

"Oh, no, grandfather," cried Lorna with zeal; "nobody knows what John Ridd is because he is so modest. I mean, nobody except me, dear." And here she turned to me again and rose upon tiptoe, and kissed me.

"I have seen a little of the world," said the old man, "but this is beyond all I have seen."

He leaned back upon his brown chair-rest and coughed a little. He sighed a good deal more and perhaps his dying heart desired to open time again with such a lift of warmth and hope as he saw in our eyes and arms. I wondered whether at this time of life, or rather on the brink of death, he was thinking of his youth and prime.

"Fools you are; be fools for ever," said Sir Ensor at last; "it is the best thing I can wish you; boy and girl, be boy and girl until you have grandchildren."

And then he turned so as not to see us and his white hair fell around him.

Chapter Nineteen

The Death of Sir Ensor Doone

I longed to see and know a great deal more about Sir Ensor Doone and hoped that he might not die for at least a week or more. No doubt he had done evil, as evil had been done him, but let us admit that he was, at least, a brave and courteous gentleman.

I will not say that Sir Ensor Doone gave his consent to my resolve about Lorna. He may have meant to bestow on us his blessing, but he died next day without taking the trouble to do it. His loss aroused great lamentation, not among the Doones alone, but also among the neighboring farmers. This grief came not only from fear that a more wicked one might succeed him, but from true admiration of his strong will and from sympathy with his misfortunes.

The day after my visit I returned to the deathbed of Sir Ensor. There was considerable confusion. No one molested me because Carver and the Counselor were minding their own affairs so as to become the new leaders. While I was there, they never came near the dying man.

He for his part never asked for anyone to come near him, not even a priest nor a monk nor a friar. But he seemed to like to have me at one side of his bed and Lorna upon the other. An hour or two before he died, when only we two were with him, he looked at us both very dimly and softly, as if he wished to do something for us, and had left it now for too late. Lorna hoped that he wanted to bless us, but he only frowned at that and let his hand drop downward and crooked one knotted finger.

"He wants something out of the bed, dear," Lorna whispered to me. "See what it is, upon your side, there."

I followed the directions and felt something hard and sharp and drew it forth. It flashed like the spray of a fountain upon us in the dark winter of the room. He could not take it in his hand, but let it hang, only making Lorna see that he meant her to have it.

"Why, it is my glass necklace!" Lorna cried in great surprise; "my necklace he always promised me. Grandfather kept it because the children wanted to pull it from my neck. May I have it now, dear grandfather?"

Except by one very feeble nod the old man could not tell her that she was doing what he wished. Then she gave me the necklace for the sake of safety and I put it in my jacket. He seemed to me to follow this and be well content.

Before Sir Ensor was buried, the greatest frost of the century had set in. The strong men broke three good pickaxes before they got through the hard brown sod, checked with flakes of frosty white, where old Sir Ensor was to lie upon his back, awaiting the darkness of the judgment day.

I stood apart from the ceremony, and indeed it would have been wiser for me to have kept away altogether, for now there was no one to protect me among those wild and lawless men. Both Carver and the Counselor had vowed a fearful vengeance on me, as I heard from Gwenny. They had not dared to meddle with me while the chief lay dying, nor did they consider it wise for a short time after that to endanger their leadership by an open breach with Lorna.

The old outlaw's funeral was a grand and moving sight; those dark and mighty men, hardened to all of sin and crime, now with heads devoutly bent, clasped hands and downcast eyes, following the long black coffin of their leader. Not a tear was shed upon him, except by Lorna. Unless in hot anger his life had been very cold and bitter and distant, and now a week had exhausted all the sorrow of those around him, a grief flowing less from affection than fear.

After all was over I strode across the moors very sadly, trying to keep the cold away by quick movement. It was freezing hard and sharp with a piercing wind to back it. The sky was banked with darkness, hard, austere and frowning.

In the very night which followed old Sir Ensor's funeral, a storm of snow began, such as was never seen before. At what time of night it first began is more than I can say, for we all went to bed soon after supper, being cold and not inclined to talk. At the evening meal an old shepherd had dropped in and foretold a heavy snowfall, with great danger to livestock. Yet despite his warnings we carelessly neglected to take precautions.

Chapter Twenty

The Great Winter

In the bitter morning I arose, knowing the time from force of habit, although the room was dark and gray. I went to the window at once, of course, and found it half covered with snow. The air was thick with snow. It was blocking up doors and roads and streams. I realized we would have to work fast to save our livestock. As we set out, it was snowing harder than it ever had snowed before.

After a deal of floundering we came all safe to the lower meadow, where most of our flock had been kept. But lo, there was no flock at all! None, I mean, to be seen anywhere, only at one corner of the field where a great drift was rolling and curling beneath the violent blast.

Our dog began to scratch at once and to howl along the sides of the drift. He knew that the sheep were buried there. We four men who had set out together began to dig in earnest. At last we drove our tunnels in and listened. The other men declared they heard nothing at all, being anxious now to abandon the matter because of the chill in their feet and knees.

Suddenly I heard a faint "ma-a-ah" coming through the snow, like a last appeal. Then we all fell to again and very soon we hauled the first sheep out. Further in, and close under the bank where they had huddled for warmth, we found all the rest of the poor sheep packed as closely as if they were in a great pie. Two or three of the weaker sheep were dead, but more than sixty were as lively as ever, though cramped and stiff for a little while.

"How shall we get them home?" John Fry, our hired man, asked in great dismay.

"You see to this place, John," I replied; "let none of them out for the present. They are better where they are."

Then of the outer sheep I took the two finest and heaviest and with one beneath my right arm and the other beneath my left, I went straight home. Sixty-six I took home in that way, two at a time on each journey. The work grew harder and harder each time as the drifts of the snow were deepening. I was resolved to try my strength against the strength of the elements, and try it I did—yes, and proved it. People talk of it to this day, but none can tell what the labor was, who have not felt that snow and wind.

Of our sheep upon the mountain and the western farm, scarcely one in ten was saved, do what we would for them. And this was not through any neglect, but from the pure impossibility of finding them at all. That great snow never ceased a moment for three days and nights, and then when all the earth was filled and the trees broke down with weight, a brilliant sun broke forth.

All our house was snowed under. The kitchen was as dark as the cellar. Several windows fell inwards through the weight of the snow against them. We were obliged to cook by candle-light. We were forced to read by candle-light. We couldn't bake because the oven was too chill.

When the sun burst forth at last under that world of white, he brought neither warmth nor cheer, only a clearer cold. That night such a frost ensued as we had never dreamed of. The kettle by the fire froze. Many men were killed, and cattle were frozen rigid in their stalls. Then I heard that fearful sound, which I had never heard before, the sharp yet solemn sound of trees burst open by the frost. Our great walnut lost three branches and has been dying ever since. Even the horses in the stables had long icicles from their muzzles almost every morning.

Of all things the most serious, in my opinion, was the impossibility of hearing from Lorna. Not that those three days alone of snow, tremendous as it was, could have blocked the country so. But the sky had never ceased for more than two days at a time, through three full weeks, to pour fresh piles of snow upon us. Nor did the wind relax a single day. As a rule it snowed all day, cleared up at night, and froze intensely; then in the morning came the snow again before the sun could come to help.

Lizzie, who read a great deal, told me how to make snowshoes for walking on the snow and sleds for skimming over the snow. With these hints I soon had built myself a pair of strong and light snowshoes. At first I could not walk, but floundered about, to the great amusement of the girls, until after a while I grew more expert.

One day I held council with my mother, for I wanted despite the snow, to see if Lorna were safe. She declared that she had seen my pining; rather than watch me grieving so, she gave me her blessing to go. I took her at her word and set off on my new snowshoes.

Chapter Twenty-One

Not too Soon

When I started on my road across the hills and glens, the most I could hope to do was to gain the crest of the hills and look into Doone Valley. Hence I might at least see by the nests still remaining and the view of the Captain's house whether Lorna still was safe. When I came to the open country, far beyond the sheltered homestead and in the full brunt of the wind, the keen blast of the cold broke upon me.

At last I got to my spy-hill, although I might never have known it except for the view it gave me. All the beautiful Doone Valley was snowed half up the sides, so that it looked like a white basin. Not a patch of grass was there, not a black branch of a tree. All was white, and the little river flowed beneath an arch of snow, if it managed to flow at all.

As I thought of Lorna, I resolved to slide the cliffs and bravely go to her, for I saw no Doones about and doubted anyway whether their guns would go off in this weather. To help me the snow came on again, thick enough to blind a man who had not spent as much time in it as I had done for days and days. I strode boldly across the valley, being now afraid of nobody.

If Lorna had looked out of the window, she would not have known me, with those snowshoes on my feet and a sheepskin over me. The house was partly drifted up, though not so much as ours was. I knocked on the door in a hesitating manner wondering whether my answer might be the muzzle of a gun. But I heard a pattering of feet and a whispering going on, and then a shrill voice through the keyhole asking, "Who's there?"

"Only me, John Ridd," I answered, after which I heard a little laughter and a little sobbing, and then the door was opened about a couple of inches, with a bar behind it. When Gwenny saw who it was, she let me in and barred the door again like lightning.

"What is the meaning of all this, Gwenny?" I asked, as I slipped about on the floor, for I could not stand there firmly with my great snowshoes on.

"Meaning enough, and bad meaning, too," the girl answered. "We are shut in here and starving and dare not let anybody in on us. I wish you were good to eat, young man. I could manage most of you myself."

I was so frightened by her eyes, full of wolfish hunger, that I could only say, "Good heavens!" having never seen the like before. Then I drew forth a large piece of bread, which I had brought in case of accidents and placed it in her hands. She leapt at it, as a starving dog leaps at the sight of his supper, and she set her teeth in it. But she stopped immediately, and then took it round the corner, no doubt to her young mistress. Though I was occupied with taking off my snowshoes, I wondered why Lorna did not come to me.

Soon, I knew the cause, for Gwenny called me. I ran and found Lorna unable to say as much as, "John, how are you?" Between the hunger, the cold, and the excitement of my coming, she had fainted away. However, in a few minutes she regained her senses.

"I never expected to see you again. I had made up my mind to die, John, and to die without your knowing it."

I shuddered at this thought. "After all, Lorna," I said, pretending to be gay, for a smile might do her good; "you do not love me as Gwenny does, for she even wanted to eat me."

"And shall, before I'm through, young man," Gwenny answered laughing. "You come in here with those red cheeks and make us think of sirloin."

"Eat up your brown bread, Gwenny. For your mistress I have something here such as she never tasted the like of. Look here, Lorna, smell it first. Annie made it." And then I showed my great mince-pie, and I told them how the mince-meat was made of golden apples and fine sirloin and spice and fruit. But Lorna would not touch a morsel, until she had thanked God for it and put a piece in Gwenny's mouth. Then I begged to know the meaning of the present state of affairs.

"The meaning is sad enough," said Lorna; "and I see no way out of it. We are both to be starved until I let them do what they like with me."

"That is to say, until you choose to marry Carver Doone, and be slowly killed by him."

"Slowly! No, John, quickly. I hate him with such bitterness that less than a week would kill me."

I told them that this state of things could be endured no longer. They agreed, but saw no means to help it. For even if Lorna could make up her mind to come away with me and live at our farm under my good mother's care, as I had urged so often, the snow was all around us, heaped as high as mountains. How could any delicate girl ever get across it?

Then I spoke, with a strange tingle upon both sides of my heart, knowing that this undertaking was a serious one which might bring the Doones out to burn down our farm.

"If I guarantee to take you safe and without much hardship, Lorna, will you come with me?"

"To be sure I will, dear," said Lorna with a smile. "I have small alternative—to starve or go with you."

"Gwenny, have you courage for it? Will you come with your young mistress?"

"Will I stay behind?" cried Gwenny in a voice that settled it. And so we began to arrange it, and I was much excited. It had to be done quickly. The Counselor had ordered that Lorna should have no food until she would obey him. He had strictly watched the house, taking turns with Carver, to ensure that none came near it bearing food. But this evening they had thought it unnecessary to remain on guard.

Now while we sat reflecting and talking—for I was never in a hurry to go when I had Lorna with me—she said, "Come to this frozen window, John, and see the Doones light their bonfire. They are having a celebration in honor of Carver and the Counselor, our new leaders."

The fire went up very merrily, blazing red and white and yellow, and the light danced on the snowdrifts. In this I saw great obstacles to what I wished to manage. For when the fire should be kindled thoroughly, would not all the valley be like a room full of candles? Thinking thus, I was half inclined to wait for another night, but on second thought I realized that this was an opportunity! All the Doones would be drunk, of course, in about three hours' time, and getting more and more in drink as the night went on. The fire itself would sink somewhat in about three hours or more, and only cast uncertain shadows friendly to my purpose. And then the outlaws must gather closer, as the cold increased on them. In their gayety any noise would be cheered as a false alarm. Most of all, and which decided once for all my action—when these wild and reckless villains should be gay with liquor, what was door or wall to stand between them and Lorna? This thought quickened me so much that I made ready to go immediately.

"Lorna, in two hours' time I shall be with you again. Keep the bar up and have Gwenny ready to answer anyone. You are safe while they are dining, dear, and drinking healths and such, and before they have done with that I shall again be with you. Have everything you care to take in a small bundle. I shall knock loudly and then wait a little, and then knock twice, very softly."

With this I folded her in my arms, and she looked up frightened at me, not having realized her danger. Just before I left, I told Gwenny over again what I had instructed her mistress.

Chapter Twenty-Two

Brought Home at Last

To my great delight I found that the weather, not often friendly to lovers, had in the most important matter done me a service. For when I had promised to take my love from the power of those wretches, the only way of escape apparently lay through the main Doone-gate. Though I might try to climb the cliffs myself, I dared not try to take Lorna up them, even if she were not half starved and partly frozen. Therefore I was at my wit's end how to get them out, the passage by the Doone-gate being long and dark and difficult, and leading to such a weary circuit among the snowy moors and hills.

But now, being homeward-bound by the shortest possible track I slipped along between the bonfire and the boundary cliffs, where I found a caved way of snow behind a sort of avalanche. Even if the Doones had been keeping watch instead of reveling, they could scarcely have discovered me. And when I came to my old ascent, where I had often scaled the cliff, it struck me that I would just have a look at my first and painful entrance, the waterslide. I never for a moment imagined that this could help me now, since I never had dared to descend it, even in the finest weather. Still I had a curiosity to know what my old friend was like, with so much snow upon him.

To my great surprise there was scarcely any snow there at all. Probably the sweeping of the northeast wind up the narrow chasm had kept it clear, although the water had no power under the bitter grip of frost. All my waterslide was now less a slide than a path of ice. Here and there the ice was fibred with frozen weed, slanting from the surface and matted so as to make a resting-place.

Lo, it was an easy track and channel, as if made for my purpose, down which I could guide a sled with Lorna sitting in it. There were only two things to be feared: a possible snowslide that would bury us or a too rapid descent that would carry us headlong into the black whirlpool at the bottom, the middle of which was still unfrozen and looking more horrible by contrast. Against this latter danger I made provision by fixing a stout bar across, but against the other we must take our chance and trust ourselves to Providence.

I hastened home at my utmost speed and told my mother to keep the house up till my return and to have plenty of fire blazing and plenty of water boiling and hot food enough for a dozen people. Mother smiled softly at my excitement, though her anxiety was great.

After this I took some brady with me for fear of what might happen in such great cold to my comrades. Also I carried some other provisions, and then I took our new light pony sled, which was not made for snow but ran as sweetly as if it had been. I dared not take the pony with it, first because his hoofs would break through the snow and second because he neighed aloud, particularly in cold weather.

Therefore I put a dozen turns of rope around my own body, twisting both the ends under at the bottom of my breast. I put a good piece of spare rope in the sled, as well as two or three fur coats, and then just as I started, out came Annie, in spite of the cold, panting for fear of missing me, with nothing on her head but with a lantern in one hand.

"Oh, John, here is the most wonderful thing! Mother had this coat stored away. Lizzie says it is a most magnificent sealskin cloak, worth at least fifty pounds."

"At any rate it is soft and warm," said I, very calmly flinging it into the bottom of the sled. "Thank Mother kindly."

With that I drew the ropes tight and set my staff in the snow and struck out with my best foot first, and the sled came after me as lightly as a dog might follow. I went on quietly and at a good speed, being only thankful that the snow had ceased and no wind had yet arisen. Having learned the signs of frost, I knew that we were in for a bitter cold night. Nevertheless I had work enough to keep me warm if I managed it. The question was, could I save my Lorna from the cold?

Daring not to risk my sled by any fall from the valley-cliffs, I dragged it very carefully up the steep incline of ice, through the narrow chasm, and so to the very spot where first I had met Lorna in my boyhood. I moored the sled quite safe at the very lip of the chasm, and then I set off up the valley, skirting along one side of it.

The bonfire was burning strongly, but with more heat than light, and many of the younger Doones were playing on the edge of it. The oldest warriors were inside the two lowest houses. All these I passed without the smallest risk or difficulty. Then I crossed with more care to the door of Lorna's house and made the sign and listened, after taking my snowshoes off.

But no one came as I had expected, nor could I see a light. And I seemed to hear a faint low sound like the moaning of the snow-wind. Then I knocked again more loudly, with a similar knocking at my heart. Receiving no answer, I set all my power at once against the door. In a moment it flew inwards and I glided along the passage with my feet still slippery. There in Lorna's room I saw, by the moonlight flowing in, a sight which drove me beyond sense.

Lorna was behind a chair, crouching in the corner. In the middle of the room lay Gwenny Carfax, dazed, but with one hand clutching the ankle of a struggling man. Another man stood above my Lorna, trying to draw the chair away. In a moment I had him round the waist, and he went out of the window with a mighty crash of glass. Luckily for him the window had no bars like some of them. Then I took the other man by the neck, and he could not plead for mercy. I bore him out of the house as lightly as I could bear a baby, yet squeezing his throat a little more than I would do to an infant. By the bright moonlight I

saw that I carried Marwood de Whichehalse, the same traitor
who had joined the Doones in their plot on Jeremy. For his
father's sake I spared him, and because he had been my school
mate. But with every muscle of my body tight with indignation
I cast him like a tenpin from me into a snowdrift. Then I looked
for the other fellow tossed through Lorna's window, and found
him lying stunned and bleeding, nor able to groan yet. This was
Charleworth, another Doone I had met before.

It was no time to linger now. I fastened my shoes in a moment
and caught up Lorna, telling Gwenny to follow me if she could
or else I would come back for her. I ran the whole distance to
the sled, caring not who might follow me. There by the time I
had set up Lorna, with the sealskin cloak over her, sturdy
Gwenny came along, having trudged in the track of my snow
shoes. I set her in beside her mistress, and then with one look
back at the valley, I hung behind the sled and launched it down
the steep and dangerous way.

Though the cliffs were black above us and the road unseen
in front and a great white grave of snow threatening, Lorna was
calm and happy. Gwenny, however, was in great fright. With
my staff from rock to rock and my weight thrown backward
broke the sled's too rapid descent and brought it safely through

Unpursued, yet looking back as if someone must be after us
we skirted round the black whirlpool and gained the frozen
meadows beyond. Here there was hard pulling, but I drew my
ropes tight and set my whole strength to the business. We
slipped along at a merry pace and in about an hour's time came
to the farmyard where all the dogs greeted us.

My heart was quivering and my cheeks were as hot at the
Doones' bonfire with wondering both what Lorna would think
of our farmyard and what my mother would think of her. Every
one came to the steps to greet us, but I put the others by and
fetched my mother forward.

"You shall see her first," I said; "is she not your daughter?
Hold the light here, Annie."

Mother's hands were quick and trembling as she opened the

nowy cloak and saw my Lorna sleeping with her black hair all disheveled. She bent and kissed Lorna's forehead and only said, "God bless her, John!"

The others carried Lorna into the house, chattering away. I went and brought Gwenny in and asked her how she could have been such a fool as to let those two vile fellows enter the house where Lorna was. She explained so naturally that I could only blame myself, for my agreement had been to give one loud knock and after that two little knocks. Well, these two drunken rogues had come, and one, being very drunk indeed, had given a great thump. The other, being three-quarters drunk, had followed his leader but feebly and had given two little thumps. Thereupon up jumped Lorna and declared that her John was at the door.

All this Gwenny told me briefly, while eating very hungrily the potful of bacon and peas I had given her. Then there came a message that Lorna awakened, and I went to see her.

In a chair was my Lorna, propped with pillows around her and her fair hands spread to the blazing fire. From the shock she knew me not at first, but gradually her senses returned and she smiled at me.

A little sob disturbed us and Mother tried to make us believe that she was only coughing, but Lorna, guessing who she was, jumped up and ran to her. She kneeled before Mother, looking up into her face.

"God bless you, my fair mistress!" said Mother, bending nearer; "God bless you, my sweet child!"

And so she went to Mother's heart even as she had come to mine.

Chapter Twenty-Three

Tom Faggus Makes a Startling Discovery

Jeremy Stickles had gone south before the frost set in for the
purpose of mustering forces to attack the Doone Valley. But the
weather had put a stop to every kind of movement, for even if
men could have borne the cold, they could scarcely be brought
to face the perils of the snow-drifts.

To tell the truth, I cared not how long this weather lasted, so
long as we had enough to eat and could keep ourselves from
freezing. For the Doones could not come prowling after Lorna
while the snow lay piled between us with the surface soft and
dry. Of course, they would soon discover where Lorna was, for
Marwood de Whichehalse was almost certain to have recognized
me. And it gave me great pleasure to think how Carver must be
angered with me for robbing him of the lovely bride whom he
was starving into matrimony. However, I was not pleased with
the possibility that they would come to burn our farm down the
first chance they could. For the present though, we were safe.

Lorna loved our house, and particularly the kitchen with its
cheerful fire, its richness, and pleasant, clean smell. And so the
time flew by. Although it was the longest winter ever known in
our land, to me it was the very shortest and most delicious, and
I believe it was the same to Lorna. But in the middle of March
there were increasing signs of a change of weather. A blessed
rain came down upon us from the southwest and the snow began
to melt.

The melting snow brought with it a rising flood, swollen from
every moorland hollow and from every spouting crag. It was
now high time to work very hard; both to make up for the farm-

work lost during the months of frost and snow, and also to be ready for a great and vicious attack from the Doones, who would burn us in our beds at the earliest opportunity.

In spite of the floods and the perilous state of the roads, Tom Faggus came to see us at last, riding his famous strawberry mare. Annie was overjoyed to see him after four months of parting. Tom had benefited by the weather that had nearly ruined everyone else, for he had sent his mare Winnie out into the evening cold when the wild horses were seeking fodder and shelter. And Winnie never came home at night without at least a score of ponies trotting after her in search of food. Tom would get them into his enclosure within five minutes. Then he fed them well and kept them until he could break them for riding. He had more than three hundred in that manner and stood to make a small fortune by his cleverness.

Then he asked us to set a date for his marriage to Annie, and we realized we could not put the date off much longer. Lorna was curious to meet this former highwayman, and so at dinner she dressed in her very best and came down to meet him. Tom could scarcely keep his eyes off Lorna's necklace, which had been restored to her by Sir Ensor Doone.

A bit later when the girls were in another room, Tom Faggus said quite suddenly—

"What do you know of the history of that beautiful maiden, good mother?"

"Not half so much as my son does," Mother answered, with a soft smile at me; "and when John does not choose to tell a thing, wild horses will not pull it out of him."

"Come, come," said Tom, smiling very pleasantly, "you two understand each other if any two on earth do. Ah, if I had only had a mother, how different I might have been!" And with that he sighed in the tone which always won over Mother and had something to do with his getting Annie.

Tom told us that he was sure he had seen my Lorna's face before, many years ago, when she was quite a little child, but he could not remember where. He could not be mistaken, he said,

for he had noticed her eyes especially. I asked him if he had
ever ventured into the Doone Valley, but he replied that he valued his life a deal too much for that. This was indeed a mystery,
for Lorna thought she had always lived in the Doone Valley and
had never been outside it.

After this he grew very wise and told us clearly that we were
both very foolish. Surely, he said, we were keeping Lorna at the
risk not only of our stock and farm, but also of our precious lives.
After all, was she worth it, even if so very beautiful? I answered
with indignation that her beauty was the least part of her goodness and that I would thank him for his opinion when I had requested it.

"Bravo, John Ridd!" he answered. "Fools will be fools, and I
might be as big a one if I were in your shoes. Nevertheless, in
the name of goodness don't let that helpless child go about with
a thing worth half the county on her."

"Oh, the ring I gave her cost only . . ."

But Tom broke in with contempt, "Not the ring, but the neck-
lace. The necklace is worth all your farm put together and your
Uncle Ben Huckaback's fortune besides, yes and all the town of
Dulverton, too."

"What," said I, "that common glass thing which she has had
since her childhood!"

"Glass, indeed! They are the finest diamonds I ever set eyes
on, and I have handled a good many."

"Surely," cried Mother with excitement, "you must be wrong,
or the young mistress would herself have known it."

"Trust me," answered Tom in his loftiest manner, "trust me,
good mother and simple John, for knowing diamonds when I
see them. In my highwayman days I would have stopped an
eight-horse coach with four armed riders for such a booty as
that. But alas, those days are over; those were days worth living
in. Ah, I never shall know the like again. How fine it was by
moonlight!"

"Mister Faggus," began my mother with a manner of some
dignity, "this is not the tone in which you have formerly spoken

o me about your previous way of life. You have won my Annie's
heart somehow, and you have won my consent through your
epentance, but I will not risk my Annie's life with a man who
earns for the highway."

But Mother, being softhearted, could not retain her wrath
against Tom, especially when she came to reflect, upon Annie's
suggestion, how natural that a young man, fond of adventure,
hould think fondly of his youth.

Chapter Twenty-Four

Jeremy in Danger

To see whether or not Tom was right about the necklace, Mother
went out to fetch Lorna, that the trinket might be examined
before the day grew dark. Lorna came in and Mother led her
up to the light, for Tom to examine her necklace. But she took
the necklace off and placed it in my mother's hands. Tom
Faggus took it eagerly and bore it to the window.

"Don't go out of sight," I said; "you cannot resist such things
as those, if they are what you think them."

"John, I'll have to trounce you yet," said Tom with good humor. "I am now a man of honor. What will you take for it, Miss
Lorna? At a guess, say now."

"I am not accustomed to sell things, sir," said Lorna. "What is
t worth, in your opinion?"

"Do you think it is worth five pounds, now?"

"Oh, no! I never had so much money as that in all my life. It
s very bright and very pretty, but it cannot be worth five pounds,
am sure."

"What a chance for a bargain! Oh, if it were not for Annie,
could make my fortune."

"But, sir, I would not sell it to you, not for twenty times fiv
pounds. My grandfather was so kind about it, and I think it be
longed to my mother."

"There are twenty-five rose diamonds in it, and twenty-fiv
other gems that cannot be matched in London. What do yo
say, Miss Lorna, to a hundred thousand pounds?"

But Lorna took the necklace very quietly from the hands o
Tom Faggus who had not half finished admiring it, and she wen
up to my mother.

"Dear mother, I am so glad," she said in a whisper; "now yo
will have it, won't you, dear? And I shall be so happy, for n
jewels in the world can repay a thousandth part of your kind
ness."

Mother didn't know what to say. Of course, she would neve
dream of taking such a gift as that, and yet she saw how sadl
Lorna would be disappointed. What she said in reply I canno
tell, for Tom went on to say that a necklace of this kind mus
have belonged to one of the highest and wealthiest families i
England.

I knew what Lorna was thinking of. She was thinking all th
time that her necklace had been taken with violence by th
Doones upon some great robbery. As we learned later, this in
deed was true, and yet the necklace honestly belonged to Lorna
How this may be explained will come to light before our tale i
done.

We said no more about the necklace for a long time afterwards
nor did Lorna wear it, now that she knew its value. She aske
me the very next day to take charge of it.

Scarcely had Tom left than Jeremy Stickles arrived, splashe
with mud from head to foot, but happy to get back again.

"Not a blessed morsel have I touched for more than twenty
four hours."

"Surely then you must be quite starving, sir," my sister Anni
replied with zeal, for she loved to see a man with an appetite
Would you like pork or mutton or deer's meat, sir?"

"Oh, deer's meat, by all means," Jeremy answered. "I hav

asted none since I left you, though dreaming of it often. Well, his is better than being chased over the moors for one's life, John. All the way from Landacre Bridge I have ridden a race for my precious life, at the peril of my limbs and neck. Three great Doones were galloping after me. It's good they were so big, or hey would have overtaken me."

He explained that as he was riding towards us, he found the oads soft and heavy with the floods. He had been riding with a soldier from the King's army. At the bridge the torrent was so great that the trooper proposed to ride back again, but Jeremy ared to cross with his horse. He had almost made the other side with difficulty and was turning around to give directions to the soldier when suddenly he saw the trooper fall headlong into the torrent. At the same instant Jeremy heard the report of a gun from behind him and felt a shock to his own body which lifted him out of the saddle.

Turning round he saw three men, two of them ready to load again, and the third with his gun unfired, waiting to get good aim at him. Then Jeremy did a gallant deed that saved his life. He saw that to swim his horse back again would be almost certain death, as affording too good a target. Therefore he struck his spurs into the horse and rode through the water straight at the man who was pointing the long gun at him. If the horse had been carried off his legs, it would have been the end of Jeremy, or the other attackers were getting ready to have another shot at him.

Luckily the horse galloped right on, no doubt being himself excited by the shots, and Jeremy lay almost flat, so as to give little space for good aim. If that fellow with the gun had had any brains, he would have shot the horse at once and then had Stickles at his mercy. Instead he aimed at Jeremy and missed him altogether, being frightened perhaps by the pistol that Jeremy aimed at him. Galloping by at full speed, Master Stickles tried to leave his mark, for he aimed his pistol at the biggest man, who was loading his gun and cursing like ten cannons. But the pistol missed fire, no doubt from the flood which had wetted it.

Jeremy, seeing three horses tethered just up the hill, knew tha
he had not yet escaped, but had more danger ahead of him. H
aimed his other pistol at one of the horses tethered there, so as t
lessen the number of his pursuers, but the powder again faile
him. He dared not stop to cut the bridles, for he heard the me
coming up the hill. He made the most of his head start, an
thanked God that his weight was light as compared to theirs.

His horse was in good condition, and though they had travele
many miles that day through heavy ground, the bath in the rive
had washed the mud off and refreshed his mount. The thre
villains came after him, with all the speed they could muste
hoping that the badness of the road would hinder Jeremy an
put him at their mercy.

Though Jeremy prayed for an Exmoor fog, none came to giv
him cover from his pursuers. Once he really despaired, for th
horse stuck fast in a soft bog after leaping a little brook. Jerem
dismounted and struggled with all his might to free the strug
gling animal. The villains, now topping the crest of the hill, wer
scarcely two hundred yards away. He heard them shout in sav
age delight.

With the calmness of despair Jeremy resolved to have on
more try for it. Scrambling over the horse's head, he gained firr
land and tugged at the bridle. The poor nag replied with all hi
power and reared his forefeet out of the quicksand.

"Now," said Jeremy to his horse, "now, my fine fellow," and h
lifted him with the bridle. The brave beast reared up on hi
trapped haunches. One more spring and he was on earth agair
Jeremy leaped on his back and stooped low, for he knew tha
they would fire. Two bullets whistled over him, as the horse
mad with fright, dashed forward.

In five minutes more he had come to the River Exe with hi
pursuers close behind him. Though a small stream ordinarily, th
Exe now ran in a foaming torrent, unbridged and too wide fo
leaping. But Jeremy's horse took the water well, and both moun
and rider were comforted by its coolness.

As the horses of the three pursuers were beginning to tir

der them, Jeremy knew that if he could only escape the quick-
nds, he was safe. He stood up in his stirrups and gave a scorn-
l cry.

Their only answer was to fire at him again, but the distance
s too great for any aim from horseback. He acknowledged
eir fire with a wave of his hat. From that moment he led them

merry chase while they still followed him, hoping to make him
y dearly if he should slip into one of the swamps. Fortunately
outdistanced them and arrived at our farm safely and in rare
petite.

"But was the poor soldier drowned?" asked Annie. "And you
ver went to look for him! How awful!"

"Shot or drowned, I know not which. But they shall pay dearly
r it."

"How was it you were struck by a bullet and only shaken the saddle? Had you a coat of mail on?" asked Lizzie.

"I happened to have a little flat bottle of the best stonew slung beneath my cloak, and filled with fine brandy. Oh, murderous scoundrels, what a fine spirit they have spilled!"

"You had better thank God," said I, "that they didn't spill y own spirit!"

Chapter Twenty-Five

Every Man Must Defend Himself

Jeremy took me aside, away from the girls, and told me the sults of his mission to get men for attacking the Doones. Wl he had reached his destination, he had found that most of King's troops had been sent elsewhere. The few soldiers rema ing had been ordered to stay where they were. Therefore thought they would gladly have come for a fight with celebrated Doones, they dared not leave their quarters beca of their instructions. However, they spared Jeremy a sin trooper, as a companion and as proof to the county justices t Jeremy had royal approval for attacking the Doones.

To these authorities Stickles was now forced to address hims although he would rather have had one regular trooper tha score of the best volunteers. These volunteers had formed g trained bands during the civil war, but now their discipline v gone, and the younger generation had seen no real fighting. E would have his own opinion and would want to argue it.

But this was not the worst of it. The officers, knowing h hard it would be to collect their men at that time of year and that state of the weather, began to make every possible exc And especially they pressed this point, that Bagworthy was

in their county. The Devonshire people affirmed vehemently
that it lay in Somerset, and the Somersetshire folk averred that it
lay in Devonshire. The truth is that the Bagworthy country was
on the border and in both counties.

Jeremy suggested very sensibly that the two counties should
unite and equally contribute to the elimination of these pests.
But here arose another difficulty, for the men of Devon said they
wouldn't march until the men of Somerset had taken the field,
and the sons of Somerset replied that they were quite ready, but
what were the Devonshire men doing? And so Jeremy returned,
without any army whatever, but with the promise of two hundred men when the roads should be more passable.

Meanwhile, what were we to do, abandoned as we were to the
mercy of the Doones, with only our hands to help us? Jeremy
agreed, when I had told him of Lorna's presence, that we could
not hope to escape an attack from the outlaws, the more especially since they knew he had returned to us. He recommended
that all the entrances to the house should be strengthened and
a watch maintained at night. He also directed me to go to Lynmouth, if a horse could pass the valley, and fetch any of the
mounted troopers who might be quartered there. Also, if any
man of courage, though capable of handling only a pitchfork,
could be found in the neighborhood, I was to try to summon
them. But our district is so thinly populated that I had little faith
in this.

Knowing how fiercely the floods were out, I resolved to travel
the high road. When I descended the hill towards Lynmouth,
however, I feared that my journey was all in vain. For the East
Lynn river was ramping and roaring frightfully, lashing whole
trunks of trees on the rocks and ripping them apart.

I followed the bank of the flood to the beach and had the luck
to see a man on the opposite side. Though I could not make him
hear a word, from the deafening roar of the torrent, I got him
to understand at last that I wanted to cross over. Upon this he
fetched another man and the two of them launched a boat and
made my shore. I gave my message and he fetched his comrades

of whom there were but four. However, to have even these was a help. I started again at full speed for my home, for the men must follow afoot. They were loyal fellows, and meeting two neighbors on the way, persuaded them to come along. As it happened I arrived at the farm two hours before the others.

It was lucky that I had come home so soon, for I found the house in a great commotion. When I asked what the matter was, Lorna answered that it was all her fault, for she alone had

frightened them. She had stolen out to the garden towards dusk. Suddenly in the elder bush across the stream a calm cruel face appeared, the face of Carver Doone.

The maiden, although so used to terror, lost all presence of mind and could neither shriek nor fly, but only gaze as if bewitched. Then Carver Doone, with his deadly smile, gloating upon her horror, lifted his long gun and pointed full at Lorna's heart. In vain she strove to turn away, but fright had stricken her stiff as stone. With the inborn love of life she tried to cover her heart, for she knew Carver's deadly aim, but her hands hung numb and heavy.

With no sign of pity in his face, no quiver of relenting, Carver Doone lowered, inch by inch, the muzzle of his gun. When it pointed to the ground, he pulled the trigger and the bullet flung the dirt all about her. It was a kind of bullying that I swore that night I would avenge. I swore in secret that I would strike down Carver Doone, or else he should strike me down.

"I have spared you this time," he said in his deep calm voice, "only because it suits my plans. But unless you come back to-morrow and teach me how to destroy that fool who took you from me, your death is here where it has been waiting."

Although his gun was empty, he struck the breech of it with his finger and then he turned away, not once looking back again. Lorna saw his giant figure striding across the meadow.

Expecting a sharp attack that night we prepared a great deal of food, for we would almost rather surrender than keep our garrison hungry. All our men were exceedingly brave, but good eaters, too.

Before the women went to bed, Lorna went up to my mother, threw herself into Mother's arms, and begged to be allowed to return to Doone Valley.

"My child, are you unhappy here?" Mother asked her, very gently, for she had begun to regard her now as a daughter of her own.

"Oh, no! Too happy, by far too happy, Mistress Ridd. I never knew rest or peace before, or met with real kindness. But I cannot be so ungrateful as to bring you all into danger for my sake alone. Let me go. You must not pay this great price for my happiness."

"Dear child, we are paying no price at all," replied my mother, embracing her. "We are not threatened for your sake only." I agreed to this and Lorna was comforted. With her hand on my breast she asked—

"Can't you keep out of this fight, John?"

"My own one," I answered, "I believe there will be nothing, but what there is I must see out."

"Shall I tell you what I think, John? It is only a fancy of mine, and perhaps it is not worth telling."

"Tell me, by all means. You know so much about the Doones and their ways."

"What I believe is this, John. You know how high the rivers are, higher than they ever were before. I believe that Doone Valley is flooded, and all the houses under water."

"You little witch!" I answered, "what a fool I must be not to think of it! Of course it is. It must be. The torrent from all the Bagworthy forest, and all the valleys above it, and the great drifts in the glen itself never could have outlet down my little waterslide. The valley must be under water, twenty feet at least. Well, if ever there was a fool, I am he, for not having thought of it."

"I remember once before," said Lorna, "when there was very heavy rain, all through the autumn and winter. The river came down with such a rush that the water was two feet deep in our rooms and we all had to camp by the cliff-edge. But the floods are even higher now."

"There has never been a flood like this," I agreed.

"I am sorry to think of all the poor women flooded out of their houses. However, there is one good result: they cannot send many men against us, with all this trouble upon them."

"You are right," I replied; "and that is why there were only three to cut off Jeremy Stickles. Now we'll beat them, if they come at all. And I defy them to fire the house. The thatch is too wet for burning."

After what Lorna had told me, I had little fear as to the result of the combat. It was not likely that the Doones could bring more than eight or ten men against us, while their homes were in such danger. To meet these we had eight good men, including Jeremy and me, all well armed and resolute, as well as five weaker helpers.

It was my great desire and my chief hope to come across Carver Doone that night and settle the score between us by a conflict man to man. As yet, since I had come to full-grown power, I had never met anyone whom I could not toss in wrestling. But now at last I had found a man whose strength was not to be laughed at. I could guess it in his face. I could tell it in his arms. I could see it in his stride and walk. Being so well used to wrestling and judging antagonists, I felt that here I had found my match.

Therefore I was not content to wait within the house, but took myself to the haystacks, knowing that the Doones were likely to begin their attack there. For they had a custom, when they visited farm houses, of lighting themselves toward picking up anything they wanted, or stabbing the inhabitants, by first creating a blaze in the haystacks.

I leaned back in the haystack and the dust of the seed and the smell came around me. Back went my head and my chin went up, and off I was into slumber, despite all my good resolutions.

Chapter Twenty-Six

Maiden Sentinels Are Best

It was not likely that the outlaws would attack until some time after the moon had risen, because it would be too dangerous to cross the flooded valleys in the darkness of the night. Except for this I would have tried harder to stay awake, but even so it was very foolish of me to abandon watch, since I sleep so soundly. Moreover I had chosen the very worst place in the world to take a nap, for I had a good chance of awaking in a bed of flames.

And so it would have been but for Lorna's vigilance. Her light

hand upon my arm woke me, not too readily. Leaping up, I
seized my club and prepared to knock down whoever it was.

"Who's that?" I cried; "stand back."

"Are you going to strike me down, John?" replied Lorna; "I
am sure I'd never get up again!"

"Lorna, is it you?" I cried. "Breaking all your orders. Come
back into the house at once!"

"How could I sleep while at any moment you might be killed?
And now is the time of real danger, for men can see to travel."

I saw at once the truth of this. The moon was high and clearly
lighted all the watered valleys. To sleep any longer might be
death, not only to myself but to all.

"The man on guard at the back of the house is fast asleep,"
she continued; "Gwenny, who let me out and came with me, has
heard him snoring for two hours. I think the women ought to
be the watch because they have had no traveling. Where do you
suppose little Gwenny is?"

"Surely not in the Doone Valley?" I was not sure, however, for
I could believe little Gwenny would dare anything.

"No," replied Lorna, "although she wanted even to do that.
But of course I would not hear of it, on account of the swollen
waters. But she is perched in yonder tree, which commands our
valley. She says that they are almost sure to cross the stream
there. If they cross, she is sure to see them, and in good time to
let us know."

"What a shame," I cried, "that the men should sleep and the
maidens be the soldiers! I will sit in that tree myself, and send
little Gwenny back to you. Go to bed, Lorna. I'll take good care
not to sleep again."

"Please don't send me away, John," she answered very mournfully; "you and I have been through perils worse than this. I
shall only be miserable indoors."

"I cannot let you stay here," I said. "It is altogether impossible. Do you suppose that I can fight, with you among the
bullets, Lorna?"

"You're right, John. I'd only do more harm than good. I'll go indoors, but not to bed. Please be careful, John."

"I will. I'll shoot them all through the haystacks!"

"Good," she answered, never doubting that I could do it. "But don't think of climbing that tree, John. Gwenny is better for that job."

Before I had been long on duty, a short figure stole towards me. I saw that it was Gwenny with some tidings.

"Ten of them crossed the water down yonder," said Gwenny, seeming to regard this as good news.

"There is no time to lose, Gwenny. Run to the house and fetch Jeremy Stickles and all the men, while I stay here and watch the haystacks."

The robbers rode into our yard as coolly as if they had been invited. Then they actually opened our stable-doors and turned our horses out, putting their own in place of them. This quite took my breath away. By this time I could see our troopers, waiting in the shadow of the house round the corner from where the Doones were, and expecting the order to fire. But Jeremy wisely kept them in readiness until the enemy advanced upon them.

"Two of you men go," it was the deep voice of Carver Doone, "and make us a light to cut their throats by. But one warning: if any man touches Lorna, I'll stab him where he stands! She belongs to me. There are two other young damsels here, whom you may take away if you please. Now for our rights! We have borne too long the insolence of these farmers. Kill every man and every child and burn the cursed place down!"

As he spoke thus I set my gunsights against his breast. The aim was sure as death itself. If I only drew the trigger Carver Doone would breathe no more. And yet—will you believe me? —I could not pull the trigger. Would to God I had done so! But I had never taken human life before. Therefore I dropped my gun and grasped again my club, which seemed a more straightforward implement.

Soon two young men came towards me, bearing torches kindled from Carver's lamp. The first set his torch to the stack within a yard of me, the smoke concealing me from him. I struck him with a back-handed blow on the elbow as he bent it, and I heard the bone of his arm break as clearly as ever I heard a twig snap.

With a roar of pain the villain fell on the ground, and his torch dropped and burnt him. The other man stood amazed at this, not yet having gained sight of me, till I caught his firebrand from his hand and threw it into his face. With that he leaped at me, but I caught him in a manner learned from wrestling and snapped his collarbone, as I laid him upon the top of his comrade.

This little success so encouraged me that I was half inclined to advance and challenge Carver to meet me, but I bore in mind that he would be apt to shoot me without warning. And what is human strength against gunpowder?

While I was hesitating thus, a blaze of light lit up the house and brown smoke hung around it. Six of our men had fired at the Doones, by Jeremy's order, as the villains came swaggering down in the moonlight ready for murder. Two of them fell and the rest hung back. They were not used to this sort of treatment.

Being unable to hold myself back any longer, I strode across the yard and marched right up to Carver Doone, whom I knew by his size in the moonlight. I took him by the beard and said, "Do you call yourself a man?"

For a moment he was so astonished that he could not answer. None had ever dared, I suppose, to look at him in that way, and he saw that he had met his equal, or perhaps his master. Then he tried to fire his pistol at me, but I was too quick for him.

"Now, Carver Doone, take warning," I said to him very soberly; "you have shown yourself a fool by your contempt of me. I may not be your match in trickery, but I am in manhood. You are a contemptible villain. Lie low in your native mud."

And with that by a quick move I laid him flat upon his back in our yard. Seeing him down the others ran, though one of them took a shot at me and wounded me very slightly. Some of them got their horses before our men came up, and some went away without them. And among these last was Captain Carver, who arose while I was feeling my wound, and strode away cursing.

We gained six very good horses, as well as the two young prisoners I had struck by the haystack. The two dead Doones were left behind. I was inclined to pursue the enemy and try to capture more of them, but Jeremy Stickles would not allow it, for he said that the advantage would be upon their side. And who could tell whether or not a second band might be ready to fall upon the farm if we left it unprotected?

One thing was quite certain, that the Doones had never before received so rude a shock and so violent a blow to their supremacy since they had become Lords of Exmoor. I knew that Carver Doone would gnash his teeth and curse the men around him for the blunder, which was really his, of carelessness and over-confidence.

Though my wound was slight, the women made such a fuss about it that I was ashamed to look Jeremy in the face. As for the two captive Doones, they were led off and later executed for their misdeeds. After this attack we resolved to wait and keep a watch upon the valley until the floods went down again.

Chapter Twenty-Seven

John Visits Ruth Huckaback

Although we had lost many cattle during that cruel winter, yet even so we had not lost money, for the few remaining fetched such prices as were never known before. We grumbled; yet on the whole we benefited by the winter, though our neighbors lost nearly everything they owned and had to be helped by us.

When we went to church, Lorna was the main attraction. People who would not come near us when the Doones were threatening with gun and fire flocked in their very best clothes to see a Lady Doone go to church. However, Lorna was not troubled, partly because of her natural dignity and gentleness, and partly because she never dreamed that the people had come to look at her.

Now it happened that I had to go on an errand to Dulverton to visit my cousin Ruth Huckaback and Uncle Ben. I arrived at their door about two hours before noon and knocked smartly. Ruth herself came and let me in, blushing very heartily, for which color I praised her health and my praises made her blush more. I kissed her and put my arm around her waist, only out of pure gallantry and my knowledge of London fashions.

Now Ruth as yet had never heard a word about dear Lorna, and when she led me into her spotless kitchen she told me how glad she was to see me, blushing more at every word. What I had always liked in Ruth was the calm straightforward gaze and beauty of her large brown eyes. Indeed I had spoken of them to Lorna as the only ones to be compared, though not for more than a moment, to her own for truth and light, but never for depth and softness.

We talked about old times at our farm. Finally, I said, "How old are you next birthday?"

"Eighteen, dear John," said Ruth.

"Do you remember how we danced that night when first you visited our farm?" I asked, "and how you were afraid of me first because I looked so tall?"

"Yes, and so very broad, John. I thought that you would eat me. But I have come to know, since then, how very kind and good you are."

"And will you come and dance again, at my wedding, Ruth?"

She nearly let fall the bottle she had in her hands. She poured out a glass of wine, but gave no other sign.

"What did you ask me, John?"

"Nothing of any importance, Ruth. Only we are so fond of

you. I mean to be married as soon as I can. Will you come and help us?"

"To be sure I will, Cousin John—unless, unless grandfather cannot spare me from the business." With this she went away to the window and stood there trying to cover up her sobs.

For my part I knew not what to do. At last I said, "Come and sit by me, dear Ruth, and listen to a long, long story, how things have happened with me."

Then I told her how, for years and years, I had loved Lorna, and of all the dangers and difficulties which had so long beset us. When all my tale was told, she asked in a low and gentle voice, but still without showing her face to me—

"And does she love you, Cousin John? Does she say that she loves you with—with all her heart?"

"Certainly she does," I answered.

She said no more, but crossed the room and kissed me gently on the forehead.

"I hope you may be very happy with—I mean in your new life," she whispered very softly. "Wait just a moment. I shall be back again directly."

With that she was out of the door in a moment, and when she came back, you would not have thought that a tear had dimmed those large bright eyes, but her hands were cold and trembling.

Uncle Reuben did not get home at all, and Ruth, who had promised to come and see us and stay for two weeks, suddenly discovered that she couldn't. I had never before realized her love for me, and now I grieved for her sake, for she was the kindest and gentlest of maidens. How I came to be forever in her debt will later be told.

Chapter Twenty-Eight

A Visit from the Counselor

While I was riding home that evening, thinking about poor Ruth, I little guessed that I was needed desperately at home. So, however, it proved to be, for as I came in after dark, my sister Lizzie met me and said, "Don't go in there, John, until I have had a talk with you."

"What are you at now?" I asked. "There is no peace for a quiet fellow."

"It is nothing we are at," she answered; "it is something very important about Lorna."

"Tell me at once," I cried.

"Do you know a man of about Gwenny's shape, nearly as broad as he is long, about six times the size of Gwenny, and with a length of snow-white hair?"

"I know the man from your description, although I have never seen him. Now where is Lorna?"

"Your Lorna is with Annie, having a good cry, I believe. She knows that this huge man is here to see her, but she begged to defer the interview till you returned."

I was almost sure that the man who had come must be the Counselor himself, and of whom I felt much keener fear than of his son Carver. Knowing that his visit promised ill I sought Lorna immediately. I led her with a heavy heart to meet the dreadful visitor in Mother's room. He pretended not to see me, but advanced with zeal to Lorna, holding out both hands at once.

"My dear niece. How well you look! Mistress Ridd," he went on, turning to Mother, "I give you credit. This is the country of good things. I never would have believed Lorna could have looked so well."

He turned to me, bowing airily. "And this must be your son John, the wrestler. Ah, since I was young, how everything is changed, madam! Except indeed the beauty of women, which seems to increase every year." Here the old villain bowed to my mother and she blushed, and made another curtsy.

"I can hardly be wrong," he went on, "in assuming that this young farmer is beloved of our poor maiden. And for my part, she is welcome to him! I have never been one of those who consider distinctions of rank and birth important. But to come to the point: I may now be regarded, I think, as this young lady's legal guardian, although I have not had the honor of being formally appointed such. As Lorna's guardian I shall give my full and ready consent to her marriage with your son, madam."

"Oh, how good of you, sir, how kind!" said Mother. "Well, I always did say that the most learned people were, almost always, the best and kindest."

"Madam, that is a great sentiment. What a fine couple they will be! And if we can add him to our band—"

"Oh, no, sir, oh no!" cried Mother. "You really must not think of it. He has always been brought up so honest—"

"Ah, yes, that does make a difference! A decided disqualification for domestic life among the Doones. But, surely, he might get over those predjudices, madam?"

"Oh, no, sir! Never. When he was only that high, sir, he couldn't steal even an apple when some boys tried to mislead him."

"Ah," replied the Counselor, shaking his white head gravely; "then I greatly fear that his case is quite incurable. But why doesn't my niece Lorna come and thank me for giving my permission."

Lorna, being challenged thus, came up and looked at the Counselor.

"For what am I to thank you, Uncle?"

"My dear niece, I have told you—for giving my permission to your marriage."

"Well, Uncle, I should be very grateful if I thought that you did so from love of me, but I know you still have something concealed from me."

"I am very generous considering what I know, for you two young people will have the rare advantage of beginning married life with a common interest to discuss. Lorna, your father killed John's father, and John's father slew yours!"

Having spoken, the Counselor leaned back on his chair. Feeling I must speak first, I said—

"Now, Sir Counselor, Sir Ensor gave his approval to our marriage. Even if your story is true—which I doubt—it makes no difference to us."

Lorna squeezed my hand as much as to say, "Right! Give it to him again, like that!"

The Counselor looked at us with great wrath in his eyes, which he tried to keep in check.

"No kind of violence can surprise us," I went on, "since the Doones first came to Exmoor. Now we are used to anything."

"You scoundrel," cried the Counselor in fury, "is that the way we are to deal with such a low-bred fool as you? To question our doings!"

"Besides," I continued quietly, "if our fathers hated one another bitterly, that is all the more reason why we should be wiser than they and make it up in this generation by good will and love."

"Lorna, do you regard this slaughter as a pleasant trifle?"

"In Doone Valley nine-tenths of what is said is false, and you are always arguing that there is little difference between truth and falsehood. Therefore, good uncle, I decline politely to believe a word of what you have told me!"

Lorna became so upset at this that even the Counselor stood back and seemed a little sorry. Since he was still our guest, I took him outside and offered him a glass of wine.

"You know, John," he said, "you are wonderfully good people on the whole. Instead of giving me up to the soldiers, as you might have done, you are giving me wine. I meant to be harsh with you tonight, but you have turned the tables on me through your simple goodness. I have not enjoyed an evening so much in ever so long."

"Sir," I said, "it makes me proud to hear that. Of all the things that please us, the first is to think that we have pleased a visitor."

That night we gave him our best old bedstead.

Chapter Twenty-Nine

The Way to Make the Cream Rise

After the Counselor had gone to bed, I scarcely knew whether he really had begun to feel good will towards us, or whether he was merely acting, so as to deceive us. Nor did I understand a little story which Lorna told me later, how she had heard during the night a sound as of someone prowling about her room, looking for something. But the noise had ceased at once, she said, when she sat up in bed and listened. Knowing how many mice we had, she took courage and fell asleep again.

After breakfast the Counselor followed Annie into the dairy to see how we managed the clotted cream, of which he had eaten a basinful. And thereupon they talked a little, and Annie thought him a fine old gentleman for praising her beloved Tom Faggus.

As Annie was explaining how we clotted the cream, the Counselor asked, "Have you ever heard that if you pass across the top, without breaking the surface, a string of beads or polished glass or anything of that kind, the cream will set three times as solid and in three times the quantity?"

"No, sir, I have never heard that," said Annie innocently. "But it is very easy to try it. I will get my coral necklace. It will not be witchcraft, will it, sir?"

"Certainly not," the old man replied; "I will make the experiment myself, and you may trust me not to be hurt, my dear. But coral will not do, my child, neither will anything colored. The beads must be of plain common glass, but the brighter they are, the better."

"Then I know the very thing," cried Annie; "as bright as bright can be, and without any color. Lorna has the very thing, a necklace of some glass beads. She will be too glad to lend it to us. I will go for it, in a moment."

"My dear, it cannot be half so bright as your own pretty eyes. But remember one thing, Annie, you must not say what it is for, or even that I am going to use it, or else the charm will be broken. Bring it here without a word if you know where she keeps it."

"To be sure I do," she answered. "John used to keep it for her. But she took it away from him last week and wore it when Tom Faggus was here. He said it was very valuable, but valuable or not, we cannot hurt it, can we, sir, by passing it over the cream-pan?"

"Hurt it!" cried the Counselor; "no, we shall do it good, my dear. It will help to raise the cream and reveal its powers!" He looked so benevolent as he said this that Annie suspected nothing, but ran away to get the necklace.

Now as luck would have it, Lorna had taken it into her head only a day or two before that I was far too valuable to be trusted with her necklace, for she feared someone might injure me to obtain it. So she coaxed me to give it to her.

Therefore Annie found it sparkling in the little secret hole, near the head of Lorna's bed. Without a word to anyone she brought it down and danced it in the air before the Counselor for him to admire its brilliance.

"Oh, that old thing!" said the gentleman in a tone of some contempt; "I remember that old thing well enough. However, for want of a better, no doubt it will answer our purpose. Three times three I pass it over. Crinkleum, crankum, grass and clover! What are you afraid of, you silly child?"

"Oh, sir, it is perfect witchcraft. What would Mother say to me. Oh, I see the cream already!"

"To be sure you do; but you must not look, or the whole charm will be broken and the devil will fly away with the pan and drown every cow you own in it."

"Oh, sir, it is too horrible."

The Counselor's eyes rolled like two blazing barrels and his white shaggy brows were knit across them and his forehead scowled. Whether the old man wished to scare her, or whether he was trying not to laugh, is more than I can tell you.

"Now," he said, in a deep, stern whisper; "not a word of this to a living soul. Neither you nor anyone else may enter this place for three hours at least. By that time the charm will have done its work. The pan will be cream to the bottom and you will bless me for a secret which will make your fortune. Put the necklace under this pan, which none must lift for a day and night. Have no fear, simple Annie, not a breath of harm shall come to you if you obey my orders."

"Oh, that I will, sir, that I will, if you only tell me what to do."

"Go to your room without so much as a single word to anyone. Bolt yourself in, and for three hours now, read the Lord's Prayer backwards."

Poor Annie was only too glad to escape upon these conditions. The Counselor kissed her upon the forehead and told her not to make her eyes red, because they were much too sweet and pretty. She ran to her bedroom, but as for reading the Lord's Prayer backwards, that was much beyond her.

Meanwhile the Counselor was gone. He bade our mother adieu with such dignity, warmth, and gratitude that she was quite won over to him. While she was raving about what a fine old gentleman he was, I entered and said, "You had better marry him, Mother. He has stolen a hundred thousand pounds." Annie had just told me of the Counselor's wonderful magic, and I had seen through his trick at once.

"John," cried my mother, turning as pale as death, "you are mad."

"He has gone off with Lorna's necklace. Fifty farms like ours can never make it good to Lorna."

Grim silence followed. I was furious at Lorna's loss and the abuse of our hospitality. But Lorna came to me softly.

"John, did you want me to think that you cared more for my money than for me?"

Then she went to my mother and took her by both hands, and said—

"Mother, I shall worry so if I see you worrying."

For my part my heart was lighter. None could say that I wanted Lorna for her money now, and perhaps the Doones would let me have her, now that her property was gone. But poor Annie was grieved. When we raised the pan and found no necklace, she was horrified and stunned. Lorna did her best to cheer Annie, but the shock was very great.

That same night Jeremy Stickles, of whose absence the Counselor must have known, came back with all equipment ready for a grand attack upon the Doones. Now the Doones knew, quite as well as we did, that this attack was threatening; and therefore we were sure to meet with good resistance and preparation.

Jeremy laughed heartily about Annie's new manner of charming the cream, but he looked very grave at the loss of the jewels, as soon as he knew their value.

"John," he said, "this is bad news. It will be difficult for you to make good this loss, as I fear that you will have to do."

"What!" cried I with my blood running cold. "We make good the loss, Master Stickles! Every farthing we have in the world and the labor of our lives to boot will never pay one tenth of it."

"Not a word to your good mother of this unlucky matter. Keep it to yourself my boy, and try to think but little of it. After all, I may be wrong. Will you keep a secret every word I am about to tell you?"

"By the honor of a man, I will, until you yourself release me."

"Agreed," said he and began his story.

Chapter Thirty

Jeremy Finds Out Something

"You know, John," said Jeremy Stickles, with a good pull at his pipe, "it has been my duty for a long time to search this neighborhood narrowly and learn everything about everybody. Well, about six or seven months before the frost set in I was riding one afternoon from Dulverton to Watchett. It was late in the afternoon and I was growing weary. The road turned suddenly down from the higher land to the very brink of the sea. Close at hand and in the corner above the yellow sands stood as snug a little house as ever I saw.

"My view of that little house, and the way the lights were twinkling, so different from the cold and darkness of the rolling sea, moved my curiosity. So I made the old horse stop. I knocked on the door and someone came and peeped out at me. I saw that it was a dark and foreign-looking woman.

"'Can I rest here for the night?' I asked, with a lift of my hat to her; 'my horse is weary from the swamps and I'm but little better. Besides that we are both starved.'

"'Yes, sir, you can rest and welcome. But there is little food. However, we do have—what do you call it?—the flesh of the pig salted.'

"'Bacon!' said I; 'what can be better?'

"After I had eaten, we began to talk, and I got on very well with my charming hostess. I became curious to know how a clever and handsome woman, as she must have been once, could have settled in this lonely inn, with only the waves for company. When she heard I was a King's agent, she was eager to tell me her story.

"By birth she was an Italian, Benita by name, who had gone to Rome to seek her fortunes. There she met a rich and noble English family. When they offered to employ her to take charge of their son and daughter, she was glad to go, for she loved the children.

"At first all things went well. They traveled through Northern Italy and the south of France, always happy. Then the lord died suddenly and his wife stayed on for six months, in her shock refusing to believe that he was dead.

"Finally the people convinced her that she should return to her native England, and with her came Benita. They landed not far from here ten or eleven years ago and set out for Watchett, where the lady owned a quiet mansion. In their party were two servants and two maids, including Benita.

"They started out bravely but made poor time. The lady was eager to reach her destination that night, and so kept the coach going even as darkness approached. She had been warned about the outlaw Doones of Exmoor, but declared, 'Drive on. I know a little of highwaymen. They never rob a lady.'

"Through the fog and mud the coach went on as best it might, until it reached the sea bank near Watchett. There they met their fate and could not fly it. Although it was past dusk, the silver light from the sea flowed in and showed them a troop of horsemen, waiting under a nearby rock, and ready to dash upon them.

"The horses were driven toward the sea and the servants cocked their guns, but the lady stood up in the carriage and neither screamed nor spoke. Before the waves came into the coach, a score of fierce men were around it. Benita, foreseeing that all their boxes would be turned inside out or carried away, snatched the most valuable of the jewels, a magnificent diamond necklace, and cast it over the little girl's head, burying it under the child's cloak in the hope of saving it.

"What followed, Benita cannot tell, having been herself stunned by a blow on the head. When she recovered her senses, the robbers were gone, and with them the little girl. The lady was sitting upright on a little rock with her dead boy's face to her bosom, for they had slain him. She herself died of shock before morning.

"This is a miserable tale," suddenly said Jeremy Stickles. "Hand me a glass of wine, my boy. What fools we are to spoil our eyes for other people's troubles." But although he carried on so, I knew that tears were in his eyes, if I had dared to look for them or show my own.

"And what was the lady's name?" I asked. "And what became of the little girl? And why did Benita stay there?"

"Well," went on Jeremy, only too glad to be cheerful again, "the Doones had taken every penny and Benita couldn't get her wages. She married a Watchett man and there they are and you may go to visit them."

"But what became of the little maid?" I repeated.

"You great fool!" cried Jeremy; "you are more likely to know than anyone else in the kingdom. As certain as I stand here that little maid is Lorna Doone!"

Chapter Thirty-One

Attack on the Doone Valley

It must not be supposed that I was altogether so thick-headed as Jeremy would have made me out. For when he described the heavy coach and the time and the weather and the season of the year, my heart began to burn within me. For then I thought of my childhood journey many years ago with John Fry. I remembered our meeting with the coach, and the foreign-looking maid, and the beautiful lady and the fine little boy. But most of all I thought of the little girl, dark-haired and very lovely and having even in those days the rich, soft look of Lorna.

But when he spoke of the necklace thrown over the head of the little girl and of her disappearance, I thought of my first sight of the Doones. I remembered the tramp of the outlaw cavalcade and the helpless child, head downward, lying across the robber's saddle. Then I recalled my own mad shout of boyish indignation and marveled at the strange coincidences in my life.

Jeremy thought it wise to conceal from me for the present the name of Lorna's mother, but I knew that I could easily discover it without him. Indeed I was half afraid to hear it, fearing that the nobler and wealthier she proved to be, the smaller was my chance of winning such a wife for plain John Ridd. He made me promise that I wouldn't tell a soul, not even Lorna, for a while yet.

"But suppose we should both be shot in this grand attack on Doone Valley. Is Lorna to remain ignorant of that which changes all her life?"

"Both shot!" cried Jeremy; "my goodness, boy, don't talk like that! And those Doones are cursed good shots, too."

I laughed, for I knew his cool bravery and never-flinching courage. In truth, no coward would have dared to talk like that.

"But when one comes to think of it," he continued, smiling to himself, "some provision should be made for even that unpleasant chance. I will leave the whole in writing, with orders for it to be opened if we are killed."

The Somerset men, dressed in yellow, were already coming down our road, singing and joking. Having no discipline at all, they made pretense to none whatever. They had dismissed their officers as being unnecessary!

"Well," said poor Jeremy, turning to me, "a pretty state of things, John! Sixty cobblers, farmers, tailors, and other craftsmen, and not a man to keep order among them except me! And I'll bet there isn't one among them can hit a barn door. The Doones will make sieves of us all."

However, he had better hopes when the Devon men appeared, as they did in about an hour's time: fine fellows, eager to prove themselves. They had not discarded their officers, but marched in good obedience to them, and were quite prepared to fight the men of Somerset, if need be, in addition to the Doones. They were dressed in red.

The yellows and the reds together numbered a hundred and twenty men, most of whom slept in our barns and stacks. Besides these we had fifteen troopers of the regular army. We were all glad when Jeremy Stickles gave orders to march. Unfortunately, the laws of England insisted that these County Guards should fight only in their own counties. So as we approached the Doone Valley, the Devon men marched to the western side and the Somerset men marched to the eastern. Each band had a cannon. A third cannon was entrusted to the fifteen regular troopers, who with ten picked soldiers from either trained band were to assault the Doone-gate itself. Jeremy and I went with this third force.

The tactics of this grand campaign appeared to me so clever that I commended "Colonel Stickles," as everybody now called him, for his great ability and mastery of the art of war. He admitted that he deserved high praise, but said that he wasn't certain of success, so large a proportion of his forces being untrained and undisciplined.

I wish I could tell all that happened in the battle, but I knew at first hand only the part I played. We twenty-five men lay back a little way from the Doone-gate. Our cannon was ready, loaded to the muzzle. Some of us had horses there, besides the sturdy beasts who had dragged the cannon and now were sniffing at it.

At last we heard the loud bang-bang which proved that the Devon and Somerset men were pouring bullets into the valley— or so at least we supposed. Therefore at double-quick march we advanced around the bend of the cliff which had hidden us, hoping to find the gate undefended and to blow down all barriers with cannon fire. And indeed it seemed likely at first to be so, for the wild and mountainous gorge of rock appeared to be deserted. Therefore we shouted a loud hurrah, as for an easy victory.

But while the sound of our cheer ran back among the crags

above us, a shrill clear whistle cleft the air for a single moment, and then a dozen guns bellowed, and all among us flew murderous lead. Several of our men rolled over, but the rest rushed on, Jeremy and I in front, while we heard the horses plunging at the loaded gun behind us.

"Now, my lads," cried Jeremy, "one dash and we are beyond them!" For he saw that the foe was overhead in the gallery of brushwood.

Our men with a brave shout answered him, for his courage was fine example, and we leaped in under the feet of the foe before they could load their guns again. But here, when the first of our band had passed, an awful crash rang behind us, with the shrieks of men, and the din of metal, and the horrible screaming of horses. The trunk of the tree had been launched overhead and crashed into the very midst of us. Our cannon was under it, and so were two men and a horse with his poor back broken. Another horse vainly struggled to rise, with his thigh-bone smashed and protruding.

Now I lost all presence of mind at this, for I loved both those good horses. Shouting for any to follow me, I dashed headlong into the cavern. Some five or six men came after me, the first of whom was Jeremy. A storm of shots whistled and pattered around me with a blaze of light and a thunderous roar.

On I leaped, like a madman, and pounced on one gunner and hurled him across his cannon, but the others had fled, and a heavy oak door closed with a bang behind them. So utterly were my senses gone and nothing but strength remaining that I caught up the cannon with both hands and dashed it at the doorway. The solid oak burst, and the gun stuck fast.

But here I looked round in vain for any to come and follow up my success. The scanty light showed me no figure moving through the length of the tunnel behind me; only a heavy groan or two went to my heart and chilled it. So I hurried back to seek Jeremy, fearing that he must be wounded.

And thus indeed I found him, as well as three other poor fellows, struck by the cannonball which had passed so close beside me. Two of the four were as dead as stones and growing cold already, but Jeremy and the other could manage to groan, just now and then. So I turned my attention to them and thought no more of fighting.

Having so many wounded and dead among us, we hesitated at the cavern's mouth, wishing for somebody to come and take command of us. But no one came, and I was grieved so much about poor Jeremy that I could only keep his head up and try to stop him from bleeding. The shot had taken him in the mouth. Two of his teeth were in his beard and one of his lips had been shot away. I laid his shattered face on my breast and nursed him as best I could.

While we stayed here, quite out of danger, a boy came up to us with a sudden rush and said, "You've got the worst of it. You'd better be off, all of you. Somerset is fighting Devon, and the Doones have beaten them both."

We few who yet remained of the force which was to have won the Doone-gate gazed foolishly at one another. For we still had some faint hopes of winning the day and recovering our reputation. We could not understand at all how Devon and Somerset, being embarked on the same cause, should be fighting with one another.

Finding nothing more to be done to carry on the battle, we rolled the cannon into the river and laid poor Jeremy and two other wounded men on a crude litter. Sadly we trudged homewards, feeling ourselves thoroughly beaten through no fault of ours.

Since the enterprise failed, I prefer not to dwell too long upon it, only to show the mischief which lay at the root of the failure. This mischief was the stupid jealousy between the yellows of Somerset and the red uniforms of Devon. Now I try to speak impartially, for I live on the borderland between both counties. Listening to one side and another I feel the truth to be about as follows:

The men of Devon had a long way to go around the hills before they could get into position on the western side of Doone

Valley. Knowing that the Somerset men would claim all the glory if allowed to shoot first, the Devon men pointed their cannon in a general direction, trusted in God for good aim, and fired. Now as Providence ordained it, the shot came scattering down upon the unfortunate men of Somerset, killing one and wounding two.

What did the men of Somerset do? Instead of waiting for their friends to send round and beg pardon they trained their gun full upon the men of Devon. Not only this but they cheered loudly when they saw four or five red coats fall on the other side of the valley. Both sides waxed hotter and hotter with the fire of destruction. If the gorge hadn't lain between them, very few would have lived to tell of it. Instead of assaulting the Doones and relieving the pressure at the Doone-gate where we were attacking, the two bands fired steadily at each other.

At last the Doones, who must have laughed at the thunder passing overhead, recalled their man from the gallery and fell on the rear of the Somerset men, slaying four beside their cannon. Then while the survivors ran away, the outlaws took the hot cannon and rolled it down into their valley. Thus of the three guns set forth that morning, only one ever came home again, and that was the gun of the Devon men, who dragged it home themselves to boast about it.

This was a melancholy end of our brave setting out. Everybody blamed everyone else, and several of us wanted to attack again immediately, but we were overruled.

Chapter Thirty-Two

Lorna Knows Her Nurse

After the ill-fated attack on the Doone Valley, the dying and
wounded caused me much grief. Jeremy Stickles lay and tossed
and thrust up his feet in agony. He looked at us ever so many
times, as much as to say, "Fools, let me die. Then I shall have
some comfort," but we comforted him and cheered him as best
we could.

To me particularly Jeremy's wound was a great misfortune in
more ways than one. It put off my chance of telling Lorna and
my mother that Lorna was not of the race that had killed my
father. For I felt that the Counselor's words had made a deep
impression on both Lorna and my mother. Then, too, Jeremy's
illness was a grievous thing to us in that we had no one now to
command the ten troopers still alive. If they left, all our house,
goods, and lives, would be at the mercy of the Doones, who were
bolder than ever after their success.

One day two men appeared at our gate, stripped to their shirts
without horses, and looking very sorrowful. They had come from
London in search of Lorna, for there was a vast fortune awaiting
her, as I had expected. They had gone first to the Doone Valley,
where they had been stripped of all their possessions. Finally
they had reached our farm.

Having Jeremy's permission, which he gave me with a nod, I
told my mother what I knew and guessed about Lorna's parent-
age. She received this with tears and wonder and thanks to God
that Lorna was not an accursed Doone. I knew that the time had
come to tell Lorna, too.

"Darling," I said, when I had found her in the garden, "are

your spirits good? Are you strong enough today to hear a tale of cruel sorrow, but which may leave you all the happier?"

"What can you mean?" she answered, trembling. "Have you come to give me up, John?"

"Not very likely," I replied; "nor do I hope such a thing would leave you all the happier. Oh, Lorna, you are far, far above me in the world and I have no right to claim you. Perhaps when you have heard my message, you will say, 'John Ridd, go away. Your life and mine are parted.'"

"Will I?" cried Lorna playfully. "You are very foolish and jealous, John!"

"Lorna, you are of a very unfortunate family," I blurted out suddenly.

"Better unfortunate than wicked," she answered with her usual quickness, leaping to a conclusion. "Tell me I am not a Doone, and I will—but I cannot love you more."

"You are not a Doone, Lorna, of that at least I am sure, though I don't know what your name is."

"And my father—your father—what I mean is . . ."

"Your father and mine never met one another. The Counselor lied. Your father was killed by an accident in France, and your mother by the Doones, or at least they caused her death and carried you away from her."

Lorna lay back on the garden bench quietly. By pressing my hand she let me know that she wanted to hear all of it. When at last my tale was done, she turned away and wept bitterly at the sad fate of her parents. But to my surprise she spoke not even a word of wrath or bitterness. She seemed to take it all as fate.

"Lorna, darling," I said at last impatiently, "don't you even wish to know what your proper name is?"

"How can it matter to me, John?" she answered. "It can never matter now, when there are none to share it. I have you. Having you I want no other. All my life is one with yours."

I was very proud and showed it. I hoped that Lorna would be

proved of noble family, and yet love me and belong to me. I led her into the house and she fell into my mother's arms.

The truth about Lorna's birth made many things clear to me. It explained why the Doones treated her better than most women they had captured, for they wanted her estate eventually. Any mistreatment would have lost them their chance at her fortune.

To discover Lorna's real name, I rode off one day to Watchett, to see Benita, Lorna's nurse of so many years before. I knocked at the door of her lonely little house.

"Who is it that wishes to enter?" came a voice from within.

"The boy who was at the pump," said I, "when your carriage broke down at Dulverton. The boy that lives at Oare. Some day, you said, you would come to see him."

"Oh, yes, I remember, certainly. My little boy with the fair white skin. I have desired to see him many times."

She was opening the door while saying this, and then she started back in fear that the little boy should have grown so.

"You cannot be that little boy. It is quite impossible!"

"Not only am I that little boy, but also I have come to tell you all about your little girl."

Her curiosity aroused, she invited me in immediately. She told me the very same story she had related to Jeremy, except that she dwelled more upon the little girl because of my interest in her.

"Would you know her again?" I asked, being stirred by these accounts of Lorna when she was five years old. "Would you know her as a full-grown maiden?"

"I think so. From the eyes of the little girl, I think that I would know her."

"The little maid is now a tall young lady, as beautiful as can be. Will you come with me to Oare tomorrow to see your little maiden?"

She promised to come. Later that evening Benita told me that Lorna's father was Lord Dugal, member of a very famous and wealthy Scottish family.

We set out the next day and arrived before dusk safe at my farm. As luck would have it, the first who came to meet us was Lorna. In her joy she ran straight up to us, and then stopped and gazed at Benita. At one glance her old nurse knew her. "Oh, the eyes, the eyes!" she cried.

Lorna, on the other hand, looked at her with some doubt and wonder, but when the foreign woman said something to her in Italian, Lorna cried, "Oh, Nita, Nita!" and threw her arms about her.

This being so, there could be no doubt as to the power of proving Lady Lorna's birth and rights. For though we had not the necklace now—thanks to Annie's foolish belief in the Counselor—we had a heavy gold ring which Lorna had given me long before. The ring had the form of a wildcat stamped upon it, the arms of the house of Lorne. For though Lorna's father was a nobleman of high and goodly lineage, her mother was of yet more ancient and renowned descent, being the last in line direct from the great chiefs of Lorne.

The Doones, knowing Lorna to be heir to large property and bearing special spite against the house of which she was the last, had brought her up with full intention of lawful marriage. Carver Doone himself had hoped to succeed to the property she owned.

Chapter Thirty-Three

Lorna Gone!

As it happened, not long afterward I had to leave home for a few days. I was the champion wrestler in our part of the country, but a mighty giant had appeared in Cornwall to challenge me. His calf was twenty-five inches around; the breadth of his shoulders was two feet and a quarter; and his height was seven feet nd three quarters. Round the chest he was seventy inches, and is hand was a foot across.

Now this man, or rather his backers, sent me a brave and aughty challenge to meet him in the ring on August first, or else ive up the championship. Though I was frightened at first, my nother and Lorna would never believe that this man could beat ne. I resolved to go and try him, if they would pay all expenses nd a hundred pounds if I conquered him.

I found the giant quite as big as they had described him, and nough to terrify anyone, but when my arms were around him, found that his strength did not match his size. I was actually fraid of crushing him. He lay on his back and smiled at me, and begged his pardon. I got my hundred pounds and made up y mind to spend every penny in presents for Mother and Lorna. nnie was already married to Tom Faggus by this time.

Coming into the kitchen with all my cash jingling I found

dear Mother glad to see me safe and sound again. Even Lizzie
was softer and more gracious than usual.

"Where is Lorna?" I asked at length, after trying not to ask
it. "I want her to come and see my money. She never saw so
much before."

"Alas!" said Mother with a heavy sigh. "She will see a great
deal more, I fear, and a great deal more than is good for her.
Whether you ever see her again will depend upon her nature,
John."

"What do you mean, Mother? Have you quarreled? Am I
never to know?"

"The Lady Lorna Dugal," said Lizzie screwing up her lips as
if the title was too grand, "has gone to London, brother John,
and is not likely to come back again. We must try to get on
without her."

"Lorna gone! And without a goodbye to me even! It is your
spite has sickened her."

"You are quite mistaken, there," replied Lizzie. "The Lady
Lorna Dugal is gone because she could not help herself. And she
wept enough to break ten hearts. But she left a letter for 'poor
John.'"

"Where is the letter, you devil?" I cried.

"The letter is in the little cupboard, near the head of Lady
Lorna's bed, where she used to keep the diamond necklace
which we helped to get stolen."

Without another word I rushed up to Lorna's room and tore
the little cupboard open. The letter was simple and loving. Part
of it ran as follows, the other parts being too personal to open to
strangers:

"Forgive me that I go without saying farewell, for I cannot
persuade the men to wait until you return. My great uncle, some
grand lord, is awaiting me at Dunster. I, who have been so lawless always, and the child of outlaws, am now to make up for
this, it seems, by living in a court of law under a guardian and
master until I am twenty-one years old. To me this appears a
dreadful thing, and very unjust and cruel; for why should I lose

my freedom through inheriting land and gold? I offered to abandon all, if they would let me go. I went down on my knees to them, and said I didn't want titles, land or money, just to stay where I was, where first I had known happiness. But they only laughed and called me 'child' and said I must talk of that to the King's minister. They had their orders and must obey them. And then, although it pierced my heart not to say one farewell, I was glad upon the whole that you were not here to dispute it. For I am almost certain that you would not, without violence to yourself, have let your Lorna go to people who never can care for her. But of one thing rest assured—no difference of rank or fortune or life itself shall ever make me swerve from my love to you. We have passed through many troubles, dangers, and disappointments, but there has never yet been doubt between us, nor ever shall be. No matter what anyone says I shall ever be your own Lorna Dugal."

Chapter Thirty-Four

Slaughter in the Marshes

Even though Lorna was not with us, we expected the Doones to attack and make an end of us, since we lay almost at their mercy now, with only four troopers left to protect us. Captain Stickles had been ordered southward with all his force, for there were rumors of trouble. Yet the Doones did not attack.

Now the reason why the Doones did not attack us was that they were preparing to meet another and more powerful assault upon their fortress. For they realized that their repulse of King's troops could not be overlooked when brought before the authorities. And no doubt they were right, because orders had been issued that these outlaws should be brought to justice at any price. Then suddenly the death of King Charles the Second threw all things into confusion and all minds into a panic.

Although the throne was to pass to James II, the King's brother, a force of rebels under the Duke of Monmouth attempted, unsuccessfully, to take over the government. The Doones, knowing they could expect nothing but destruction from the regular government, threw in their lot with the rebels. Even Tom Faggus, Annie's husband, joined the rebel bands.

So it happened that Annie came weeping to me one day and said pleadingly, "John, Tom has gone off with the rebels, and you must, you must go after him."

Reluctantly I agreed, for the Doones were now too busy with the rebellion to think of bothering with us or our farm. But when my mother heard that I was committed by word of honor to a wild-goose chase among the rebels after Tom Faggus, she simply stared and would not believe it. At last, however, we convinced her that I was in earnest and must be off in the early morning. And so I went.

After an adventurous trip I arrived at Bridgewater, which I found full of the Duke's soldiers, if men may be called so, half of whom had never fired a gun before. There were rumors that a battle was to take place that night. However, by this time I had been taught to pay little attention to rumors. Having sought vainly for Tom Faggus among these poor country warriors I went to bed, being as weary as weary can be.

I was awakened roughly by a woman who told me to get out and fight, for the battle was on. Through the open window I heard the distant roll of guns, and the beating of drums. Perhaps Tom Faggus might be there and shot at any moment, leaving my poor Annie a widow. I arose, dressed myself, woke my horse, and set out to see the worst of it, though I had no intentions of taking part in the battle.

It was an awful thing to hear the sounds of raging fight and the howls of poor men hit fatally, and shattered from wrath to wailing. Finally I came to a broad open moor. The rising summer sun showed me a ghastly scene.

Would that I had never been there! Flying men, flung back
from dreams of victory and honor, only glad to have the luck of
life and limbs to fly with, tore past. They were covered with mud
and slime, reeking with sweat and blood, which they could not
stop to wipe, cursing every stick that hindered them.

Seeing me riding to the front, the fugitives called to me to
make no utter fool of myself, for the great guns had come. The
fight was over. All the rest was slaughter.

"It's all up with the Duke of Monmouth!" shouted one big fellow, a miner, whose weapon was a pickaxe. "No use to fight any
more. Go home again, young man."

Upon this I stopped my horse, desiring not to be shot for nothing, and eager to aid some poor sick people, who tried to lift their
arms to me. As I was tending one of the wounded, I felt warm
lips laid against my cheeks quite softly, and then a little push.
Behold it was a horse leaning over me! I arose in haste, and
there stood Winnie, Tom Faggus's famous mare! She looked at
me with pleading eyes and scraped one foot impatiently, entreat-
ing me to follow her.

A cannon-bullet, fired low, ploughed the marsh slowly and
almost ended poor Winnie, but she went bravely on. With those
reckless cannons bellowing a few hundred yards off, I'd have
given that year's hay-crop for a bit of hill to hide behind. At
Doone Valley I had fought, even against cannon, with some spirit
and fury, but now I saw nothing to fight about. Rather I saw
in every poor corpse a reason for not fighting.

The last scene of this pitiful play was now acting, just as I
rode up. The cavalry of the King, with their horses at full speed,
dashed from either side upon the helpless mob of countrymen. A
few weapons feebly challenged them, but the King's soldiers
leaped, with swords drawn, into the scattering shattered mass.
Right and left they hacked and hewed. I could hear the snap-
ping of scythes beneath them and see the flash of their sweeping
swords. How it must end was plain enough, even to one like me
who had never seen a battle before. But Winnie led me away to
the left, and as I could not help the people, nor stop the slaugh-

ter, I was only too glad to follow her, especially as I found the cannon balls coming very rudely near me.

Chapter Thirty-Five

John in Danger

Winnie stopped in front of a low black shed. There I found her sniffing gently, but with great emotion, at the body of Tom Faggus. Poor Tom appeared to be a corpse, and I turned away, unable to keep altogether from weeping. But the mare either could not understand or else would not believe it. She looked at me as much as to say, "He is all right."

Upon this I took courage and handled poor Tom. He groaned very feebly, as I raised him up, and there was the wound, a great savage one, gaping and welling in his right side. I bound it up with some of my linen to stanch the flow of blood, and gave him a little bandy and water.

After that he seemed better, and a little color came into his cheeks. He looked at Winnie and knew her, and put her nose in his clammy hand. Then he managed to whisper, "Is Winnie hurt?"

"Not a bit!" I answered.

"Then neither am I. Put me upon her back, John!"

I was surprised and scarcely knew what to do, for it seemed murder to put such a man on horseback, where he would probably bleed to death. But he told me that unless I obeyed his orders, he would tear off all my bandages and accept no further aid from me.

While I was hesitating, a storm of horsemen went galloping by, reminding me that Tom was certain to be killed as a rebel if

found here. After much difficulty I got him into his saddle.
"Lean forward, Tom. It will stop your wound from bleeding."

"God bless you, John. I am safe," he whispered, fearing to
open his lungs much. "Who can come near my Winnie? Look
out for yourself, John Ridd." He sucked his lips, and the mare
went off, as easy and swift as a swallow.

"Well," thought I, as I looked at my horse, who was thoroughly
weary, "I have done a very good thing, no doubt, and ought to
be thankful to God for the chance. But as for getting away unharmed with all these scoundrels about me! No wonder Tom
said, 'Look out for yourself!' I shall look out from a prison window, or perhaps from a noose!"

I resolved to wait in the shed awhile, for my horse required
a good rest. I was weary, too, and went to sleep for three or
four hours, when a rough shaking brought me back to the world
again. I looked up with a mighty yawn, and saw about twenty
foot-soldiers.

"This shed is not yours," I said, when they had roughly aroused
me; "what business have you here?"

"Bad business for you," said one, "for it will lead you to the
gallows."

"Will you pile your arms outside," I said, "and try a bit of fair
play with me?" For I disliked these men sincerely and would
have liked to teach them a lesson.

These savage-looking men laughed at the idea of my having
any chance against some twenty of them, but I knew that the
place was in my favor. It was small enough so that only two
could come at me at once. Therefore I laid aside my gun and the
two pistols. They set their weapons against the wall, and turned
up their coat sleeves jauntily. Then they began to hesitate.

"You go first, Bob," I heard them say. "You are the biggest of
us, and Dick is the best wrestler. We'll back you up, boy."

Then Bob and Dick made a rush, and the others followed
quickly. But as Bob ran at me most stupidly, not even knowing
how to place his hands, I caught him with my knuckles at the

back of his neck, and with the sway of my right arm sent him over the heads of his comrades.

Meanwhile Dick the wrestler had grappled me, expecting to show off his art, but being quite a lightweight, in a second he was flying after his companion Bob. These two men were hurt so badly that the rest had no desire to encounter similar misfortune. So they hung back whispering, and before they had made up their minds, I rushed into the midst of them. The suddenness and the weight of my rush took them wholly by surprise, and they fell away, hustling over one another, so that my only difficulty was not to tumble over them.

I had taken my gun out with me, but the pair of pistols I had left behind, so I took two from the fallen wariors. I leaped upon my horse and said goodbye to that mongrel lot. They shot at me, but their bullets found no mark and I thanked God for my deliverance, for they would have strung me up from the nearest tree, without trial. Now my way was home, for I had rescued Tom from the mischief into which he had fallen.

While thinking of my adventures I fell in with another group of soldiers, from whom there was no escape. They met me, swaggering very heartily, with their barrels of cider, like so many cannon, across the road.

"We have won the victory, and mean to enjoy it. Down from your horse and have a drink of cider with us, you giant rebel."

"I am no rebel. My name is John Ridd. I belong to the side of the King, and I want some breakfast."

Those fellows were truly hospitable, that much I will say for them, and we got along well together. As we were enjoying ourselves, up came the soldiers I had just beaten at the shed. Now these men upset everything. My new-found friends swore that I was no rebel, but the most loyal subject and finest-hearted fellow they'd ever met, while the men from the shed swore I was a rebel and would be hanged.

A fight began between the two groups, and it was in my power to take my horse and go, but somehow I felt it was a mean thing

o slip off so. While I was hesitating a superior officer rode up,
with his sword drawn and his face angry.

"Is this how you waste my time," he cried striking with the
lat of his sword, "when you ought to be catching a hundred
prisoners worth ten pounds apiece to me? Who is this young
fellow we have here? Speak up; who are you? How much will
your mother pay for your body?"

"My mother will pay nothing for me," I answered. "I am no
rebel, but an honest, loyal farmer."

"Ha, ha! A farmer are you? Those fellows always pay the best.
We'll hang you from my favorite tree."

Colonel Kirke made a sign to his men, and before I could
think of resistance, stout new ropes were flung around me. With
three men on either side, I was led along very painfully. I saw
that I was in a ticklish situation, and likely to get the worst of it,
for the face of the Colonel was hard and stern. Though the men
might pity me, yet they must obey their orders or themselves be
put to death.

When I pleaded with the Colonel, he only gave command that
I should be struck in the mouth. When Bob, whom I had flung
so hard out of the shed, did this, I thrust forth my teeth and
injured him far worse than he injured me.

When we came to the fatal tree, we saw two men hanging
there already, as innocent perhaps as I was. Though ordered by
the Colonel to look steadfastly upon them, I could not bear to do
so. At this he called me a paltry coward and promised my
clothes to any man who would spit upon me. This vile thing
Bob, being angered no doubt by the smarting wound of his
knuckles, bravely stepped forward to do for me, trusting no
doubt to the rope I was led with.

But unluckily as it proved for him, my right arm was free for
a moment. I dealt him such a blow that he never spoke again.
At the sound and sight of that bitter stroke, the other men drew
back. Colonel Kirke, now black in the face with fury and vexation, gave orders for his men to shoot me and cast me into the
nearby ditch.

The men raised their guns and pointed at me, waiting for the word to fire. I spread my hands before my eyes, not being so brave as some men, and hoping in some foolish way to cover my heart with my elbows. A cold sweat broke over me as the Colonel, prolonging his enjoyment, began slowly to say, "Fire."

But while he was yet dwelling on the "F" the hoofs of a horse dashed out on the road, and a horseman flung himself between me and the guns. So narrowly was I saved that one man could not check his trigger. His musket went off, and the ball grazed the horse, frightening him exceedingly. He began to lash out with his heels all around, and the Colonel was glad to keep clear of him. The men made excuse to lower their guns, not really wishing to shoot me.

"What is this, Captain Stickles?" cried Kirke, the more angry because he had shown his cowardice. "Do you dare, sir, to come between me and my lawful prisoner?"

"No. Listen a moment, Colonel," replied my old friend Jeremy, and his voice was the sweetest sound I had heard for many a day; "for your own sake, listen." He looked so full of important tidings that Colonel Kirke made a sign to his men not to shoot me till further orders. Then he went aside with Stickles, but in spite of my anxiety, I could not catch what passed between them. But I feel that the name of my old friend, Justice Jeffreys, was spoken more than once.

"Then I leave him in your hands, Captain Stickles," said Kirke at last, though his dark face was hideous with baffled malice "and I shall hold you answerable for the custody of this prisoner."

"Colonel Kirke, I will answer for him," Jeremy said with a grave bow. "John Ridd, you are my prisoner. Follow me, John Ridd."

I wrung the hand of Jeremy Stickles, and he almost wept as he answered, "Turn for turn, John. You saved my life from the Doones, and by the mercy of God, I have saved you from a far worse company."

Chapter Thirty-Six

John Sees Lorna in London

Jeremy advised me to flee at once, but I refused. "Now that I have been taken prisoner," I declared, "my name is known. If I fly, the farm is lost and my mother and sister will starve. I have done no harm. I have borne no weapons against the King, nor desired the success of his enemies. If they have anything to try me for, I will stand my trial."

"Then to London you must go, my son. There is no such thing as trial here. But hurry, John. I have influence with Lord Churchill, who is a man of sense."

When we reached London, what moved me most was the thought that here Lorna lived, and walked, and perhaps remembered now and then the old days in the good farmhouse. Although I would make no approach to her, any more than she had done to me, yet there was a chance of seeing her somehow and learning how her mind was set. If against me, all should be over. But if she loved me still, as in my heart of hearts I hoped, then would I care for no one. Rank and title, wealth and grandeur, all should go to the winds before they scared me from my own true love.

I discovered that Lady Lorna was in the charge of Earl Brandir, her poor mother's uncle. I learned, too, that Lady Lorna went to the chapel at Whitehall where the King himself worshiped.

One Sunday I obtained admittance to the antechamber of the chapel. Here I took care to be in waiting, before the royal procession entered. You may suppose that my heart beat high when the King and Queen appeared and entered, but my heart beat

faster when Lorna appeared. She entered modestly and shyly.
Would she see me, or would she pass? Was there instinct in our
love?

By some strange chance she saw me. Though her eyes had
been kept carefully on the floor, suddenly she looked up, and
her eyes met mine. She made me a courtly bow, but her cheeks
were as red as my own.

Upon the whole I was satisfied. Lorna had seen me and had
not tried to snub me. As I waited, a lean man with a yellow
beard came up to me and gave me a letter. Lorna had sent me
a message to come and see her.

When I came to Earl Brandir's house, where Lorna was staying,
my natural modesty made me go around to the servant's entrance. Here, to my great surprise, who should let me in but little
Gwenny Carfax, whose very existence I had almost forgotten.
But she looked ashamed, and turned away, and would hardly
speak to me. I followed her to a little room where shortly afterward the door opened and Lorna entered. She came to me, and
in an instant was weeping on my breast.

"Oh, John, why have you behaved so? Why haven't you written me for so long?"

"Because," I answered, "you didn't write me to tell me where
you were."

"What!" cried Lorna in amazement. I told her over and over
again that not a single syllable of any message from her, or tidings of her welfare, had reached me or any one of us, since the
letter she had left behind.

Lorna rang a bell and little Gwenny Carfax came in with a
grave and sullen face.

"Gwenny," began my Lorna, in a tone of high rank and dignity; "go and fetch the letters which I gave you at various times
to send to John Ridd."

"How can I fetch them when they are gone?"

But after a moment she admitted that she had kept the letters
because she wanted Lorna to marry someone of higher rank than
poor John Ridd. I was so glad at having Lorna once again and

true to me through everything that I would have forgiven Gwenny for treason or forgery.

I was resolved not to have a word to say until Lorna had made up her mind how to act for her own happiness.

"Now, John," she cried, "my mind has been made up that you must be my husband for—well, I will not say how long, lest you should laugh at my folly. But I believe it was from the first time I saw you. Now, after all this age of loving, shall a trifle sever us?"

I told her that it was no trifle, but a most important thing, to abandon wealth and honor and the life at court. But Lorna told me that my ancestry of good honest men was as fine as anyone's in England.

I was introduced to her uncle, Lord Brandir, and got along well with him. He looked upon me as an excellent youth, who had rescued Lorna from the Doones, whom he cordially hated. Learning that I had thrown two of them out of the window, he patted me on the back and declared that his doors would ever be open to me, and that I could not come too often.

It was his son, Alan Brandir, who had been killed by Carver Doone as the price of talking to Lorna. Lord Brandir did not know that Alan had been slain, but always hoped that he would return some day to marry Lorna. Because he was old and feeble, we thought it best not to tell him that Alan Brandir lay below the sod in Doone Valley.

One evening towards September I was able to do the Earl a favor that moved him deeply. I saved him from a pair of villainous fellows who were trying to rob and kill him. As it happened, the two robbers were in great disfavor with the King, so that I earned the gratitude of both Lord Brandir and the King. I was knighted for my services and given a coat of arms. Lorna was delighted and proud of me, calling me "Sir John" often, half in fun and half in earnest.

Chapter Thirty-Seven

Not to Be Put Up With

Growing anxious about the farm and my mother, I longed to get back. I was now released from any obligations and given permission to return to Oare. Lorna, too, longed to be back in the country, but she was obliged to remain in London for awhile yet, and so I went alone.

With the passing of winter the Doones no longer kept to their valley. Misdeed followed misdeed until they committed an outrage that we could not tolerate. They surprised a farmer's wife and child one evening while the good man was away in the fields. When poor Christopher Babcock came home that evening, he found his baby murdered and his wife stolen away. The shock of this loss drove him half crazy.

We agreed to this: if the Doones would not return Margery, Christopher's wife, as well as the man who had slain the babe, then I would lead an expedition into the valley to wipe them out.

Since no one else wanted to take this word to the Doones, I volunteered to do so. Carver greeted my demands scornfully. After much attempted persuasion, I saw that it was no use. I did my best to look calmly at him and to say with a quiet voice, "Farewell, Carver Doone, this time. Our day of reckoning is near."

"You fool, it is come," he cried, leaping aside into the crack of rock by the doorway: "Fire!"

Except for the quickness of spring and readiness, learned in many a wrestling bout, that trick would have ended me. But scarce was the word "Fire!" out of his mouth than I was out of range by a single bound behind the rocky pillar of the opening. In this jump I was so brisk that the men could not be checked with their fingers on the triggers. The valley sang with a roar behind it down the avenue of crags.

Amazed at the treachery of this scheme, I ran at top speed away from these vile fellows. Before they could reload I had escaped, but with a heart and mind bitter at their wickedness.

Without any further hesitation I agreed to take command of the honest men who were burning to punish and destroy these outlaws. One condition I made; namely, that the Counselor should be spared, if possible, because, even though he had stolen the necklace, he had been good to Annie on several occasions.

The men met at our house. Tom Faggus joined us, too, being now quite healed of his wound. He was made second in command to me. Even Uncle Ben Huckaback came over to help us with his advice and presence, for he had never forgiven the old outrage upon him.

The Doones looked with ridicule upon our preparations. After repulsing King's troopers and the militia of two counties, was it likely that they would yield their fortress to a band of farmers? We, for our part, felt the power of this reasoning, and knew that we could succeed only through superior judgment and clever planning. From these things we took warning. Having failed through overconfidence, could we not now make the enemy fail through the same cause?

Hence, what we devised was this: to lure from home a part of the robbers and fall by surprise on the other part. Thus we caused a rumor to be spread that a large heap of gold was collected at a mine near the Wizard's Quicksand; this was the lure by which we hoped to tempt some of the Doones to ride forth.

Chapter Thirty-Eight

A Long Account Settled

Having resolved on a night assault, we fixed upon Friday evening because the moon would be full. Some of the farmers and the miners, who also had a grudge against the Doones, would account for those of the outlaws who rode forth to plunder the rumored gold. As soon as we knew that this party of robbers was out of hearing from the valley, we were to pretend to attack at the Doone-gate. Actually, however, the main attack was to come from the rear, by means of my old waterslide.

Upon the whole I rejoiced that Lorna was not present now. It would have been sad to have all her kindred and old associates, though she had kept apart from them, being put to death without ceremony, or else putting all of us to death. For all were resolved this time to have no more shilly-shallying, but to go through with a nasty business. It was "your life or mine."

There was hardly a man among us who had not suffered bitterly from the villains now before us. One had lost his cow, perhaps; another had lost a wife; another, a daughter. Nearly everyone had lost at least a haystack. All were eager to stamp out these outlaws.

We were not to begin our climb up the waterslide until we heard a musket fired from the heights, where John Fry was stationed, in the very place where I had been used to sit and watch for Lorna. John Fry was to fire his gun when he heard the commotion which indicated that the false attack on the Doone-gate was beginning.

We waited a very long time. Suddenly an awful noise rang out.

"The signal, my lads!" I cried. "Now hold on by the rope, and keep your guns pointing to heaven, lest we shoot one another by accident."

At the Doone-gate the forces under Tom Faggus were making their sham attack. We stole up the meadow quietly. The earliest notice any Doone had of our presence was the blazing of the log cabin, where Carver lived. It was my especial privilege to set this house on fire. And I must confess that I rubbed my hands, with a strong delight and comfort, when I saw the home of that man, who had fired so many other houses, having its turn of smoke and blaze.

We took good care, however, to burn no innocent women or children in that righteous destruction, for we brought them all out beforehand. One child I noticed as I saved him, a fair and handsome little fellow, the son of Carver, whom Carver loved if he loved anybody. The boy climbed on my back and rode. Much as I hated his father, it was not in my heart to say or do a thing to upset him.

In the smoke and rush and fire the women believed that there were a hundred of us. Away they ran to the battle at the Doone-gate.

"All Doone-town is on fire!" we heard them shrieking as they went; "a hundred soldiers are burning it with a dreadful great man at the head of them."

Soon, just as I expected, back came the Doone warriors, leaving but two or three at the gate, and burning with wrath to crush us under foot. All the valley glowed with light now, but the finest sight of all was to see those haughty men striding toward us darkly, reckless of their end, but resolute to have two lives for every one. A finer dozen of young men could not have been found in the world perhaps, nor a braver, nor a viler one.

Seeing how few there were of them, I was very loath to fire, although I covered the leader, who appeared to be dashing Charleworth Doone. They were at easy distance now, brightly shown by the fire-light, yet unaware of where we were. I thought that we might take them prisoners, but my followers had other ideas. They saw a fair shot at the men they hated, and the chance was too much for their charity. A dozen muskets rang out, and half the Doones dropped lifeless, like so many logs of firewood.

The rest of the Doones leaped at us like so many demons. They fired wildly, not seeing us well among the bushes, and then they clubbed their muskets or drew their swords, and furiously drove at us. For a moment, although we were twice their number, we fell back before the power of their attack.

I withheld my hand awhile, for I was looking for Carver. One thing I saw, which I long remembered, was Christopher Babcock's giving his life to get Charley's, for he had discovered that Charley now held his wife Margery. Without a weapon he rushed up to Charley and killed him, though he died himself in the struggle. And Margery Babcock came and wept and hung upon her dead husband, and died that summer of heart-disease.

I like not to tell of slaughter, but that was a night of fire and slaughter and long-harbored revenge. Before the daylight broke upon that March morning, the only Doones still left alive were the Counselor and Carver. And of all the dwellings of the Doones, not even one was left.

Carver had been with the party that had ridden out to steal the gold at the mine. Through his fearful strength and his perfect coolness, he had managed to escape, even though every other Doone with him had been slain. For Lorna's sake, I was vexed at his bold escape, since it was no light thing to have at large a man of such power and resourcefulness and desperation.

The Counselor I had spied during the height of the battle creeping away on all fours like a sheep. I ran up to him at full speed.

"John," he said. "Sir John, you will not play falsely with your ancient friend among these violent fellows. I look to you to protect me, John."

"I'll let you go on two conditions," I said, gently taking him by the arm; "the first is that you tell me truly who it was that slew my father."

"I will tell you truly and frankly, John, however painful to me to confess it. It was my son, Carver."

"I thought as much all along," I answered; "but the fault was none of yours, sir, for you were not even present."

"If I had been there, it would not have happened. I am always opposed to violence. Therefore, let me haste away. This scene is against my nature."

"You shall go directly, Sir Counselor, after meeting my other condition, that you place in my hand Lorna's diamond necklace."

"The thing is not in my possession. Carver, my son, has it. What are jewels to me, young man, at my time of life?"

I might have believed him, if I hadn't seen him make a suspicious movement. I thrust my hand inside his coat and drew forth Lorna's necklace, purely sparkling in the moonlight. Because I pitied him, I gave him one of the diamonds from the necklace and then let him go.

Chapter Thirty-Nine

At the Altar

Soon after I had left London, Earl Brandir had died. After a series of legal complications and heavy fees, Lorna was at last free to leave London and marry me. I could scarce believe my fortune when I looked upon her beauty, gentleness, and sweetness mingled with enough humor and warmth to be never tiring.

On our wedding day there was great to-do. Mother, and Annie, and Lizzie, and even cousin Ruth Huckaback made a sweeping of dresses that I scarcely knew where to place my feet. Then Lorna came to me down the aisle, and took my left hand in her right, and I prayed God that it were soon over.

Lorna looked so glorious that I was afraid of glancing at her, yet took in all her beauty. She was nervous, no doubt, though nobody noticed it but me. Her dress was of pure white, touched with faint lavender, and as simple as need be. I was afraid to look at her, except when each of us said, "I will;" and then each dwelled upon the other.

It is impossible to describe my joy and pride when after ring and all were done, and the parson had blessed us, Lorna turned to look at me with a subdued glance. Her eyes told me such a depth of comfort that I was almost amazed, thoroughly as I knew them.

But suddenly a shot rang through the church and those eyes were filled with death!

Lorna fell across my knees in the very moment that I was going to kiss her, as the bridegroom is supposed to do. A flood of blood came out upon the yellow wood of the altar steps, and at my feet lay Lorna, trying to tell me some last message out of her faithful eyes. I lifted her up and petted her and coaxed her, but it was no good. The only sign of life remaining was a spurt of bright red blood.

Of course, I knew who had done it. There was but one man in the world who could have done such a thing! I leaped upon our best horse, and the men fell back before me. I had no sort of weapon. Unarmed and regardless of my strange attire I went out to find justice!

With my vicious horse at a furious speed, I rode on. A few hundred yards ahead of me rode a man on a great black steed, and I knew that the man was Carver Doone.

"Your life or mine," I said to myself, "as God wills it. But we two live not upon this earth one more hour together."

I knew the strength of the great man, and I knew that he was armed with a gun, if he had had time to load again after shooting Lorna. But at any rate he had pistols and a horseman's sword, as well. Nevertheless I had no more doubt of killing the man before me than a cook has of roasting a headless fowl.

Although he was so far in front of me and riding as hard as he could, I saw that he had something on the horse in front of him, something which needed care and stopped him from looking backward. In the whirl of my wits I fancied that this was Lorna, until the scene I had been through fell across my hot brain and heart. But as he made a turn, I saw that he was bearing his little child, little Ensie, whom I had rescued from the burning house on the night of the slaughter. Ensie also saw me and stretched his hands and cried to me, for the face of his father frightened him.

Carver Doone, with a vile oath, thrust spurs into his weary horse and laid one hand on a pistol. I knew then that he had not reloaded his musket since his shot at Lorna. A cry of triumph rose from the black depths of my heart. What cared I for pistols? I had no spurs, nor did my horse need them, for he was as fresh as ever. I knew that the black steed in front would be in our reach soon.

His rider knew this too, and having no room in the rocky channel to turn and fire, drew rein and plunged into the black ravine leading to the Wizard's Quicksand. I followed my enemy carefully, steadily, even leisurely, for I had him, as in a pitfall, from which there was no escape. He thought that I feared to approach him, for he knew not where he was, and his low disdainful laugh came back. "Let him laugh who wins," thought I. Rising from my horse's back I tore a limb from a gnarled oak tree.

Carver Doone turned the corner suddenly on the black and bottomless quicksand. With a start of fear he reined back his horse, and I thought he would have turned on me. But instead he again rode on, hoping to find a way round the side.

Now there is a way between the cliff and the quicksand, for those who know the ground thoroughly, or have time enough to search for it, but for him there was no road, and he lost some time in seeking it. Upon this he made up his mind, and wheeling, fired, and then rode at me.

His bullet struck me somewhere, but I took no heed of that. Fearing only his escape I laid my horse across the way, and with the limb of the oak struck full on the forehead his charging steed. Before the slash of his sword came near me, the man and horse rolled over, and nearly bore my own horse down with the power of their charge.

Carver Doone was somewhat stunned and for a moment could not arise. Meanwhile I leaped on the ground and waited, as though in the ring for wrestling. Then the little boy Ensie ran to me, clasped my leg, and looked up at me, and the terror in his eyes made me almost fear myself.

"Ensie, dear," I said quite gently, grieving that he should see his wicked father killed, "run up there around the corner and try to find a pretty bunch of flowers." The child obeyed me, hanging back, and looking back, and then laughing, while I prepared for business. There and then I might have killed my enemy with a single blow while he lay unconscious, but it would have been foul play.

With a sullen and black scowl Carver gathered his mighty limbs, and arose, and looked round for his weapons, but I had put them well away. Then he came to me and gazed, being used to frighten young men thus.

"I would not harm you, lad," he said, with a lofty style of sneering. "I have punished you enough for most of your impertinence. For the rest I forgive you, because you have been good and gracious to my little son. Go and be contented."

For answer I struck him on the cheek, lightly and not to hurt him, but to make his blood leap up. I would not soil my tongue by speaking to a man like this.

There was a level space of grass between us and the quicksand. To this place I led him. I think he felt that his time was come. I think he knew from my knitted muscles and arched breast that he had found his master. At any rate a paleness came, an ashy paleness on his cheeks, and the vast calves of his legs bowed in, as if he were out of training.

Seeing this, villain though he was, I offered him first chance. I stretched forth my left hand as I do to a weaker antagonist, and I let him have the first hug of me. But in this I was too generous, having forgotten my pistol wound and the cracking of one of my ribs. Carver Doone caught me round the waist with such a grip as never yet had been laid upon me.

I heard my rib go. I grasped an arm, and tore the muscle out of it as the string comes out of an orange. Then I took him by the throat. In vain he tugged and strained and twisted. He dashed his bleeding fist into my face and flung himself on me with gnashing jaws. Beneath the iron of my strength, for God that day was with me, I had him helpless in two minutes, and his fiery eyes lolled out.

"I will not harm you any more," I cried, so far as I could for panting. "Carver Doone, you are beaten. Admit it, and thank God for it, and go your way and repent."

It was all too late. Even if he had yielded in his frenzy, even if he had admitted for the first time in his life he had found his master, it was all too late.

The black quicksand had him by the feet. The sucking of the ground drew on him like the thirsty lips of death. In our fury we had forgotten where we were. I myself could scarcely leap, with the last spring of overtired legs, from the engulfing grave of slime. He fell back. Then he tossed his arms to heaven, and they were black to the elbow, and the glare of his eyes was ghastly. I could only gaze and pant, for my strength was no more than an infant's from the fury and the horror. Scarcely could I turn away while, joint by joint, he sank from sight.

Chapter Forty

Given Back

When the little boy came back with the flowers which he had managed to find, the only sign left of his father was a dark brown bubble upon a new-formed patch of blackness. But the center of the quicksand was heaving and sullenly grinding its jaws.

With pain and ache both of mind and body, and shame at my own fury, I heavily mounted my horse again and looked down at the innocent Ensie. Would this playful loving child grow up like his cruel father and end a godless life of hatred with a death of violence? He lifted his face toward me, as if to answer, "No, I will not," but the words he spoke were these—

"Don"—for he never could say, "John"—"oh Don, I am so glad that nasty man is gone away. Take me home, Don. Take me home."

It has been said of the wicked, "Not even their own children love them." And I could easily believe that Carver Doone's cold-hearted ways had scared from him even his favorite child. But it did hurt me to take into my arms the child of the man I had just slain.

I had lost a great deal of blood and was rather faint and weary. When we came towards the farm, I seemed to be riding in a dream almost, and the voices seemed to wander from a distant muffling cloud. Only the thought of Lorna's death, like a heavy knell, was tolling in the belfry of my brain.

I tottered into the old farmhouse like a young child. "I have killed him," was all I said, "even as he killed Lorna. Now let me see my wife. She belongs to me none the less, though dead."

"You cannot see her now, dear John," said Ruth Huckaback, coming forward. "Annie is with her now, John."

"What has that to do with it? Let me see my dead one, and die."

All the women fell away and whispered, and looked at me with side-glances, for my face was as hard as flint. Ruth alone stood by me, and dropped her eyes, and trembled. She whispered gently, "John, she is not your dead one. She may even be your living one yet, your wife, your home, and your happiness. But you must not see her now."

"Is there any chance for her?"

"God in heaven knows, dear John. But the sight of you so battered would be certain death to her. Now come first and be healed yourself."

I obeyed her like a child, whispering only as I went, for none but myself knew her goodness, "Almighty God will bless you, Ruth, for the good you are doing now."

If it had not been for this little maid, Lorna would have died at once. But the moment I left to pursue Carver, Ruth came forward and took command of everyone. She made them bear Lorna home at once, with the door of the church as a stretcher. She probed the wound in her side and extracted the bullet, and then with cold water staunched the flowing of the blood. Ruth did all this while Lorna lay insensible and all the other women declared she was dead.

At the very moment when all the rest had decided that Ruth was a simple idiot to try to save Lorna from certain death, a flutter in my darling's throat made them pause and look and hope. For days she lay at the very verge of death, kept alive by nothing but the care, the skill, the tenderness, and perpetual watchfulness of Ruth. She took the whole task of healing on herself and with God's help bore it through. Lorna recovered long before I did.

For the grief was on me still of having lost my love and lover at the moment she was mine. With the black cauldron of the Wizard's Quicksand boiling in my heated brain I had no faith in the tale they told. I believed that Lorna lay dead in the churchyard while these rogues were lying to me.

One day I was sitting in my bedroom, for I could not get downstairs and there was no one strong enough to carry me, even if I would have allowed it. Presently a little knock sounded through my gloomy room, and supposing it to be the doctor I tried to rise and make my bow. But to my surprise it was little Ruth.

She ran towards me with sparkling eyes, and then suddenly stopped. I saw entire amazement in her face.

"Can you receive visitors, Cousin John? Why, they never told me of this! I knew that you were weak, but not that you were dying. What is that basin for?"

"I have no intention of dying, Ruth. That basin is for the doctor's purpose. He has been bleeding me twice a week for the last six weeks. Nothing else has kept me alive."

"Nothing else has killed you, nearly. There!" and she set her little boot across the basin and crushed it. "Not another drop shall they have from you."

I was surprised to see Ruth excited, and I tried to soothe her with my feeble hand as she knelt before me.

"Dear Ruth, the doctor must know best."

"Well you leave it to me, John! I have saved your Lorna's life. And now I will save yours, which is a far easier business."

"You have saved my Lorna's life! What do you mean by talking so?"

"Only what I say, Cousin John. Have you ever known me to tell a lie?"

"I do not understand," was all I could say for a very long time.

"Will you understand if I show you Lorna? I have feared to do it, for the sake of you both. But now Lorna is well enough, if you think that you are, Cousin John. Surely you will understand when you see your wife."

In a moment Ruth was back with Lorna. Ruth banged the door and ran away, and Lorna stood before me. I felt my life come back. I felt the joy of living now, and the power of doing it.

Little more have I to tell. The doctor was turned out at once, and slowly I recovered my former strength, with a darling wife and good food.

As I write this story, Lorna never tires of being with me and talking of the many fears and troubles, dangers and discouragements, and worst of all the bitter partings which we used to suffer. Lorna has inherited great stores of money, though we never draw upon them except for some poor neighbor. Tom Faggus has finally settled down to a good respectable life with

Annie, bringing his children up to honesty as the first of all qualifications. Lizzie has married one of the officers who had been stationed with us at the time of the Doone-trouble. Ruth Huckaback is not married yet, though there is one deeply in love with her who may win her.

Little Ensie Doone I sent to school at my own expense, having changed his name for fear of what anyone might do to him. I call him "Ensie Jones," and I hope that he will be a credit to us, for the bold adventurous nature of the Doones broke out in him, and we have got him into the army where he has distinguished himself.

Of Lorna, of my lifelong darling, I will not talk, for it is not proper that a man should exalt his pride. Year by year her beauty grows with the growth of goodness, kindness, and true happiness. But whenever we become too forgetful, I bring us both back to forgotten sadness by the two words, "Lorna Doone."

PRIDE AND PREJUDICE

Pride
and Prejudice

BY

JANE AUSTEN

ADAPTED BY
OLLIE DEPEW
Professor of English
Southern Oregon College of Education
Ashland, Oregon

EDITED BY
HERBERT SPENCER ROBINSON
Adjunct Professor of English
Pace College, New York City

J. J. LITTLE & IVES CO., INC. • NEW YORK

Contents

CONTENTS

160

PRIDE AND PREJUDICE

Chapter One

Mr. Bingley, a Handsome, Rich Young Bachelor Comes Upon the Scene, and Mrs. Bennet Forms Plans for One of Her Five Daughters

A single man in possession of a good fortune must be in want of a wife. This truth is so well fixed in the minds of all, that when such a man enters a neighborhood he is considered by the surrounding families as the rightful property of some one or other of their daughters.

"My dear Mr. Bennet," said Mrs. Bennet to him one day, "have you heard that Netherfield Park[1] is rented at last?"

Mr. Bennet replied that he had not.

"But it is," returned she; "for Mrs. Long has just been here, and she told me all about it."

Mr. Bennet made no answer.

"Do you not want to know who has taken it?" cried his wife impatiently.

"*You* want to tell me, and I have no objection to hearing it."

"Why, my dear, Mrs. Long says that Netherfield is taken by a young man of large fortune from the north of England. He came down on Monday to see the place and was so much delighted with it that he took it at once. Some of his servants are to be in the house by the end of next week."

"What is his name?"

"Bingley."

"Is he married or single?"

"Oh! single, my dear, to be sure! A single man of large fortune. What a fine thing for our girls!"

"How so? How can it affect them?"

---

[1] The name of a large country mansion and its grounds.

"My dear Mr. Bennet," replied his wife, "how can you be so tiresome! You must know that I am thinking of his marrying one of them."

"Is that his purpose in settling here?"

"Nonsense, how can you talk so! But it is very likely that he *may* fall in love with one of them, and therefore you must visit him as soon as he comes."

"I see no cause for that. You and the girls may go. Or you may send them by themselves, which perhaps will be still better. You are as handsome as any of them, and Mr. Bingley might like you the best of the party."

"My dear, you flatter me. I certainly *have* had my share of beauty, but I do not pretend to be anything unusual now. When a woman has five grown-up daughters, she ought to stop thinking of her own beauty."

"In such cases, a woman has not often much beauty to think of."

"But, my dear, you must indeed go and see Mr. Bingley when he comes into the neighborhood."

"It is more than I plan, I assure you."

"But think of your daughters. Only think what a fine place it would be for one of them. Indeed you must go, for it will be impossible for *us* to visit him if you do not."

"I dare say Mr. Bingley will be very glad to see you, and I will send a few lines by you to assure him of my hearty consent to his marrying whichever he chooses of the girls, though I must throw in a good word for my little Lizzy."

"You will do no such thing. Lizzy is not a bit better than the others. She is not half so handsome as Jane nor half so good-humored as Lydia."

"They have none of them much to recommend them," replied he. "They are all silly and ignorant like other girls, but Lizzy has something more of quickness than her sisters."

"Mr. Bennet, how can you abuse your own children in such a way? You delight in vexing me. You have no mercy on my poor nerves."

"You mistake me, my dear. I have a high respect for your nerves. They are my old friends. I have heard you mention them these twenty years at least."

"Ah! you do not know what I suffer."

"But I hope you will get over it, and live to see many rich young men come into the neighborhood."

"It will be no use to us if twenty such should come, since you will not visit them."

"Depend upon it, my dear, that when there are twenty, I shall visit them all."

Mr. Bennet was so odd a mixture of quick parts, sarcastic humor and reserve, that twenty-three years of marriage had not made his wife understand his nature. She was a woman of little understanding, and uncertain temper. When she was vexed she fancied herself nervous. The business of her life was to get her daughters married; her other interest was visiting and news.

Mr. Bennet was among the first of those who visited Mr. Bingley. He had always intended to visit him, though to the last always telling his wife that he should not go, and till the evening after the visit was paid, she had no knowledge of it. It was then learned of in the following manner. Mr. Bennet, seeing his daughter busy trimming a hat, suddenly said to her:

"I hope Mr. Bingley will like it, Lizzy."

"We are not in a way to know *what* Mr. Bingley likes," said her mother in a vexed tone, "since we are not to visit."

"But you forget, mama," said Elizabeth, "that we shall meet him at the assemblies and that Mrs. Long has promised to introduce him."

"I do not believe Mrs. Long will do any such thing. She has two nieces of her own. She is a selfish deceitful woman, and I have no good opinion of her."

"Nor I," said Mr. Bennet. "I am glad that you do not depend on her serving you."

Mrs. Bennet would not reply to him, but, unable to contain herself, began scolding one of her daughters.

"Don't keep coughing so, Kitty, for heaven's sake! Have a little mercy on my nerves. You tear them to pieces. When is your next ball to be, Lizzy?"

"Two weeks from tomorrow."

"So it is," cried her mother, "and Mrs. Long does not come back till the day before. It will be impossible for her to introduce him, for she will not know him herself."

"Then, my dear, you may have the advantage of your friend; you may introduce Mr. Bingley to *her*."

"Impossible, Mr. Bennet, impossible, when I do not know him myself. How can you be so teasing?"

"Two weeks is certainly very little time. One cannot know what a man really is by the end of two weeks. But if *we* do not venture, somebody else will. I will take it on myself to introduce him."

The girls stared at their father. Mrs. Bennet said only, "Nonsense, nonsense!"

"What!" cried he. "Do you mean to say that the stress that is laid on the forms of introduction is nonsense? I cannot quite agree with you *there*. What say you, Mary? For you are a young lady of deep reflection, I know, and read great books and make extracts."

Mary wished to say something very sensible, but did not know how.

"While Mary is adjusting her ideas," he continued, "let us return to Mr. Bingley."

"I am sick of Mr. Bingley," cried his wife.

"I am sorry to hear *that*, but why did you not tell me so before? If I had known as much this morning, I certainly would not have called on him."

The surprise of the ladies was just what he wished.

"How good it was in you, my dear Mr. Bennet; I was sure you loved your girls too well to neglect such a duty. Well, how pleased I am! And it is such a good joke, too, that you should have gone this morning and never said a word about it till now."

"Now, Kitty, you may cough as much as you choose," said Mr.

Bennet, and as he spoke he left the room, weary with the raptures of his wife.

"What an excellent father you have, girls," said she when the door was shut. "I do not know how you will ever reward him for his kindness. Or me either, for that matter. Lydia, my love, though you *are* the youngest, I dare say Mr. Bingley will dance with you at the next ball."

"Oh," said Lydia stoutly, "I am not afraid. I'm the tallest, though I *am* the youngest."

But not all of Mrs. Bennet's questions, nor those of her five daughters, could draw from Mr. Bennet any clear description of Mr. Bingley. They were able to learn something from their neighbor, Lady Lucas. Her report was highly favorable. Sir William Lucas had been delighted with Mr. Bingley. He was quite young, handsome, agreeable, and to crown the whole, he meant to be at the next assembly with a large party. Nothing could be more delightful!

"If I can but see one of my daughters happily settled at Netherfield," said Mrs. Bennet to her husband, "and all the others equally well married, I shall have nothing to wish for."

Chapter Two

Mr. Darcy, a Handsome, Very Rich and Very Proud Young Bachelor Comes Upon the Scene

In a few days Mr. Bingley returned Mr. Bennet's visit, and sat about ten minutes with him in his library. He had hopes of a sight of the young ladies, of whose beauty he had heard much, but he saw only the father. The ladies were more fortunate, for they were able to see from an upper window that he wore a blue coat and rode a black horse.

An invitation to dinner was soon afterward sent, and already Mrs. Bennet had planned the courses that were to do credit to her housekeeping, when an answer came which put off the dinner. Mr. Bingley had to be in London the next day. Mrs. Bennet was quite disturbed. She could not imagine what business he could have in town so soon after his arrival. She began to fear that he might be always flying about from one place to another, and never settled at Netherfield as he ought to be. Lady Lucas quieted her fears a little by starting the idea of his being gone to London only to get a large party for the ball.

A report soon followed that Mr. Bingley was to bring twelve ladies and seven gentlemen with him to the assembly. The girls grieved over such a number of ladies, but the day before the ball they heard that he had brought only six with him from London, his five sisters and a cousin.

But when Mr. Bingley and his party entered the assembly room, they were seen to be only five altogether—Mr. Bingley, his two sisters, the husband of the eldest, and another young man. His sisters were fine women with an air of fashion. His brother-in-law, Mr. Hurst, merely looked the gentleman. But his friend Mr. Darcy soon drew the attention of the room by his fine, tall person, handsome features, and noble bearing. Within five minutes after his entrance the report was all abroad that he had ten thousand pounds[1] a year. He was looked at with great admiration for about half the evening, till his manners turned opinion against him. He was discovered to be proud, to be above his company, and above being pleased. Then, not all of Pemberley, his large estate in Derbyshire, could save him from having a most forbidding appearance and being unworthy to be compared with his friend, the pleasant mannered Mr. Bingley.

Mr. Bingley had soon got to know all the principal people in the room. He was lively and danced every dance, was vexed that the ball closed so early, and talked of giving one himself at Netherfield. What a contrast between him and Mr. Darcy, who

---

[1] The pound sterling, the monetary unit of Great Britain, was formerly worth about five dollars.

danced only twice, once with Mrs. Hurst and once with Miss Bingley, and spent the rest of the evening walking about the room, speaking now and then to one of his own party. All agreed that he was the proudest, most disagreeable man in the world, and everybody hoped that he would never come there again. Among the most violent against him was Mrs. Bennet, for he had slighted one of her daughters.

Elizabeth Bennet because of the scarcity of gentlemen, had had to sit down for two dances. During part of that time Mr. Darcy had been standing near enough for her to overhear a talk between him and Mr. Bingley, who came from the dance for a few minutes to press his friend to join it.

"Come, Darcy," said he, "I hate to see you standing about by yourself in this dull manner. You had much better dance."

"I certainly shall not. Your sisters are dancing, and there is not another woman in the room with whom it would not be a punishment to me to dance."

"Upon my honor," cried Bingley, "I never met with so many pleasant girls in my life as I have this evening, and several of them, you see, are very pretty."

"*You* are dancing with the only handsome girl in the room," said Mr. Darcy, looking at Jane Bennet.

"Oh, she is the most beautiful creature I ever saw! But there is one of her sisters sitting down just behind you who is very pretty and, I dare say, very agreeable."

"Which do you mean?" And turning around, he looked for a moment at Elizabeth, till catching her eye, he withdrew his own and coldly said, "She is not handsome enough to tempt *me*. You had better return to your partner and enjoy her smiles, for you are wasting your time with me."

Mr. Darcy walked off, and Elizabeth remained with no very cordial feelings toward him. She told the story, however, with great spirit among her friends, for she had a lively, playful nature, and delighted in anything ridiculous.

The evening altogether passed off pleasantly enough to the whole family. Mrs. Bennet had seen her eldest daughter Jane much admired by the Netherfield party. Mr. Bingley had danced with her twice. Jane was as much pleased by this as her mother could be, though in a quieter way. Elizabeth felt Jane's pleasure. Mary had heard herself mentioned as the most accomplished girl in the neighborhood. Kitty and Lydia had not once been without partners. They returned therefore in good spirits to Longbourn, their home. They found Mr. Bennet still up.

"Oh, my dear Mr. Bennet," cried Mrs. Bennet, as she entered the room, "we have had a most delightful evening, a most excellent ball. I wish you had been there. Jane was so admired. Everybody said how well she looked. Mr. Bingley thought her quite beautiful and danced with her twice, and she was the only person in the room that he asked a second time. First of all, he asked Miss Lucas. I was so vexed, but he did not admire her at all; nobody can, you know. He danced the next two with Jane. Then he danced with Miss King, then with Maria Lucas, and then with Jane again, and then with Lizzy, and the—"

"Say no more of his partners!" cried Mr. Bennet impatiently. "Oh, that he had sprained his ankle in the first dance!"

"I am quite delighted with him," continued Mrs. Bennet. "He is so handsome! And his sisters are charming women. I never in my life saw anything like their dresses. The lace on Mrs. Hurst's gown—"

Here Mr. Bennet cried out against any description of finery. She then told him, with much bitterness, about the shocking rudeness of Mr. Darcy.

"But Lizzy does not lose much by not suiting *his* fancy," she added. "He is a most disagreeable, horrid man, not at all worth pleasing. So high and so conceited there was no enduring him! He walked here, and he walked there, fancying himself so very great! Not handsome enough to dance with! I wish you had been there, my dear, to have given him one of your set-downs. I detest the man."

Chapter Three

The Five Miss Bennets Talk Over the Ball
with Their Friend Charlotte Lucas

When Jane and Elizabeth were alone, Jane told her sister how very much she admired Mr. Bingley.

"He is just what a young man ought to be," said she, "sensible, good-humored, lively. And I never saw such happy manners, so much ease with such perfect good breeding!"

"He is also handsome," replied Elizabeth, "which a young man ought likewise to be, if he possibly can. His character is therefore complete."

"I was very much flattered by his asking me to dance a second time. I did not expect such a compliment."

"*I* did for you. But that is one great difference between us. Compliments always take *you* by surprise, and *me* never. What could be more natural than his asking you again? He could not help seeing that you were about five times as pretty as any other woman in the room. Well, he certainly is very agreeable, and I give you leave to like him. You have liked many a stupider person."

"Why, Lizzy!"

"Oh, you never see a fault in anybody. All the world are good and agreeable in your eyes. I never heard you speak ill of a human being in my life."

"I would wish not to be hasty in thinking ill of anyone, but I always speak what I think."

"I know you do, and it is *that* which makes the wonder. With *your* good sense, to be so honestly blind to the follies and nonsense of others! To pretend to see only good in people is common enough—one meets that everywhere. But to take the good in everybody's character and say nothing of the bad—that quality belongs to you alone. And so you like this man's sisters, too, do you? Their manners are not equal to his."

"Certainly not—at first. But they are very pleasing when you talk with them. Miss Bingley is to live with her brother and keep his house. I think we shall find a very charming neighbor in her."

Elizabeth listened in silence. With more quickness and less gentleness than her sister, she was very little disposed to like them. They were in fact very fine ladies, and able to be agreeable when they chose. They had been educated in one of the private schools in town and had a fortune of twenty thousand pounds.[1] They were in the habit of being with people of rank, and were therefore likely to think well of themselves and meanly of others. Bingley had been of age two years. Between him and Darcy there was a very steady friendship, in spite of a great difference of character. Darcy liked Bingley for his easy, open manner and yielding nature. Bingley was by no means lacking in understanding, but Darcy was clever. He was at the same time haughty and reserved, and his manners, though well-bred, were not inviting. Bingley was sure of being liked wherever he was; Darcy was always giving offense.

Within a short walk of Longbourn lived the family of Sir William Lucas. Lady Lucas was a very good kind of woman, not too clever to be a valuable neighbor to Mrs. Bennet. They had several children. The eldest of them, a sensible young woman about twenty-seven, was Elizabeth's close friend. The morning after the assembly brought Miss Lucas to Longbourn to hear and to talk of the ball.

"*You* began the evening well, Charlotte," said Mrs. Bennet to Miss Lucas. "*You* were Mr. Bingley's first choice."

"Yes, but he seemed to like his second better."

"Oh, you mean Jane, I suppose, because he danced with her

[1] About a hundred thousand dollars.

twice. To be sure that *did* seem as if he admired her—indeed I rather believe he *did*—I heard something about it—something about Mr. Robinson, but I hardly know what."

"Perhaps you mean what I overheard between him and Mr. Robinson. Did I not mention it to you? Mr. Robinson asked him if he did not think there were a great many pretty women in the room, and *which* he thought the prettiest? And he answered at once, 'Oh, Miss Jane Bennet, beyond a doubt; there cannot be two opinions on that point.'"

"Upon my word! Well, that was very decided indeed—that does seem as if—but, however, it may all come to nothing, you know."

"Mr. Darcy is not so well worth listening to as his friend, is he?" said Charlotte. "Poor Elizabeth! not handsome enough to tempt him to dance!"

"He is such a disagreeable man that it would be quite a misfortune for Lizzy to be liked by him," said Mrs. Bennet. "Mrs. Long told me last night that he sat close to her for half an hour without once opening his lips."

"Are you quite sure?" said Jane. "I certainly saw Mr. Darcy speaking to her."

"Yes—because she asked him at last how he liked Netherfield, and he could not help answering her. But she said he seemed very angry at being spoken to."

"Miss Bingley told me," said Jane, "that he never speaks much unless among his close friends. With *them* he is very agreeable."

"I do not believe a word of it, my dear. If he had been so very agreeable, he would have talked to Mrs. Long. But I can guess how it was; everybody says that he is eaten up with pride. I dare say he had heard somehow that Mrs. Long does not keep a carriage and had come to the ball in a hack chaise."

"I do not mind his not talking to Mrs. Long," said Charlotte Lucas, "but I wish he had danced with Elizabeth."

"Another time, Lizzy," said her mother, "I would not dance with *him*, if I were you."

"I believe I may safely promise you *never* to dance with him."

"His pride," said Charlotte, "does not offend *me* so much, because there is an excuse for it. One cannot wonder that so very fine a young man, with family, fortune, everything in his favor, should think highly of himself. He has a *right* to be proud."

"That is very true," replied Elizabeth, "and I could easily forgive *his* pride if he had not hurt *mine*."

"Pride," said Mary, who aspired to be considered a deep thinker, "is a very common failing, I believe. Human nature is quite prone to it. Most of us feel proud of some quality or other, real or imaginary. Vanity and pride are different things. A person may be proud without being vain. Pride rises from a good opinion of ourselves; vanity from what we would have others think of us."

"If I were as rich as Mr. Darcy," cried a young Lucas who had come with his sister, "I should not care how proud I was. I would keep a pack of foxhounds and drink a bottle of wine every day."

"Then you would drink a great deal more than you ought," said Mrs. Bennet. "If I were to see you at it, I should take away your bottle at once."

The boy declared that she should not. She replied that she would, and the argument ended only with the visit.

Chapter Four

The Young People Meet Again in a Party at the Home of Charlotte Lucas

The ladies of Longbourn soon visited those of Netherfield. The visit was returned in due form. Jane Bennet's pleasing manners won the good will of Mrs. Hurst and Miss Bingley. Jane was pleased with their attention, but Elizabeth still saw pride in their treatment of everyone, and could not like them. However, she thought their kindness to Jane, such is it was, had a value, arising as it probably did from their brother's interest in her. For it was plain to all that he *did* admire her. And to Elizabeth it was plain that Jane was in a way to be very much in love, though people in general would never guess it, for Jane was not one to wear her heart on her sleeve. Elizabeth spoke of this to her friend Charlotte Lucas.

"Bingley likes Jane without doubt," said Charlotte, "but he may never do more than like her if she does not help him on."

"But she does help him on as much as her nature will allow. If he cannot see her regard for him, he must be a simpleton."

"Remember, Elizabeth, that he does not know Jane as you do."

"But if a woman likes a man and does not try to conceal it, he must find it out."

"Perhaps he must, if he sees enough of her. But though Bingley and Jane meet often, they always see each other in large parties. Jane should make the most of every time when she has his attention. When she is sure of him, there will be time for falling in love as much as she chooses."

"Your plan is a good one," replied Elizabeth, "where nothing is in question but the wish to be well married. If I should set out to get a rich husband, or any husband, I should adopt the plan. But these are not Jane's feelings. As yet she cannot even be certain of her own mind. She has known him only a fortnight. She danced four dances with him. She saw him one morning at his own house, and has since dined in company with him four times. This is not quite enough to make her understand his character."

"Not as you mean it. Had she merely *dined* with him, she might only have learned whether he had a good appetite. But you must remember that four evenings have been spent together —and four evenings may do a great deal. I wish Jane success with all my heart, and if she were married to him tomorrow she would have as good a chance of happiness as if she were to be studying his character for a year. Happiness in marriage is entirely a matter of chance. To know the nature of each other does not aid the chance of happiness in the least. And it is better to know as little as possible of the faults of the person with whom you are to pass your life."

"You make me laugh, Charlotte, but you are wrong. You know you are wrong, and that you would never act in this way yourself."

Watching Mr. Bingley's attentions to her sister, Elizabeth was far from knowing that she was herself becoming of some interest to his friend Mr. Darcy. At the ball he had scarcely thought her pretty, and when they next met, he looked at her only to criticize. But no sooner had he made it clear to himself and his friends that she had hardly a good feature in her face, than he began to find it was made very intelligent by her dark eyes. Her manners were not those of the fashionable world, but he was caught by her easy playfulness. He began to wish to know more of her. He listened as she talked with others, and his doing so drew her notice. It was at Sir Williams Lucas's, where a large party had gathered.

"What does Mr. Darcy mean," she said to Charlotte, "by listening to me talk with Colonel Forster?"

"That is a question which Mr. Darcy only can answer."

"But if he does it any more, I shall certainly let him know that I see what he is about." To her, Mr. Darcy was only the man who made himself agreeable nowhere and who had not thought her handsome enough to dance with.

"I am going to open the piano, Elizabeth, and you know what follows," said Charlotte.

"You are a very strange friend," said Elizabeth, "always wanting me to play and sing before anybody and everybody! I would rather not perform before those in the habit of hearing the best performers."

But Charlotte insisted, and she went to the piano. Her performance was pleasing, though by no means unusual. After a song or two, her place at the piano was eagerly taken by her sister Mary, who, being the only plain one in the family, worked hard for musical skill and was always eager to display it.

Mary had neither talent nor taste, and her manner was too serious and self-important. Elizabeth, easy and careless, had been listened to with much more pleasure, though she did not play half so well. At the end of a long concerto, Mary was glad to gain praise by playing dance music for her younger sisters, who with some of the Lucases and two or three officers, joined eagerly in dancing at one end of the room.

Sir William turned to Darcy and said, "What a charming amusement for young people this is, Mr. Darcy! There is nothing like dancing, after all."

"Certainly, sir, and it is in vogue everywhere. Every savage can dance."

Sir William only smiled. "You have a house in town, I believe?"

Mr. Darcy bowed.

"I once had some thoughts of fixing in town myself—for I am fond of good society. But I did not feel quite certain that the air of London would agree with Lady Lucas."

He paused in hopes of an answer, but Darcy did not make any. Elizabeth at that moment was moving toward them, and Sir William, struck with the notion of doing a very gallant thing, called out to her:

"Why are you not dancing? Mr. Darcy, you cannot refuse to dance, I am sure, when so much beauty is before you." And taking her hand, he would have given it to Mr. Darcy, who was not unwilling to receive it, but she drew back and said to Sir William:

"Indeed, sir, I have not the least intention of dancing. Please do not suppose that I moved this way to beg for a partner."

Mr. Darcy gravely asked her to dance, and Sir William added:

"Though this gentleman dislikes dancing in general, he can have no objection, I am sure, to dancing with such a partner as you."

"Mr. Darcy is all politeness," said Elizabeth, smiling as she turned away.

Darcy was thinking of her with some pleasure when Miss Bingley came up and said:

"I can guess what you are thinking of. You are thinking how

awful it would be to pass many evenings in such society. I am quite of your opinion. I was never more annoyed! The noise, the nothingness, and yet the self-importance of all these people!"

"You are totally wrong. My mind was agreeably engaged. I have been thinking on the very great pleasure which a pair of fine eyes in the face of a pretty woman can give."

Miss Bingley looked at him and asked what lady had caused such thoughts.

"Miss Elizabeth Bennet," Darcy replied.

"Miss Elizabeth Bennet!" repeated Miss Bingley. "What a surprise! How long has she been such a favorite? And when am I to wish you joy?"

He listened to her with perfect indifference, and as his calm manner led her to believe that all was safe, her wit flowed long.

Chapter Five

Jane Bennet, on a Visit to Mr. Bingley's Sisters, Becomes Ill

Mr. Bennet's income was from a landed estate which, unfortunately for his daughters, could be inherited only by a male heir.[1] At his death, therefore, the property would not be inherited by his wife or daughters but would go to a distant kinsman named Collins. Mrs. Bennet's father, a Meryton attorney, had left her four thousand pounds,[2] a fortune ample for her situation in life, but hardly enough to support five daughters. She had

---

[1] At this time, many large landed estates were "entailed"; that is, the whole estate was inherited by the eldest son or, lacking a son, the next male heir in line. This law served to keep large estates from being broken up among several heirs, and thus kept together the land and wealth necessary to maintain a class of nobles and "gentlemen."

[2] About twenty thousand dollars.

a sister in Meryton, married to a Mr. Philips who had been a clerk in her father's law office but had now succeeded him in the business. She had also a brother in London engaged in trade.

Longbourn was only one mile from Meryton, and the young ladies usually went there three or four times a week to visit their aunt Philips. The two youngest girls, Kitty and Lydia, visited there very often. Their minds were more vacant than their sisters', and when nothing better offered, a walk to Meryton would amuse their morning hours and furnish talk for the evening. However bare of news the country in general might be, they could always learn some from their aunt. At present, they were made happy by the arrival of a militia regiment, which was to remain the whole winter, and Meryton was the headquarters.

Every day their visits to their aunt added something to their knowledge of the officers' names and connections, and at length they began to know the officers themselves. Now they could talk of nothing but officers. Mr. Bingley's large fortune, the mention of which gave joy to their mother, was worthless in their eyes when set against the uniform of an officer. After listening one morning to their chatter on this subject, Mr. Bennet said coolly:

"From all I can gain from your talk, you must be two of the silliest girls in the country."

Kitty was abashed and made no answer. But Lydia paid no attention to his words, and went on speaking of Captain Carter and her hopes of seeing him before he went the next morning to London.

"I am surprised, my dear," said Mrs. Bennet, "that you should be so ready to think your own children silly. If I wished to think slightingly of anybody's children, it should not be of my own."

"If my children are silly, I hope to be always aware of it."

"Yes—but as it happens, they are all of them very clever."

"I must so far differ from you as to think our two youngest daughters uncommonly foolish."

"My dear Mr. Bennet, you must not expect such girls to have the sense of their father and mother. When they get to our age,

I dare say they will not think about officers any more than we do. I remember the time when I liked a red coat myself very well —and, indeed, so I do still in my heart. If a smart young colonel with five or six thousand a year should want one of my girls, I shall not say nay to him. I thought Colonel Forster looked very fine the other night at Sir William's in his uniform."

"Mama," cried Lydia, "my aunt says that Colonel Forster and Captain Carter do not go so often to Miss Watson's as they did when they first came. She sees them now very often standing in Clarke's library."

A footman came in with a note for Jane. It came from Netherfield, and the servant waited for an answer. Mrs. Bennet's eyes sparkled with pleasure, and she was eagerly calling out while her daughter read:

"Well, Jane, who is it from? What is it about? What does he say? Well, Jane, make haste and tell us; make haste, my love."

"It is from Miss Bingley," said Jane, and then read it aloud.

My dear Friend,

If you are not so merciful as to dine today with Louisa and me, we shall be in danger of hating each other for the rest of our lives. A whole day's talk between two women can never end without a quarrel. Come as soon as you can after you receive this letter. My brother and the gentlemen are to dine with the officers. Yours ever,

Caroline Bingley.

"With the officers!" cried Lydia. "I wonder my aunt did not tell us of *that*."

"Dining out!" said Mrs. Bennet; "that is very unlucky."

"Can I have the carriage?" said Jane.

"No, my dear, you had better go on horseback, because it seems likely to rain, and then you must stay all night."

"That would be a good plan," said Elizabeth, "if you were sure that they would not offer to send her home."

"Oh, but the gentlemen will use Mr. Bingley's chaise to go to Meryton, and the Hursts have no horses here."

"I had much rather go in the carriage."

"But, my dear, your father cannot spare the horses, I am sure. They are needed at the farm, Mr. Bennet, are they not?"

"They are needed at the farm much oftener than I can get them."

It was settled that Jane must go on horseback, and her mother went with her to the door with many cheerful forecastings of a bad day. Her hopes were answered; Jane had not been gone long before it rained hard. Her sisters were uneasy for her, but her mother was delighted. The rain fell the whole evening without stopping. Jane certainly could not come back.

"This was a lucky idea of mine, indeed!" said Mrs. Bennet more than once, as if the credit of making it rain were all her own.

The next morning breakfast was scarcely over when a servant from Netherfield brought the following note for Elizabeth:

My dearest Lizzy,

I find myself very unwell this morning, which, I suppose, is caused by my getting wet yesterday. My kind friends will not hear of my returning home till I am better. They insist also on my seeing the doctor—therefore do not be alarmed if you should hear of his having been to see me—and but for a sore throat and headache there is not much the matter with me.

Jane.

"Well, my dear," said Mr. Bennet, when Elizabeth had read the note aloud, "if your daughter should have a dangerous illness, if she should die, it would be a comfort to know that it was all in pursuit of Mr. Bingley, and under your orders."

"Oh, I am not at all afraid of her dying. People do not die of little trifling colds. She will be taken good care of. As long as she stays there, it is all very well. I would go and see her if I could have the carriage."

Elizabeth, feeling really anxious, decided to go to her, though the carriage was not to be had. As she was no horsewoman, she would walk.

"How can you be so silly," cried her mother, "as to think of such a thing, in all this dirt! You will not be fit to be seen when you get there."

"I shall be very fit to see Jane—which is all I want."

"Is this a hint to me, Lizzy," said her father, "to send for the horses?"

"No indeed, I wish to walk. The distance is nothing, only three miles. I shall be back by dinner."

Elizabeth walked on, crossing field after field at a quick pace, jumping over stiles and springing over puddles. She came at last in view of the house, with weary ankles, dirty stockings, and a face glowing with the warmth of exercise.

She was shown into the breakfast-parlor, where all but Jane were gathered, and where she was greeted with a great deal of surprise. That she should have walked three miles so early in the day, in such dirty weather and by herself, was almost unbelievable to Mrs. Hurst and Miss Bingley. They received her, however, very politely; and in their brother's manner, there was something better than politeness; there was good humor and kindness. Mr. Darcy said very little, and Mr. Hurst nothing at all.

She learned that Jane had slept ill, and though up, was very feverish and not well enough to leave her room. Elizabeth was glad to be taken to her at once. Jane was delighted to see her. She was not equal, however, to much talk, and when Miss Bingley left them together, she spoke only of the very great kindness that had been shown her. Elizabeth silently attended to her needs.

When breakfast was over, they were joined by Miss Bingley and Mrs. Hurst. Elizabeth began to like them when she saw how much care they showed for Jane. The doctor came, said that she had caught a violent cold, which she must try to get the better of, and advised her to return to bed. The advice was followed willingly, for the fever made her head ache severely.

Elizabeth did not quit her room for a moment, nor were the other ladies often absent; the gentlemen being out, they had in fact nothing to do elsewhere.

When the clock struck three, Elizabeth unwillingly said she must go. Miss Bingley invited her to remain at Netherfield for the present, and Elizabeth most thankfully accepted. A servant was sent to Longbourn to tell the family of her stay and to bring back a supply of clothes.

Chapter Six

Elizabeth Bennet Nurses Her Sister and Sees More of the Disagreeable Mr. Darcy

At five o'clock the two ladies retired to dress, and at half-past six Elizabeth was called to dinner. To the civil inquiries which then poured in, she could not make a very favorable answer. Jane was by no means better. The sisters, on hearing this, said three or four times how much they were grieved, how shocking it was to have a bad cold, and how they disliked being ill themselves, and then thought no more of the matter. Their carelessness toward Jane when she was not before them awoke in Elizabeth her old dislike.

But their brother's anxiety about Jane was sincere, and his attentions to herself kept her from feeling an intruder. She had very little notice from any but him. Miss Bingley was taken up with Mr. Darcy, her sister scarcely less so. As for Mr. Hurst, by whom Elizabeth sat, he lived only to eat, drink, and play cards, and had nothing to say to her. When dinner was over she went back to Jane.

Miss Bingley began abusing her as soon as she was out of the

room. Her manners were very bad indeed, a mixture of pride
and pertness; she had no style, no taste, no beauty. Mrs. Hurst
thought the same, and added:

"She has nothing to recommend her but being a good walker.
I shall never forget how she looked this morning. She really
looked almost wild."

"She did, indeed, Louisa. I could hardly keep my face straight.
Why must *she* be scampering about the country because her
sister has a cold? Her hair so untidy, so blowzy!"

"Yes, and her skirts six inches deep in mud."

"But this was all lost upon me," said Bingley. "I thought Miss
Bennet looked very well when she came into the room this morning."

"*You* noticed it, Mr. Darcy, I am sure," said Miss Bingley.
"You would not wish to see *your* sister making such a sight of
herself."

"Certainly not."

"To walk three, four, five miles, or whatever it is, above her
ankles in dirt, and alone, quite alone! What could she mean by
it?"

"It shows a love for her sister that is very pleasing," said
Bingley.

"I am afraid, Mr. Darcy," said Miss Bingley, in a half whisper,
"that this adventure has rather changed your opinion of her fine
eyes."

"Not at all," he replied; "they were brightened by the exercise."
A short pause followed this speech, and Mrs. Hurst began again:

"I have a high regard for Jane Bennet. She is really a very
sweet girl, and I wish with all my heart she were well married.
But with such a father and mother, and such low connections,
I am afraid there is no chance of it."

"I think I have heard you say that their uncle is an attorney in
Meryton," said Mrs. Hurst.

"Yes, and they have another who lives somewhere near Cheapside."

They both laughed heartily.

"If they had uncles enough to fill *all* Cheapside," cried Bingley, "it would not make them one jot less agreeable."

"But it must lessen their chance of marrying men of any station in the world," said Darcy.

To this speech Bingley made no answer. But his sisters agreed heartily, and again laughed at their dear friend's vulgar relations.

However, they went to her room on leaving the dining-parlor, and sat with her till summoned to coffee. She was still very poorly, and Elizabeth would not quit her at all till late in the evening, when Jane had fallen asleep. Then it seemed to her rather right than pleasant that she should go downstairs herself. On entering the drawing-room she found the whole party at cards and was at once invited to join them. She said she would amuse herself for the short time she could stay below with a book. Mr. Hurst looked at her with surprise.

"Do you prefer reading to cards?" said he. "That is rather strange."

Elizabeth walked toward a table where a few books were lying. Bingley offered to fetch her others, all that his library had.

"And I wish my collection were larger for your benefit and my own credit. But I am an idle fellow, and though I have not many books, I have more than I ever look into."

Elizabeth said that she could suit herself perfectly with those books already in the room.

"What a delightful library you have at Pemberley, Mr. Darcy," said Miss Bingley.

"It ought to be good," he replied; "it has been the work of many generations."

"And then you have added so much to it yourself. You are always buying books. I am sure you neglect nothing that can add to the beauties of that noble place. Charles," turning to her brother, "when you build *your* house, I wish it may be half as delightful as Pemberley."

"I wish it may."

"Is Miss Darcy much grown since the spring?" said Miss Bingley. "Will she be as tall as I am?"

"I think she will. She is now about Miss Elizabeth Bennet's height, or rather taller."

"How I long to see her again! I never met anybody who delighted me so much. Such beauty, such manners, and so accomplished at her age!"

"It is amazing," said Bingley, "how young ladies can have patience to be so very accomplished as they all are."

"All young ladies accomplished! My dear Charles, what do you mean?"

"Yes, all of them, I think. They all paint tables, cover screens, and net purses. I scarcely know anyone who cannot do all this."

"I am far from agreeing with you that all are accomplished," said Darcy. "I cannot boast of knowing more than half a dozen that are really accomplished."

"Nor I, I am sure," said Miss Bingley.

"Then," said Elizabeth, "you must include a great deal in your idea of an accomplished woman."

"Yes, I do include a great deal in it."

"Oh, certainly!" cried Miss Bingley. "To be really accomplished, a woman must have a thorough knowledge of music, singing, drawing, dancing, and the modern languages. And besides all this, she must have a certain something in her air and manner of walking, and the tone of her voice."

"All this she must have," said Darcy, "and to all this she must yet add something more important, the improvement of her mind by extensive reading."

"I am not surprised that you know *only* six accomplished women. I rather wonder now at your knowing *any*," said Elizabeth.

Mrs. Hurst and Miss Bingley both cried out that they knew many such women. At this moment Mr. Hurst called them to order with bitter complaint of their lack of attention to the game. All talk was thereby at an end, and Elizabeth soon after left the room.

Chapter Seven

Mrs. Bennet Visits Her Daughter and Comes into Conflict with Mr. Darcy

Elizabeth passed the night in her sister's room, and in the morning had the pleasure of seeing her better. But she asked to have a note sent to Longbourn urging her mother to visit Jane and form her own judgment of her condition. Mrs. Bennet, with her two youngest girls, reached Netherfield soon after the family breakfast.

Had she found Jane in any danger, Mrs. Bennet would have been very miserable. But being satisfied on seeing her that her illness was not alarming, she had no wish to remove her from Netherfield. She would not listen, therefore, to Jane's request to be taken home. Neither did the doctor, who arrived about the same time, think it at all advisable. After sitting a little while with Jane, the mother and three daughters went into the breakfast-parlor. Bingley met them with hopes that Mrs. Bennet had not found her daughter worse than she had expected.

"Indeed I have, sir," was the answer. "She is a great deal too ill to be moved. The doctor says we must not think of moving her. We must trespass a little longer on your kindness."

"Moved!" cried Bingley. "It must not be thought of. My sister, I am sure, will not hear of it."

"You may depend upon it, madam," said Miss Bingley with cold civility, "that she shall have every possible care while she remains with us."

Mrs. Bennet was profuse in her thanks. "If it was not for such good friends I do not know what would become of her, for she is very ill indeed. She suffers a great deal, though with the greatest patience in the world, for she has the sweetest temper I ever met with. I often tell my other girls they are nothing to *her*. You have a sweet room here, Mr. Bingley, and a charming view over that gravel walk. I do not know a place in the country that is equal to Netherfield. You will not think of quitting it in a hurry, I hope, though you have but a short lease."

"Whatever I do is done in a hurry," replied he. "And if I should decide to quit Netherfield, I should probably be off in five minutes. At present, however, I feel quite fixed here."

"That is exactly what I should have expected of you," said Elizabeth.

"You begin to understand me, do you?" cried he, turning toward her.

"Oh, yes—I understand you perfectly."

"I wish I might take this for a compliment, but to be so easily seen through is, I am afraid, pitiful."

"That is as it happens. It does not follow that a complex character is more or less to be admired than such a one as yours."

"Lizzy," cried her mother, "remember where you are, and do not run on in the wild manner that you do at home."

"I did not know before," said Bingley, "that you were a student of character. It must be an amusing study."

"Yes, but complex characters are the *most* amusing. They *do* have at least that advantage."

"The country," said Darcy, "can supply but few subjects for such a study. In a country neighborhood you move in a very confined and unvaried society."

"But people themselves alter so much that there is something new to be seen in them forever."

"Yes, indeed," cried Mrs. Bennet, offended by his manner of mentioning a country neighborhood. "There is quite as much of *that* going on in the country as in town."

Everybody was surprised; and Darcy, after looking at her for a moment, turned silently away. Mrs. Bennet fancied she had gained a complete victory over him, and went on:

"I cannot see that London has any great advantages over the

country, for my part, except the shops and public places. The country is a great deal pleasanter, is it not, Mr. Bingley?"

"When I am in the country," he replied, "I never wish to leave it. When I am in town, it is pretty much the same with me. Each has its advantages, and I can be equally happy in either."

"Yes—that is because you have the right disposition. But that gentleman," looking at Darcy, "seemed to think the country was nothing at all."

"You quite mistook Mr. Darcy, mama," said Elizabeth, blushing for her mother. "He only meant that there were not so many people to be met with in the country as in town."

"Nobody said there were. But as to not meeting with many people in the neighborhood, I believe there are few neighborhoods larger. I know we dine with twenty-four families."

Nothing but concern for Elizabeth could enable Mr. Bingley to keep a straight face. His sister was less kind, and turned her eyes toward Mr. Darcy with a meaning smile. Elizabeth, for the sake of saying something that might turn her mother's thoughts, now asked her if Charlotte Lucas had been at Longbourn since *her* coming away.

"Yes, she called yesterday with her father. What an agreeable man Sir William is, Mr. Bingley—so genteel and so easy! He has always something to say to everybody. *That* is my idea of good breeding. Those persons who fancy themselves very important, and never open their mouths, quite mistake the matter."

"Did Charlotte dine with you?"

"No, she would go home. I fancy she was needed about the mince pies. For my part, Mr. Bingley, *I* always keep servants that can do their own work; *my* daughters are brought up differently. But the Lucases are very good sort of girls, I assure you. It is a pity they are not handsome!"

"She seems a very pleasant young woman," said Bingley.

"Oh, dear, yes. But you must own she is very plain. Lady Lucas herself has often said so, and envied me Jane's beauty. I do not like to boast of my own child, but to be sure, Jane—one

loes not often see anybody better looking. It is what everybody
,ays."

The general pause which followed made Elizabeth tremble
est her mother should be exposing herself again. She longed to
speak but could think of nothing to say. After a short silence
Mrs. Bennet began repeating her thanks to Mr. Bingley for his
:indness to Jane. Mr. Bingley was kind and civil in his answer,
and forced his sister to be civil also. Mrs. Bennet was satisfied,
and soon afterward ordered her carriage. Upon this, Lydia, the
youngest of her daughters, put herself forward. The two girls
had been whispering to each other during the whole visit, and
he result of it was that Lydia should remind Mr. Bingley that
he had promised to give a ball at Netherfield.

Lydia was a stout, well-grown girl of fifteen, with a fine com-
plexion and good-humored face. She had high animal spirits
and the manner of one sure of herself. She reminded Bingley of
his promise, adding that it would be the most shameful thing in
he world if he did not keep it. His answer to this sudden attack
was delightful to Mrs. Bennet's ear.

"I am perfectly ready to keep my promise. When your sister
s well again, you shall name the very day of the ball. But you
would not wish to be dancing while she is ill."

"Oh, it would be much better to wait till Jane is well, and by
hat time most likely Captain Carter will be at Meryton again.
And when you have given *your* ball," Lydia added, "I shall insist
on their giving one also. I shall tell Colonel Forster it will be
quite a shame if he does not."

Mrs. Bennet and her younger daughters then left, and Elizabeth went back to Jane, leaving her own and her relations' behavior to the remarks of the two ladies and Mr. Darcy. He, however, would not join in their censure of *her*, in spite of Miss Bing-
ey's witticisms on *fine eyes*.

Chapter Eight

Elizabeth Bennet Wears Out Her Welcome

The day passed much as the day before had done. Mrs. Hurst
and Miss Bingley had spent some hours of the morning with Jane
who continued, though slowly, to mend. In the evening Elizabeth joined their party in the drawing-room. Mr. Hurst and Mr.
Bingley were at cards, and Mrs. Hurst was watching their game.
Mr. Darcy was writing, and Miss Bingley, seated near him, was
watching the progress of his letter and sending messages to his
sister.

"How delighted your sister will be to have such a letter!" cried
Miss Bingley.

He made no answer.

"You write very fast. How can you manage to write so even?"

"You are mistaken. I write rather slowly."

"How many letters you must have to write in the course of the
year! Letters of business too! How tiresome I should think
them!"

"It is fortunate, then, that they fall to my lot instead of to
yours."

"Pray tell your sister that I long to see her."

"I have already told her so once, by your wish."

"Tell your sister I am delighted to hear of her improvement on
the harp. But do you always write such charming long letters
to her, Mr. Darcy?"

"They are generally long, but whether always charming it is
not for me to say."

"It is a rule with me that a person who can write a long letter
with ease always writes well."

"That will not do for Darcy, Caroline," cried her brother. "He does *not* write with ease. He studies too much for words of four syllables. Do you not, Darcy?"

"My style of writing is very different from yours."

"Oh," cried Miss Bingley, "Charles writes in the most careless way. He leaves out half his words and blots the rest."

"My ideas flow so rapidly that I have not time to express them —by which means my letters sometimes make no sense at all."

"You are proud of your defects in writing," said Darcy, "because you believe they come from speed of thought. Everyone is proud of the power to do anything with speed, no matter whether it is done well or not. When you told Mrs. Bennet this morning that if you ever decided to leave Netherfield you should be gone in five minutes, you meant it to be a sort of compliment to yourself. Yet what is there to be proud of in a haste that must leave business undone and can be of no real advantage to any one?"

"Now," cried Bingley, "this is too much, to remember at night all the foolish things that were said in the morning. And yet upon my honor, I believed what I said of myself to be true, and I believe it now."

"I dare say you believed it, but I am by no means sure that you would be gone with such speed. If, as you were mounting your horse, a friend were to say, 'Bingley, you had better stay till next week,' you would probably do it—and at another word might stay a month."

"To yield readily—easily—to the wishes of a friend is no merit with you?" asked Elizabeth.

"To yield without reason is no compliment to the understanding of either."

"Miss Bennet," cried Bingley, "if Darcy were not such a great tall fellow, compared with myself, I should not yield to him half so easily. I declare I do not know a more commanding person than Darcy, at his own house especially, and of a Sunday evening when he has nothing to do."

Mr. Darcy smiled, but Elizabeth thought she could see that he was rather offended, and therefore checked her laugh.

"I see your purpose, Bingley," said Darcy. "You dislike an argument and want to silence me."

"Arguments are too much like disputes," said Bingley. "If you and Miss Bennet put off your arguments until I am out of the room, I shall be very thankful. And then you may say whatever you like of me."

"What you ask," said Elizabeth, "is no sacrifice on my side. And Mr. Darcy had much better finish his letter."

Darcy took her advice and did finish his letter. When that business was over, he asked Miss Bingley and Elizabeth for some music. Miss Bingley moved to the piano at once, and Mrs. Hurst sang with her sister.

Elizabeth could not help noticing, as she turned over some music books that lay on the piano, how often Mr. Darcy's eyes were fixed on her. She could hardly suppose that she could be an object of admiration to so great a man, and yet that he should look at her because he disliked her was still more strange. She could only suppose that she drew his notice because there was something about her more wrong, according to his ideas of right, than in any other person present. But she liked him too little to care for his opinion of her.

After playing some Italian songs, Miss Bingley began a lively Scotch air. Soon afterward Mr. Darcy, drawing near Elizabeth, said to her:

"Do you not feel that this is a good time for dancing a reel?"

She smiled but made no answer. He repeated the question, with some surprise at her silence.

"Oh," said she, "I heard you before, but I could not decide what to say in reply. You wanted me, I know, to say 'Yes,' that you might have the pleasure of despising my taste. I have therefore made up my mind to tell you that I do not want to dance a reel at all—and now despise me if you dare."

"Indeed I do not dare."

Elizabeth had rather expected to offend him, and was amazed at his gallant reply. But there was a mixture of sweetness and archness in her manner which made it hard for her to offend anybody. Moreover, Darcy had never been so bewitched by any woman as he was by her. He really believed that if it were not for her low connections, he should be in some danger.

Miss Bingley saw enough to be jealous, and her great anxiety for the recovery of her dear friend Jane, arose from her wish to get rid of Elizabeth. She often tried to provoke Darcy into disliking Elizabeth by talking of their supposed marriage and planning his happiness in such a union.

"I hope," said she, as they were walking together in the shrubbery the next day, "you will give your mother-in-law a few hints to hold her tongue. And do try to cure the younger girls of running after the officers. And, oh yes, do let the portraits of your uncle and aunt Philips be placed in the gallery at Pemberley. Put them next to your great-uncle the judge. They are in the same profession, you know, only in different lines. As for your Elizabeth's picture, you must not try to have it taken, for what painter could do justice to those beautiful eyes?"

"It would not be easy, indeed, to catch their expression. But their color and shape and the eyelashes, so very fine, might be copied."

At that moment they were met from another walk by Mrs. Hurst and Elizabeth herself.

"I did not know that you intended to walk," said Miss Bingley, in some confusion lest they had been overheard.

"You used us ill," answered Mrs. Hurst, "in running away without telling us that you were coming out."

Then taking the other arm of Mr. Darcy, she left Elizabeth to walk by herself. The path was wide enough for only three. Mr. Darcy felt their rudeness and said:

"This walk is not wide enough for our party. We had better go into the avenue."

But Elizabeth, who had not the least wish to remain with them, laughingly answered:

"No, no; stay where you are. You make a charming group, and the picture would be spoiled by a fourth. Good-bye."

She then ran gaily off, rejoicing as she rambled about, in the thought of being at home again in a day or two. Jane was already so much better as to intend leaving her room for a couple of hours that evening.

Chapter Nine

Elizabeth Sees More of the Unsociable Darcy, Jane Recovers, and They Return Home

When Jane entered the drawing-room she was warmly welcomed by her two friends. Elizabeth had never seen them so agreeable. Mr. Darcy spoke polite good wishes for her health. Mr. Hurst also made her a slight bow and said he was "very glad." But Bingley was full of joy and attention. The first half hour he spent in piling up the fire lest she should suffer from the change of room. And he had her move to the other side of the fireplace that she might be farther from the door. He then sat down by her and talked scarcely to anyone else. Elizabeth saw it all with great delight.

When tea was over, Mrs. Hurst asked for the card table—but in vain. Miss Bingley had learned that Mr. Darcy did not wish for cards. Mr. Hurst had therefore nothing to do but to stretch himself on one of the sofas and go to sleep. Darcy took up a book. Miss Bingley did the same; and Mrs. Hurst sat playing with her bracelets and rings, joining now and then in her brother's talk with Jane.

Miss Bingley's attention was quite as much taken up watching Mr. Darcy's progress through *his* book as in reading her own. She often asked him something, or looked at his page. She could not win him, however, to any talk; he merely answered her questions and read on. At last she gave a great yawn and said:

"How pleasant it is to spend an evening in this way! I declare after all there is no enjoyment like reading! How much sooner one tires of anything than of a book!"

No one made any reply. She then yawned again, threw aside her book, and looked round the room for some amusement. Hearing her brother speak of a ball to Jane, she turned suddenly toward him and said:

"By the way, Charles, are you really thinking of a dance at Netherfield? If I am not much mistaken, there are some among us to whom a ball would be more punishment than pleasure."

"If you mean Darcy," cried her brother, "he may go to bed, if he chooses, before it begins. As for the ball, it is quite a settled thing."

Miss Bingley made no answer, and soon afterwards got up and walked about the room. Turning to Elizabeth, she said:

"May I persuade you to take a turn about the room? It is very restful after sitting so long."

Elizabeth was surprised but agreed at once. And now Mr. Darcy looked up and closed his book. He was invited to join them, but refused, saying that he could think of but two reasons for their walking up and down the room together, and his joining them would interfere.

"What can he mean? I am dying to know what can be his meaning—do you know what he means by that?" asked Miss Bingley.

"Not at all," said Elizabeth. "But depend upon it, he means to be severe on us. Our surest way to disappoint him will be to ask nothing about it."

But Miss Bingley asked him what were the two reasons.

"You either have secrets to talk of, or you know that you appear to great advantage in walking. If the first, I should be in your way; if the second, I can admire you much better as I sit by the fire."

"Oh! shocking!" cried Miss Bingley. "How shall we punish him for such a speech?"

"Nothing so easy," said Elizabeth. "Tease him—laugh at him. Knowing him as you do, you must know how it is to be done."

"But upon my honor I do *not*. I do assure you that I have not yet learned *that*."

"Mr. Darcy is not to be laughed at!" cried Elizabeth. "That is a great advantage, and uncommon I hope, for I dearly love a laugh."

"The wisest and the best of men," said he, "and the wisest and best of their actions, may be made ridiculous by a person whose first object in life is a joke."

"Certainly," replied Elizabeth, "there are such people, but I hope I am not one of *them*. I hope I never laugh at what is wise or good. Follies, nonsense and whims *do* amuse me, and I laugh at them. But these, I suppose, are just what you are without."

"Perhaps that is not possible for anyone. But it has been the study of my life to avoid weaknesses, which often expose a strong understanding to ridicule."

"Such as vanity and pride."

"Yes, vanity is a weakness indeed. But pride—persons of real understanding, will always keep it under good control."

Elizabeth smiled. "Mr. Darcy has no defect. He owns it himself."

"No," said Darcy, "I have made no such claim. I have faults enough, but they are not, I hope, faults of understanding. My temper, I believe, is a little too unyielding. I cannot forget the follies and vices of others so soon as I ought, nor their offences against myself. My temper would perhaps be called resentful. My good opinion once lost is lost forever."

"*That* is a failing indeed!" cried Elizabeth. "But you have chosen your fault well. I really cannot *laugh* at it. You are safe from me."

"There is, I believe, in everyone some natural defect, which not even the best education can overcome."

"And *your* defect is a tendency to hate everybody."

"And yours," he replied with a smile, "is wilfully to misunderstand them."

"Do let us have a little music," cried Miss Bingley, tired of talk in which she had no share. "Louisa, you will not mind my waking Mr. Hurst?"

Her sister made not the smallest objection, and the piano was opened. Darcy was not sorry. He began to feel the danger of paying Elizabeth too much attention.

Elizabeth wrote the next morning to her mother, asking that the carriage be sent for them in the course of the day. But Mrs. Bennet had planned on her daughter's remaining at Netherfield till the following Tuesday, which would exactly finish Jane's week. She therefore sent them word that they could not possibly have the carriage before Tuesday. In a postscript she added that if Mr. Bingley and his sisters pressed them to stay longer, she could spare them very well.

Elizabeth then urged Jane to borrow Mr. Bingley's carriage. He heard with real sorrow that they were to go so soon, and tried to persuade Jane that it would not be safe for her—that she was not well enough. But Jane was firm where she felt herself to be right.

To Mr. Darcy it was good news—Elizabeth had been at Netherfield long enough. She attracted him more than he liked —and Miss Bingley was uncivil to *her* and more teasing than usual to himself. Miss Bingley told Jane when they parted of the pleasure it would always give her to see her either at Longbourn or Netherfield, and embraced her most tenderly. She even shook hands with Elizabeth, who took leave of the whole party in the liveliest spirits.

They were not welcomed home very warmly by their mother. Mrs. Bennet wondered at their coming, and thought them very wrong to give so much trouble, and was sure Jane would have caught cold again. But their father, though very brief in his expressions of pleasure, was really glad to see them. He had felt their importance in the family circle; the evening family talk had lost much of its interest and almost all its sense by the absence of Jane and Elizabeth.

They found Mary, as usual, deep in study, with some new remarks of threadbare morality to make. Kitty and Lydia had news for them of a different sort. Much had been done and said in the regiment; several of the officers had dined lately with their uncle, and it had been hinted that Colonel Forster was going to be married.

Chapter Ten

Mr. Collins, Another Young Bachelor, Neither Handsome nor Rich, Comes Upon the Scene

"I hope, my dear," said Mr. Bennet to his wife, as they were at breakfast the next morning, "that you have ordered a good dinner today, because I am expecting an addition to our family party."

"What do you mean, my dear? I know of nobody that is coming, unless Charlotte Lucas should happen to call. And I hope *my* dinners are good enough for her. I do not believe she often sees such at home."

"The person I speak of is a gentleman and a stranger."

Mrs. Bennet's eyes sparkled. "A gentleman and a stranger! It is Mr. Bingley, I am sure. Why, Jane—you never dropped a word of this, you sly thing! Well, I am sure I shall be very glad to see Mr. Bingley. But—good Lord! how unlucky! there is not a bit of fish to be got today. Lydia, my love, ring the bell. I must speak to the housekeeper this moment."

"It is *not* Mr. Bingley," said her husband. "It is a person whom I never saw in my life."

This roused a general surprise, and he had the pleasure of being eagerly questioned by his wife and five daughters at once. After amusing himself some time with their curiosity, he explained:

"About a month ago I received this letter, and about two weeks ago I answered it, for I thought it should have early attention. It is from my cousin, Mr. Collins, who, when I am dead, may turn you all out of this house as soon as he pleases."

"Oh, I cannot bear to hear that mentioned!" cried his wife. "Pray do not talk of that odious man. I do think it is the hardest thing in the world that your estate should not go to your own children." And she continued to rail bitterly against the cruelty of settling an estate away from a family of five daughters in favor of a man whom nobody cared anything about.

"It certainly is most wicked of Mr. Collins to inherit Longbourn," said Mr. Bennet. "But if you will listen to this letter, you may perhaps be a little softened toward him."

"No, that I am sure I shall not be. I hate such false friends. Why could he not keep on quarreling with you, as his father did before him?"

"Well, you must hear the letter," said Mr. Bennet.

Hunsford, near Westerham, Kent
October 15.

Dear Sir,

I have often wished to heal the breach between your family and mine. For some time I have held back, fearing it might seem disloyal to the memory of my father to be on good terms with anyone with whom he had always disagreed. My mind, however, is now made up.

I received ordination[1] at Easter, and am now serving the parish of the Right Honorable Lady Catherine de Bourgh, of Rosings Park, widow of Sir Lewis de Bourgh. As rector here, I shall make every effort to act with grateful respect toward her

---

[1] Made a clergyman.

ladyship, and be ever ready to perform the rites and ceremonies of the Church of England.

As a clergyman, I feel it my duty to promote peace. I therefore offer you my good will, and the fact that I am heir to Longbourn will, I hope, not lead you to refuse my offered olive branch. I regret that Longbourn must pass away from your charming daughters, and I assure you that I am ready to make them all possible amends—but more of this hereafter.

If you have no objection to receive me, I shall visit you Monday, November 18, by four o'clock, and stay till the end of the week following. Lady Catherine does not object to my absence now and then on a Sunday, provided that some other clergyman is engaged to take my place. I remain, dear sir, with respectful greetings to your wife and daughters, your well-wisher and friend.

William Collins.

"At four o'clock, therefore, we may expect this peace-making gentleman," said Mr. Bennet, as he folded up the letter. "He seems to be a most polite young man, upon my word, and I do not doubt will be a valuable acquaintance, if Lady Catherine should be so kind as to let him come to us again."

"There is some sense in what he says about the girls," said Mrs. Bennet. "If he wishes to make them any amends, I shall not be the person to discourage him."

"It is hard," said Jane, "to guess in what way he can mean to make us amends. But the wish is certainly to his credit."

Elizabeth was struck with his great respect for Lady Catherine. "He must be a very odd person. I cannot make him out. There is something very self-important in his style. And what can he mean by apologizing for being next in line to inherit Longbourn. We cannot suppose he would help it if he could. Can he be a sensible man, sir?"

"No, my dear, I think not. There is a mixture of the servile and the self-importance in his letter which promises to amuse me well. I am impatient to see him."

"His letter," said Mary, "does not seem defective. The idea of the olive branch perhaps is not wholly new, yet I think it is well expressed."

To Kitty and Lydia, neither the letter nor their cousin William Collins was of any interest. He would not come in a scarlet coat, and it was now some weeks since they had cared about a man in any other color. As for their mother, Mr. Collins's letter had done away much of her ill will, and she was ready to receive him with a degree of friendliness which amazed her husband and her daughters.

Mr. Collins arrived on time, and was received with great politeness by the whole family. Mr. Bennet indeed said little, but the ladies were ready enough to talk, and Mr. Collins seemed in no need of encouragement. He was a tall, heavy-looking young man of twenty-five. His air was grave and stately, and his manners very formal. He had not been long seated before he complimented Mrs. Bennet on having so fine a family of daughters. He had heard, he said, much of their beauty, but fame had fallen short of the truth. He added that he did not doubt her seeing them all, in due time, well married. This gallantry was not much to the taste of some of his hearers, but Mrs. Bennet, who quarreled with no compliments, answered most readily:

"You are very kind sir, and I wish with all my heart it may prove so, for else they will be poor enough."

"You are thinking, perhaps, of the loss to them of this estate."

"I am indeed, sir. It is a sad affair to my poor girls, you must confess. Not that I mean to find fault with *you* for it."

"I am aware, madam, of the hardship to my fair cousins, and could say much on the subject, but that I am cautious of appearing too forward. But I can assure the young ladies that I come prepared to admire them. I will not say more until we are better acquainted."

He praised the room and all the furniture. His praise of everything would have touched Mrs. Bennet's heart, but for her thought that he was looking at it all as his own future property.

The dinner too was highly admired. He begged to know which of his fair cousins had cooked it. But here he was set right by Mrs. Bennet, who told him a little sharply that they were very well able to keep a good cook and that her daughters had nothing to do in the kitchen. He begged pardon for having displeased her. In a softened tone she declared herself not at all offended.

Chapter Eleven

Mr. Collins Picks a Wife from among the Miss Bennets; and Mr. Wickham, another Young Bachelor, Handsome, but Not Rich, Comes Upon the Scene

During dinner Mr. Bennet scarcely spoke at all, but when the servants had withdrawn, he thought it time to have some talk with his cousin. He therefore started a subject, in which he was sure his guest would shine, by remarking that Mr. Collins was very fortunate in having such a patroness as Lady Catherine de Bourgh. He could not have chosen a better subject. Mr. Collins spoke in high praise of Lady Catherine. On this subject his manner was more stately even than usual. He had never in his life, he said, seen such behavior in a person of rank—such willingness to stoop to others. She had been kind enough to approve of both the sermons which he had already had the honor of preaching before her. She had also asked him twice to dine at Rosings. And she had sent for him once to make up a card table in the evening. Lady Catherine was called proud by many people, he knew, but she had always spoken to him as she would to any other gentleman. She did not object to his joining in the society of the neighborhood, nor to his leaving his parish now and then for a week or two to visit his relations. She had even advised him to marry as soon as he could, if he found the proper sort of wife. She had once paid him a visit in his humble parsonage and had spoken well of all the changes he had been making. She had even suggested some herself—some shelves in the closets up-stairs.

"I dare say she is a very agreeable woman," said Mrs. Bennet. "It is a pity that great ladies in general are not more like her. Does she live near you, sir?"

"The garden of my humble house is just across a lane from Rosings Park, her ladyship's residence."

"I think you said she was a widow, sir? Has she any family?"

"She has one only daughter, the heiress of Rosings and of very extensive property."

"Ah!" cried Mrs. Bennet, shaking her head, "then she is better off than many girls. And what sort of young lady is she? Is she handsome?"

"She is a most charming young lady indeed. As to beauty, Lady Catherine herself says that she is far more than handsome, for there is that in her face which marks the young woman of high birth. And I have more than once said to Lady Catherine that her daughter seemed born to be a duchess. Unfortunately her ill health has prevented her making that progress in many accomplishments which she could not otherwise have failed of. But she is very agreeable and often drives by my humble house in her little pony carriage."

"Has she been presented at court?" asked Mrs. Bennet. "I do not remember her name among the ladies at court."

"Her state of ill health unhappily prevents her being in town. Because of this, as I told Lady Catherine myself one day, the British court has lost one of its brightest ornaments. Her lady-ship seemed pleased with the idea, and you may imagine that I am happy whenever possible to offer those little delicate com-pliments which are always pleasing to ladies."

Mr. Bennet listened to him with the keenest enjoyment, keep-ing at the same time the most serious face, with a glance now and then toward Elizabeth, his partner in amusement.

But by tea-time the dose had been enough, and when tea was

over Mr. Bennet was glad to invite him to read aloud to the ladies. Mr. Collins willingly agreed, and a book was brought. But on seeing it, he started back, and begging pardon, said that he never read novels. Kitty stared at him, and Lydia exclaimed. Other books were brought, and after some time he chose Fordyce's Sermons. Lydia gaped as he opened the book, and before he had read three pages she broke in with:

"Mama, uncle Philips is talking of turning away Richard, and if he does, Colonel Forster will hire him. My aunt told me so herself on Saturday. I shall walk to Meryton tomorrow to hear more about it, and to ask when Mr. Denny comes back from town."

Lydia was bid by her two eldest sisters to hold her tongue, but Mr. Collins, much offended, laid aside his book and said:

"I have often noticed how little young ladies are interested in serious books, though they are written solely for their benefit. It amazes me, I confess."

Then turning to Mr. Bennet, he offered himself for a game of cards.

Mr. Collins was not a sensible man, and this lack had been very little overcome by education. He had gone to one of the universities, but had merely passed the usual time there, without forming any useful acquaintance. The control which his father had held him in, had given him great humility of manner, but this was a good deal offset by the self-conceit of a weak head, living in retirement, and early unexpected prosperity when a lucky chance had recommended him to Lady Catherine de Bourgh when the parsonage of Hunsford became vacant. The respect which he felt for her high rank, mingled with a very good opinion of his own authority as a clergyman, made him a mixture of self-importance and humility.

Having now a good house and very sufficient income, Mr. Collins intended to marry, and in seeking friendship with the Bennet family, he had a wife in view, meaning to choose one of the daughters if he found them to his liking. This was his plan of amends for inheriting their father's estate.

The first evening Jane Bennet became his settled choice. The next morning he had a talk with Mrs. Bennet. It began with his parsonage-house and led naturally to his hopes that a mistress for it might be found at Longbourn. Mrs. Bennet was all smiles and general encouragement, but she cautioned against the choice he had fixed on.

"As to my *younger* daughters, I could not take upon me to say —I could not positively say—but my *eldest* daughter is likely to be very soon engaged."

Mr. Collins had only to change from Jane to Elizabeth; and it was soon done—done while Mrs. Bennet was stirring the fire.

Mrs. Bennet now had hopes that she might soon have two daughters married. The man whom she could not bear to speak of the day before was now high in her good graces.

Lydia's walk to Meryton was not forgotten. Every sister except Mary agreed to go with her. Mr. Collins was to attend them, at the request of Mr. Bennet, who was most anxious to get rid of him and have his library to himself. Though prepared, as he told Elizabeth, to meet with folly in every other room in the house, he was used to be free from it in his library. Mr. Collins, being in fact much better fitted for a walker than a reader, was well pleased to close his large book and go.

When they entered Meryton, the eyes of the younger ones went wandering the street in search of the officers, and nothing less than a very smart bonnet, or a really new muslin in a shop window, could recall them. They soon met the very Mr. Denny whose return from London Lydia came to inquire about. With him was a stranger, a young man whom he introduced as Mr. Wickham, who had just received a commission in their regiment. The strange young man was completely charming, with a fine face, a good figure, and very pleasing manners. The whole party were still standing and talking together when the sound of horses drew their notice, and Darcy and Bingley were seen riding down the street.

They rode up and began the usual greetings, Bingley the prin-

cipal speaker, and Jane the principal object. He was then, he said, on his way to Longbourn to ask about her. Mr. Darcy, trying not to fix his eyes on Elizabeth, was suddenly arrested by sight of the stranger. Elizabeth, happening to see the faces of both as they looked at each other, was amazed at the effect of the meeting. Both changed color; one looked white, the other red. Mr. Wickham after a few moments touched his hat—a greeting which Mr. Darcy just barely returned. What could be the meaning of it?

In another minute Mr. Bingley, without seeming to have noticed what passed, took leave and rode on with his friend.

Mr. Denny and Mr. Wickham walked with the young ladies to the door of Mr. Philips's house. There they made their bows and left, in spite of Lydia's urging them to come in, and even in spite of Mrs. Philips's throwing up the parlor window and loudly seconding the invitation.

Mrs. Philips was always glad to see her nieces. She received Mr. Collins with her very best politeness, which he returned with as much more. To Lydia's inquiry about Mr. Wickham she could tell her only that Mr. Denny had brought him from London, and that he was to have a lieutenant's commission in the corps. She had been watching him the last hour, she said, as he walked up and down the street.

Kitty and Lydia kept up the watch, but unluckily no one passed the windows now except a few of the officers who, in comparison with the stranger, were becoming "stupid, disagreeable fellows." Some of them were to dine with the Philipses the next day. Their aunt promised to make her husband call on Mr. Wickham and invite him also, if the family from Longbourn would come in the evening. This was agreed to, and Mrs. Philips said that they would have a nice, comfortable, noisy game of lottery-tickets and a little bit of hot supper afterwards. The thought of such pleasures was very cheering, and they all parted in good spirits.

As they walked home, Elizabeth told Jane what she had seen pass between Mr. Darcy and Mr. Wickham. But though Jane would have defended either or both had they appeared to be wrong, she could no more explain such behavior than her sister.

Chapter Twelve

Elizabeth Bennet Hears Ill Report of Mr. Darcy

Next day at the proper hour Mr. Collins and his five cousins went to Meryton. The girls had the pleasure of hearing, as they entered the Philips drawing-room, that Mr. Wickham would be there for dinner.

When they had all taken their seats, Mr. Collins was free to look around him and admire. He was so much struck with the size and furniture of the apartment that he declared he might almost suppose himself in the small summer breakfast-parlor at Rosings. When Mrs. Philips understood from him what Rosings was, when she had heard the description of only one of Lady Catherine's drawing-rooms and found that the chimney piece alone had cost eight hundred pounds, she felt all the force of the compliment. Her opinion of his importance grew with what she heard, and she planned to tell it all among her neighbors as soon as she could.

When Mr. Wickham walked into the room, Elizabeth felt that she had not been mistaken in forming a high opinion of him. The officers were in general a very gentlemanlike set, and the best of them were of the present party, but Mr. Wickham was as far beyond them all in person, air, and manner, as *they* were beyond the broad-faced, stuffy uncle Philips.

Mr. Wickham was the happy man toward whom almost every woman's eye was turned, and Elizabeth was the happy woman by whom he finally seated himself. The agreeable manner in which he fell into talk, though it was only on its being a wet night and the chance of a rainy season, made her feel that the commonest, dullest topic might be made interesting.

In the presence of such rivals as Mr. Wickham and the officers, Mr. Collins seemed likely to go unnoticed. To the young ladies he certainly was nothing. But he had still a kind listener in Mrs. Philips, and was, by her watchfulness, well supplied with coffee and muffin. When the card tables were placed, he had a chance to return her favor by sitting down to whist.

"I know very little of the game," he said, "but I shall be glad to learn, for in my situation of life—" Mrs. Philips was very thankful for his willingness to oblige, but could not wait for his reason.

Mr. Wickham did not play at whist, and with ready delight was he received at the other table between Elizabeth and Lydia. At first there seemed danger that Lydia would take all his attention, for she was a great talker. But she was also very fond of lottery-tickets, and soon grew too eager in making bets and winning prizes, to have attention for anyone. Mr. Wickham was then free to talk to Elizabeth, and she was very willing to hear him. What she chiefly wished to hear was what was between him and Mr. Darcy.

Mr. Wickham began the subject himself. He asked how far Netherfield was from Meryton. Being told, he asked how long Mr. Darcy had been staying there.

"About a month," said Elizabeth and then, unwilling to let the subject drop, added, "He is a man of very large property in Derbyshire, I understand."

"Yes," said Wickham, "his estate there is a noble one. A clear ten thousand a year. I have been connected with his family from my childhood."

Elizabeth could not help looking surprised.

"You may well be surprised, Miss Bennet, after seeing the very cold manner of our meeting yesterday. Do you know Mr. Darcy very well?"

"As well as I ever wish to," cried Elizabeth warmly. "I have spent four days in the same house with him, and I think him very disagreeable."

"I have no right to give *my* opinion," said Wickham. "I have known him too long and too well to be a fair judge."

"He is not at all liked here. Everybody is disgusted with his pride."

Wickham only shook his head. "With *him* I believe that does not often happen. The world is blinded by his fortune or frightened by his high manners, and sees him only as he chooses to be seen. I wonder whether he is likely to be in this country much longer."

"I do not know, but I *heard* nothing of his going away when I was at Netherfield. I hope your plans to be here will not be changed by his being in the neighborhood."

"Oh, no—it is not for *me* to be driven away by Mr. Darcy. If *he* wishes to avoid seeing *me*, he must go. We are not on friendly terms, and it always gives me pain to meet him, but I have no reason for avoiding *him*. His father, the late Mr. Darcy, was one of the best men that ever breathed and the truest friend I ever had. Though this Mr. Darcy's behavior to me has been most unfair, I verily believe I could forgive him anything but disgracing the memory of his father."

Elizabeth listened with all her heart, but would not ask him more. He began to speak on more general topics, Meryton, the neighborhood, the society, seeming highly pleased with all that he had yet seen.

"It was the prospect of constant society," he added, "which caused me to enter this regiment. And my friend Denny tempted me by his account of Meryton. I have been a disappointed man, and my spirits will not bear solitude. A military life is not what I was intended for. I was brought up for the church, and I should at this time have been in charge of a most valuable parish, had it pleased the gentleman we were speaking of just now."

"Indeed!"

"Yes—the late Mr. Darcy intended me to have the best parish

in his gift. He was my godfather and meant to provide for me well, and thought he had done it. But the parish was given elsewhere."

"Good heavens!" cried Elizabeth, "but how could *that* be? Why did you not go to law for your rights?"

"There was no hope from law. A man of honor could not have doubted the late Mr. Darcy's intention, but his son chose to doubt it—or to treat it as merely a recommendation, and to say that I had lost all claim by my extravagance—in short anything or nothing was excuse enough. I have a warm temper, and I may perhaps have sometimes spoken my opinion *of* him and *to* him, too freely. I can think of nothing worse. But the fact is, that we are very different sort of men, and that he hates me."

"This is quite shocking! He deserves to be publicly disgraced."

"Some time or other he *will* be—but it shall not be by *me*. Till I can forget his father, I can never defy or expose *him*."

Elizabeth honored him for such feelings and thought him handsomer than ever. "But what," said she after a pause, "caused him to behave so cruelly?"

"A thorough dislike of me—a dislike which is due partly to jealousy. Had the late Mr. Darcy liked me less, his son might have borne with me better. His father's liking for me irritated him, I believe, very early in life."

"I had not thought Mr. Darcy so bad as this—though I have never liked him. I had supposed him to despise his fellow-creatures in general, but did not suspect him of such injustice as this! I *do* remember his boasting one day at Netherfield of having an unforgiving temper."

"I will not trust myself on the subject," replied Wickham. "*I* can hardly be just to him."

Elizabeth was again deep in thought, and after a time said: "To treat in such a manner the godson, the friend, the favorite of his father!" She could have added, "A young man, too, like *you*," but she only said, "And one, too, who had been his companion from childhood, as I think you said."

"The greatest part of our youth was passed together. *My*

father began life in the law, but he gave up everything to be of use to the late Mr. Darcy, and gave all his time to the care of the Pemberley property. Just before my father's death Mr. Darcy promised to provide for me."

"How strange!" cried Elizabeth. "How awful! I wonder that the very pride of this Mr. Darcy has not made him be just to you! He should have been too proud to be dishonest—for dishonesty I must call it."

"It *is* strange," replied Wickham, "for almost all his actions may be traced to pride, and pride has often been his best friend. It has brought him nearer to virtue than any other feeling. But in his behavior to me there were stronger impulses even than pride."

"Can such pride as his have ever done him good?"

"Yes. It has often led him to give his money freely, to help his tenants, and relieve the poor. Family pride has done this. He has also *brotherly* pride, which makes him a very kind and careful guardian of his sister. You will hear him generally cried up as the best of brothers."

"What sort of girl is Miss Darcy?"

He shook his head. "It gives me pain to speak ill of a Darcy. But she is too much like her brother—very, very proud. As a child she was pleasing, and very fond of me; and I have given hours and hours to her amusement. But she is nothing to me now. She is a handsome girl, about fifteen or sixteen. Since her father's death she has been in London, where a lady lives with her and looks after her education."

After many pauses and many trials of other subjects, Elizabeth could not help coming back once more to the first, and saying:

"I am surprised at his friendship with Mr. Bingley! How can Mr. Bingley, who seems good-humor itself, be friends with such a man? How can they suit each other? Do you know Mr. Bingley?"

"Not at all."

"He is a sweet-tempered, charming man. He cannot know what Mr. Darcy is."

"Probably not. But Mr. Darcy can please where he chooses, if he thinks it worth his while. Among those who are his equals he is a very different man from what he is to the less prosperous. His pride never deserts him, but with the rich he is just, sincere, honorable, and perhaps agreeable."

Mr. Wickham then asked Elizabeth in a low voice whether Mr. Collins knew the family of de Bourgh very well.

"Lady Catherine de Bourgh," she replied, "has very lately put him in charge of a parish. I hardly know how Mr. Collins came to her notice, but he certainly has not known her long."

"You know of course that Lady Catherine de Bourgh is an aunt of the present Mr. Darcy."

"No, indeed, I did not. I knew nothing at all of Lady Catherine till the day before yesterday."

"Her daughter will have a very large fortune, and it is believed that she and her cousin Darcy will marry and unite the two estates."

This news made Elizabeth smile, as she thought of poor Miss Bingley. Vain indeed must be all her attentions to Mr. Darcy, vain and useless her affection for his sister, and her praise of himself, if he were already engaged to another.

"Mr. Collins," said she, "speaks highly both of Lady Catherine and her daughter. But from what he says of her, I believe I should not admire her."

"I have not seen her for many years, but I very well remember that I never liked her," said Wickham.

They continued talking together till supper put an end to cards and gave the rest of the ladies their share of Mr. Wickham's attentions. There could be no talk in the noise of Mrs. Philips's supper-party, but his manners pleased everybody. Whatever he said was said well, and whatever he did was done gracefully. Elizabeth went away with her head full of him. She could think of nothing but him and of what he had told her, all the way home. But there was not time for her even to mention his name as they went, for neither Lydia or Mr. Collins was once silent, Lydia talking constantly about lottery-tickets, and what she had won and lost; and Mr. Collins about the polite treatment he had received from Mr. and Mrs. Philips.

Chapter Thirteen

The Five Miss Bennets Are Invited to a Ball, and Elizabeth Is Engaged for the First Dance by Mr. Collins

Elizabeth told Jane the next day what had passed between Mr. Wickham and herself. Jane listened with concern. She could not believe that Mr. Darcy was so unworthy of Mr. Bingley's regard. And if Mr. Wickham had endured such unkindness, that was enough to waken all her tender feelings. Nothing, therefore, remained for her but to think well of them both.

"We have both been deceived in some way or other. Some causes, which we cannot guess, have separated them without actual blame, perhaps, on either side. It is very distressing. One does not know what to think."

"I beg your pardon; one knows exactly what to think."

But Jane could think with certainty on only one point—that Mr. Bingley, if he *had* been imposed on, would have much to suffer when the affair became public.

The young ladies were called from the shrubbery where this talk passed, by the arrival of Mr. Bingley and his sisters. They came to give their personal invitation for the ball at Netherfield, which was fixed for the following Tuesday. The two ladies were delighted to see their dear friend Jane again, called it an age since they had met, and asked what she had been doing with herself since their separation. They paid as little attention as possible to Mrs. Bennet, said not much to Elizabeth, and nothing at all to the others. They were soon gone again, rising from their seats with a speed which took their brother by surprise, and hurrying off as if eager to escape.

Mrs. Bennet chose to think of the Netherfield ball as given for Jane, and was very pleased to have the invitation from Mr. Bingley himself, instead of by card. Jane pictured to herself a happy evening with her two friends and their brother. Elizabeth thought of dancing a great deal with Mr. Wickham, and of seeing in Darcy's looks and behavior proof of all Wickham had told her. Kitty and Lydia too meant to dance half the evening with Mr. Wickham, but he was by no means the only partner who could satisfy them. And even Mary said that she had no objection to going.

"While I can have my mornings to myself," said she, "I think it no sacrifice to join now and then in an evening of entertainment. Society has claims on us all. I consider periods of amusement to be desirable for everybody."

Elizabeth asked Mr. Collins whether he intended to accept Mr. Bingley's invitation. She was rather surprised to find that he was far from dreading a rebuke either from the Archbishop or Lady Catherine de Bourgh by venturing to dance.

"A ball of this kind," he said, "given by a young man of character, can have no evil tendency. I am so far from objecting to dancing myself that I shall hope to be honored with the hands of all my fair cousins in the course of the evening. And I take this time to ask you for the two first dances."

Elizabeth felt herself completely taken in. She had fully expected to be asked by Wickham for those very dances, and to have Mr. Collins instead! There was no help for it, however. It now first struck her that *she* was selected from among her sisters as worthy to become the mistress of Hunsford parsonage, and to help form a card table at Rosings in the absence of more important visitors. She now began to notice his frequent compliments on her wit and liveliness. It was not long before her mother gave her to understand that the idea of their marriage was very agreeable to *her.* Elizabeth, however, did not choose to take the hint, being well aware that a serious dispute must follow any reply. Mr. Collins might never make the offer, and till he did, it was useless to quarrel about him.

From the day of the invitation to the day of the ball, there was so much rain that they could not walk to Meryton once. No aunt, no officers, no news—the very shoe-roses[1] for the Netherfield ball had to be sent for. Even Elizabeth found some trial of her patience in weather which kept her from seeing Mr. Wickham. And nothing less than a dance on Tuesday could have made Kitty and Lydia endure such a Friday, Saturday, Sunday, and Monday.

Chapter Fourteen

The Ball at Mr. Bingley's

Not till Elizabeth entered the drawing-room at Netherfield and looked in vain for Mr. Wickham among the cluster of red coats there gathered, had she had a doubt of his being present. She had dressed with more than usual care and in high spirits, trusting that his heart might be won completely in the course of the evening. But now came the dreadful thought of his being purposely omitted for Mr. Darcy's sake. His friend Mr. Denny, of whom Lydia eagerly inquired for Wickham, told him that Wickham had been obliged to go to town on business the day before and was not yet returned. He added with a meaningful smile:

"I imagine his business would not have called him away just now if he had not wished to avoid a certain gentleman here."

This part of the news, unnoticed by Lydia, was caught by Elizabeth. Wickham had stayed away because Darcy was to be there. Every feeling against Darcy was so sharpened by disap-

---

[1] Rosettes for slipper or shoe.

pointment that she could hardly reply with civility when he afterward came to speak to her. Patience with Darcy was injury to Wickham. She decided against any talk with him, and turned away with an ill humor which she could not wholly overcome even in speaking to Mr. Bingley, whose blind liking for Darcy provoked her.

But Elizabeth was not formed for ill humor, and it could not dwell long on her spirits. Having told all her griefs to Charlotte Lucas, whom she had not seen for a week, she spoke of her odd cousin, Mr. Collins, and pointed him out for Charlotte's notice. The two dances, however, brought a return of distress. Mr. Collins, awkward and solemn, apologizing instead of attending to what he was doing, and often moving wrong without knowing it, gave her all the shame and misery which such a partner for a couple of dances can give.

She danced next with an officer, and had the pleasure of talking of Wickham and of hearing that he was liked by all. When those dances were over, she returned to Charlotte Lucas, and was talking with her when she suddenly found herself being spoken to by Mr. Darcy. He took her so much by surprise in asking for a dance that, without knowing what she did, she accepted. He walked away again at once, and she was left to fret over her own want of presence of mind. Charlotte tried to console her.

"I dare say you will find him very agreeable."

"Heaven forbid!—*That* would be the greatest misfortune of all!—to find a man agreeable whom one is determined to hate!— Do not wish me such an evil."

When the dancing began, however, and Darcy approached to claim her hand, Charlotte cautioned her in a whisper not to be a simpleton and allow her fancy for Wickham to make her unpleasant to a man of ten times his importance. Elizabeth made no answer, and took her place in the set, amazed at the dignity of being allowed to stand opposite Mr. Darcy, and reading in the looks of others their equal amazement in beholding it.

They stood for some time without speaking a word, and she began to imagine that their silence was to last through the dance. Then thinking that it would be greater punishment to make him talk, she made some comment on the dance. He replied and was again silent. After a pause of some minutes she spoke a second time with:

"It is *your* turn to say something now, Mr. Darcy. *I* talked about the dance, and *you* ought to make some kind of remark on the size of the room or the number of couples."

He smiled and said that whatever she wished him to say should be said.

"Very well. That reply will do for the present. Perhaps by and by I may state that private balls are much pleasanter than public ones. But *now* we may be silent. One must speak a little, you know. It would look odd to be silent for half an hour together. Yet for *some*, conversation ought to be so arranged as to give them the trouble of saying as little as possible."

"Are you speaking your own feelings, or do you imagine that you are speaking mine?"

"Both," replied Elizabeth archly. "We are each unsocial, unwilling to speak unless we expect to say something that will amaze the whole room and be handed down as a proverb."

"That is not your own character, I am sure," said he. "How near it may be to *mine* I cannot say. *You* think it a true picture no doubt."

They were again silent till they had gone down to dance. Then he asked her if she and her sisters did not very often walk to Meryton. She answered that they did, and could not resist the temptation to add:

"When you met us there the other day, we had just met a new friend."

The effect was immediate. A deeper shade of haughtiness spread over his features, but he said not a word, and Elizabeth, though blaming herself for her own weakness, could not go on. At length Darcy spoke, and in a strained manner said:

"Mr. Wickham is blessed with such happy manners as may cause him to *make* friends—whether he may *keep* them is less certain."

"He has been so unlucky as to lose *your* friendship," replied Elizabeth, "and in a manner which he is likely to suffer from all his life."

Darcy made no answer. At that moment Sir William Lucas came close to them, meaning to pass through the set to the other side of the room. But on seeing Darcy he stopped to compliment him on his dancing partner.

"I must hope to have this pleasant evening repeated, especially when a certain event, my dear Miss Elizabeth," (glancing at her sister and Bingley), "shall take place."

Sir William's words seemed to strike Darcy with force. His eyes turned with a very serious expression toward Bingley and Jane, who were dancing together. Then he turned to his partner and said:

"Sir William has made me forget what we were talking of."

"I do not think we were speaking at all. We have tried two or three subjects already and what we are to talk of next I cannot imagine. I remember hearing you once say, Mr. Darcy, that you hardly ever forgave. You are very cautious, I suppose, never to allow yourself to be blinded by prejudice?"

"I am," said he with a firm voice.

"Those who never change their opinion should be sure of judging properly at first."

"May I ask to what your question tends?"

"I am trying to make out your character," said she, trying to shake off her gravity. "But I do not get on at all. I hear such different accounts of you that I am puzzled greatly."

"I can readily believe that reports of me may vary greatly," he coldly replied.

She said no more and they went down the other dance and parted in silence. But in Darcy's breast there was a powerful feeling toward her, which soon caused her to be pardoned and turned all his anger against another. They had not been separated long when Miss Bingley came toward her, and with a look of civil disdain said:

"I hear you are quite delighted with George Wickham! Your sister has been talking to me about him and asking me a thousand questions. I find that the young man forgot to tell you that he is the son of old Wickham, the late Mr. Darcy's steward. Let me advise you, as a friend, not to believe all he says. As to Mr. Darcy's using him ill, it is perfectly false. On the contrary, he has been always very kind to him, though George Wickham has treated Mr. Darcy in a most shameful manner. I do not know the particulars, but I know very well that Mr. Darcy is not in the least to blame, and that he cannot bear to hear George Wickham mentioned. My brother thought he could not well avoid inviting him with the officers, but we were glad to find that he had taken himself out of the way."

"I have heard you accuse him of nothing worse than of being the son of Mr. Darcy's steward," said Elizabeth angrily, "and he told me *that* himself."

"I beg your pardon," said Miss Bingley, turning away with a sneer. "Excuse my interference. It was kindly meant."

Elizabeth went to look for Jane, who had undertaken to ask Bingley about Wickham. Jane met her with a glow of happiness, showing how well she was satisfied with the evening. Elizabeth read her feelings, and at that moment everything else gave way before the hope of Jane's being in the fairest way for happiness.

"What have you learned about Mr. Wickham?" said she with a face as smiling as her sister's. "But perhaps you have been too pleasantly engaged to think of any third person, in which case you may be sure of my pardon."

"No," replied Jane, "I have not forgotten him, but I have nothing satisfactory to tell you. Mr. Bingley does not know the whole of his history, and he knows nothing of that part which has offended Mr. Darcy. But from what he said, as well as by what his sisters have said, I am afraid Mr. Wickham has deserved to lose Mr. Darcy's regard."

"Mr. Bingley does not know Mr. Wickham himself?"

"No, he never saw him till the other morning at Meryton."

"Then, since he does not know all the story," said Elizabeth, "and has learned the rest from Darcy himself, I shall still think of both as I did before."

They were joined by Mr. Bingley, and Elizabeth withdrew to Charlotte Lucas. Mr. Collins came up to them and told her with great pride that he had just made a most important discovery.

"I have found out," said he, "by accident, that there is now in the room a near relation of my patroness, Lady Catherine de Bourgh. I happened to overhear the gentleman himself speak her name. How wonderfully these things occur! Who would have thought of my meeting with a *nephew* of Lady Catherine in this assembly! I am now going to pay my respects to him."

"You are not going to introduce yourself to Mr. Darcy?"

"Indeed I am. I shall beg his pardon for not having done it earlier." And with a low bow he left her to attack Mr. Darcy.

Elizabeth eagerly watched and saw Mr. Collins begin with a solemn bow, and though she could not hear a word of it, she felt as if hearing it all. She saw in the motion of his lips the words "apology," "Hunsford," and "Lady Catherine de Bourgh." It vexed her to see him expose himself to such a man. Mr. Darcy replied with distant civility, made a slight bow and moved away. Mr. Collins returned to Elizabeth.

"Mr. Darcy seemed much pleased," he said. "He answered me with the utmost civility, and even paid me the compliment of saying he believed Lady Catherine never bestowed her favors on persons unworthy of them. It was really a very handsome thought. Upon the whole, I am much pleased with him."

When they sat down to supper, Elizabeth was vexed to find that her mother was talking to Lady Lucas freely, openly, and of nothing but her expectation that Jane would be soon married to Mr. Bingley. Mrs. Bennet spoke of the advantages of the match. Mr. Bingley was such a charming young man, and so rich, and living but three miles from them. It was such a comfort to think how fond the two sisters were of Jane, and to be certain

that they too must wish for the marriage. It was such a fin
thing for her younger daughters, as Jane's marrying so well mus
throw them in the way of other rich young men. She ended witl
many good wishes that Lady Lucas might soon be equally for
tunate, though plainly she did not believe there was a chance o
it.

Elizabeth reminded her mother that Mr. Darcy, who sat op
posite to them, could overhear her. Her mother only scolded her

"What is Mr. Darcy to me that I should be afraid to say any
thing *he* may not like to hear?"

Elizabeth blushed and blushed again with shame and vexa
tion. She could not help glancing at him, and though he was no
always looking at her mother, she believed that his attention wa
fixed on her. His face showed a composed and steady gravity.

When supper was over, singing was talked of. Mary, afte
very little entreaty, went forward and obliged the company witl
several songs. Any such chance was delightful to her. Mary'
powers were by no means fitted for such a display; her voice wa
weak and her manner affected. Elizabeth was in agonies. Sh
looked at Jane to see how she bore it, but Jane was talking t
Bingley. She looked at his two sisters and saw them send smilin;
glances to each other, and at Darcy who was quiet and grave
She looked for help, lest Mary should be singing all night. He
took the hint, and when Mary had finished her song, said aloud

"That will do, child. You have delighted us long enough. Le
the other young ladies have time to exhibit."

Mary pretended not to hear, but left the piano. Elizabeth wa
sorry for her, and sorry for her father's speech. Others of th
party were now invited to furnish music.

"If I," said Mr. Collins, "were able to sing, I should have grea
pleasure in obliging the company with a song, for I look on musi
as a very innocent pastime, as well suited to a clergyman as t
other people. I do not mean that we can give too much of ou
time to music, for there are other things to be done. The recto
of a parish has much to do. In the first place, he must make sucl
an agreement for tithes as may be right to himself and not offen

sive to his patron. He must write his own sermons; and the time that remains will not be too much for his parish duties and the care of his dwelling."

With a bow to Mr. Darcy he finished his speech, which had been spoken so loud as to be heard by half the room. Many stared—many smiled, but no one looked more amused than Mr. Bennet. Mrs. Bennet said in a half-whisper to Lady Lucas that he was a very clever, good kind of young man.

To Elizabeth it seemed that if her family had made an agreement to expose themselves as much as they could during the evening, they could not have played their parts with more spirit or finer success. She did not know whether the silent contempt of Darcy or the sneering smiles of the ladies were more painful.

The rest of the evening brought her little amusement. Mr. Collins stayed by her side, and though he could not persuade her to dance with him again, put it out of her power to dance with others. In vain did she urge him to dance with somebody else. As to dancing, he said, he did not care for it; he had danced only to please her, and now he wished only to remain by her the whole evening. She owed her greatest relief to her friend Charlotte, who often joined them and good-naturedly talked with Mr. Collins herself. Elizabeth thought that at least she was free of any more notice by Mr. Darcy who, though often standing within a very short distance of her, never came near enough to speak.

Chapter Fifteen

Mr. Collins Will Not Take No for an Answer

The Bennet party were the last to leave Netherfield, for Mrs. Bennet had so managed that they had to wait for their carriage a quarter of an hour. This gave Elizabeth time to see how heartily they were wished away by some of the family. Mrs. Hurst and her sister scarcely opened their mouths except to complain of being tired. They passed over every attempt of Mrs. Bennet at friendly talk, and by so doing threw all into a silence, which was very little relieved by the long speeches of Mr. Collins, who praised Mr. Bingley and his sisters for their entertainment and politeness to their guests. Darcy said nothing at all. Mr. Bennet, in equal silence, was enjoying the scene. Mr. Bingley and Jane were standing together, a little apart from the rest, talking only to each other. Elizabeth kept as steady a silence as either Mrs. Hurst or Miss Bingley. Even Lydia was too weary to utter more than "Lord, how tired I am!" with a violent yawn.

When at length they arose to leave, Mrs. Bennet was most pressing in her hopes of seeing the whole family soon at Longbourn. She reminded Mr. Bingley of how happy he would make them by eating a family dinner with them at any time. Bingley was all grateful pleasure and promised to visit her after his return from London, where he was to go the next day for a short time.

Mrs. Bennet left the house under the delightful belief that she would see Jane settled at Netherfield in the course of three or four months. Of having Elizabeth married to Mr. Collins she thought with equal certainty and with some, though not equal, pleasure. Elizabeth was the least dear to her of all her children, and she thought the match was quite good enough for *her*.

The next day Mr. Collins made his formal offer of marriage. He had decided to do it without loss of time, as his leave of absence lasted only to the following Saturday. He set about it in a very orderly manner. On finding Mrs. Bennet, Elizabeth and one of the younger girls together soon after breakfast, he said to the mother:

"May I hope, madam, that you will agree when I ask for a private talk with your daughter Elizabeth in the course of this morning?"

Before Elizabeth had time for anything but a blush of surprise, Mrs. Bennet answered, "Oh dear, yes—certainly. I am sure Lizzy will be very happy—I am sure she can have no objection. Come,

Kitty, I want you upstairs." And gathering her work together, she was hastening away, when Elizabeth called out:

"Please do not go. Mr. Collins must excuse me. He can have nothing to say to me that anybody need not hear. I am going away myself."

"No, no, nonsense, Lizzy. You will stay where you are." And upon Elizabeth's seeming really, with vexed looks, about to escape, she added, "Lizzy, I *insist* upon your staying and hearing Mr. Collins."

Elizabeth would not disobey her command. And a moment's thought having convinced her that it would be wisest to get it over as soon and as quietly as possible, she sat down again. Mrs. Bennet and Kitty walked off, and as soon as they were gone, Mr. Collins began.

"Believe me, my dear Miss Elizabeth, your modesty only adds to your other perfections. Indeed you would have been less charming in my eyes had there *not* been this little unwillingness to hear me. But let me assure that I have your mother's permission to speak. You can hardly doubt the purpose of my proposed talk with you, however your natural modesty may lead you to pretend otherwise. My attentions have been too marked to be mistaken. Almost as soon as I entered the house I singled you out as the companion of my future life. But before I am run away with by my feelings on this subject, perhaps I should state my reasons for marrying—and for coming here to select a wife, as I certainly did."

The idea of Mr. Collins, with all his solemn composure, being run away with by his feelings, brought Elizabeth so near laughing that she could not use the short pause he allowed to make any attempt to stop him from continuing.

"My reasons for marrying are, first, that I think it a right thing for every clergyman to set the example of matrimony in his parish. Secondly, that it will add very greatly to my happiness. Thirdly—which perhaps I ought to have mentioned earlier—it is the advice of Lady Catherine de Bourgh. Twice has she given me her opinion (unasked too!) on this subject. It was but the

very Saturday night before I left Hunsford—when we were playing cards, while Mrs. Jenkinson was arranging Miss de Bourgh's
footstool—that she said. 'Mr. Collins, you must marry. A clergyman like you must marry. Choose properly, choose a gentle-
woman for *my* sake. And for your *own* sake, let her be an active,
useful sort of person, not brought up high, but able to make a
small income go a good way. This is my advice. Find such a
woman as soon as you can, bring her to Hunsford, and I will
visit her.' And allow me to say that the notice and kindness of
Lady Catherine de Bourgh will be among the advantages I have
to offer you. You will find her manners beyond anything I can
describe. And she will not object to your wit and liveliness, when
tempered with the silence and respect due her rank. It remains
now to tell you why I came to Longbourn instead of looking for
a wife in my own neighborhood, where there are many charming
young women. But as I am to inherit this estate after the death
of your father, I wished to choose a wife from among his
daughters, that the loss might be felt as little as possible when
the sad event takes place—which, however, may not be for several years. This was my motive, and I think it will not sink me in
your esteem. As to property, I shall make no demands on your
father, since I know that he would not be able to meet them,
and that one thousand pounds in the 4 per cents, which will not
be yours till after your mother's death, is all that you will ever
be entitled to. But on that head, you may be sure that no reproach shall ever pass my lips when we are married."

It was now necessary for Elizabeth to interrupt him. "You are
too hasty, sir," she cried. "You forget that I have made no answer. Let me do it without further loss of time. I thank you
for the honor of your proposal, but I must decline."

"I know well enough," replied Mr. Collins, with a formal wave
of the hand, "that it is usual with young ladies to refuse the man
whom they secretly mean to accept, when he first speaks. I know
too that sometimes the refusal is made a second or even a third
time. I am therefore not discouraged by what you have just said,
and shall hope to lead you to the altar ere long."

"Upon my word, sir," cried Elizabeth, "I am not one of those young ladies (if such young ladies there are) who are so daring as to risk the chance of being asked a second time. I am perfectly serious in my refusal. You could not make *me* happy, and I am the last woman in the world who would make *you* so. And if your friend Lady Catherine were to know me, she would find me entirely unfit for the place."

"If I were certain that Lady Catherine would think so," said Mr. Collins very gravely—"but I am sure that her ladyship would approve of you. And you may be certain that when I have the honor of seeing her again I shall speak in the highest terms of your modesty, economy, and other good qualities."

"Indeed, Mr. Collins, you must let me judge for myself, and believe what I say. I wish you very happy and very rich, and by refusing your hand, do all in my power to prevent your being otherwise. In making me the offer, you must have satisfied your feelings with regard to my family, and may take the Longbourn estate whenever it falls, without any self-reproach. This matter is, therefore, finally settled." And rising, she would have left the room, but Mr. Collins spoke again.

"When I do myself the honor of speaking to you next on this subject, I shall hope to have a more favorable answer. As I said, I know that it is the custom of young ladies to refuse a man on the first proposal. Perhaps you have even now said as much to encourage me as I should expect."

"Really, Mr. Collins," cried Elizabeth with some warmth, "you puzzle me greatly. If what I have said can seem like encouragement, I do not know how to speak my refusal in a way to convince you that it is one."

"You must give me leave to flatter myself, my dear cousin, that your refusal is merely words. My reasons for believing it are these:—It does not appear to me that my offer is unworthy your acceptance. My position, my connections with the family of de Bourgh are highly in my favor. And you should remember that in spite of your many attractions, it is by no means certain that another offer of marriage may ever be made you, as your property is unhappily so small. I must therefore believe that you are not serious in refusing me."

"I would rather be paid the compliment of being believed sincere. I thank you again and again for the honor you have done me, but I cannot accept your offer. My feelings in every way forbid it. Can I speak plainer?"

"You are always charming!" cried he with an air of awkward gallantry, "and I feel sure that when you have spoken with your parents, my offer will be accepted."

Elizabeth would make no reply, and in silence left the room. If he went to her father, he would receive a refusal spoken in such words and such manner as could not be mistaken for the coquetry of a young woman.

Chapter Sixteen

Mr. Collins Withdraws His Offer

Mr. Collins was not left long alone. Mrs. Bennet had dawdled about in the hall to watch for the end of the conference. When she saw Elizabeth open the door and with quick step pass her toward the staircase, she entered the breakfast-room and began speaking in warm tones on the happy prospect of his marriage to Elizabeth. Mr. Collins spoke with equal pleasure, adding that he believed he had every reason to be satisfied, since the refusal given him would naturally come from bashful modesty.

This report, however, startled Mrs. Bennet. She would have been glad to think that her daughter had meant to encourage him by refusing him, but she dared not believe it and could not help saying so.

"But depend upon it, Mr. Collins," she added, "Lizzy shall be brought to reason. I will speak to her about it myself at once.

She is a very headstrong, foolish girl, and does not know her own interest, but I will *make* her know it."

"Pardon me, madam," cried Mr. Collins, "but if she is really headstrong and foolish, she might not be a very suitable wife. Perhaps it would be better not to force her, because if she has such defects of temper, she could not add to my happiness."

"Sir, you quite misunderstand me," said Mrs. Bennet, alarmed. "Lizzy is only headstrong in such matters as these. In everything else she is as good-natured a girl as ever lived. I will go at once to Mr. Bennet, and we shall very soon settle it with her, I am sure."

She would not give him time to reply, but hurrying at once to her husband, called out as she entered the library:

"Oh, Mr. Bennet; we are all in an uproar! You must come and make Lizzy marry Mr. Collins, for she vows she will not have him, and if you do not make haste he will change his mind and not have *her*."

Mr. Bennet raised his eyes from his book as she entered, and fixed them on her face with a calm unconcern which was not in the least altered by the news.

"I have not the pleasure of understanding you," said he when she had finished her speech. "Of what are you talking?"

"Of Mr. Collins and Lizzy. Lizzy declares she will not have Mr. Collins, and Mr. Collins begins to say that he will not have Lizzy!"

"And what am I to do? It seems a hopeless business."

"Speak to Lizzy about it yourself. Tell her that you insist upon her marrying him."

"Let her be called down. She shall hear my opinion."

Mrs. Bennet rang the bell, and Elizabeth was sent for to come to the library.

"Come here, child," said her father as she appeared. "I understand that Mr. Collins had made you an offer of marriage. Is it true?" Elizabeth replied that it was. "Very well—and this offer of marriage you have refused?"

"I have, sir."

"Very well, we now come to the point. Your mother insists upon your accepting it. Is not that so, Mrs. Bennet?"

"Yes, or I will never see her again."

"An unhappy choice is before you, Elizabeth. Your mother will never see you again if you do *not* marry Mr. Collins, and I will never see you again if you *do*."

Elizabeth could not but smile at such an outcome to such a beginning. But Mrs. Bennet was greatly disappointed.

"What do you mean, Mr. Bennet, by talking in this way? You promised me to *insist* upon her marrying him."

"My dear," replied her husband, "I have a small favor to ask. Allow me the free use of my understanding and of my room. I shall be glad to have the library to myself as soon as may be."

Not yet, however, did Mrs. Bennet give up the point. She talked to Elizabeth again and again, coaxed and threatened her by turns.

Mr. Collins, meanwhile, was thinking on what had passed. He thought too well of himself to understand why his cousin could refuse him; and though his pride was hurt, he suffered in no other way. His regard for her was quite imaginary, and the possibility of her being headstrong and foolish, as her mother had said, kept him from feeling any regret.

While the family were in this confusion, Charlotte Lucas came to spend the day with them. She was met in the hall by Lydia who, flying to her, cried in a half-whisper, "I am glad you have come, for there is such fun here! What do you think has happened this morning? Mr. Collins has made an offer to Lizzy, and she will not have him."

Charlotte had hardly time to answer before they were joined by Kitty, who came to tell the same news. And no sooner had they entered the breakfast-room where Mrs. Bennet was alone, than she too began on the subject, calling on Miss Lucas for pity, and begging her to persuade Lizzy to accept Mr. Collins.

"Pray do, my dear Charlotte," she added in a sad tone, "for nobody is on my side, nobody takes part with me, nobody feels for my poor nerves."

Charlotte's reply was spared by the entrance of Jane and Elizabeth.

"Ah, there she comes," continued Mrs. Bennet, "looking as if she cared for nothing but her own way. I tell you what, Lizzy, if you take it into your head to go on refusing every offer of marriage in this way, you will never get a husband at all—and I am sure I do not know who is to maintain you when your father is dead. *I* shall not be able to keep you—and so I warn you. I have done with you from this very day. I told you in the library, you know, that I should never speak to you again, and you will find me as good as my word. I have no pleasure in talking to undutiful children. Not that I have much pleasure indeed in talking to anybody. People who suffer as I do from nervous complaints can have no great pleasure in talking. Nobody can tell what I suffer! But it is always so. Those who do not complain are never pitied."

Her daughters listened in silence, knowing that trying to soothe her would only throw her into a worse temper. She talked on, till they were joined by Mr. Collins, who entered with an air more stately than usual. On seeing him, Mrs. Bennet said to the girls:

"Now I do insist that all of you hold your tongues, and let Mr. Collins and me have a little talk together."

Elizabeth passed quietly out of the room. Jane and Kitty followed, but Lydia stood her ground, determined to hear all she could. Charlotte walked to the window and pretended not to hear.

"Oh, Mr. Collins!" Mrs. Bennet began in a doleful voice.

"My dear madam, let us forever be silent on this point. Far be it from me," he said in a voice that marked his displeasure, "to resent the behavior of your daughter. But you will not, I hope, consider me as showing any lack of respect to your family by withdrawing my offer to your daughter. I had not as yet asked you and Mr. Bennet, and I have accepted my refusal from your daughter's lips instead of your own. I have meant well through the whole affair. My object has been to secure a suitable com-

panion for myself with due concern for the advantage of all your
family. If my *manner* has been at all wrong, I here beg leave to
apologize."

Chapter Seventeen

Mr. Bingley Runs Away from Love

The discussion of Mr. Collins's offer was now nearly at an end.
Elizabeth had only to suffer from some peevish remarks of her
mother. As for Mr. Collins, *his* feelings were chiefly expressed
not by trying to avoid her, but by stiffness of manner and resentful silence. He scarcely ever spoke to her, and his attentions
were given for the rest of the day to Charlotte Lucas.

The morrow brought no improvement in Mrs. Bennet's ill humor or ill health. Mr. Collins was also in the same state of angry
pride. Elizabeth had hoped that he might shorten his visit, but
his plan did not change. He had always meant to remain until
Saturday, and until Saturday he still meant to stay.

After breakfast the girls walked to Meryton to learn if Mr.
Wickham had returned. He joined them on their entering the
town and went with them to their aunt's, where his absence was
well talked over. To Elizabeth, he frankly said that he had been
absent on purpose.

"I found," he said, "as the time drew near, that I had better
not meet Darcy, that to be in the same room for so many hours
together might be more than I could bear, and that unpleasant
scenes might arise."

Wickham and another officer walked back with them to Longbourn. His returning with them had a double advantage; Elizabeth felt all the compliment it offered to herself, and it gave the
opportunity to introduce him to her father and mother.

Soon after their return a letter from Netherfield was brought to Jane. Elizabeth saw her face change as she read it. Jane finished the letter, put it away, and tried to join with her usual cheerfulness in the general talk. But Elizabeth felt an anxiety which drew her attention even from Wickham. No sooner had he and his companion taken leave than a glance from Jane invited her to follow her upstairs. When they had gained their own room, Jane, taking out the letter, said:

"This is from Caroline Bingley. What it contains has surprised me a good deal. The whole party have left Netherfield by this time and are on their way to town, and without any intention of coming back again. You shall hear what she says."

She then read the first sentence aloud, which stated that they had just decided to follow their brother to London at once, and would dine that day in Grosvenor Street, where Mr. Hurst had a house. The next was in these words: "I do not pretend to regret anything I shall leave except your society, my dearest friend. We will hope at some future time to enjoy many returns of the delightful hours we have known together, and in the meanwhile we may lessen the pain of separation by frequent letters. I depend on you for that. When my brother left us yesterday, he believed that the business which took him to London might be done in three or four days, but we are certain it cannot be so, and feel sure that when Charles gets to town he will be in no hurry to leave it again. So we have decided to follow him there, that he may not have to spend his time in a comfortless hotel. Many of my friends are already there for the winter. I sincerely hope your Christmas may be gay and that your beaux will be so many that you will not feel the loss of the three who are leaving."

"It is plain by this," added Jane, "that he comes back no more this winter."

"It is only plain that Miss Bingley does not mean he *should*."

"Why will you think so? It must be his own doing. He is his own master. But you do not know *all*. I *will* read you the passage which particularly hurts me. I will hold back nothing from *you.* 'Mr. Darcy wishes to see his sister, and we are eager to meet Georgiana Darcy again. Louisa and I have every reason to hope that she will one day be our sister. My brother admires her greatly already, and he will now be able to see her often. Her family too all wish for this marriage.'

"Is it not clear enough, dear Lizzy," said Jane as she finished the letter, "that Caroline does not expect or wish me to be her sister? She believes that her brother cares nothing for me, and if she suspects my feelings for him, she means (most kindly!) to put me on my guard. Can there be any other opinion on the subject?"

"Yes, there can; for mine is totally different. Miss Bingley sees that her brother is in love with you, and wants him to marry Miss Darcy. She follows him to town in the hope of keeping him there, and tries to persuade you that he does not care about you."

Jane shook her head.

"Indeed, Jane, you ought to believe me. No one who has ever seen you together can doubt his affection. Miss Bingley, I am sure, cannot. She is not such a simpleton. Could she have seen half so much love in Mr. Darcy for herself, she would have ordered her wedding clothes. But the case is this:—we are not rich enough or grand enough for them. And she is anxious to see her brother married to Miss Darcy, because such family connection might help her to marry Mr. Darcy. And she might, if Miss de Bourgh were out of the way. But, my dearest Jane, you cannot believe that because Miss Bingley tells you her brother greatly admires Miss Darcy, he admires you less than when he took leave of you on Tuesday, or that she can persuade him that he is very much in love with Georgiana Darcy instead of with you."

"If we thought alike of Caroline Bingley," replied Jane, "your words might make me quite easy. But I fear you are not just to Caroline. She would not wilfully deceive anyone. All that I can hope in this case is that she is deceived herself."

"That is right. You could not have started a more happy idea, since you will not take comfort in mine. Believe her to be deceived by all means. You have now done your duty by her and must fret no longer."

"But, my dear sister, can I be happy, even supposing the best, in marrying a man whose sisters and friends are all wishing him to marry elsewhere?"

"You must decide for yourself," said Elizabeth. "If after thinking it over, you find that disappointing his two sisters is more than the happiness of being his wife, I advise you to refuse him."

"How can you talk so?" said Jane, faintly smiling. "You know that though I should be grieved to disappoint them, I should marry him nevertheless."

"I thought you would. And that being the case, I can see no cause to pity you."

"But if he returns no more this winter, it will all be over! A thousand things might arise in six months!"

The idea of his returning no more Elizabeth treated with scorn. It was merely Caroline's wish, and that wish, however artfully spoken, could not greatly influence a young man so independent of everyone. She told her sister as forcibly as possible what she thought, and soon had Jane hoping that Bingley would return to Netherfield and answer every wish of her heart.

They agreed that Mrs. Bennet should hear only that the family had left for the time being. But even this report gave her a great deal of concern, and she bewailed it as so very unlucky that the ladies should happen to go away just as they were all getting so friendly together. She consoled herself by thinking that Mr. Bingley would soon return and be dining again at Longbourn.

Chapter Eighteen

Mr. Collins Makes a Third Choice

On Thursday the Bennets were dining with the Lucases, and during most of the day Charlotte was so kind as to listen to Mr. Collins. Elizabeth found time to thank her.

"It keeps him in a good humor," she said, "and I am more obliged to you than I can say."

Charlotte said that she was pleased to be useful, and that it amply repaid her. But Charlotte's kindness went farther than Elizabeth had any idea of. Her object was nothing less than to turn Mr. Collins's attention toward herself, and when they parted at night she would have felt almost sure of success if he were not to leave Longbourn so very soon. But in this fear she did injustice to the fire and independence of his character. The shortness of the time led him to escape out of Longbourn House the next morning with great slyness and hasten to Lucas Lodge to throw himself at her feet.

He was anxious to avoid the notice of his cousins, for he was not willing to have his plans known till he was sure of success. Already he felt almost sure, for Charlotte had been encouraging. And his welcome was flattering. Charlotte saw him from an upper window as he walked toward the house, and set out to meet him by accident in the lane. But little had she dared to hope for such a speedy courtship.

In as short a time as Mr. Collins's long speeches would allow, everything was settled between them. As they entered the house, he was urging her to name the day that was to make him the happiest of men. His natural stupidity must keep his courtship from any charm that could make a woman wish to prolong it.

And Charlotte, who accepted him solely for the sake of being settled in marriage, cared not how soon the settlement was gained.

Sir William and Lady Lucas gave their consent joyfully. Mr. Collins was a good match for their daughter, to whom they could give little fortune, and his prospects of future wealth were good. Lady Lucas began at once to wonder how many years longer Mr. Bennet was likely to live. The younger girls formed hopes of *coming out* a year or two sooner than they might otherwise have done, and the boys were relieved of their fear of Charlotte's dying an old maid. Charlotte herself was composed. She had gained her point and had time to think it over. Mr. Collins, to be sure, was neither sensible nor agreeable. But still he would be her husband. Without thinking highly either of men or of matrimony, marriage had always been her object. It was the only honorable outcome for well-educated young women of small fortune. At the age of twenty-seven, without having ever been handsome, she felt that she had been lucky. Her chief worry was the surprise it must cause Elizabeth Bennet, whose friendship she valued beyond that of any other person. Elizabeth would wonder, and probably would blame her. And Charlotte's feelings must be hurt by her surprise and disapproval.

Therefore she charged Mr. Collins when he went back to Longbourn to dinner, to drop no hint of what had passed before any of the family. The promise was of course very dutifully given, but it was hard to keep. Questions burst forth at once about his long absence. Moreover, he was at the same time longing to give out the news of his success in love.

As he was to begin his journey too early on the morrow to see any of the family, he took leave of the ladies that night. Mrs. Bennet, with great politeness, said how happy they should be to see him at Longbourn again, whenever his other engagements might allow him to visit them.

"My dear madam," he replied, "this invitation is what I have been hoping to receive, and you may be very certain that I shall return as soon as possible."

They were all astonished, and Mr. Bennet, who wished for no return, said at once:

"But is there not danger of displeasing Lady Catherine, my good sir? You had better neglect your relations than run the risk of offending her."

"My dear sir," replied Mr. Collins, "I thank you for this friendly caution, and you may depend upon my not taking such a step without her ladyship's approval."

"You cannot be too much on your guard. Risk anything rather than her displeasure, and if you find it likely to be raised by your coming to us again, stay quietly at home. We shall take no offence."

"Believe me, my dear sir, you have my gratitude, and you will soon receive from me a letter of thanks for your regard during my stay. As for my fair cousins, though I shall soon return, I now take the liberty of wishing them health and happiness, not excepting my cousin Elizabeth."

The ladies then withdrew, all of them surprised to find that he planned a quick return. Mrs. Bennet wished to understand by it that he thought of turning his attention to one of her younger girls, and Mary might be willing to accept him. But on the following morning every hope of this kind was done away. Charlotte Lucas called soon after breakfast and in a private talk with Elizabeth told her the event of the day before.

The thought of Mr. Collins's fancying himself in love with Charlotte had come to Elizabeth within the last day or two, but she had not thought that Charlotte could encourage him. Her surprise, therefore, was so great at first that she could not help crying out:

"Engaged to Mr. Collins! My dear Charlotte—impossible!"

The steady look which Charlotte had kept in telling her story gave way to a confusion, but she soon gained back her composure and calmly replied:

"Why should you be surprised, my dear Elizabeth? Do you think no other woman could have a good opinion of him because he was not so happy as to succeed with you?"

But Elizabeth had now recollected herself, and was able to say that she wished her all happiness.

"I see what you are feeling," said Charlotte. "You must be surprised, very much surprised—as Mr. Collins so lately was wishing to marry you. But when you have had time to think it all over, I hope you will be satisfied with what I have done. I am not romantic, you know. I never was. I ask only a comfortable home, and considering Mr. Collins's character and position in life, I believe that my chance of happiness with him is as fair as most people can boast on entering the marriage state."

Elizabeth quietly answered "No doubt," and after an awkward pause they returned to the rest of the family. Charlotte did not stay much longer, and Elizabeth was then left to think of what she had heard. It was a long time before she became at all willing to accept the idea of so unsuitable a match. She had always felt that Charlotte's opinion of marriage was not exactly like her own, but she had not thought that Charlotte would be willing to marry merely for worldly advantage. Charlotte the wife of Mr. Collins! And to the pang of seeing her friend sunk in her esteem was added the fear that she could not be happy in the lot she had chosen.

Elizabeth was sitting with her mother and sisters, thinking on what she had heard from Charlotte and wondering whether she should mention it to the family, when Sir William Lucas himself appeared, sent by his daughter to announce her engagement. He unfolded the matter—to an audience not merely wondering but unbelieving. Mrs. Bennet cried out that he must be entirely mistaken, and Lydia, always unguarded and often uncivil, loudly exclaimed:

"Good Lord! Sir William, how can you tell such a story? Do you not know that Mr. Collins wants to marry Lizzy?"

Sir William's good breeding carried him through it all, and Elizabeth, to relieve him, now put herself forward to say that she had heard of it from Charlotte herself. She tried to put a stop to the unbelief of her mother and sisters by earnest good wishes for the couple, in which she was joined by Jane.

Mrs. Bennet was too much overpowered to say a great deal while Sir William remained. But no sooner had he left them than her feelings found a rapid vent. In the first place, she could not believe the whole of the matter. Secondly, she was very sure that Mr. Collins had been taken in. Thirdly, she trusted that they would never be happy together. And fourthly, that the match might be broken off, that Elizabeth was the real cause of all the mischief, and that she herself had been very ill used by them all. On the last two points she dwelt during the rest of the day. Indeed, it was a week before she could see Elizabeth without scolding her. A month passed away before she could speak to Sir William or Lady Lucas without being rude, and many months were gone before she could at all forgive their daughter.

Mr. Bennet said only that he was pleased to learn that Charlotte Lucas, whom he used to think sensible, was as foolish as his wife, and more foolish than his daughters!

Jane confessed herself a little surprised at the match, but she said less of that than of her earnest desire for their happiness. Kitty and Lydia were far from envying Charlotte, for Mr. Collins was only a clergyman, and the affair was to them only a piece of news to be spread at Meryton.

Lady Lucas was now able to triumph over Mrs. Bennet in the prospect of having a daughter well married. She called at Longbourn rather oftener than usual to say how happy she was, though Mrs. Bennet's sour looks and ill-natured remarks might have been enough to drive happiness away.

Between Elizabeth and Charlotte there was a restraint which kept them silent on the subject. Elizabeth felt that no real confidence could ever exist between them again.

The promised letter of thanks from Mr. Collins arrived on Tuesday. He spoke of his happiness in gaining the love of Miss Lucas, and then explained that it was with the view of enjoying her society that he had been so ready to accept their kind invitation to come again to Longbourn. He hoped to be able to return on Monday fortnight. Lady Catherine, he added, so heartily approved his marriage that she wished it to take place as soon as possible.

Mr. Collins's return was no longer a matter of pleasure to Mrs. Bennet. She was now as much disposed to complain of it as her husband. It was very strange that he should come to Longbourn instead of to Lucas Lodge. It was also very troublesome. She hated having visitors in the house while her health was so bad, and lovers were of all people the most disagreeable.

Chapter Nineteen

Jane Bennet Still Thinks the Best of Everyone

Jane had sent Caroline Bingley an early answer to her letter and was counting the days till she might hope to hear again. Neither Jane nor Elizabeth was comfortable on this subject. Day after day passed away without bringing any other tidings of Mr. Bingley than the report heard in Meryton of his coming no more to Netherfield the whole winter, a report which Mrs. Bennet never failed to say was an outright falsehood.

Even Elizabeth began to fear—not that Bingley did not care for Jane, but that his sisters would be able to keep him away. The united efforts of his two unfeeling sisters and of the overpowering Darcy, aided by the attractions of Miss Darcy and the amusements of London, might be too much, she feared, for the strength of his love for Jane.

Mr. Collins returned on Monday fortnight, but his welcome at Longbourn was not quite so gracious as it had been on his first visit. He was too happy, however, to need much attention. He spent most of every day at Lucas Lodge, and sometimes returned to Longbourn only in time to make an apology for his absence before the family went to bed.

Mrs. Bennet was really in a most pitiable state. The very mention of the match threw her into an agony of ill humor, and wherever she went she was sure of hearing it talked of. The sight of Charlotte Lucas was odious to her. As her successor in Longbourn House, she looked on her with jealous dislike. Whenever Charlotte spoke in a low voice to Mr. Collins, Mrs. Bennet was sure they were talking of the Longbourn estate, and planning to turn her and her daughters out as soon as Mr. Bennet should be dead. She complained bitterly of all this to her husband.

"It is very hard," she said, "to think that Charlotte Lucas should ever be mistress of this house, that I should be forced to make way for *her*, and live to see her take my place in it!"

"My dear, do not give way to such gloomy thoughts. Let us hope for better things. *I* may outlive them both."

This was not very consoling to Mrs. Bennet, and therefore, instead of making any answer, she went on as before.

At last a letter came to Jane from Caroline Bingley. It stated among other things that they were all settled in London for the winter, adding that her brother regretted not having time to see his friends at Longbourn before he left Netherfield.

Hope was over, entirely over. When Jane could read the rest of the letter, she found little that could give her any comfort. Caroline wrote much of Georgiana Darcy, boasting joyfully of her hopes to see her soon married to her brother Charles. She wrote with great pleasure of his being often at Mr. Darcy's house, and of plans there for new furniture.

Elizabeth heard it in silent anger. That Charles Bingley was really fond of Jane she doubted no more than she had ever done. And much as she liked him, she could not think without anger of his easy-going nature which now made him the slave of his family and friends and led him to give up the happiness of himself and of Jane, at their wishes.

A day or two passed before Jane had courage to speak of her feelings to Elizabeth. But at last, as Mrs. Bennet left them together after a longer than usual complaint about Netherfield and its master, she could not help saying:

"Oh, that my dear mother had more command over herself! She can have no idea of the pain she gives me by speaking ill of him. But it cannot last long. He will be forgot, and we shall be as we were before."

Elizabeth looked at Jane in doubt, but said nothing.

"Indeed you have no reason to doubt that," cried Jane, slightly coloring. "He may live in my memory, but that is all. I have nothing either to hope or fear, and nothing to reproach him with. It has been an error of fancy on my side."

"My dear Jane!" cried Elizabeth, "you are too good. I do not know what to say to you. I feel as if I had never done you justice or loved you as you deserve. *You* wish to think all the world good, and are hurt if I speak ill of anybody. As for myself, there are few people whom I really love and still fewer of whom I think well. The more I see of the world, the less I can believe in what appears to be merit or sense. For instance, think of Charlotte's marriage. I cannot explain it!"

"My dear Lizzy, do not give way to such feelings as these. They will ruin your happiness. You do not make allowance enough for differences in disposition. Think of Charlotte's prudent, steady character. Remember that she is one of a large family, that as to fortune it is a good match. And be ready to believe, for everybody's sake, that she may feel something like regard and esteem for him."

"To oblige you, I would try to believe almost anything, but no one else could be benefited by such a belief as this. For if I thought that Charlotte had any regard for him, I should only think worse of her understanding than I now do of her heart. My dear Jane, Mr. Collins is a pompous, narrow-minded, silly man. You know he is, as well as I do, and you must feel, as well as I do, that the woman who marries him cannot have a proper

way of thinking. You shall not defend her, though it is Charlotte Lucas. You shall not, for the sake of one person, change the
meaning of principle and right."

"I think your language is too strong in speaking of both," replied Jane. "And I hope you will be convinced of it by seeing
them happy together. But enough of this. I beg you, dear Lizzy,
not to pain me by thinking *that person* to blame, and saying
your opinion of him has sunk. We must not be so ready to
fancy ourselves injured on purpose. We must not expect a lively
young man to be always so guarded and thoughtful. It is very
often nothing but our own vanity that deceives us. Women
fancy that admiration means more than it does."

"And men take care that they should. I am far from thinking
Mr. Bingley's conduct was intentionally wrong, but without planning to do wrong, or to make others unhappy, there may be error
and misery. Thoughtlessness, want of attention to other people's
feelings, will do the business. But if I go on, I shall displease you,
by saying what I think of persons you esteem. Stop me while
you can."

"You still think that his sisters influenced him?"

"Yes, and his friend Darcy."

"I cannot believe it. Why should they try to influence him?
They can only wish his happiness, and if he is attached to me,
no other woman can make him happy."

"They may wish many things besides his happiness. They may
wish him to marry a girl who has money, great family, and pride."

"Beyond a doubt, they *do* wish him to choose Miss Darcy,"
replied Jane. "But this may be from better feelings than you
think. They have known her much longer than they have known
me; no wonder if they love her better. But whatever may be
their own wishes, if they believed him attached to me, they
would not try to part us, and if he were so, they could not succeed. By thinking so of them, you are making everybody act
unnaturally and wrong, and me most unhappy. I do not wish to
think ill of him or his sisters. Let me take it in the best light
in which it may be understood."

Elizabeth could not oppose such a wish; and from this time, Mr. Bingley's name was scarcely ever mentioned between them. But Mrs. Bennet still wondered and longed for his return. Her best comfort was that he must be back again in the summer.

Mr. Bennet treated the matter differently. "So, Lizzy," he said one day, "your sister is crossed in love, I find. Next to being married, a girl likes to be crossed in love a little now and then. It is something to think of and gives her a sort of distinction among her companions. When is your turn to come? Let Wickham be *your* man. He is a pleasant fellow and would jilt you very well."

"Thank you, sir, but a less agreeable man would satisfy me. We must not all expect Jane's good fortune."

"True," said Mr. Bennet, "but it is a comfort to think that, whatever of that kind may befall you, you have a mother who will always make the most of it."

The Longbourn family saw Mr. Wickham often, and liked him more and more. All that he had suffered from Mr. Darcy was now publicly known, and all were pleased to think how much they had always disliked the man even before they had known anything of the matter. Jane Bennet was the only one who always pleaded for allowance and urged the possibility of mistakes— but by everybody else Mr. Darcy was spoken of as the worst of men.

After a week spent in seeing Charlotte and planning for future happiness, Mr. Collins was called from her by the arrival of Saturday. He took leave of the family at Longbourn with as much solemnity as before, wished them health and happiness again, and promised Mr. Bennet another letter of thanks.

Chapter Twenty

Elizabeth Is Warned Against Falling in Love with Mr. Wickham, and Charlotte Lucas Is Married

On the following Monday Mrs. Bennet had the pleasure of welcoming her brother and his wife from London, who came as usual to spend the Christmas at Longbourn. Mr. Gardiner was a sensible, gentleman-like man, greatly superior to his sister Mrs. Bennet, both by nature and by education. Mrs. Gardiner, who was several years younger than Mrs. Bennet and Mrs. Philips, was an agreeable, intelligent woman and a great favorite with all her Longbourn nieces, who went often to stay with her in town.

The first part of Mrs. Gardiner's business on her arrival was to distribute her presents and describe the newest fashions. When this was done, it came her turn to listen. Mrs. Bennet had many griefs to tell and much to complain of. They had all been very ill-used since she last saw her sister-in-law. Two of her girls had been on the point of marriage, and after all, nothing came of it.

"I do not blame Jane," she went on, "for Jane would have got Mr. Bingley if she could. But Lizzy! Oh, sister, it is very hard to think that she might have been Mr. Collins's wife by this time, but for her own fault. He made her an offer in this very room, and she refused him. And now Lady Lucas will have a daughter married before I have. The Lucases are very artful people indeed, sister. They are all for what they can get. I am sorry to say it of them, but so it is. It makes me very nervous and ill to be hindered so in my own family, and to have neighbors who think of themselves before anybody else. However, your coming just at this time is a great comfort, and I am very glad to hear what you tell us of long sleeves."

When alone with Elizabeth afterwards, Mrs. Gardiner spoke

more on the subject. "It seems likely to have been a good match for Jane," she said. "I am sorry nothing came of it. But a young man so easily falls in love with a pretty girl for a few weeks, and then when they are apart so easily forgets her. These things happen so often!"

"It does not so often happen," said Elizabeth, "that others can persuade a young man of independent fortune to think no more of a girl whom he was in love with only a few days before. He was wholly taken up by Jane. At his own ball he offended two or three young ladies by not asking them to dance, and I spoke to him twice myself without getting an answer. Is not general carelessness of all others the very heart of love?"

"Poor Jane! I am sorry for her, because with her nature she may not get over it soon. It had better have happened to *you*, Lizzy. You would have laughed yourself out of it sooner. But do you think she would be willing to go back with us? Change of scene and perhaps a little relief from home may be as useful as anything."

Elizabeth was highly pleased with this plan.

"I hope," added Mrs. Gardiner, "that she will not happen to see this young man. We live in a different part of town; all our friends are so different, and we go out so little that it is not likely they should meet at all, unless he really comes to see her."

"And *that* will not be, for he is now in the hands of his friend who would never allow him to call on Jane in such a part of London! Mr. Darcy may have *heard* of such a place as Gracechurch Street, but he would never enter it. And depend upon it, Mr. Bingley never stirs without him."

"So much the better. I hope they will not meet at all. But does not Jane write to the sister? *She* will not be able to help calling."

"She will drop Jane entirely."

But in spite of what she said, Elizabeth did not look at the matter as entirely hopeless. It was possible that Mr. Bingley's affection might be revived, and the influence of his friends overcome by being again with Jane.

Jane accepted her aunt's invitation with pleasure. She only hoped that she might sometimes see Caroline Bingley without any danger of seeing her brother.

The Gardiners stayed a week at Longbourn, and what with the Philipses, the Lucases, and the officers, there was not a day without its engagement. Mrs. Bennet had so carefully provided for the entertainment of her brother and sister that they did not once sit down to a family dinner. When the party was for home, some of the officers always made part of it, of which Mr. Wickham was sure to be one.

About ten or a dozen years ago, before her marriage, Mrs. Gardiner had spent some time in that very part of Derbyshire to which he belonged. They therefore knew many people in common. She had seen Pemberley and known the late Mr. Darcy by report perfectly well. On learning of the present Mr. Darcy's treatment of Wickham, she called to mind that she had heard Mr. Fitzwilliam Darcy spoken of as a very proud, ill-natured boy.

Having heard Elizabeth praise Mr. Wickham so warmly, she noticed them together. Their interest in each other was plain enough to make her a little uneasy. She spoke to Elizabeth the first time she had with her alone:

"You are too sensible a girl, Lizzy, to fall in love merely because you are warned against it. Therefore I am not afraid of speaking openly. Seriously, I would have you be on your guard. I have nothing to say against *him*. He is a most interesting young man, and if he had the fortune he ought to have, I should think you could not do better. But as it is—you must not let your fancy run away with you. You have sense, and we all expect you to use it. Your father would depend on *you*, I am sure."

"My dear aunt, this is being serious indeed."

"Yes, and I hope you will be serious likewise."

"Well, then, you need not be alarmed. I will take care of myself, and of Mr. Wickham too. He shall not be in love with me if I can prevent it."

"Elizabeth, you are not serious now."

"I beg your pardon. I will try again. At present I am not in love with Mr. Wickham; no, I certainly am not. But he is the most agreeable man I ever saw—and if he becomes really attached to me—I believe it will be better that he should not. I should be very sorry to make any of you unhappy, but since we see every day young people entering into engagements without fortune, how can I promise to be wiser than so many others? All that I can promise you, therefore, is not to be in a hurry. In short, I will do my best."

"Perhaps it will be as well if you do not *remind* your mother so often to invite him here."

"As I did the other day," said Elizabeth with a conscious smile; "very true. But he is not always here so often. It is on your account that he has been invited so often this week. You know my mother's idea of constant company for her friends."

Mr. Collins returned soon after the Gardiners had gone, but as he took up his abode with the Lucases, his arrival was no great worry to Mrs. Bennet. His marriage day was now nearing fast, and she was at length able to say in an ill-natured tone that she "*wished* they might be happy." Thursday was to be the wedding day, and on Wednesday Charlotte paid her farewell visit. When she rose to leave, Elizabeth, ashamed of her mother's ungracious manner, went with her out of the room. As they went downstairs together, Charlotte said:

"I shall depend on hearing from you very often, Elizabeth."

"*That* you certainly shall."

"And I have another favor to ask. Will you come and see me at Hunsford?"

Elizabeth could not refuse, though she foresaw little pleasure in the visit.

"My father and Maria are to come to me in March," added Charlotte, "and I hope you will be of the party. Indeed, Elizabeth, you will be as welcome to me as either of them."

The wedding took place; the bride and bridegroom set off for Hunsford from the church door.

Charlotte's first letters were read by Elizabeth with a good deal of eagerness to know how she would speak of her new home, how she would like Lady Catherine, and how happy she would dare say herself to be. Charlotte wrote cheerfully, seemed surrounded with comforts, and mentioned nothing which she could not praise. The house, furniture, neighborhood, and roads, were all to her taste. Lady Catherine was most friendly and obliging. It was Mr. Collins's picture of Hunsford and Rosings rather softened. Elizabeth felt that Charlotte had written and acted on every point exactly as she might have foreseen. She must wait for her own visit there to know the rest.

Chapter Twenty-One

Elizabeth and Jane Visit in London

Jane had already written a few lines to announce their safe arrival in London. Elizabeth hoped that when she wrote again, she might have something to say of the Bingleys. Her second letter stated that she had been a week in town without either seeing or hearing from Caroline Bingley. She accounted for this by supposing that her last letter to Caroline from Longbourn had failed to reach her.

"My aunt," her letter went on, "is going tomorrow into that part of the town, and I shall take the opportunity of calling on her."

She wrote again when the visit had been paid. "I did not think Caroline in spirits, but she was very glad to see me and asked why I had given her no notice of my coming to London. I was right, therefore; my last letter had never reached her. I asked about her brother, of course. He was well, but so much engaged with Mr. Darcy that they scarcely ever saw him. I found that

Miss Darcy was expected to dinner. I wish I could see her. My visit was not long, as Caroline and Mrs. Hurst were going out. I dare say I shall soon see them here."

Elizabeth shook her head over this letter. She felt that only by accident could Mr. Bingley learn of Jane's being in town.

Four weeks passed away, and Jane saw nothing of him. She tried to think that she did not regret it, but she could no longer be blind to Miss Bingley's lack of interest in her. After Jane had waited at home for two weeks, and found every day a fresh excuse for her friend, she did at last appear. But the shortness of her stay and her change of manner would not allow Jane to deceive herself any longer. She made a slight apology for not calling before, and said not a word of wishing to see her again.

Jane's letter about Caroline's visit gave Elizabeth some pain. But at least, she thought, Jane would no longer be duped. All expectation as to the brother was now quite over. She would not even wish for any renewal of his attentions. His character sank on every review of it. As a punishment for him, as well as a possible advantage to Jane, she seriously hoped he might really soon marry Darcy's sister who, by Wickham's account, would make him regret what he had thrown away.

About this time Elizabeth noticed that Wickham's attentions to herself were over; he was the admirer of someone else. She was watchful enough to see it all, but she could see it without pain. Her heart had been but slightly touched, and her vanity was satisfied with believing that *she* would have been his choice had either been provided with an income. Ten thousand pounds was the greater charm of the young lady to whom he was now making himself agreeable. Elizabeth, less clear-sighted perhaps in this case than in Charlotte's, did not quarrel with him for his wish to gain independence. On the contrary, nothing she thought, could be more natural, and she could very sincerely wish him to be happy.

All this she wrote to Mrs. Gardiner, and thus went on: "I know now that I have never been much in love. My feelings are kind toward *him,* and I cannot find that I hate Miss King at all, but think her a very good sort of girl. There can be no love in all this. Kitty and Lydia take this much more to heart than I do. They are young in the ways of the world, and are not yet willing to believe that handsome young men must have something to live on, as well as the plain."

With no greater events than these in the Bennet family did the sometimes dirty and sometimes cold January and February pass away. March was to take Elizabeth to Hunsford. She had not at first thought very seriously of going, but Charlotte, she soon found, was depending on it, and she gradually learned to think of the visit with greater pleasure. She longed to see Charlotte again, and absence had weakened her disgust of Mr. Collins. She was to travel with Sir William and his second daughter, Maria. They were to spend a night in London on the way. The only pain was in leaving her father, who would certainly miss her and who so little liked her going that he told her to write to him and almost promised to answer her letter.

The farewell between herself and Mr. Wickham was friendly; on his side even more. She parted from him convinced that whether married or single, he must always be her model of the agreeable and pleasing.

It was a journey of only twenty-four miles to London, and they began it early so as to be there by noon. As they drove to Mr. Gardiner's door, Jane was at the drawing-room window watching for them. When they entered the hall, she was there to welcome them. Elizabeth, looking earnestly in her face, was pleased to see it healthy and lovely as ever. On the stairs were troops of little boys and girls, whose shyness kept them from coming lower. All was joy and kindness. The day passed most pleasantly away, the morning in bustle and shopping, and the evening at one of the theaters.

Elizabeth managed to sit by her aunt, and their first talk was of Jane. Elizabeth was grieved to hear that though Jane always struggled to keep in good spirits, there were times of sadness.

It was reasonable, however, to hope that they would not continue long. Mrs. Gardiner then teased her niece about Wickham's leaving her, and praised her for bearing it so well.

"But, my dear Elizabeth," she added, "what sort of girl is Miss King? I should be sorry to think our friend would marry for money."

"My dear aunt, last Christmas you were afraid of his marrying me, because neither of us had property. Now, because he is trying to get a girl with only ten thousand pounds, you are sorry to think he may be marrying for money."

"If you will only tell me what sort of girl Miss King is, I shall know what to think."

"She is a very good kind of girl, I believe. I know no harm of her."

"But he paid her not the smallest attention till her grandfather's death made her mistress of his fortune."

"No—why should he? If he ought not to win *my* affection because I had no money, what reason could there be for making love to a girl whom he did not care about and who was equally poor?"

"But to turn his attentions toward her so soon as she came into this property!"

"If *she* does not object to it, why should *we?*"

"*Her* not objecting does not justify *him.* It only shows her lacking in something herself—sense or feeling."

"Well," said Elizabeth, "have it as you choose. *He* shall be money-loving, and *she* shall be foolish."

"No, Lizzy, that is what I do *not* choose. I should be sorry to think ill of a young man who has lived so long in Derbyshire."

"Oh, if that is all! I have a very poor opinion of young men who live in Derbyshire. I am sick of them all. Thank heaven, I am going tomorrow where I shall find a man who has not one agreeable quality, who has neither manner nor sense. Stupid men are the only ones worth knowing, after all."

"Take care, Lizzy; that speech hints of disappointment."

Before she left, Elizabeth had the happiness of an invitation to go with her uncle and aunt in a tour of pleasure which they were taking in the summer.

"We are not quite decided how far it shall carry us," said Mrs. Gardiner, "but perhaps to the Lakes." [1]

"My dear, dear aunt," she cried joyfully. "What delight! You give me fresh life and vigor. Adieu to disappointment and anger. What are men to rocks and mountains? Oh, what happy hours we shall spend!"

Chapter Twenty-Two

Mr. Collins Is the Proud Host

The next day's journey was interesting to Elizabeth. When they left the high road for the lane to Hunsford, every eye was in search of Hunsford parsonage and every turning was expected to bring it in view. At length they saw it, the garden sloping to the road, the green pales and the laurel hedge, everything as had been described. Mr. Collins and Charlotte appeared at the door, and the carriage stopped at the small gate which led by a short gravel walk to the house. In a moment they were all out of the chaise, Mrs. Collins was welcoming them with the liveliest pleasure, and Elizabeth was glad indeed that she had come. Mr. Collins's manner was as formal as it had always been; he kept Elizabeth some minutes at the gate to ask after all her family. As soon as they were in the parlor, he welcomed them a second time to his "humble abode" and repeated all his wife's offers of refreshment.

Elizabeth fancied that, in pointing out the good proportion

[1] The region of lakes and mountains in Westmorland and Cumberland.

of the room and its furniture, he spoke chiefly to her, as if wishing to make her feel what she had lost in refusing him. When he said anything of which his wife might be ashamed—which certainly was not seldom—in general, Charlotte wisely did not hear. After they had sat long enough to admire every article of furniture in the room, from the sideboard to the fender, and given an account of their journey and all that had happened in London, Mr. Collins invited them to take a stroll in the garden. Here, leading the way through every walk and crosswalk, and scarcely allowing them a chance to utter the praises he asked for, he pointed out every view, every field, and told them how many trees were in the most distant clump. But of all the views which his garden— or the country, or the kingdom—could boast, none was to be compared with the view of Rosings, which they could see through an opening in the trees that bordered the park in front of his house. It was a handsome modern building, well set on rising ground.

From his garden Mr. Collins would have led them round his two meadows, but the ladies, not having shoes to meet the remains of a white frost, turned back. Sir William went with him, while Charlotte took Maria and Elizabeth over the house, well pleased, probably, to show it without her husband's help. It was rather small, but well built and convenient. When Mr. Collins could be forgotten, there was really a great air of comfort throughout, and by Charlotte's real enjoyment of it, Elizabeth supposed that he must be often forgotten.

Elizabeth had already learned that Lady Catherine was still at Rosings. It was spoken of again while they were at dinner.

"You will have the honor of seeing Lady Catherine de Bourgh next Sunday at church," Mr. Collins said, "and you will be delighted with her. And I have no doubt that she will include you all in every invitation with which she honors us during your stay here. Her behavior to my dear Charlotte is charming. We dine at Rosings twice every week, and are never allowed to walk home. Her ladyship's carriage is always ordered for us. I *should* say, one of her ladyship's carriages, for she has several."

"Lady Catherine is a very good neighbor indeed," added Charlotte.

"Very true, my dear, that is exactly what I say. She is the sort of woman whom one cannot honor and admire too much."

About the middle of the next day, as Elizabeth was in her room getting ready for a walk, a sudden noise below seemed to throw the whole house into confusion. Then she heard somebody running upstairs in a great hurry and calling loudly for her. She opened the door and met Maria on the landing-place, who, breathless with excitement, cried out:

"Oh, my dear Elizabeth, make haste and come into the dining room, for there is such a sight to be seen! I will not tell you what it is. Make haste and come down this moment."

Down they ran into the dining room, which fronted the lane, to see this wonder. It was two ladies stopping in a low carriage at the garden gate.

"And is this all?" cried Elizabeth. "I thought at least that the pigs had got into the garden, and here is nothing but Lady Catherine and her daughter!"

"La! my dear," said Maria, quite shocked at the mistake, "it is not Lady Catherine. The old lady is Mrs. Jenkinson, who lives with them. The other is Miss de Bourgh. Only look at her. She is quite a little creature. Who would have thought she could be so thin and small!"

"She is very rude to keep Charlotte out of doors in all this wind. Why does she not come in?"

"Oh, Charlotte says she hardly ever does. It is the greatest of favors when Miss de Bourgh comes in."

"I like her appearance," said Elizabeth, struck with other ideas. She thought: "She looks sickly and cross. Yes, she will do for Darcy very well. She will make him a very proper wife."

Mr. Collins and Charlotte were both standing at the gate talking with the ladies. Sir William was standing in the doorway, bowing whenever Miss de Bourgh looked that way.

At length there was nothing more to be said; the ladies drove on, and the others returned into the house. Mr. Collins no sooner saw the two girls than he began to speak of their good fortune; the whole party had been asked to dine at Rosings the next day.

Mr. Collins's pleasure was complete. To show the grandeur of his patroness to his wondering visitors, and to let them see her civility toward himself and his wife was exactly what he had wished for.

"I confess," said he, "that I should not have been at all surprised by her ladyship's asking us on Sunday to drink tea and spend the evening at Rosings. I rather expected that would happen. But who could have thought she would invite us to dine there so soon after your arrival!"

Chapter Twenty-Three

Dinner with Lady Catherine de Bourgh

Scarcely anything was talked of the whole day or next morning but their visit to Rosings. Mr. Collins was careful to tell them what to expect, that the sight of such rooms, so many servants, and so splendid a dinner might not overpower them. When the ladies were going away to dress for the event, he said to Elizabeth:

"Do not make yourself uneasy about your dress. Lady Catherine does not expect to see us in such dress as becomes herself and daughter. I would advise you merely to put on your best clothes. Lady Catherine will not think the worse of you for being simply dressed. She likes to have the difference of rank observed."

While they were dressing, he came two or three times to their different doors, to urge them to hurry, as Lady Catherine did not like to be kept waiting for her dinner. Such accounts of her ladyship and her manner of living quite frightened Maria Lucas, who had been little used to company, and she looked forward to her visit to Rosings with fear.

As the weather was fine, they had a pleasant walk of about half a mile across the park. Every park has its beauty and its views, and Elizabeth saw much to be pleased with, though she could not be in such raptures as Mr. Collins expected the scene to arouse in her, and was not greatly affected when he told her the number of windows in front of the house and their original cost.

When they went up the steps to the hall, Maria's alarm grew at every step, and even Sir William did not look calm. Elizabeth's courage did not fail her. She had heard nothing of Lady Catherine that spoke her awful from any great talents or unusual virtue, and the mere stateliness of money and rank she thought she could witness without fear.

From the entrance hall, they followed the servants to the room where Lady Catherine, her daughter, and Mrs. Jenkinson were sitting. Her ladyship arose to greet them. Sir William had just courage enough to make a very low bow and take his seat without saying a word. Maria, frightened almost out of her senses, sat on the edge of her chair, not knowing which way to look. Elizabeth found herself quite equal to the scene and could look calmly at the three ladies before her. Lady Catherine was a tall, large woman, with strongly marked features, which might once have been handsome. Her air was not pleasing, nor was her manner of receiving them such as to make them forget their lower rank. In her face and manner, Elizabeth saw some likeness to Mr. Darcy. But Miss de Bourgh, pale and sickly, spoke very little, except in a low voice to Mrs. Jenkinson.

At dinner, there were all the servants and all the silver which Mr. Collins had promised. He took his seat at the bottom of the table, by her ladyship's wish, and looked as if he felt that life could furnish nothing greater. He carved, and ate, and praised. Every dish was praised first by him and then by Sir William, who was now enough recovered to echo whatever his son-in-law said, in a manner which Elizabeth wondered Lady Catherine could bear. But Lady Catherine seemed pleased by their great admiration and gave most gracious smiles, especially when any dish on the table proved a novelty to them.

There was not much talk. Elizabeth, seated between Charlotte and Miss de Bourgh, was ready to speak whenever there was an opening, but Charlotte was listening to Lady Catherine, and Miss de Bourgh said not a word to her all dinner-time. Mrs. Jenkinson was chiefly employed in watching how little Miss de Bourgh ate, urging her to try some other dish, and fearing she was not well. Maria thought speaking out of the question, and the gentlemen did nothing but eat and admire.

When they returned to the drawing room, there was little to be done but to hear Lady Catherine talk, which she did without pause, till coffee was brought in. She gave her opinions in the firm manner of one not used to having her judgment denied. She offered Charlotte a great deal of advice as to the management of their affairs, told her how to care for her cows and poultry. Nothing was beneath this great lady's attention which could furnish her with a chance to dictate to others. She addressed a variety of questions to Maria and Elizabeth, but especially to Elizabeth, of whom she knew the least, and who, she said to Mrs. Collins, was a very genteel, pretty kind of girl. She asked how many sisters she had, whether they were older or younger, whether any of them were likely to be married, whether they were handsome, where they had been educated, what carriage her father kept, and what had been her mother's maiden name. Elizabeth felt all the impertinence of her questions, but answered them very composedly.

"Your father's estate is to be inherited by Mr. Collins, I think," she said. "For your sake," turning to Charlotte, "I am glad of it, but otherwise I see no reason for passing over the female line. It was not done in Sir Lewis de Bourgh's family. Do you play and sing, Miss Bennet?"

"A little."

"Oh, then some time or other we shall be happy to hear you. Our piano is a good one, probably better than—you shall try it some day. Do your sisters play and sing?"

"One of them does."

"Why did you not all learn? You ought all to have learned. Do you draw?"

"No, not at all."

"What, none of you?"

"Not one."

"That is very strange. Your mother should have taken you to town every spring for the benefit of teachers."

"My mother would have gone, but my father hates London."

"Has your governess left you?"

"We never had a governess."

"Five daughters brought up at home without a governess! I never heard of such a thing. Your mother must have been quite a slave to your education."

Elizabeth could hardly help smiling, as she assured Lady Catherine that such had not been the case.

"But who taught you? Who attended to you? Without a governess you must have been neglected."

"Compared with some families, I believe we were, but such of us as wished to learn never lacked the means. We were always encouraged to read and had all the teachers that were necessary. Those who chose to be idle certainly might."

"Yes, no doubt. But that is what a governess will prevent, and if I had known your mother, I should have advised her most strongly to engage one. I always say that nothing is to be done in education without steady and regular instruction, and nobody but a governess can give it. It is wonderful how many families I have helped by finding governesses for them. I am always glad to get a young person a good place. Four nieces of Mrs. Jenkinson have been very well placed by me. Only the other day I recommended another young person, whom I had accidentally heard of, and the family was quite delighted with her. Mrs. Collins, did I tell you of Lady Metcalf's calling yesterday to thank me? She finds Miss Pope a great treasure. 'Lady Catherine,' she said, 'you have given me a treasure.' Are any of your younger sisters out,[1] Miss Bennet?"

"Yes, ma'am, all."

"All! The younger ones out before the elder are married! Your younger sisters must be very young?"

"Yes, my youngest is not sixteen. Perhaps *she* is full young to be in company. But really, ma'am, I think it would be very hard upon younger sisters not to have their share of society and fun because the eldest may not have the chance to marry early."

"Upon my word," said her ladyship, "you give your opinion very plainly for so young a person. Pray, what is your age?"

"With three younger sisters grown up," replied Elizabeth, smiling, "your ladyship can hardly expect me to own it."

Lady Catherine seemed quite shocked not to have a direct answer, and Elizabeth fancied herself to be one of the few who had ever dared to trifle with such dignified impertinence.

"You cannot be more than twenty, I am sure; therefore you need not conceal your age."

"I am not twenty-one."

Lady Catherine, Sir William, and Mr. and Mrs. Collins sat down to cards, while Elizabeth and Maria had the honor of joining in a game with Miss de Bourgh and Mrs. Jenkinson. Their table was very stupid. Scarcely a word was said that did not relate to the game, except when Mrs. Jenkinson spoke her fears of Miss de Bourgh's being too hot or too cold, or having too much or too little light. A great deal more passed at the other table. Lady Catherine was generally speaking—stating the mistakes of the three others or telling some story of herself. Mr. Collins was agreeing to everything her ladyship said, thanking her every time he won, and apologizing if he thought he won too often. Sir William did not say much. He was storing his mind with stories and noble names.

When Lady Catherine and her daughter had played as long as they chose, the carriage was offered to Mrs. Collins, and the

---

[1] Allowed to enter into society.

party then gathered round the fire to hear Lady Catherine foretell what weather they were to have on the morrow.

Sir William stayed only a week at Hunsford, but his visit was long enough to convince him that his daughter was most comfortably settled, with such a husband and such a neighbor as were not often met with. While Sir William was with them, Mr. Collins gave his mornings to driving him out in his gig and showing him the country. When he went away at the end of a week, Elizabeth was thankful to find that they did not see the more of Mr. Collins. Most of the time between breakfast and dinner he passed at work in the garden, reading and writing, and looking out of the window in his own book-room which fronted the road. The room in which the ladies sat was to the back. Elizabeth at first had rather wondered that Charlotte should not prefer the dining-parlor for common use, as it was on the front and a larger and pleasanter room. But she soon saw that Charlotte had a good reason for what she did; Mr. Collins would have been much less in his own book-room, had they sat in a room fronting the road. From where they sat, they could see nothing of what went on in the lane outside. But they learned from Mr. Collins what carriages went along and when Miss de Bourgh drove by in her phaeton, of which he never failed to come and tell them, though it happened almost every day.

Chapter Twenty-Four

Colonel Fitzwilliam, Another Young Bachelor of High Birth but No Great Wealth, Comes Upon the Scene

Very few days passed in which Mr. Collins did not walk to Rosings, and not many in which his wife did not go likewise.

Now and then they were honored with a call from her ladyship, and nothing escaped her eyes during these visits. She looked at their work, and advised them to do it differently. She found fault with the arrangement of the furniture, or charged the housemaid with carelessness. If she took any refreshment, she seemed to do it only for the sake of finding out that Mrs. Collins's joints of meat were too large for her family.

Elizabeth soon learned that though this great lady was not an officer of the law, she was the most active agent in her own parish, the smallest concerns of which were carried to her by Mr. Collins. And whenever any of the villagers became quarrelsome or too poor, she sallied out to settle the matter and scold them into peace and plenty.

Upon the whole, Elizabeth spent her time pleasantly enough. There were half hours of pleasant talk with Charlotte, and the weather was so fine that she could be often out of doors. Her favorite walk was along the open grove which edged that side of Rosings park, where she felt beyond the reach of Lady Catherine's eyes.

She had heard soon after her arrival that Mr. Darcy was expected at Rosings. His arrival was soon known at the parsonage, and on the following morning Mr. Collins hastened to Rosings to pay his respects. Mr. Darcy had brought with him a Colonel Fitzwilliam, the younger son of his uncle, Lord ———. To the great surprise of all, when Mr. Collins returned, they came with him. Charlotte had seen them from her window and, running into the girls' room, told them what an honor they must expect, adding:

"I may thank you for this courtesy, Elizabeth. Mr. Darcy would never have come so soon to see me."

Elizabeth had scarcely time to say that she could claim no credit, before they were announced by the doorbell. Colonel Fitzwilliam, who led the way in, was about thirty, not handsome, but in person and manner most truly the gentleman. Mr. Darcy looked just as he used to look, and had his usual reserve, saying little. Colonel Fitzwilliam talked pleasantly with the ease of a well-bred man, but Darcy, after a few words on the house and garden to Mrs. Collins, sat for some time without speaking to anybody. At length, however, he spoke to Elizabeth to ask about her family. She answered him in the usual way, and after a moment's pause, added:

"My sister Jane has been in London these three months. Have you never happened to see her there?"

She knew that he never had, but she wished to see whether he would show any sign of knowing what had passed between the Bingleys and Jane. She thought he looked a little confused as he answered that he had never been so fortunate as to meet Miss Bennet. The subject was dropped, and the gentlemen soon afterward went away.

Colonel Fitzwilliam's manners were very much admired at the parsonage, and the ladies all felt that he must add greatly to the pleasure of their visits at Rosings. But it was not till Easter day, almost a week later, that they had an invitation to Rosings, and then they were merely asked on leaving church, to come there in the evening. For the last week they had seen very little of either Lady Catherine or her daughter. Colonel Fitzwilliam had called at the parsonage more than once during the time, but Mr. Darcy they had only seen at church.

Her ladyship received them civilly, but it was plain that their coming was by no means so prized as when she could get nobody else. She was, in fact, almost entirely taken up by her nephews, speaking to them chiefly, and to Darcy much more than to any other person in the room.

Colonel Fitzwilliam seemed really glad to see them. Anything was a welcome relief to him at Rosings. Moreover, Mrs. Collins's pretty friend had caught his fancy. He now seated himself by her and talked so agreeably of traveling and staying at home, of new books and music, that Elizabeth had never been half so well entertained in that room before. They talked with so much spirit and flow as to draw the attention of Mr. Darcy. His eyes had been turning toward them again and again, with a look of in-

terest. Her ladyship, after a while, shared the same feeling and
called out:

"What is that you are saying, Fitzwilliam? What is it you are
talking of? What are you telling Miss Bennet? Let me hear
what it is."

"We are speaking of music, madam," said he, when no longer
able to avoid a reply.

"Of music! Then speak aloud. It is of all subjects my delight.
There are few people in England, I suppose, who have more
true enjoyment of music than myself, or a better natural taste.
How does Georgiana get on in music, Darcy?"

Mr. Darcy spoke with affectionate praise of his sister's progress.

"I am very glad to hear it. Pray tell her from me that she
cannot expect to excel if she does not practice a great deal. I
have told Miss Bennet several times that she will never play
really well unless she practices more. Mrs. Collins has no piano,
but she is very welcome, as I have often told her, to come to
Rosings every day and use the one in Mrs. Jenkinson's room. She
would be in nobody's way, you know, in that part of the house."

Mr. Darcy looked a little ashamed of his aunt's ill-breeding and
made no answer.

When coffee was over, Colonel Fitzwilliam reminded Elizabeth of having promised to play for him. She went to the piano
and he drew a chair near her. Lady Catherine listened to half
a song and then talked, as before, to her other nephew, till he
walked away from her. Moving in his usual deliberate manner
toward the piano, he stationed himself so as to look directly at
Elizabeth. She saw what he was doing and turned to him with an
arch smile, and said:

"You mean to frighten me by coming in all this state to hear
me? But I will not be alarmed; there is a stubbornness about me
that never can bear to be frightened at the will of others."

"I shall not say that you are mistaken," he replied, "because
you do not really believe I could wish to frighten you. I have
known you long enough to know that you sometimes like to say
what you do not really think."

Elizabeth laughed heartily at this picture of herself and said to Colonel Fitzwilliam, "Your cousin will teach you not to believe a word I say. I am very unlucky to meet with a person so well able to expose my real character. Indeed, Mr. Darcy, it is very unkind of you, and may cause such things to come out as will shock your relations to hear."

"I am not afraid of you," said he, smilingly.

"Pray let me hear what you have to accuse him of," cried Colonel Fitzwilliam. "I should like to know how he behaves among strangers."

"You shall hear, then—but prepare yourself for something very dreadful. The first time I ever saw him was at a ball—and at this ball, he danced only four dances! I am sorry to pain you—but it was so. He danced only four dances, though gentlemen were scarce, and more than one young lady was sitting down in want of a partner. Mr. Darcy, you cannot deny the fact."

"I had not at that time the honor of knowing any lady there except in my own party."

"True; and nobody can ever be introduced in a ballroom. Well, Colonel Fitzwilliam, what do I play next? My fingers wait your orders."

"Perhaps," said Darcy, "I should have asked for an introduction, but I am not readily liked by strangers."

"Shall we ask him the reason for this?" said Elizabeth, still speaking to Colonel Fitzwilliam. "Shall we ask him why a man of sense and education is not readily liked by strangers?"

"I can answer your question," said Fitzwilliam, "without asking him. It is because he will not give himself the trouble to make them like him."

"I certainly have not the talent which some people have," said Darcy, "of talking easily with those I have never seen before."

"My fingers," said Elizabeth, "do not move over this keyboard in a masterly way. But then I have always supposed it to be my own fault—because I would not take the trouble to practice."

Darcy smiled and said, "You are perfectly right. You have used your time much better."

Here Lady Catherine called out to know what they were talking of. Elizabeth at once began playing again. Lady Catherine came up and, after listening for a few minutes, said to Darcy:

"Miss Bennet would not play at all badly if she practiced more and could have a London teacher. She has a very good notion of fingering, though her taste is not equal to Anne's. Anne would have been a delightful performer if her health had made it possible."

Elizabeth looked at Darcy to see how readily he agreed to his cousin's praise, but neither at that moment not at any other could she see any sign of love on his part.

Lady Catherine continued her remarks on Elizabeth's playing, mixing with them many instructions on how to play and how to improve her taste. Elizabeth listened politely and, at the request of the gentlemen, remained at the piano till her ladyship's carriage was ready to take them all home.

Chapter Twenty-Five

Mr. Darcy's Strange Behavior

Elizabeth was sitting by herself the next morning and writing to Jane, while Mrs. Collins and Maria were gone on business into the village, when she was startled by a ring at the door. She thought it might be Lady Catherine, and was putting away her half-finished letter that she might escape being questioned about it, when the maid opened the door and, to her great surprise, Mr. Darcy, and Mr. Darcy only, entered the room.

He seemed surprised too on finding her alone and apologized for his intrusion, saying he did not know the other ladies were out. They sat down, and when her inquiries after Rosings were made, seemed in danger of sinking into total silence. She must think of something to say.

"How very suddenly you all left Netherfield last November, Mr. Darcy! Mr. Bingley and his sisters were well, I hope, when you left London."

"Perfectly so—I thank you."

She found that she was to have no other answer—and after a short pause, added:

"I have understood that Mr. Bingley does not plan to return to Netherfield again?"

"I have never heard him say so. It is probable that he may spend very little of his time there in future. I should not be surprised if he were to give up the place as soon as a tenant is found."

Elizabeth made no answer. She was afraid of talking longer of Bingley and, having nothing else to say, left him the trouble of finding a subject.

He took the hint and soon began with, "This seems a very comfortable house. Lady Catherine, I believe, did a great deal to it when Mr. Collins first came to Hunsford."

"I believe she did—and I am sure she could not have been kind to a more grateful person."

"Mr. Collins seems very fortunate in his choice of a wife."

"Yes, indeed. Charlotte has an excellent understanding— though I am not certain that her marrying Mr. Collins is the wisest thing she ever did."

"It must be very agreeable to her to be settled so near her own family and friends."

"I should never have said Mrs. Collins was settled *near* her family," cried Elizabeth. "It is nearly fifty miles."

"Anything beyond the very neighborhood of Longbourn, I suppose, would appear far to you."

As he spoke there was a sort of smile which Elizabeth fancied she understood; he supposed her to be thinking of Jane and Netherfield, and she blushed as she answered:

"I do not mean to say that a woman may not be settled too near her family. But I believe Charlotte would not call herself *near* her family under less than *half* the present distance."

He drew his chair a little toward her and said, "*You* cannot have a right to such very strong attachment to any place. *You* have not always lived at Longbourn."

Elizabeth looked surprised. He showed some change of feeling, drew back his chair, took a newspaper from the table, and glancing over it, said in a colder voice:

"Are you pleased with this region?"

A short talk on the country followed, on both sides calm and concise, and soon was ended by the entrance of Charlotte and her sister, just returned from their walk. They were surprised to see Mr. Darcy, who explained that he had not expected to find Miss Bennet alone, apologized again and, after sitting a few minutes longer without saying much to anybody, went away.

"What can be the meaning of this!" said Charlotte as soon as he was gone. "My dear Elizabeth, he must be in love with you, or he would never have called on us in this friendly way."

But when Elizabeth told of his silence, it did not seem very likely to be the case, even to Charlotte's wishes. His visit, they decided, was probably made for want of something to do. All field sports were over; within doors there were Lady Catherine, books, and a billiard-table; but gentlemen cannot be always within doors.

The nearness of the parsonage, or the pleasantness of the walk to it, or of the people who lived in it, led Darcy and his cousin to walk thither almost every day.

They called at various times, sometimes separately, sometimes together, and now and then with their aunt, Lady Catherine. It was plain that Colonel Fitzwilliam came because he had pleasure in their society. Elizabeth was reminded, by her pleasure in being with him and by his open admiration of her, of her former favorite, George Wickham.

But why Mr. Darcy came so often to the parsonage was harder to understand. It could not be for society, as he often sat there ten minutes together without opening his lips. And when he did speak, it seemed for the sake of courtesy, not from interest in their company. Mrs. Collins did not know what to make of him. Colonel Fitzwilliam now and then laughed at him for being dull, proving that he was generally different. Charlotte would have liked to believe this the effect of love for her friend Elizabeth, and she set herself to find out. She watched him whenever they were at Rosings and whenever he came to the parsonage. He certainly looked at Elizabeth a great deal, but it was an earnest, steadfast gaze, and she often doubted whether there was much admiration in it; sometimes it seemed nothing but absence of mind.

She had once or twice said to Elizabeth that he seemed to be fond of her, but Elizabeth always laughed at the idea. Mrs. Collins did not press the subject, fearing to raise hopes which might end in disappointment. In her opinion there could be no doubt that Elizabeth's dislike would vanish if she thought him to be in her power. In her kind plans for Elizabeth, she sometimes thought of marrying her to Colonel Fitzwilliam. He was much the pleasantest man, and he certainly admired her.

More than once did Elizabeth in her ramble within the park unexpectedly meet Mr. Darcy. It was certainly an ill chance, she felt, that brought him where no one else came. To prevent its ever happening again, she took care to tell him at the first meeting that it was a favorite walk of hers. How a meeting could happen a second time, therefore, was very odd! Yet it did, and even a third time. It seemed like a wilful ill-nature or a wish to punish himself, for on these meetings it was not merely a few formal words and an awkward pause and then away; but he actually thought he must turn back and walk with her. He never said a great deal, nor did she give herself the trouble to talk or to listen much.

It struck her in the course of their third meeting that he was asking some odd questions—about her pleasure in being in that part of the country, her love of lonely walks, and her opinion of Mr. and Mrs. Collins's happiness. And in speaking of Rosings and her not perfectly understanding the house, he seemed to expect that whenever she came into that country again she would be staying *there* too. Could he have Colonel Fitzwilliam in his thoughts? It distressed her a little, and she was quite glad to find herself at the gate of the parsonage again.

Chapter Twenty-Six

Elizabeth Hears of Darcy's Part in Her Sister's Disappointment

Elizabeth was engaged one day as she walked in the park, reading Jane's last letter, and noticing that Jane had not written in good spirit, when she looked up to see that Colonel Fitzwilliam was meeting her. Putting away the letter and forcing a smile, she said:

"I did not know before that you ever walked this way."

"I have been making the tour of the park," he replied, "as I generally do every year, and intend to stop at the parsonage. Are you going much farther?"

"No, I should have turned in a moment."

And then she did turn, and they walked toward the parsonage together.

"Do you really leave on Saturday?" said she.

"Yes—if Darcy does not put it off again. He arranges the business just as he pleases."

"I do not know anybody who seems more to enjoy the power of doing what he likes than Mr. Darcy."

"He likes to have his own way very well," replied Colonel Fitzwilliam. "But so do we all. It is only that he has better means of having it than many others, because he is rich, and many others are poor. I speak feelingly. A younger son, you know, must be used to self-denial and dependence."

"In my opinion, the younger son of an earl can know very little of either. Now, seriously, when have you lacked money to go wherever you chose or get anything you had a fancy for?"

"Perhaps I cannot say that I have experienced many hardships of that nature. But in matters of greater weight I may suffer from lack of money. Younger sons cannot marry where they like."

"Unless they like women of fortune, which I think they very often do."

"Our habits of expense make us too dependent, and there are not many in my rank of life who can afford to marry without some thought of money."

"Is this," thought Elizabeth, "meant for me?" She colored at the idea, but said in a lively tone, "And what is the usual price of an earl's younger son? Unless the elder brother is very sickly, I suppose you would not ask more than fifty thousand pounds."

He answered her in the same style, and she dropped the subject, saying:

"I suppose Mr. Darcy enjoys full power over his sister too."

"No," said Colonel Fitzwilliam, "I am joined with him as her second guardian."

"Are you indeed? And pray what sort of guardians do you make? Does she give you much trouble? Young ladies of her age are sometimes a little difficult to manage, and if she has the true Darcy spirit, she may like to have her own way."

He looked at her earnestly, and asked her why she thought Miss Darcy likely to give them any uneasiness. She had somehow or other got pretty near the truth, she thought, and added hastily:

"You need not be frightened. I never heard any harm of her. She is a very great favorite with Mrs. Hurst and Miss Bingley. I think I have heard you say that you know them."

"I know them a little. Their brother is a great friend of Darcy's."

"Oh, yes," said Elizabeth drily, "Mr. Darcy takes a great deal of care of him too."

"Care of him! Yes, I really believe Darcy *does* take care of him in those points where he most needs care. He told me in our journey here that he had lately saved a friend from a most imprudent marriage. He gave no names, and I only thought it to be Bingley from believing him the kind of young man to get into a scrape of that sort, and from knowing them to have been together the whole of last summer. I understand there were some strong objections to the lady."

"And what arts did he use to separate them?"

"He did not tell me of his own arts," said Fitzwilliam, smiling. "He only told me what I have now told you."

Elizabeth made no answer and walked on, her heart swelling with anger. They talked on other matters till they reached the parsonage. There, shut into her own room as soon as the visitor left them, she could think of all that she had heard. That Darcy had had a part in the separation of Bingley and Jane she had never doubted, but she had always charged Caroline Bingley with most of it. Now she understood that *he* was the cause of all that Jane had suffered and still suffered. "There were some strong objections to the lady" were Colonel Fitzwilliam's words. To Jane herself there could be no objection, all loveliness and goodness as she was, her excellent mind improved, her manners charming. Neither could anything be said against her father. And when she thought of her mother, she would not allow that any objections *there* had great weight with Mr. Darcy. No, his pride would have a deeper wound from the family's lack of importance than from their want of sense! She was quite decided at last that he had been partly moved by this worst kind of pride, and partly by the wish to see Mr. Bingley married to his sister.

The anger and tears brought on a headache, which grew worse toward the evening. This, added to her unwillingness to see Mr. Darcy, decided her not to go with her cousins to Rosings, where they were to drink tea. Mrs. Collins, seeing that she was really unwell, did not press her to go, but Mr. Collins feared that Lady Catherine would be rather displeased by her staying at home.

Chapter Twenty-Seven

A Very Darcy-like Proposal

When they were gone, Elizabeth, as if intending to anger herself as much as possible against Darcy, began to read again all the letters which Jane had written her there. They contained no actual complaint, but she noticed now, what she had not so clearly felt at first reading, an absence of Jane's old cheerfulness. This cheerfulness, arising from a mind at ease with itself and kindly disposed toward everyone, had been scarcely ever clouded. And Darcy had shamefully boasted that he had inflicted this misery upon her sister! It was some relief to think that his visit to Rosings was to end the day after the next, and a still greater relief to think that in less than a fortnight she would be with Jane again, able to help her recover her spirits by all that sisterly affection could do.

She could not think of Darcy's leaving without remembering that his cousin was to go with him. But Colonel Fitzwilliam had made it clear that he had no intentions at all, and agreeable as he was, she did not mean to be unhappy about him. While settling this point, she was suddenly roused by the sound of the doorbell. Her spirits were a little fluttered by the idea of its being Colonel Fitzwilliam, who had once before called late in the evening, and might now have come to ask about her.

To her utter amazement, not Colonel Fitzwilliam but Mr. Darcy walked into the room. In a hurried manner he at once began to ask after her health, saying he had come in the hope of hearing that she was better. She answered him with cold civility. He sat down for a few moments and then, getting up, walked about the room. Elizabeth was surprised, but said not a word. After a silence of several minutes, he came toward her and in a hurried manner began:

"In vain I have struggled. It will not do. My feelings will not be overcome. You must allow me to tell you how ardently I admire and love you."

Elizabeth stared, colored, doubted, and was silent. This he took for sufficient encouragement, and he went on, speaking of all that he felt and had long felt for her. He spoke well, but there were feelings besides those of the heart to be expressed. His sense of her inferior rank—of its being a degradation—of family objections, which his better judgment had opposed to his love. All this he dwelt on with a warmth which seemed to him due to the rank and importance that he was wounding.

In spite of her deeply rooted dislike, she could not help feeling the compliment of such a man's affection. She was at first sorry for the pain he was to receive. But as he went on to speak of his great love, which had overcome him in spite of himself, she lost all pity in anger. She tried to calm herself to answer him with dignity when he should have done. As he spoke his hope that his love would now be rewarded by her hand, she could see that he had no doubt of her favorable answer. He *spoke* of anxiety, but his face showed real security.

When he ceased, the color rose in her cheeks, and she said: "If I could *feel* grateful, I would now thank you. But I cannot—I have never wished for your good opinion, and you have certainly given it most unwillingly. I am sorry to cause pain to anyone, but it should not last long. The reasons which have led you to struggle against your regard for me should help you to overcome it."

Mr. Darcy, who was leaning against the mantelpiece with his eyes fixed on her face, seemed to catch her words with surprise, then turned pale with anger. He struggled for composure, and would not open his lips till he had gained it. The pause was to Elizabeth quite dreadful. At length, in a voice of forced calmness, he said:

"And this is all the reply which I am to have! I might, perhaps, wish to be told why, with so little civility, I am thus refused. But it is of small importance."

"I might as well ask," replied she, "why with so plain a purpose of insulting me, you tell me that you liked me against your will and against your reason. This should be some excuse, if I *was* uncivil. But I have other reasons. You know I have. Do you think that I would ever be willing to marry a man who has ruined the happiness of a most beloved sister? I have every reason in the world to think ill of you."

At these words he changed color, but the emotion was short, and she saw with anger that he listened with an air of being wholly unmoved by regret. He even looked at her with a smile of doubt.

"Can you deny that you have done it?" she said.

"I have no wish to deny that I did everything in my power to separate my friend from your sister, or that I rejoice in my success. Toward *him* I have been kinder than toward myself."

"But it was not merely this affair," she said, "on which my dislike is founded. Long before it had taken place, your character was unfolded to me by Mr. Wickham."

"You take great interest in that gentleman," said Darcy in a less controlled tone and with a heightened color.

"Who that knows what his misfortunes have been can help feeling an interest in him?"

"His misfortunes!" repeated Darcy scornfully; "yes, his misfortunes have been great indeed."

"And of your making!" cried Elizabeth with energy. "You have reduced him to a state of poverty. You have kept from him what was his due. You have done all this! And yet you can treat the mention of his misfortunes with scorn."

"And this," cried Darcy as he walked with quick steps across the room, "is your opinion of me! This is what you think of me! I thank you for giving it so fully. But perhaps," he added, stopping in his walk and turning toward her, "if I had flattered you by denying that I ever tried to withhold my regard, my offences might have been overlooked. Your pride has been hurt by my honest confession that I have been held back by reason, by everything. But I am not ashamed of those feelings. They are natural and just. Could you expect me to rejoice in forming connections in life so much beneath my own?"

Elizabeth felt herself growing more angry every moment; yet she tried to the utmost to speak calmly.

"You are mistaken, Mr. Darcy, if you think that the way you have spoken had any other effect but to spare me the concern which I might have felt in refusing you, had you behaved in a more gentlemanlike manner."

She saw him start at this, but he said nothing, and she continued:

"You could not have made me the offer of your hand in any possible way that would have tempted me to accept it."

He gazed at her with a look of mingled doubt, surprise, and wounded pride. She went on:

"From the very first moment that I knew you, I have seen in your manners conceit and a selfish disdain of the feelings of others. And I had not known you a month before I felt you were the last man in the world whom I could wish to marry."

"You have said quite enough, madam. I understand your feelings and am now ashamed of what my own have been. Forgive me for having taken up so much of your time, and accept my best wishes for your health and happiness."

And with these words he hastily left the room, and Elizabeth heard him the next moment open the front door and quit the house.

The tumult of her mind was now painfully great. From actual weakness she sat down and cried for half an hour. Her amazement as she thought on what had passed grew greater and greater. That she should have an offer of marriage from Mr. Darcy! That he should have been in love with her for so many months—so much in love as to wish to marry her in spite of all that had made him prevent his friend from marrying her sister. It was almost unbelievable! It was gratifying to have awakened so strong an affection. But his hateful pride, his shameless confession of what he had done to Jane, his unfeeling cruelty, which he did not even try to deny, toward Mr. Wickham—all this overcame the pity which thought of his love had for a moment excited.

Chapter Twenty-Eight

Mr. Darcy's Letter

Elizabeth awoke the next morning to the same thoughts with which she had closed her eyes. She could not yet recover from the surprise of what had happened. It was impossible to think of anything else. Soon after breakfast she went out for air and exercise. She was going directly to her favorite walk, but remembering that Mr. Darcy sometimes came there, she stopped and instead of entering the park, turned up the lane and walked along beside the park railing.

After walking two or three times along that part of the lane, she was tempted by the pleasantness of the morning to stop at the gates and look into the park. Every day was now adding to the leaves of the early trees. She was on the point of taking up again her walk when she caught a glimpse of a gentleman among the trees, moving that way. Fearful of its being Mr. Darcy, she was hastening on, but he was now near enough to see her and, stepping forward with eagerness, called her name. It was Mr. Darcy. He came forward holding out a letter, saying with a haughty look:

"I have been walking in the grove some time in the hope of meeting you. Will you do me the honor of reading that letter?" And then, with a slight bow, he turned again and was soon out of sight.

Expecting no pleasure but with strong curiosity, Elizabeth opened the letter and saw two sheets of paper, closely written throughout. Going her way along the lane, she began to read. It was dated from Rosings, at eight o'clock in the morning, and was as follows:—

I write without any intention of paining you, or humbling myself, by dwelling on wishes which cannot be too soon forgotten. But my character required this letter to be written and read.

Two offences you last night charged me with. The first was that I had separated Mr. Bingley from your sister. The other was that I had ruined the prospects of Mr. Wickham. If in explaining my acts I should offend you further, I can only say that I am sorry.

I had not been long at Netherfield before I saw, as others did, that Bingley was greatly attracted toward your sister. But it was not till the evening of the dance at Netherfield that I had any thought of his being serious; I had often seen him in love before. I learned from what Sir William Lucas said that Bingley's attention to your sister had given rise to a general belief that they would be married. Then I began to notice that his interest was beyond what I had ever seen in him. Your sister I also watched. Her look and manners were open, cheerful, and engaging as ever, and I believed that she was not as yet greatly attached to him. But if *you* have not been mistaken here, *I* must have been in error. If being thus misled, I have caused your sister pain, your anger against me has not been unreasonable.

My objections to the marriage were not merely those which I last night spoke of as to my own case; the want of connection could not be so great an evil to my friend as to me. But there were other causes, causes which I tried in my own case to forget —the total want of propriety so often shown by your mother and by your three younger sisters, and sometimes even by your father. Pardon me. It pains me to offend you.

When Bingley left Netherfield for London, he intended to return. But his sisters' uneasiness was equal to my own, and seeing that no time was to be lost in separating the two, we decided to join him in London. We therefore went—and there I pointed out to him the certain evils of such a choice. I admit that I told him that his love was not returned, that her heart was not likely to be easily touched. He had before believed that she returned his affection. But Bingley has great natural modesty, and a stronger dependence on my judgment than on his own. It was not hard to convince him that he had deceived himself. To persuade him against returning to Netherfield was then easy. I cannot blame myself for having done this. There is but one part of my conduct in the whole affair on which I cannot look with satisfaction. It is that I stooped to conceal from him that your sister was in town. I knew it myself, as it was known to Miss Bingley, but he even yet does not know of it. Perhaps this deceit was beneath me. It is done, however, and it was done for the best. If I have wounded your sister's feelings, it was done unknowingly.

As to my having injured Mr. Wickham, a more weighty charge, I can refute that charge only by laying before you the whole of his connection with my family. He is the son of a very respectable man, who for many years managed all the Pemberley estates. His faithfulness to his trust naturally inclined my father to be kind and liberal to him and to his son. He supported George Wickham, who was his godson, at school and afterward at Cambridge—as his own father would have been unable to give him a gentleman's education. My father was fond of this young man, whose manners were always engaging, and had the highest opinion of him. He intended to provide for him in the church, hoping that would be his profession. As for myself, it is many years since I first began to think of him in a very different manner. The lack of principle which he was able to keep from my father's knowledge, could not escape the eyes of one nearly the same age, who saw him in unguarded moments. Here again I shall give you pain—but I must tell you his real character.

My father died about five years ago, and in his will advised me that if Wickham went into the church he should be given charge of a valuable family parish. There was also a gift of one thousand pounds. Wickham's own father did not live long after this. Within half a year Wickham wrote me that he had decided against going into the church, and hoped he might be given other property in place of the post in the church. He said he had thought of studying law. I knew that he ought not to be a clergyman, and he was given three thousand pounds. All connection between us seemed now finished. I thought too ill of him to invite him to Pemberley. He lived chiefly, I believe, in town, but his studying law was a mere pretense. He led a life of idleness and sport. For about three years I heard little of him; then he wrote me again asking for the position in the church. He said— and I had no great trouble in believing him—that he was greatly in need of money, that he did not like the law, and had decided to go into the church if he could have the place which my father had intended for him. You can hardly blame me for refusing him. He was violent in his abuse of me to others, and in his letters to me. After this, all connection between us was over. How he lived, I know not. But last summer he again most painfully put himself into my notice.

I must now tell you a matter which I would wish to forget, and which nothing but your right understanding of my motive could make me unfold to any human being. Having said this much, I feel no doubt of your secrecy. My sister, who is more than ten years my junior, was left to the guardianship of Colonel Fitzwilliam and myself. Last summer she went with a companion, Mrs. Younge, to Ramsgate, and there also went Mr. Wickham, undoubtedly with some plan in mind, for he knew already Mrs. Younge, in whose character we were greatly deceived. By her aid he was able to see Georgiana, who remembered his kindness to her as a child. She was led to believe herself in love and agreed to elope with him. She was then but fifteen, which must be her excuse. I am happy to add that I owed the knowledge of it to herself. I joined her a day or two before the intended elopement, and then Georgiana, grieved to offend a brother whom she almost looked up to as a father, told me the whole story. Regard for my sister's credit and feelings prevented any public exposure of Wickham, but I wrote to him, and he left the place at once. Mrs. Younge was of course removed from her duties. Wickham's chief object was, of course, my sister's fortune, and also perhaps the hope of revenging himself on me. His revenge would have been complete indeed.

This is a faithful narrative of everything between us. I hope it will lead you to acquit me of cruelty toward Mr. Wickham. You may wonder why all this was not told you last night. But I was not then master enough of myself to know what could or ought to be told. The truth of all this you can learn from Colonel Fitzwilliam, who from our kinship, friendship, and business connections has known of it from the first. If your dislike of *me* should cause you to doubt all this, you can have no reason to doubt him. That you may have time to see him, I shall try to put this letter in your hands in the course of the morning. I will only add, God bless you.

Fitzwilliam Darcy.

Chapter Twenty-Nine

Elizabeth Changes Her Opinion of Darcy

Elizabeth read the letter with eagerness. That he had believed Jane's heart to be untouched, she thought at once to be false. And his account of the real, the worst objections to the match made her too angry to have any wish to do him justice. He spoke no regret for what he had done. His letter was haughty; it was all pride and insult.

But when she read his account of Mr. Wickham, which, if true, must overthrow every good opinion of him, her feelings were yet more painful. Surprise and even horror oppressed her. She wished to disbelieve it entirely, saying over and over, "This must be false! This cannot be! This must be the grossest falsehood!" And when she had gone through the whole letter, she put it hastily away, feeling that she would never look at it again.

But it would not do; in half a minute the letter was unfolded again and she again began reading all that related to Wickham. The story of his connection with the Darcy family was exactly what he had told her himself. And the kindness of the elder Mr. Darcy, though she had not before known how kind, all agreed with his own words. But when she came to the will, the difference was great. What Wickham had said was fresh in her memory; there was falsehood on one side or the other.

Again she read. But every line proved more clearly that the affair could be given a turn which must make Mr. Darcy entirely blameless. Of Mr. Wickham's former way of life, nothing had been known in Meryton but what he told himself. She tried to recall some trait of goodness that might excuse him from the attacks of Mr. Darcy. She could see him in every charm of air and manner, but she could remember no more solid good than general liking which his social powers had gained him. And alas! the story of his wish to elope with Miss Darcy was proven by what had passed between Colonel Fitzwilliam and herself only the morning before. Last of all, she was referred for the truth of it all to Colonel Fitzwilliam himself.

She remembered that Wickham had boasted of having no fear of seeing Mr. Darcy—that Mr. Darcy might leave the country, but that *he* should stand his ground. Yet he had stayed away from the Netherfield ball the very next week. She remembered also that till the Netherfield family had left the country, he had told his story to no one but herself, but after they had left, it had been everywhere known. He had been willing to sink Darcy's character, though he had said to her that respect for the father would always prevent his speaking ill of the son. Every lingering struggle in his favor grew fainter and fainter.

She recalled that Bingley, when questioned by Jane about the affair, had said that Darcy was blameless. And proud as were his

ıanners, she had never seen in him anything unprincipled or un-
ıst. Even Wickham had allowed him merit as a brother, and
ıe had often heard him speak so affectionately of his sister as
ɔ prove him capable of *some* kind feeling. She grew positively
shamed of herself.

"How blind and prejudiced have I been!" she cried. "I, who
ave prided myself on my abilities! who have often scorned the
enerous trustfulness of my sister and pleased my vanity in use-
·ss and blamable distrust. Had I been in love, I could not have
ɛen more blind. But vanity, not love, has been my folly
leased with the attention of Wickham, and offended by the neg-
·ct of Darcy, I drove reason away. Till this moment I never
ıew myself."

She read again what he said of Jane and Bingley. He declared
ɛ did not know of Jane's attachment, and she could not help
membering what Charlotte's opinion had been—that Jane
ıould show her preference openly. She knew that it was not
ıne's nature to do so.

When she came again to that part of the letter in which her
mily were mentioned in such wounding yet truthful words, her
nse of shame was great. The justice of his words struck her too
rcibly for denial. Jane's disappointment had in fact been the
ork of her nearest relations. Elizabeth felt depressed beyond
ıything she had ever known before. After wandering along the
ne for two hours, reconciling herself as well as she could to a
ıange so sudden and so important, weariness and recollection of
·r long absence caused her at length to return home. She en-
red the house with the wish of appearing cheerful as usual.

She was told at once that the two gentlemen from Rosings had
lled while she was out. Mr. Darcy only for a few minutes to
ke leave, but Colonel Fitzwilliam had been sitting with them
least an hour, hoping for her return, and had talked of walking
ter her till she could be found. Elizabeth could only *pretend*
be sorry she had missed him. She really rejoiced at it; Colonel
tzwilliam was no longer an interest; she could think only of her
tter.

Mr. Darcy and Colonel Fitzwilliam left Rosings the next mor
ing. Mr. Collins, having been waiting near the gates to mal
them his parting bow, was able to bring home the pleasing nev
that they seemed in good spirits. To Rosings he then hastene
to console Lady Catherine and her daughter. On his return l
brought back a message from her ladyship, that she felt herse
so dull as to make her wish they would all dine with her.

Elizabeth could not see Lady Catherine without recollectir
that had she chosen it, she might by this time have been pr
sented to her as her future niece. Nor could she think without
smile of what her ladyship's manner would have been. "Wh
would she have said? How would she have behaved?" were que
tions with which she amused herself.

They first spoke of the absence of her two nephews. "I believ
nobody feels the loss of friends so much as I do," said Lac
Catherine. "I am greatly attached to these young men and kno
them to be so much atttached to me! They were so sorry to g
But so they always are. Darcy seemed to feel it most, more
think than last year."

Lady Catherine remarked after dinner that Elizabeth seeme
out of spirits, probably because she did not like to go home aga
so soon. "But if that is the case, you must write to your moth
to stay a little longer. Mrs. Collins will be very glad of yo
company, I am sure. You will have been here only six weeks.
expected you to stay two months. I told Mrs. Collins so befo
you came. Mrs. Bennet could certainly spare you for another tv
weeks."

"But my father cannot. He wrote last week to hurry my r
turn."

"Oh, your father of course can spare you if your mother ca
And if you will stay another *month*, it will be in my power to tal
one of you as far as London, for I am going there early in Jun
for a week. There will be room for one of you—and indeed,
the weather should happen to be cool, I could take you both,
you are neither large."

"You are very kind, madam; but I believe we must keep our original plan."

Lady Catherine seemed resigned. "Mrs. Collins, you must send a servant with them. You know I always speak my mind, and I cannot bear the idea of two young women traveling by themselves. It is highly improper. You must manage to send somebody. I have the greatest dislike in the world to that sort of thing. When my niece Georgiana went to Ramsgate last summer, I made a point of her having two menservants go with her."

"My uncle is to send a servant for us," said Elizabeth.

"Oh, your uncle! He keeps a manservant, does he? I am very glad you have somebody who thinks of those things. Where shall you change horses? Oh, at Bromley, of course. If you mention my name at the Bell Inn, you will be given the best attention."

Lady Catherine had many other questions to ask about their journey, and as she did not answer them all herself, it was necessary to listen, which Elizabeth believed to be lucky for her; otherwise, with a mind so taken up with Darcy's letter, she might have forgotten where she was.

The letter she was in a fair way of soon knowing by heart. She studied every sentence, and her feelings toward its writer were at times widely different. When she remembered the style of his proposal, she was still full of anger. But when she recalled how unjustly she had thought of him, her anger was turned against herself. His affection for her excited gratitude; his character won her respect. But she could not for a moment repent her refusal or feel the slightest wish ever to see him again. For her own past behavior toward him, there was vexation and regret, and for the unhappy faults of her family of which he had reminded her, yet heavier vexation and regret. They were hopeless of remedy. Her father, contented to laugh at his youngest daughters, would never exert himself to restrain their wild giddiness. Her mother, with manners so far from right herself, could not see the need. Elizabeth had often joined with Jane in trying to check

Kitty and Lydia who, supported by their mother, could not be moved. Kitty, weak-spirited and entirely under Lydia's influence, had been always vexed by their advice. Lydia, self-willed and careless, would scarcely give them a hearing. They were ignorant, idle, and vain. While there was an officer in Meryton, they would flirt with him. And while Meryton was within a walk of Longbourn, they would be going there forever.

Anxiety on Jane's behalf was another concern. Mr. Darcy's letter, by bringing back all her former good opinion of Bingley, made her feel the more what Jane had lost. His affection had been sincere, and he was clear of all blame, unless one could blame his too great dependence on his friend. How sad then was the thought that Jane's happiness had been lost to her by the folly of her own family!

Chapter Thirty

Elizabeth's Visit to Charlotte Comes to an End

Visits to Rosings were made as often during the last week of Elizabeth's stay as they had been at first. The very last evening was spent there. Her ladyship again asked about their journey, and told them so carefully the best method of packing gowns in the only right way that Maria, on her return to the parsonage, undid all the work of the morning and packed her trunk afresh.

When they parted, Lady Catherine wished them a good journey and invited them to come again to Hunsford next year. Miss de Bourgh exerted herself so far as to curtsey and hold out her hand to both.

On Saturday morning Elizabeth and Mr. Collins met for breakfast a few minutes before the others appeared.

"The favor of your company has been much felt, I assure you," began Mr. Collins. "We know how little there is to tempt any-one to our humble home. Our plain manner of living, our small rooms and few servants, and the little we see of the world must make Hunsford very dull to a young lady like you. But I hope you will believe that we are grateful for your coming, and that we have done everything in our power to make you spend your time pleasantly."

Elizabeth was eager with her thanks. She had spent six weeks with great enjoyment, and the pleasure of being with Charlotte and the kind attentions she had received from everyone must make *her* the one to feel obliged. Mr. Collins was pleased, and with a more smiling solemnity replied:

"You may carry back a very favorable report of us. Lady Cath-erine's great attentions to Mrs. Collins you have seen daily. Al-together, I trust it does not appear that Charlotte has made an unfortunate—but on this point, I will be silent. Only let me say that I can from my heart wish you an equally happy marriage. My dear Charlotte and I have but one mind and one way of thinking. We seem to have been made for each other."

Elizabeth could safely say that she firmly believed and re-joiced in his domestic comforts. She was not sorry, however, when the entrance of Charlotte put an end to their talk. Poor Charlotte! it was sad to leave her to such society! But she had chosen it with her eyes open, and though plainly sorry to see Elizabeth go, she did not seem to ask for pity. Her home, her parish, and her poultry, and all the attention they required had not yet lost their charms.

At length the carriage arrived. Mr. Collins handed Elizabeth in and Maria followed. The door was on the point of being closed when he suddenly reminded them, with some appearance of shock, that they had forgotten to leave any message for the ladies of Rosings.

"But," he added, "you will of course wish to send your grateful thanks for their kindness to you while you have been here."

Elizabeth made no objection; the door was then allowed to be shut, and the carriage drove off.

"Good gracious!" cried Maria after a few minutes' silence, "it seems but a day since we first came! And yet how many things have happened!"

"A great many indeed," said Elizabeth with a sigh.

"We have dined nine times at Rosings, besides drinking tea there twice! How much I shall have to tell!"

Elizabeth thought, "And how much I shall have to conceal."

Within four hours of their leaving Hunsford, they reached Mr. Gardiner's house in London, where they were to remain a few days.

Jane looked well, and Elizabeth had little chance to study her spirits, amid the many engagements which the kindness of her aunt had planned for them. But Jane was to go home with her, and at Longbourn there would be time enough.

It was the second week in May in which Elizabeth, Jane, and Maria set out from London for the town where Mr. Bennet's carriage was to meet them. As they entered the town and drew near the inn, they saw both Kitty and Lydia looking out of a dining-room window upstairs. These two girls had been more than an hour in the town, happily visiting the milliner, and making a salad lunch. After welcoming their sisters, they showed a table set out with such cold food as an inn usually has on hand, saying, "Isn't this a nice surprise?"

"And we mean to treat you all," added Lydia; "but you must lend us the money, for we have just spent ours at the shop out there. Look here, I have bought this bonnet. I do not think it is very pretty, but I thought I might as well buy it as not. I shall pull it to pieces as soon as I get home and see if I can make it up any better."

And when her sisters said it was ugly, she added with unconcern, "Oh, but there were two or three much uglier in the shop. And when I have bought some prettier-colored satin to trim it with fresh, I think it will be very passable. Besides, it will not much matter what one wears this summer after the regiment has left Meryton. And they are going in two weeks."

"Are they indeed?" cried Elizabeth, greatly pleased to hear it.

"They are going to be camped near Brighton, and I do so want papa to take us all there for the summer! Mamma too would like to go, of all things! Only think what a miserable summer we shall have otherwise!"

"Yes," thought Elizabeth, "*that* would be a delightful plan, indeed, and completely do for us at once. Good heaven! Brighton, and a whole campful of soldiers, to us, who have been overset already by one poor regiment, and the monthly balls at Meryton."

"Now I have some news for you," said Lydia as they sat down to table. "What do you think? It is good news, and about a certain person that we all like."

Jane and Elizabeth looked at each other, and the waiter was told that he need not stay. Lydia laughed and said:

"You thought the waiter must not hear, as if he cared! I dare say he often hears worse things said than I am going to say. But he is an ugly fellow! I am glad he is gone. I never saw such a long chin in my life. Well, but now for my news. It is about dear Wickham. There is no danger of his marrying Mary King. She has gone down to her uncle at Liverpool, gone to stay. Wickham is safe."

"And Mary King is safe!" added Elizabeth, "safe from a marriage imprudent as to fortune."

"She is a great fool for going away, if she liked him."

"But I hope there is no strong attachment on either side," said Jane.

"I am sure there is not on *his*," said Lydia. "He never cared three straws about her. Who *could* about such a nasty little freckled thing?"

Elizabeth was shocked to think that, though she could not have spoken with such coarseness, she had felt in her own breast the coarse sentiment!

As soon as all had eaten and the elder ones had paid, the carriage was ordered. After some trouble the whole party, with all their boxes, workbags, and parcels, and the unwelcome addition of Kitty's and Lydia's purchases, were seated in it.

"How nicely we are crammed in!" cried Lydia. "I am glad I bought my bonnet, if only for the fun of having another band-box! Well, now let us be quite comfortable and snug, and talk and laugh all the way home. And in the first place, let us hear what has happened to you all, since you went away. Have you seen any pleasant men? Have you had any flirting? I was in great hopes that one of you would have got a husband before you came back. Jane will be quite an old maid soon, I declare. She is almost twenty-three! Lord, how ashamed I should be of not being married before twenty-three! Aunt Philips does so want you to get husbands! She says Lizzy had better have taken Mr. Collins, but *I* do not think there would have been any fun in it. Lord! how I should like to be married before any of you."

Elizabeth listened to Lydia and Kitty's talk as little as she could, but there was no escaping the many mentions of Wickham's name.

Their welcome at home was most kind. Mrs. Bennet rejoiced to see that Jane was as beautiful as ever, and more than once during dinner did Mr. Bennet say to Elizabeth: "I am glad you are back, Lizzy."

Their party in the dining-room was large, for almost all the Lucases came to meet Maria and hear the news. Lady Lucas was asking Maria across the table all about the welfare and the poultry of her daughter Charlotte. Mrs. Bennet was busy collecting news of the newest fashions from Jane, who sat some way below her. And Lydia, in a voice rather louder than any other person's, was telling the many pleasures of the morning to anybody who would hear her.

"Oh, Mary," she cried, "I wish you had gone with us, for we had such fun! We laughed and talked so loud that anybody might have heard us ten miles off!"

To this, Mary very gravely replied, "Far be it from me to scorn such pleasures. They are doubtless suitable to the general feminine mind. But I confess they would have no charms for *me*. I should much prefer a book."

But of this answer Lydia heard not a word. She seldom lis-

tened to anybody for more than half a minute, and never listened
to Mary at all.

Elizabeth had not been many hours at home before she found
that the plan to move to Brighton, of which Lydia had given
them a hint at the inn, had been spoken of between her parents.
She saw too that her father had not the smallest intention of
going, but his answers were so vague that her mother, though
often disheartened, had never yet given up hope.

Chapter Thirty-One

*Elizabeth Tells Jane What She Has Learned of Darcy and
Wickham, and They Decide to Say Nothing
More of the Matter*

The next morning Elizabeth told Jane of Mr. Darcy's proposal.
Jane's first great surprise was soon over, for her admiration of
Elizabeth caused her to regard such a proposal as perfectly natural. She was sorry that Mr. Darcy had spoken in a manner so
little suited to recommend him, but still more was she grieved for
the unhappiness which her sister's refusal must have given him.

"Indeed," replied Elizabeth, "I am heartily sorry for him. But
you do not blame me for refusing him?"

"Blame you! Oh, no."

"But you blame me for having spoken so warmly of Wickham."

"No—I do not know that you were wrong in saying what you
did."

"But you *will* know it when I have told you what happened the
very next day."

She then spoke of the letter, telling all it had had to say of
George Wickham. What a stroke was this for poor Jane, who

would willingly have gone through the world believing evil of no one!

"I do not know when I have been more shocked," said she. "Wickham so very bad! It is almost past belief. And poor Mr. Darcy! Dear Lizzy, only think of what he must have suffered. Such a disappointment! And then with the knowledge of your ill-opinion of him, having to tell such a thing of his sister! It is really too distressing!"

"Well, I know that you will do Mr. Darcy ample justice, and therefore I am growing every moment more unconcerned. If you lament over him much longer, my heart will be as light as a feather."

"And poor Wickham. There is such a look of goodness in his face—such an openness and gentleness in his manner!"

"There certainly was some great mistake in the education of those two young men. One has got all the goodness and the other all the appearance of it."

"I never thought Mr. Darcy so lacking in the *appearance* of it as you used to do."

"And yet I meant to be very clever in taking such a dislike to him without any reason. It gives such an opening for wit to have a dislike of that kind. One cannot be always laughing at a man without now and then stumbling on something witty."

"Lizzy, when you first read that letter, I am sure you could not treat the matter as you do now."

"Indeed I could not. I was very unhappy. And with no one to speak to of what I felt, no Jane to comfort me and say that I had not been so very weak and vain and silly as I knew I had been! Oh, how I wanted you! There is still one point on which I want your advice. I want to be told whether I ought, or ought not, to make our friends in general understand Wickham's character."

Jane paused a little and then replied: "Surely there can be no need to expose him so dreadfully. What is your own opinion?"

"That it ought not to be done. The story of Mr. Darcy's sister was meant to be kept as much as possible to myself. And if I try to undeceive people as to the rest of his conduct, who would believe me? The general prejudice against Mr. Darcy is so strong that it would be the death of half the good people in Meryton to try to place him in an amiable light. I am not equal to it. Wickham will soon be gone, and then it will not matter to anybody here what he really is."

"You are quite right. To have his errors made public might ruin him forever. He is now perhaps sorry for what he has done. We must not make him desperate."

Elizabeth had now got rid of two of the secrets which had weighed on her for the past two weeks. But there was still something lurking behind. She dared not tell Jane how sincerely she had been valued by Charles Bingley. Nothing less than a perfect understanding between the two could justify her in throwing off this last secret.

"And then," she thought, "if that very unlikely event should ever take place, Bingley can tell it in a much more agreeable manner himself."

She saw that Jane was not happy, that she still had a very tender affection for him, and that all her good sense and all her wishes to be cheerful before her friends were needed to check those regrets which must have been harmful to her own health and their peace of mind.

"Well, Lizzy," said Mrs. Bennet one day, "what is your opinion *now* of this sad business of Jane's? I cannot find out that Jane saw anything of him in London. I do not suppose there is the least chance in the world of her ever getting him now. There is no talk of his coming to Netherfield again in the summer; and I have inquired of everybody, too, who is likely to know."

"I do not believe that he will ever live at Netherfield any more."

"Oh, well! it is just as he chooses. Nobody wants him to come. Though I shall always say that he used my daughter very ill, and she should not have put up with it. Well, my comfort is that if Jane should die of a broken heart, then he will be sorry for what he has done."

As Elizabeth could not take comfort from any such idea, she made no answer.

"And so the Collinses live very comfortable, do they?" went on her mother soon afterwards. "Well, well, I only hope it will last. And what sort of table do they keep? Charlotte is a fine manager, I dare say. If she is half as sharp as her mother, she is saving enough. There is nothing wasted in *their* housekeeping, I dare say."

"No, nothing at all."

"Yes, yes. *They* will take care not to outrun their income. *They* will never be in need of money. Well, much good may it do them! I suppose they often talk of having Longbourn when your father is dead. They look upon it quite as their own, I dare say."

"It is a matter which they could not mention before me."

"No. It would have been strange if they had. But I make no doubt they often talk of it between themselves."

Chapter Thirty-Two

Lydia Bennet Goes to Stay at Brighton

It was the last week of the regiment's stay in Meryton, and all the young ladies in the neighborhood were drooping fast. Elizabeth and Jane alone were still able to eat, drink, and sleep in the usual manner. Kitty and Lydia, whose misery was great, could not understand such hard-heartedness in any of the family.

"Good heaven! What is to become of us! What are we to do!" they would often cry out in the bitterness of woe. "How can you be smiling so, Lizzy?"

Their mother shared all their grief; she remembered what she had herself endured on a like occasion, five-and-twenty years ago.

"I am sure," said she, "I cried for two days together when Colonel Millar's regiment went away. I thought my heart would break."

"I am sure *mine* will break," said Lydia.

"If we could only go to Brighton!" sighed Mrs. Bennet.

"Oh, yes! If we could only go to Brighton! But papa is so set against it."

"A little sea-bathing would set me up forever."

"And Aunt Philips is sure it would do *me* a great deal of good," added Kitty.

Such were the words of regret sounding always through the Longbourn house. Elizabeth felt anew the justice of Mr. Darcy's objections, and never had she been so near to pardoning him.

But Lydia's gloom soon cleared away, for she had an invitation from Mrs. Forster, the wife of the colonel of the regiment, to visit her at Brighton. Mrs. Forster was a very young woman, very lately married, in spirits quite like Lydia herself.

The rapture of Lydia, her praise of Mrs. Forster, the delight of Mrs. Bennet, and the grief of Kitty are scarcely to be described. Lydia flew about the house in restless joy, laughing and talking with more noise than ever, while the luckless Kitty bemoaned her fate in peevish unreason.

"I cannot see why Mrs. Forster should not ask *me* as well as Lydia," said she, "though I am *not* her close friend. I have just as much right to be asked as Lydia has, and more too, for I am two years older."

Elizabeth could not help secretly advising her father not to let Lydia go. She reminded him of Lydia's general ill-behavior, the little she would gain from the friendship of such a woman as Mrs. Forster, and the danger of such a companion at Brighton, where need for restraint must be greater than at home. He heard her quietly, and then said:

"Lydia will never be easy till she has exposed herself in some

public place or other, and we can never expect her to do it with
so little effect on her family as away from home."

"If you knew," said Elizabeth, "of the very great harm to us
all which has already arisen from Lydia's manner, I am sure you
would look on this more seriously."

"Already arisen!" repeated Mr. Bennet. "What, has she frightened away some of your lovers? Poor little Lizzy! But do not be
cast down. Such sqeamish young men as cannot bear to be connected with a little folly are not worth a regret."

"Excuse me—for I must speak plainly. If you will not take
the trouble of checking her spirits and teaching her better, she
will soon be beyond control. Her character will be fixed, and she
will, at sixteen, be a common flirt. Kitty will follow wherever
Lydia leads. Vain, ignorant, idle, and uncontrolled! They will
be scorned and despised wherever they are known, and their
sisters will often share in the disgrace!"

Mr. Bennet saw that her whole heart was in the subject, and
affectionately taking her hand, he said:

"Do not make yourself uneasy, my love. Wherever you and
Jane are known you must be respected and valued. You will not
appear to less advantage for having a couple of—or I may say,
three—very silly sisters. We shall have no peace at Longbourn
if Lydia does not go to Brighton. Let her go, then. Colonel
Forster is a sensible man, and will keep her out of mischief. She
is luckily too poor to be an object of prey to anybody. At
Brighton she will be of less importance as a flirt than she was
here. The officers will find women better worth their notice. Let
us hope, therefore, that her being there may teach her her own
unimportance. At any rate, she cannot grow much worse without
causing us to lock her up for the rest of her life."

With this answer Elizabeth was forced to be content. But she
left him disappointed and sorry. Had Lydia and her mother
known of her talk with her father, their indignation could hardly
have been expressed in the united voices of the two. To Lydia,
a visit to Brighton included every possibility of happiness. She

saw in fancy the streets of that gay bathing-place covered with officers, and herself surrounded by scores of them, at present unknown. She saw all the glories of the camp, its tents stretched forth in beauteous even lines, crowded with the young and the gay, and dazzling with scarlet. And to complete the view, she saw herself seated beneath a tent, tenderly flirting with at least six officers at once.

On the very last day of the regiment's stay in Meryton, Mr. Wickham dined with other officers at Longbourn. So little did Elizabeth wish to part with him in good humor that on his making some inquiry as to her visit, she mentioned that Colonel Fitzwilliam and Darcy had spent three weeks at Rosings, and asked him if he knew Colonel Fitzwilliam.

He looked surprised, displeased, alarmed. But with a returning smile, he replied that he had formerly seen him often, and asked her how she had liked him. Her answer was warmly in his favor. With a careless air Wickham soon afterward added, "How long did you say that he was at Rosings?"

"Nearly three weeks."

"And you saw him often?"

"Yes, almost every day."

"His manners are very different from his cousin's."

"Yes, very different. But I think Mr. Darcy improves as you learn to know him."

"Indeed!" cried Wickham with a look which did not escape her. "And may I ask—" But checking himself, he added in a gayer tone, "Is it in manners that he improves?"

"When I said that he improved on knowing him, I meant that his character was better understood."

Wickham's alarm now appeared in a deeper color and a troubled look. For a few minutes he was silent, then he turned to her again and said in the gentlest of tones:

"You who so well know my feelings toward Mr. Darcy, will know how I rejoice that he is wise enough to put on even the *appearance* of what is right. But his altered manner may have

been put on for the benefit of his aunt, of whose good opinion
he stands much in awe. And of course he wishes to forward the
match between himself and Miss de Bourgh."

Elizabeth could not help smiling at this. She saw that he
wanted to talk on the old subject of his wrongs, but she would
not encourage him. They parted at last with politeness and possibly a mutual wish never to meet again.

When the party broke up, Lydia returned with Mrs. Forster
to Meryton, from whence they were to set out early the next
morning for Brighton. The parting from her family was rather
noisy than sad. Kitty was the only one who shed tears, but she
wept from vexation and envy. Mrs. Bennet wished her daughter
all happiness, and urged her to miss no opportunity of enjoying
herself as much as possible, advice hardly necessary to Lydia.
The more gentle farewells of her sisters were lost in the loud
good-byes of Lydia.

Chapter Thirty-Three

A Tour of the Pemberley Estate

When the time fixed for beginning the northern tour was nearing,
Elizabeth had a letter from Mrs. Gardiner saying that business
would keep Mr. Gardiner from setting out till in July, and that he
must be in London again within a month. As that left too short a
period for them to go so far as planned, they must give up the
Lakes and take a shorter tour. The present plan was to go into
Derbyshire. In that country there was enough to be seen to
occupy their three weeks. And to Mrs. Gardiner the region had
a strong attraction, for she had formerly passed some years of
her life there.

Elizabeth was greatly disappointed. She had set her heart on seeing the Lakes and still thought there might have been time enough. But it was her business to be satisfied—and certainly her temper to be happy; and all was soon right again. It was impossible for her to see the word Derbyshire without thinking of Pemberley and its owner. "But surely," she thought, "I may enter his county and rob it of a few petrified spars without his seeing me."

The weeks between did pass away at last, and Mr. and Mrs. Gardiner with their four children did at length appear at Longbourn. The children were to be left under the care of their cousin Jane, whose steady sense and sweet temper fitted her for caring for them in every way—teaching them, playing with them, and loving them.

The Gardiners stayed only one night at Longbourn and set off the next morning with Elizabeth, in pursuit of novelty and amusement. One enjoyment was certain—good companionship with health and temper to bear any hardship of travel, and cheerfulness, affection, and intelligence to make the most of all. Their route took them through such well known places as Oxford, Blenheim, Warwick, Kenilworth, Birmingham. Then to the little town of Lambton, the scene of Mrs. Gardiner's former home, they bent their steps, after having seen all the principal wonders of the country.

Within five miles of Lambton, Elizabeth learned from her aunt, was Pemberley. It was not in their direct road nor more than a mile or two out of it. In talking over their route the evening before, Mrs. Gardiner spoke of a wish to see the place again. Mr. Gardiner was quite willing, and Elizabeth was asked for her approval.

"My love, should you not like to see a place of which you have heard so much?" said her aunt. "A place, too, with which you have some connection; Wickham passed all his youth there, you know."

Elizabeth was distressed. She felt that she had no business at Pemberley, and was forced to pretend she did not wish to see it.

She said she was tired of great houses; after going over so many, she had no more pleasure in fine carpets or satin curtains.

"If it were merely a fine house richly furnished," said Mrs. Gardiner, "I should not care about it myself; but the grounds are delightful. They have some of the finest woods in the country."

Elizabeth said no more—but her mind could not agree. There was the chance of meeting Mr. Darcy, while viewing the place. It would be dreadful! She blushed at the very idea, and thought it would be better to speak openly to her aunt than to run such a risk. But this she would do only if she learned that Mr. Darcy was now at Pemberley. When she went to her room at night, she asked the chamber-maid if Pemberley was not a very fine place, what was the name of its owner, and whether the family was there for the summer. A most welcome "No" followed the last question. Her fears being removed, she now felt a great curiosity to see the house, and the next morning she was able to say that she had really no dislike for a visit to Pemberley. To Pemberley, therefore, they were to go.

As they drove along, Elizabeth watched for the first sight of Pemberley woods, and when at length they turned in at the lodge, her spirits were in a high flutter. The park was very large with great variety of ground. They entered it in one of its lowest points and drove for some time through a beautiful wood, stretching over a wide distance. Her mind was too full for speech, but she saw and admired every remarkable spot and point of view.

The road gradually climbed for half a mile to the top of a slope, where the wood ceased, and Pemberley House came suddenly into view, set on the opposite side of a valley, down which the road now began to wind. It was a large, handsome, stone building, standing well on rising ground and backed by a ridge of high woody hills and fronted by a stream, its banks neither formal nor falsely adorned. Elizabeth had never seen a place for which nature had done more, or where natural beauty had been so little changed by bad taste.

They were all warm in their praise, and at that moment she felt that to be mistress of Pemberley might be something! They went down the hill, crossed the bridge, and drove to the door. Now all her fear of meeting its owner returned. She dreaded lest the chamber-maid had been mistaken. On asking to see the place, they were led into the hall.

The housekeeper came, a respectable-looking, elderly woman, much less fine and more civil than she had any notion of finding her. They followed her into the dining-parlor, a large room, handsomely fitted up. Elizabeth went to a window to enjoy its view. She looked on the river, the trees scattered in its banks, and the winding valley, as far as she could trace it, with delight. As they passed into other rooms, from every window there were beauties to be seen. The rooms were lofty and handsome, and their furniture suitable to the fortune of their owner, but neither gaudy nor uselessly fine, with less of splendor and more real elegance than the furniture of Rosings.

"And of this place," she thought, "I might have been mistress! Instead of viewing these rooms as a stranger, I might have rejoiced in them as my own, and welcomed to them as visitors my uncle and aunt. But no," she thought, "that could never be; my uncle and aunt would have been lost to me; I should not have been allowed to invite them."

This was a lucky thought—it saved her from something like regret. She longed to ask the housekeeper whether her master was really absent, but did not have the courage. At length, however, the question was asked by her uncle, and she turned away with alarm while Mrs. Reynolds replied that he was, adding, "But we expect him tomorrow with a large party of friends."

How rejoiced was Elizabeth that their own journey had not been delayed a day! Her aunt now called her to look at a picture. She went forward and saw the likeness of Mr. Wickham, hanging among several other small pictures, over the mantelpiece. Her aunt asked her, smilingly, how she liked it. The housekeeper came forward and told them that it was the picture of a young gentleman, the son of her late master's steward, who had been brought up by the late master at his own expense. "He is now gone into the army," she added, "but I am afraid he has turned out very wild."

Mrs. Gardiner looked at her niece with a smile, but Elizabeth could not return it.

"And that," said Mrs. Reynolds, pointing to another of the pictures, "is my master—and very like him. It was drawn at the same time as the other—about eight years ago."

"It is a handsome face," said Mrs. Gardiner, looking at the picture. "But, Lizzy, you can tell us whether it is like him."

Mrs. Reynolds's respect for Elizabeth seemed to grow on hearing that she knew the master. "Does that young lady know Mr. Darcy?"

Elizabeth colored and said: "A little."

"In the gallery upstairs you will see a finer, larger picture of him than this. This room was my late master's favorite room, and these small pictures are just as they were then. He was very fond of them."

Elizabeth now understood why Mr. Wickham's picture was still there. Mrs. Reynolds then called their attention to one of Miss Darcy, drawn when she was only eight years old. "She plays and sings so well—in the next room is a new piano just come for her —a present from my master. She comes here tomorrow with him."

Mr. Gardiner, whose manners were easy and pleasant, encouraged her to talk. She seemed to have great pleasure, either from pride or attachment, in talking of her master and his sister.

"Is your master much at Pemberley in the course of the year?"

"Not so much as I could wish, sir. But I dare say he may spend half his time here. And Miss Darcy is always down for the summer months."

"Except," thought Elizabeth, "when she goes to Ramsgate."

"If your master would marry, you might see more of him."

"Yes, sir; but I do not know when *that* will be. I do not know who is good enough for him."

Mr. and Mrs. Gardiner smiled. Elizabeth could not help saying, "It is very much to his credit that you should think so."

"I say no more than the truth, and what everybody will say that knows him," replied the housekeeper. Elizabeth thought this was going pretty far, and she heard with amazement the housekeeper add: "I have never had a cross word from him in my life, and I have known him ever since he was four years old."

To Elizabeth this praise was strangest of all; that he was not a good-tempered man had been her firmest opinion. She longed to hear more and was grateful to her uncle for saying, "There are very few people of whom so much can be said. You are lucky in having such a master."

"Yes, sir, I know I am. I could not meet with a better. But I always said that they who are good-natured when children are good-natured when they grow up. And he was always the sweetest-tempered, most generous-hearted boy in the world."

Elizabeth almost stared at her. "Can this be Mr. Darcy!" she thought.

"His father was a fine man," said Mrs. Gardiner.

"Yes, ma'am, that he was indeed. And his son will be just like him—just as good to the poor."

Elizabeth listened, wondered, doubted, and longed to hear more. Mrs. Reynolds could interest her on no other points. She told them of the pictures, the size of the rooms, and the price of the furniture, in vain. Mr. Gardiner was highly amused by the kind of family pride she showed in praising her master, and soon led again to the subject. She dwelt with energy on his many merits as they went together up the great staircase.

"He is the best landlord and the best master that ever lived. Not like the wild young men nowadays, who think of nothing but themselves. There is not one of his tenants or servants but will give him a good name. Some people call him proud, but I am sure I never saw anything of it. To my fancy, it is only because he does not rattle away like other young men."

"In what a pleasing light does this place him!" thought Elizabeth.

"This fine account of him," whispered Mrs. Gardiner to Elizabeth as they walked, "does not quite agree with his behavior to our poor friend, Mr. Wickham."

"Perhaps we might be deceived."

They were shown into a very pretty sitting-room, newly fitted up with greater elegance and lightness than the apartments below. This, the housekeeper said, had just been done to give pleasure to Miss Darcy. She spoke of how surprised and pleased she would be on first entering the room. "And this is always the way with him," she added. "Whatever can give his sister any pleasure is sure to be done in a moment. There is nothing he would not do for her."

In the gallery were many family portraits. Elizabeth walked on in search of the only face which would be known to her. At last it arrested her—she saw a striking likeness of Mr. Darcy, with such a smile over the face as she remembered to have sometimes seen when he looked at her. She stood several minutes before the picture in earnest gaze, and returned to it again before they left the gallery. Mrs. Reynolds said it had been made in his father's lifetime.

There was certainly at this moment in Elizabeth's mind a more gentle feeling toward him than she had ever felt in the best of their acquaintance. What praise is more valuable than the praise of an intelligent servant? As a brother, a landlord, a master, how many people's happiness were in his hands! How much of good or evil must be done by him! Yet every idea that had been brought forward by the housekeeper was favorable to his character.

When all the house that was open to the public had been seen, they went downstairs and, taking leave of the housekeeper, were turned over to the gardener, who met them at the hall door. As they walked across the lawn toward the river, Elizabeth turned back and paused to look again at the building. As she stood thus, the owner of it himself suddenly came forward from the road which led back to the stables.

Chapter Thirty-Four

The Master of Pemberley Returns Home Unexpectedly

They were within twenty yards of each other, and so sudden was his coming that it was impossible to avoid his sight. Their eyes instantly met, and the cheeks of each were overspread with the deepest blush. He started and for a moment stood still from surprise. Then he came forward and spoke to her, if not in perfect composure, at least in perfect civility.

She met him with an awkwardness not to be overcome, scarcely daring to lift her eyes to his face, and hardly knowing what answer she returned to his polite inquiries after her family. The idea of her being found there! The few minutes that followed were some of the most uncomfortable of her life. Nor did he seem much more at ease. His manner had none of its usual slow calm; his words came hurriedly, and he asked more than once when she had left Longbourn and how long she had been in Derbyshire. Then every idea seemed to fail him, and after standing a few moments without saying a word, he suddenly took leave.

Elizabeth turned and walked after the other, over-powered by shame and vexation. Her coming there was the most unfortunate, the most ill-judged thing in the world! How strange it must appear to him! It might seem as if she had purposely thrown herself in his way again! Oh! why had she come? Or why did he thus come a day before he was expected? Had they been only ten minutes sooner, they should have missed seeing him, for it was plain that he had at that moment arrived. She blushed again and again over the awkward meeting. And his manner, so strangely altered—what could it mean? That he should even speak to her was amazing—but to speak with such courtesy, to inquire after her family! Never in her life had she seen his manners so little dignified, never had he spoken with such gentleness. What a contrast to their last meeting in Rosings Park, when he put his letter into her hand! She knew not what to think nor how to account for it.

They had now entered a beautiful walk by the side of the water, and every step was bringing forward a nobler fall of the ground or a finer reach of the woods which they were nearing. Elizabeth replied to the appeals of her uncle and aunt and turned her eyes to such objects as they pointed out, but she saw no part of the scene. Her thoughts were all fixed on that one spot of Pemberley House, whichever it might be, where Mr. Darcy then was. She longed to know what at that moment was passing in his mind, what he thought of her, and whether, in spite of everything, she was still dear to him. Whether he had felt more of pain or of pleasure in seeing her she could not tell, but there had been *that* in his voice which was not like ease.

Mr. Gardiner said he would like to go round the whole park but feared it might be beyond a walk. With a proud smile, the gardener told them that it was ten miles round. It settled the matter, and they went on along the usual circuit, which brought them again, after some time, down a slope among hanging woods, to the edge of the stream. They crossed it by a small bridge and were again in sight of the mansion house. Mrs. Gardiner, who was not a great walker, could go no farther, and thought only of returning to the carriage by the nearest way. Elizabeth, therefore, had to go with them toward the house.

They went slowly, for Mr. Gardiner, who was very fond of fishing, was so much taken up watching the trout in the water and talking to the gardener about them, that he advanced but little. While wandering on in this slow manner, they were again surprised by sight of Mr. Darcy, coming toward them and at no great distance. Elizabeth prepared herself to speak with calmness. She saw that he had lost none of his recent courtesy, and to be equally polite she began, as they met, to speak of the beauty of the place. But she had not got beyond "delightful" and "charming" when she stopped—he might misunderstand her purpose in praising Pemberley. Her color changed and she said no more.

She now introduced her uncle and aunt, at his request. He seemed surprised to learn who they were, and entered at once into talk with Mr. Gardiner. Elizabeth was pleased that he should know she had some relations for whom there was no need to blush. She listened to all that passed between them and gloried in every sentence of her uncle, which marked his intelligence, his taste, or his good manners.

The talk soon turned to fishing, and she heard Mr. Darcy invite him to fish there as often as he chose while he was in the neighborhood, offering at the same time to supply him with fishing tackle and pointing out those parts of the stream where there was usually most sport. Mrs. Gardiner, who was walking arm in arm with Elizabeth, gave her a look of wonder. Elizabeth said nothing, but over and over she was asking herself, "Why is he so altered? It cannot be for *me*, it cannot be for *my* sake that his manners are so softened. It is impossible that he should still love me."

After walking some time in this way, the two ladies in front, the two gentlemen behind, they went down to the brink of the river to see some curious waterplant. Here Mrs. Gardiner, weary with the long walk, took her husband's arm. Mr. Darcy and Elizabeth walked on together. She wished him to know that she had come to the place thinking he was away. She began by saying that his return was very unexpected.

"Your housekeeper told us that you would not be here till tomorrow. And before we left Bakewell, we understood that you were not expected for a few days yet."

He said that business with his steward had caused him to come a few hours before the rest of the party with whom he had been traveling. "They will join me early tomorrow, and among them are some who will claim your attention—Mr. Bingley and his sisters."

Her thoughts went back to the time when Mr. Bingley's name had been last mentioned between them, and if she might judge from his face, *he* was thinking of the same.

"There is also one other person in the party," he said after a pause, "who will wish to be known to you. Will you allow me, or do I ask too much, to introduce my sister during your stay at Lambton?"

Her surprise at such a request was too great for her to know in what manner she agreed to it. She knew that any wish that Miss Darcy might have to know her must be the work of her brother. She was flattered and pleased, and glad to know that his anger at her high-handed refusal of his proposal had not made him think really ill of her. His wish to introduce his sister to her was a compliment of the highest kind.

They soon outstripped the others, and when they had reached the carriage, Mr. and Mrs. Gardiner were half a quarter of a mile behind. He then asked her to walk into the house, but she said she was not tired, and they stood together on the lawn. At such a time, much might have been said, and silence was very awkward. She wanted to talk, but there seemed a pitfall in every subject. At last she remembered that she had been traveling, and they talked of Matlock and Dovedale with great industry. Yet time and her aunt moved slowly; her patience and her ideas were nearly worn out before her uncle and aunt came up. They were all pressed to go into the house and have some refreshment, but this was declined, and they parted with the utmost politeness on each side. Mr. Darcy handed the ladies into the carriage, and as it drove off, Elizabeth saw him walking slowly toward the house.

"He is perfectly well behaved, polite, and modest," said her uncle.

"There *is* something a little stately in him, to be sure," replied her aunt, "but it is in his air and is not unbecoming. I can now say with the housekeeper that though some people may call him proud, *I* have seen nothing of it."

"I was never more surprised. His behavior to us was more than civil; it was really attentive. And there was no need for such attention; his acquaintance with Elizabeth was very trifling."

"But, Lizzy," said her aunt, "how came you to tell us that he was so disagreeable?"

Elizabeth said that she had liked him better when they met at Rosings than before, and that she had never seen him so pleasant as this morning.

"But he may be a little variable in his friendliness," said her uncle. "Your great men often are, and I shall not take him at his word about fishing. He might change his mind another day and warn me off his grounds."

Elizabeth felt that they had entirely mistaken his character, but said nothing.

"From what we have seen of him," said Mrs. Gardiner, "I would not think that he could have behaved in so cruel a way to anybody as he did to poor Wickham. He does not have an ill-natured look. On the contrary, there is something pleasing about his mouth when he speaks. And there is something of dignity in his face that gives one a favorable idea of his heart. And to be sure, the housekeeper did give him a flaming character! I could hardly help laughing sometimes. But he is a liberal master, I suppose, and *that* in the eye of a servant takes in every virtue."

Elizabeth now gave them to understand, in as guarded a manner as she could, that she had heard while visiting Charlotte that his character was by no means so faulty, nor Wickham's so upright as they had been led to believe, and that large sums—more than his due—had actually been granted Wickham.

Chapter Thirty-Five

The Darcys and the Bingleys Again

The next day Elizabeth, with her aunt and uncle, had been walking about the inn with some friends, and had returned to the inn to dress for dining with the same family, when they saw a carriage driving up the street. Elizabeth knew the livery and guessed what it meant. Her uncle and aunt were all surprise, and her manner as she spoke, joined to what they had seen, now opened to them a new idea on the business. They now felt that there was no other way of accounting for such attentions from Mr. Darcy than by supposing an interest in their niece.

Elizabeth felt herself so anxious to please the sister she feared that every power of pleasing would fail her. She walked up and down trying to compose herself, and saw such looks of surprise in her uncle and aunt as made everything worse.

Miss Darcy and her brother appeared, and this fearful introduction took place. To her surprise Elizabeth saw that Miss Darcy was at least as ill at ease as herself. She had heard that Miss Darcy was very proud, but a very few minutes convinced her that she was only very shy. It was hard to gain any talk from her beyond a word or two.

She was tall, larger than Elizabeth, and though little more than sixteen, her figure was well formed, womanly, and graceful. She was less handsome than her brother, but there was sense and good humor in her face, and her manners were modest and gentle.

They had not been long together before Darcy told her that Bingley was also coming to visit her. She had barely time to express her pleasure when his quick step was heard on the stairs, and in a moment he entered the room. All Elizabeth's anger against him had been long done away, but if she had still felt any, it could hardly have stood against the frank pleasure he showed in seeing her again. He asked in a friendly, though general way, about her family, and looked and spoke with the same good-humored ease as always.

Mr. and Mrs. Gardiner had long wished to see him, and the thought which had just arisen of Mr. Darcy and their niece caused them to turn toward each young man with an earnest though guarded inquiry. They soon saw that at least one of the young men knew what it was to love. Of Elizabeth's feelings they were a little in doubt, but that Mr. Darcy was overflowing with admiration was plain enough.

Elizabeth, on her side, had much to do. She wanted to understand the feelings of each of her visitors; she wanted to compose her own, and to make herself agreeable to all. But Bingley was ready, Georgiana was eager, and Darcy determined, to be pleased. On seeing Bingley, her thoughts naturally flew to her sister. She longed to know whether any of his thoughts were directed in a like manner. Sometimes she could fancy that he talked less than usual, and once or twice that he looked at her as if trying to trace a likeness to Jane. He once asked her, when all the rest were busy otherwise whether *all* her sisters were at Longbourn. There was not much in the question, but there was a look and a manner which gave it meaning. Between him and Miss Darcy, who had been set up as a rival to Jane, no look appeared on either side that spoke of particular regard.

It was not often that she could turn her eyes on Mr. Darcy, but whenever she did catch a glimpse, she saw a look of general pleasure. Never, even in the company of his friends at Netherfield or his dignified relations at Rosings, had she seen him so eager to please, so free from reserve. When they rose to leave, he called on his sister to join him in wishing to see Mr. and Mrs. Gardiner and Miss Bennet to dinner at Pemberley before they left the country. Miss Darcy, with a shyness that marked her little in the habit of giving invitations, readily obeyed, and the day after the next was fixed on.

Mr. and Mrs. Gardiner now saw that their niece was much better acquainted with Mr. Darcy than they had before any idea of; it was plain that he was very much in love with her. Of Mr. Darcy they now, therefore, wished to think well; and in what they had seen of him, there was no fault to find.

As for Elizabeth, her thoughts were at Pemberley on this evening more than on the last, and the evening was not long enough for her to decide what were her feelings toward *one* in that mansion. She lay awake two whole hours, trying to make them out. She certainly did not hate him. No, hatred had vanished long ago, and she had almost as long been ashamed of ever feeling a dislike against him. She now felt for him respect, esteem, good will, and even gratitude. Gratitude, not merely for having once loved her, but for loving her still well enough to forgive her manner in refusing him, and all the unjust words she had spoken at that time. He who, she had thought, would avoid her as his enemy, was eager for the good opinion of her friends and bent on making her known to his sister. Such a change in a man of so much pride excited her gratitude—for to love, ardent love, it must be attributed.

It had been settled in the evening between the aunt and niece that Miss Darcy's courtesy in coming to them on the very day of her arrival at Pemberley, ought to be returned. They were, therefore, to call on her at Pemberley the following morning. Elizabeth was pleased, though when she asked herself the reason, she had very little to say in reply. Mr. Gardiner left them soon after breakfast. Fishing plans had been made the day before, and he was to meet some of the gentlemen at Pemberley.

Elizabeth, knowing as she now did that Miss Bingley's dislike of her had been caused by jealousy, could not help feeling that Miss Bingley would not be pleased to see her at Pemberley. On reaching the house, they were met by Miss Darcy, who was sitting with Mrs. Hurst, Miss Bingley, and Mrs. Annesley, the lady with whom she lived in London. Georgiana's welcome was very kind, but timid from shyness and fear of doing wrong. Mrs. Hurst and Miss Bingley welcomed them only by a curtsey. On their being seated, there was a pause, awkward as such pauses must always be. It was first broken by Mrs. Annesley, a genteel, agreeable-looking woman, and between her and Mrs. Gardiner, with some help from Elizabeth, the talk was carried on. Georgiana Darcy looked as if she wished for courage to join in, and sometimes did venture a short sentence when there was least danger of its being heard. At last Elizabeth received a cold inquiry from Miss Bingley about the health of her family. She answered with equal brevity, and the other said no more.

Servants entered with cold meat, cake, and a variety of all the finest fruits, but this did not take place till after many a meaning look and smile from Mrs. Annesley to Georgiana, to remind her of her post. There was now occupation for the whole party; for though they could not all talk, they could all eat, and the beautiful heaps of grapes, nectarines, and peaches soon collected them round the table.

Elizabeth hardly knew whether she had most feared or wished for the appearance of Mr. Darcy. But on his entering the room, though only a moment before she had wished to see him, she began to regret that he came. He had been some time with the fishermen by the river, and had left them on learning from Mr. Gardiner that the ladies of his family intended to visit Georgiana that morning.

Elizabeth now made an effort to be entirely at ease, a state of mind not easily kept; because she saw the attention of the whole party directed toward them and that they became watchful of his behavior from the moment he came into the room. Miss Darcy exerted herself much more to talk. Elizabeth saw that he was anxious for his sister and herself to get to know each other, and helped forward the talk between them as much as possible. Miss Bingley saw all this likewise, and took the first opening to say with sneering politeness:

"Miss Elizabeth, are not the militia gone from Meryton? They must be a great loss to *your* family."

In Darcy's presence she dared not mention Wickham's name, but Elizabeth knew that she was thinking of him, and she had a moment's distress at the ill-natured attack but was able to answer in a calm tone. While she spoke, a glance showed her Darcy with a higher color earnestly looking at her, and his sister overcome with confusion and unable to lift up her eyes. Miss Bingley had not known what pain she would be giving her beloved friend, but had intended only to attack Elizabeth by reminding Darcy of all the follies by which some of the Bennet family were connected with that regiment. She had never heard of Georgiana Darcy's intended elopement. To no person had it been told where secrecy was possible, except to Elizabeth.

Their visit did not last long, and while Mr. Darcy went with them to their carriage, Miss Bingley spoke her opinion of Elizabeth's person, behavior, and dress. But Georgiana would not join her. Her brother's liking was enough to gain her favor; his judgment could not err, and he had spoken in such praise of Elizabeth as to leave Georgiana no power to find her otherwise than lovely and charming. When he returned to the room, Miss Bingley could not help saying:

"How very ill Elizabeth Bennet looks this morning. I never in my life saw anyone so much altered as she is since the winter. She is grown so brown and coarse! Louisa and I were saying that we should not have known her again."

Mr. Darcy replied coolly that he saw no other change than her being rather tanned from traveling in the summer.

"Well, for my part," she said, "I never could see any beauty in her. Her face it too thin; her skin has no brightness, and her features are not at all handsome. Her nose lacks character. And as for her eyes, which have sometimes been called so fine, I could never see anything unusual in them. They have a sharp, shrewish look, which I do not like at all."

Mr. Darcy looked somewhat nettled but remained silent.

"I remember when we first knew her how amazed we all were to find that she was supposed to be a beauty. I recollect your saying one night, after they had been dining at Netherfield, 'She a beauty! I should as soon call her mother a wit!' But afterward she seemed to grow on you, and I believe you thought her rather pretty at one time."

"Yes," replied Darcy, "but *that* was only when I first knew her. Now I think her one of the handsomest women I know."

He then went away, and Miss Bingley was left to all the pleasure of having forced him to say what gave no one any pain but herself.

Mrs. Gardiner and Elizabeth talked as they returned of all that had passed during their visit, and of everybody they had seen there, except the person who was most in their mind. They talked of his sister, his friends, his house, his fruit, of everything but himself. Yet Elizabeth was longing to know what Mrs. Gardiner thought of him, and Mrs. Gardiner would have been highly pleased by her niece's beginning the subject.

Chapter Thirty-Six

Distressing News from Home

Elizabeth had been a good deal disappointed not to find a letter from Jane on their first arrival at Lambton inn, and this disappointment had been renewed each of the mornings that had now been spent there. But on the third, she received two letters from her, one of which was marked that it had been mis-sent elsewhere. Elizabeth was not surprised at it, as Jane had written the direction very ill. They had just been starting to walk as the letters came in, and her uncle and aunt, leaving her to enjoy them in quiet, set off by themselves. She read first the mis-sent letter, written five days ago:

Dearest Lizzy, something has taken place of a most serious nature. I am afraid of alarming you—we are all well. What I have to say is about poor Lydia. A message came at twelve last night, just as we were all gone to bed, from Colonel Forster, to say that she has gone off to Scotland with one of his officers. To own the truth, with Wickham! I am very, very sorry. So reckless a match on both sides! But I am willing to hope for the best, that he has been misunderstood. At least he has not married her for money, for he must know my father can give her nothing. How thankful I am that we never let our father and mother know what has been said against him! We must forget it ourselves. They were off Saturday night about twelve, it is thought, but were not missed till yesterday morning at eight. The message to us was sent off at once. Lydia left a few lines for Mrs. Forster, speaking of her purpose to elope with Wickham. I must stop, for I cannot be long from my poor mother. I am afraid you will not be able to make it out, but I hardly know what I have written.

On finishing this letter, Elizabeth seized the other, and hastily opening it, read as follows (it had been written a day later than the first one):

Dearest Lizzy, I hardly know what I should write, but I have bad news for you. Reckless as a marriage between Mr. Wickham and our poor Lydia would be, we are now anxious to know that a marriage has taken place. Colonel Forster came yesterday, not many hours after his message. Though Lydia's short letter to Mrs. Forster gave them to understand that they were going to Gretna Green,[1] Wickham's friend Denny says that he does not believe Wickham ever intended to go there or to marry Lydia at all. All that is known is that they were seen on the London road. I know not what to think. Our distress, my dear Lizzy, is very great. My father and mother believe the worst, but I cannot think so ill of Wickham. Many things might make it better for them to be married privately in London than to follow their first plan to go to Gretna Green. I grieve to say that Colonel Forster does not depend upon their marriage; he shook his head when I

---

[1] A village in Scotland to which couples eloped from England, to be married.

spoke of my hopes, and said he feared Wickham was not a man to be trusted. My poor mother is really ill and keeps to her room. As to my father, I never in my life saw him so troubled. Poor Kitty is being blamed for having kept their attachment a secret, but as they had asked her to do so, one cannot wonder. I cannot help earnestly begging you all to come here as soon as possible. I know my dear uncle and aunt so well that I am not afraid to ask it. My father is going to London with Colonel Forster to try to find her. Colonel Forster must be at Brighton again tomorrow evening. In such trouble, my uncle's advice and help would be everything in the world.

"Oh! where is my uncle?" cried Elizabeth darting from her seat as she finished the letter. But as she reached the door, it was opened by a servant, and Mr. Darcy came in and started at sight of her pale face and distressed manner. She, in whose mind could be no thought but of Lydia, hastily cried, "I beg your pardon, but I must leave you. I must find Mr. Gardiner this moment on business that cannot be delayed; I have not an instant to lose."

"Good God! what is the matter?" cried he with more feeling than politeness. "Let me, or let the servant go after Mr. and Mrs. Gardiner. You are not well enough; you cannot go yourself."

Elizabeth's knees trembled under her, and she felt how little would be gained by going herself. Calling back the servant, therefore, she told him in breathless words to fetch her uncle and aunt at once. Then she sat down, looking so miserably ill that Darcy said in a tone of gentleness and pity:

"Let me call your maid. Is there nothing you could take to relieve you?—a glass of wine? shall I get you one? You are very ill."

"No, I thank you," she replied, trying to recover herself. "There is nothing the matter with me. I am quite well. I am only distressed by some dreadful news which I have just had from home."

She burst into tears and for a few minutes could not speak another word. Darcy could only wait in pitying silence. At length, she spoke again. "I have just had a letter from Jane, with such dreadful news. It cannot be kept from anyone. My youngest sister has eloped with—with Mr. Wickham. They are gone off together from Brighton. *You* know him too well to doubt the rest. She has no money, nothing that can tempt him to—marry her."

Darcy was fixed in amazement. "When I think," she added, in a yet more distressed voice, "that *I* might have prevented it! *I* knew what he was. If I had but explained some part of what I learned, to my own family! But it is all, all too late now."

"I am grieved, indeed," cried Darcy, "grieved—shocked. But is it certain?"

"Oh, yes! They left Brighton together on Sunday night and were traced almost to London, but not beyond. My father is gone to London, and Jane has written to beg my uncle to come at once. We shall be off, I hope, in half an hour. But nothing can be done; I know very well that nothing can be done. How are they even to be found? It is every way horrible!"

Darcy shook his head in silent agreement, but he seemed scarcely to hear her. He was walking up and down the room, his brow frowning, his air gloomy. Elizabeth saw and thought she understood. Her power was sinking; everything *must* sink under this deepest family disgrace. Covering her face with her handkerchief, she was soon lost to everything else but grief for Lydia.

At last Darcy spoke, in a manner which showed grief for her, but likewise restraint. "I am afraid you have been long wishing me gone. Would to heaven that anything could be either said or done on my part that might help such distress. But I will not torment you with vain wishes. This unfortunate affair will, I fear, prevent my sister's seeing you at Pemberley today."

"Oh, yes. Be so kind as to apologize for us to Miss Darcy. Say that urgent business calls us home at once. Conceal the unhappy truth as long as it is possible. I know it cannot be long."

He gave his promise of secrecy, again expressed his sorrow for her distress, wished it a happier end than there was at present reason to hope, and with one serious, parting look, went away.

She saw him go with regret, and in this early example of what Lydia's act must produce, found additional grief. Never, since reading Jane's second letter, had she had a hope of Wickham's meaning to marry Lydia. No one but Jane, she thought, could flatter herself with such a hope.

She had never noticed that Lydia had any regard for Wickham, but she knew that Lydia had wanted only encouragement to attach herself to anybody. Sometimes one officer, sometimes another, had been her favorite, as their attentions raised them in her opinion. Her affections had flitted from one to another, but there was always someone.

Elizabeth was wild to be at home—to share with Jane in the cares that must now fall wholly upon her, with a father absent, and a mother helpless.

Mr. and Mrs. Gardiner had hurried back in alarm, supposing by the servant's account that their niece was taken suddenly ill. When Elizabeth read the two letters aloud, though Lydia had never been a favorite with them, they were filled with horror by the news. Not Lydia only, but all were concerned in it. Mr. Gardiner promised every help in his power. Elizabeth, though expecting no less, thanked him with tears of gratitude. At the end of an hour they were on the road to Longbourn.

"I have been thinking it over again, Elizabeth," said her uncle as they drove from the town. "It is unlikely that any young man would elope without marriage with a girl of family, and who was actually staying in his colonel's home."

"Do you really think so?" cried Elizabeth, brightening up for a moment.

"I think so too," said Mrs. Gardiner. "It would be too great a violation of honor and self interest. I cannot think so ill of Wickham. Can you yourself, Lizzy, believe him capable of it?"

"Not of forgetting his own interest. But of every other lack of honor I can believe him capable."

"They may have gone to London for lack of money to take them to Gretna Green. It might strike them that they could be married in London at less cost."

"But why all the secrecy? Why must their marriage be private? Oh, no, no, this is not likely. And his particular friend Denny, you see by Jane's letter, did not believe he ever intended to marry her. Wickham will never marry a woman without some money. He cannot afford it. And what attractions has Lydia beyond youth, health, and good humor that could make him give up the chance of marrying well?"

"But can you think that Lydia is so lost to everything but love of him as to be willing to live with him on any other terms than marriage?"

"Really," replied Elizabeth with tears in her eyes, "I do not know what to say. Perhaps I am not doing her justice. But she is very young, and has been allowed to spend her time in the most idle and heedless manner. Since the regiment has been quartered in Meryton, nothing but love, flirtation, and officers has been in her head. And we all know that Wickham has every charm of manner that can win a woman."

"But Jane does not think so ill of him."

"Of whom does Jane ever think ill? But Jane knows as well as I do what Wickham really is. We both know that he has no honesty or honor, that he is as false as he is deceitful."

"And do you really *know* all this?" cried Mrs. Gardiner, wondering how she had learned it.

"I do, indeed," replied Elizabeth, coloring. "I told you the other day of his behavior to Mr. Darcy, which I am not at liberty to tell you in detail. His lies about the whole Pemberley family are endless. From what he said of Miss Darcy, I expected to see a proud, disagreeable girl. Yet he must know that she is as gentle and unpretending as we have found her."

"But does Lydia know nothing of all this that you and Jane seem so well to understand?"

"Oh, no—that is the worst of all. Till I visited Charlotte at Hunsford, where I saw so much of Mr. Darcy, I did not know the truth myself. And when I returned home, I told only Jane. I had no reason to believe that Lydia and Wickham would ever be fond of each other. When first he came into the regiment she was ready enough to admire him, but so were we all. Every girl in or near Meryton was out of her senses about him for the first two months. But he never paid *her* any marked attention, and after a time her fancy for him gave way, and others of the regiment who gave her more attention became her favorites."

Chapter Thirty-Seven

Mr. Collins Writes a Letter of Sympathy

They traveled as rapidly as possible and, sleeping one night on the road, reached Longbourn by dinner time the next day. The little Gardiners were standing on the steps of the house when the carriage drove up to the door. The joyful surprise that lighted up their faces and showed itself in capers and frisks was the first pleasing sign of welcome. Elizabeth jumped out, and, after giving each of them a hasty kiss, hurried into the hall, where Jane came running downstairs from her mother's room to meet them.

Mrs. Bennet, as might be expected, received them with tears and moans of regret, abuses of Wickham, and complaints of her own sufferings and ill-usage. "If I had been able," she said, "to carry my point of going to Brighton with all my family, *this* would not have happened. But poor dear Lydia had nobody to take care of her. Why did the Forsters ever let her go out of their sight? I am sure there was some great neglect on their side, for she is not the kind of a girl to do such a thing if she had been well looked after. I always thought they were very unfit to have the charge of her, but I was overruled as I always am. Poor dear child! And now here's Mr. Bennet gone away, and I know he will fight Wickham and then he will be killed, and what is to become of us all? The Collinses will turn us out before he is cold in his grave."

Mr. Gardiner told her that he meant to be in London the very next day. "And as soon as I get to town, I shall make him come home with me to Gracechurch Street, and then we may plan together what is to be done."

"And when you get to town," said Mrs. Bennet, "find them, wherever they may be, and if they are not married already, *make* them marry. As for wedding clothes, do not let them wait for that, but tell Lydia she shall have as much money as she chooses to buy them, after they are married. And above all things, keep Mr. Bennet from fighting. Tell him what a dreadful state I am in, that I am frightened out of my wits and have such tremblings, such flutterings all over me, such spasms in my side and pains in my head, and such beating at my heart that I can get no rest by night or day. Oh, brother, how kind you are! I know you will manage it all."

In the afternoon when Elizabeth had a half hour with Jane alone, she asked, "Did Colonel Forster appear to think ill of Wickham himself? Does he know his real character?"

"He did not speak so well of him as he formerly did. He believed him to be reckless and extravagant. It is said that he left Meryton greatly in debt, but I hope this may be false."

"Oh, Jane, if we had told what we knew of him, this could not have happened! My poor father! how he must have felt it!"

"I never saw anyone so shocked. He could not speak a word, and my mother was taken ill at once and the whole house in such confusion!"

"It has been too much for you. You do not look well. You have had every care and anxiety upon yourself alone."

"Mary and Kitty have been very kind, and Aunt Philips came on Tuesday, after my father went away, and stayed till Thursday with me. She was a great comfort to us. And Lady Lucas has been very kind; she walked here on Wednesday morning to offer her help or any of her daughters, if they could be of use to us."

"She had better have stayed at home," cried Elizabeth. "Perhaps she *meant* well, but under such a misfortune as this, one cannot see too little of one's neighbors. They can be no help,

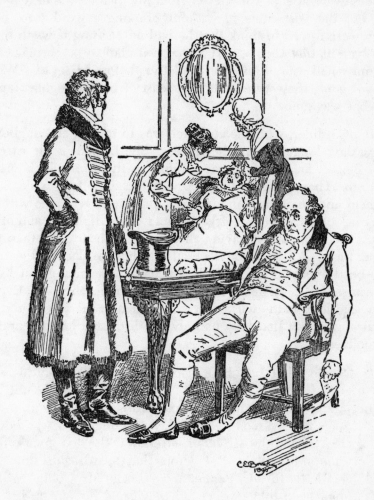

and sympathy is unbearable. Let them triumph over us at a distance and be satisfied."

They were in hopes of a letter from Mr. Bennet the next morning, but the post came in without bringing a word from him. They were forced to think that he had no pleasing news to send, but even of *that* they would have been glad to be certain. Mr. Gardiner had waited only for the letters before he set off. When he was gone, they were certain at least of having regular report of what was going on.

Mrs. Gardiner, with the children, was to remain at Longbourn a few days longer, to aid her nieces. She helped in the care of Mrs. Bennet and was a great comfort to them in their hours of freedom. Their Aunt Philips also visited them often, as she said, to cheer and hearten them up, though as she never came without bringing some fresh news of Wickham's waste of money and other faults, she went away leaving them more disheartened than she found them. All Meryton seemed striving to blacken the man who but three months before had been almost an angel of light. He was said to be in debt to every tradesman in the place. Everybody said he was the wickedest young man in the world, and all began to find out that they had always distrusted his appearance of goodness.

Mr. Gardiner left Longbourn on Sunday; on Tuesday his wife had a letter from him. It told them that he had sought out Mr. Bennet and persuaded him to come to his home. He promised to write again very soon. Every day at Longbourn was now a day of anxiety, and the arrival of letters was the first great object of every morning's affair. But before they heard again from Mr. Gardiner, a letter for Mr. Bennet arrived from Mr. Collins, which, as Jane had been told to open all that came for him in his absence, she opened and read. It was as follows:

My dear Sir:

I feel called upon, by our kinship and my situation in life, to condole with you on the great trouble you are now suffering under. We learned of this yesterday by a letter from Lady Lucas. Be sure, my dear sir, that Mrs. Collins and myself sympathize with you and all your family in your present distress, which must be of the bitterest kind. The death of your daughter would have been a blessing compared to this. My dear Charlotte tells me that this misbehavior of your daughter has come from too much freedom granted her by you and Mrs. Bennet. But I am inclined to think that her character must be naturally bad, or she could not be guilty of such evil at so early an age. However that may be, you are greatly to be pitied. In this opinion I am joined by Mrs. Collins and by Lady Catherine and her daughter, to whom I have related the affair. They agree with me in thinking that this false step in one daughter will injure the fortunes of all the others. For who, as Lady Catherine herself says, will connect themselves with such a family? And this leads me to think on a certain event of last November, when I was near to being involved in all your sorrow and disgrace. Let me advise you, my dear sir, to console yourself as much as possible, and throw off your unworthy child for ever. I am, dear sir, etc., etc.

When Mr. Gardiner wrote again, he had nothing of a pleasant nature to send. It was not known, he stated, that Wickham had a single relation with whom he kept up connection, and it was certain that he had no near kin living. It did not appear that he was on terms of close friendship with any of the officers of the regiment. There was no one, therefore, who would be likely to know of his whereabouts. His debts would be a strong reason for his hiding himself. Colonel Forster reported that more than a thousand pounds would be needed to clear his debts at Brighton, where he owed a good deal to tradesmen, and had gambling debts still larger. He added that they might expect to see Mr. Bennet at home on the following day, which was Saturday. He had at last agreed to return home and leave his brother-in-law to do what might be done.

"What, is he coming home, and without poor Lydia!" cried

Mrs. Bennet. "Surely he will not leave London before he has found them. Who is to fight Wickham and make him marry her, if he comes away?"

As Mrs. Gardiner began to wish to be at home, it was settled that she and her children should travel to London in the coach that was to bring its master back to Longbourn. Mrs. Gardiner went away still in doubt about Elizabeth and her Pemberley friend. His name had never been mentioned again by her niece, and the letters which Mrs. Gardiner had half expected to follow them to Longbourn did not come. Elizabeth had received none since her return that could have come from Pemberley.

When Mr. Bennet arrived, he seemed to have all his usual composure. He said as little as he had ever been in the habit of saying, made no mention of the business that had taken him away, and it was some time before his daughters had courage to speak of it. It was not till the afternoon, when he joined them at tea, that Elizabeth ventured to speak on the subject. Then she spoke only of her sorrow for what he must have endured. He replied, "Say nothing of that. Who should suffer but myself? It has been my own doing, and I ought to feel it."

"You must not be too severe upon yourself," replied Elizabeth.

"No, Lizzy, let me once in my life feel how much I have been to blame. I am not afraid of being over-powered by it. It will pass away soon enough." At this moment Jane came for her mother's tea. "This is a parade," he cried, "which does one good; it gives such a state to misfortune! Another day I will do the same. I will sit in my library, in my dressing gown, and give as much trouble as I can. Or maybe I shall wait till Kitty runs away."

"I am not going to run away, papa," said Kitty, fretfully. "If *I* should ever go to Brighton, I would behave better than Lydia."

"*You* go to Brighton! No, Kitty, I have at last learned to be cautious, and you will feel the effects of it. No officer is ever to enter this house again. You shall go to no balls, unless you dance with one of your sisters. And you are never to stir out of doors

till you can prove that you have spent ten minutes every day in a
sensible manner."

Kitty, who took all these threats in a serious light, began to cry.

"Well, well," said he, "do not make yourself unhappy. If you
are a good girl for the next ten years, I will take you to a review
at the end of them."

Chapter Thirty-Eight

Good News at Last!

Next day as Jane and Elizabeth were walking together in the
shrubbery behind the house, the housekeeper came to say that
a letter had come from Mr. Gardiner. Away ran the girls through
the hall, into the breakfast-room, thence to the library. Their
father was in neither place. They were on the point of seeking
him upstairs with their mother, when they were met by the but-
ler, who said: "If you are looking for the master, he is walking
toward the little grove."

They ran through the hall once more and across the lawn after
their father, who was slowly walking toward a small wood. Jane,
who was not so light nor so much in the habit of running as Elizabeth, soon lagged behind, while her sister, panting for breath,
came up to him, and eagerly cried out: "Oh, papa, what news?
What news? Is it good or bad?"

"What is there of good to be expected?" said he, taking the
letter from his pocket. "But perhaps you would like to read it."

Elizabeth caught it from his hand. Jane now came up. "Read
it aloud," said their father, "for I hardly know myself what it is
about."

> Gracechurch Street, Monday,
> August 2.

My dear Brother,

Soon after you left me on Saturday, I was able to find out in what part of London your daughter is. I have seen them both. They are not married, but if you are willing to carry out a contract, which I have ventured to make on your behalf, I hope it will not be long before they are. You are to give your daughter her equal share of the five thousand pounds which will come to your children after the death of yourself and wife. And you are to allow her during your life one hundred pounds a year. It seems that Wickham's debts are not so great as generally believed to be. I am happy to say there will be some little money, even when all are paid, to settle on my niece. If you send me full powers to act in your name, there will not be the smallest need for you to come to town again. Send back your answer as soon as you can, and be careful to write fully. My niece is to be married from my house. She comes to us today. I shall write again as soon as anything more is decided on.

> Yours, etc.
> Edw. Gardiner.

"And have you answered the letter?" asked Elizabeth.

"No, but it must be done soon."

"Oh, my dear father," she cried, "come back and write at once. Think how important every moment is in such a case."

"Let me write for you," said Jane, "if you dislike the trouble yourself."

"I dislike it very much," he replied, "but it must be done." And so saying, he turned back with them and walked toward the house.

"The terms," said Elizabeth, "I suppose must be met."

"Met! I am only ashamed of his asking so little. But there are two things that I want very much to know: one is how much money your uncle has laid down, and the other is how I am ever to pay him. No man in his senses would marry Lydia for such a small sum as one hundred a year during my life, and fifty after I am gone."

"That is very true," said Elizabeth, "though I had not thought of it before. His debts paid and something still to remain! Oh! it must be my uncle's doing! Generous, good man, I am afraid he has robbed himself. A small sum could not do all this."

"No," said her father, "Wickham's a fool if he takes her with less than ten thousand pounds. I should be sorry to think so ill of him, in the very beginning of our connection."

"Ten thousand pounds! Heaven forbid! How is half such a sum to be repaid?"

Mr. Bennet made no answer, and each of them, deep in thought, kept silent till they reached the house. Their father then went to the library to write, and the girls walked into the breakfast-room. They now wondered whether their mother knew of what had happened. They went to the library and asked their father if they should make it known to her. He was writing and, without raising his head, coolly replied:

"Just as you please."

"May we take my uncle's letter to read to her?"

"Take whatever you like, and get away."

Elizabeth took the letter from his writing-table, and they went upstairs together. Mary and Kitty were both with Mrs. Bennet. After a slight preparation for good news, the letter was read aloud. Mrs. Bennet could hardly contain herself. As soon as Jane had read Mr. Gardiner's hope of Lydia's being married soon, her joy burst forth.

"She will be married!" she cried. "She will be married at sixteen! My good, kind brother! I knew how it would be—I knew he would manage everything. How I long to see her, and to see dear Wickham too! But the clothes, the wedding clothes! I will write to my sister Gardiner about them at once. Lizzy, run down to your father and ask him how much he will give her. But stay, I will go myself. Ring the bell, Kitty, for Hill. I will put on my things in a moment. My dear, dear Lydia! How merry we shall be together when we meet!"

"We believe," said Jane, "that Uncle Gardiner has pledged himself to assist Mr. Wickham with money."

"Well," cried her mother, "it is all very right. Who should do it but her own uncle? If he had not had a family of his own, I and my children must have had all his money, you know, and it is the first time we have ever had anything from him except a few presents. Well! I am so happy. In a short time, I shall have a daughter married. Mrs. Wickham! How well it sounds. And she was only sixteen last June. I will go to Meryton as soon as I am dressed and tell the good, good news to my sister Philips. And as I come back, I can call on Lady Lucas and Mrs. Long. Kitty, run down and order the carriage. An airing would do me a great deal of good, I am sure. Oh, here comes Hill. My dear Hill, have you heard the good news? Miss Lydia is going to be married!"

Mr. Bennet's letter was soon written. He begged to know the full amount of what he owed his brother-in-law, but he was too angry with Lydia to send any message to her. He had often wished that instead of spending his whole income he had laid by a yearly sum for his children and his wife, if she outlived him. He now wished it more than ever. Had he done so, the duty of persuading one of the most worthless men in Great Britain to be Lydia's husband might have rested in its proper place. But he was determined to find out, if possible, how much his brother-in-law had paid, and to repay him as soon as possible.

The good news quickly spread through the house and with the same speed passed through the neighborhood. The good-wishes for Lydia's well-doing which had been heard before from all the spiteful old ladies in Meryton lost little of their spirit in this change of fortune because, with such a husband, her misery was considered certain. To be sure, however, it would have been more for the interest of talk, had Miss Lydia Bennet been thrown upon charity or, better still, been secluded from the world in some distant farmhouse.

It had been two weeks since Mrs. Bennet had been downstairs, but on this happy day she again took her seat at the head of her table, and in high spirits. She was busily searching through the neighborhood for a proper home for her daughter, and without knowing what their income might be, passed over many as not good enough.

"Haye Park might do," she said, "if the Gouldings would move out—or the great house at Stoke, if the drawing-room were larger. But Ashworth is too far off! I could not bear to have her ten miles from me. As for Purvis Lodge, the attics are dreadful."

Her husband allowed her to talk on while the servants remained. But when they had withdrawn, he said to her, "Mrs. Bennet, before you take any or all these houses for your son and daughter, let us come to a right understanding. Into *one* house in this neighborhood they shall never come. I will not have either of them at Longbourn."

A long dispute followed, but Mr. Bennet was firm. It soon led to another; Mrs. Bennet found to her amazement and horror that her husband would not advance a penny to buy wedding clothes for his daughter.

Elizabeth was now most heartily sorry that she had, from the distress of the moment, been led to tell Mr. Darcy of their fears for her sister. Since Lydia's marriage would so shortly give the proper end to the elopement, they might hope to conceal it from all those who were not on the spot. She had no fear of its spreading farther through his means, but at the same time, there was no one whose knowledge of it would have wounded her so much. His wish to gain her regard, which she had believed he had shown, could not survive such a blow as this. She was humbled; she was grieved; she repented, though she hardly knew of what. She longed for his esteem, now that she could no longer hope for it. She wanted to hear of him when there seemed the least chance of doing so. She was convinced that she could have been happy with him, when it was no longer likely they should meet.

What a triumph for him, as she often thought, could he know that the proposal which she had spurned only four months ago would now have been gladly and gratefully received! He was

generous, she doubted not, but while he was mortal, there must
be a triumph. She now began to understand that he was exactly
the man who would most suit her. His understanding and temper, though unlike her own, would have answered all her wishes.
By her ease and liveliness, his mind might have been softened,
his manners improved. And from his judgment and knowledge of
the world, she must have received benefit of greater importance.
But no such happy union could now teach the admiring world
what a perfect marriage really was.

Chapter Thirty-Nine

Lydia Bennet Is Married

Mr. Gardiner soon replied to Mr. Bennet's letter, and asked that
the cost of marriage settlement never be mentioned to him again.
"Mr. Wickham," he wrote, "has the promise of a post in a regiment now quartered in the North. It is an advantage to have it
so far away; and I hope that among different people, they will
both be more prudent. I have written to Colonel Forster asking
him to assure the various creditors of Mr. Wickham in and near
Brighton of speedy payment. And will you give yourself the
trouble to see his creditors in Meryton, of whom I enclose a list
according to his report, and give them the same assurance?
Wickham has given in all his debts; I hope, at least, that he has
not deceived us. Lydia wishes to see you all before she leaves for
the North. She is well and begs to be remembered to you and
her mother. Yours etc.   Edw. Gardiner."

Elizabeth and Jane agreed in wishing for the sake of all that
Lydia should be noticed on her marriage by her parents. Mr.
Bennet was persuaded to act as they wished. And their mother

had the pleasure of knowing that she should be able to show her married daughter in the neighborhood before she was banished to the North. When Mr. Bennet wrote again to his brother-in-law, therefore, he sent his permission for them to come, and it was settled that as soon as the marriage ceremony was over they should proceed to Longbourn. Elizabeth was surprised, however, that Wickham should agree to such a plan, and had she followed her own wishes, any meeting with him would have been avoided.

The wedding day arrived, and Jane and Elizabeth felt for Lydia probably more than she felt for herself. The carriage was sent to meet them, and they were to return in it by dinner-time. Their arrival was dreaded by both Jane and Elizabeth, and by Jane especially, who gave Lydia the feeling which she would have had herself had she been the culprit, and was wretched in the thought of what Lydia must endure.

They came. The family were gathered in the breakfast room to receive them. Smiles decked the face of Mrs. Bennet as the carriage drove up to the door. Her husband looked grave; her daughters alarmed, anxious, uneasy.

Lydia's voice was heard in the hall; the door was thrown open, and she ran into the room. Her mother stepped forward, embraced her, and welcomed her with rapture. She gave her hand with an affectionate smile to Wickham, and wished them both joy. Mr. Bennet, to whom they then turned, scarcely opened his lips. The easy manner of the young couple was indeed enough to provoke him. Lydia was Lydia still, untamed, wild, noisy, and fearless. She turned from sister to sister, for their good wishes, and when they all sat down, looked eagerly round the room, took notice of some little changes in it, and said with a laugh that it was a long while since she had been there. Wickham was at ease also. Elizabeth sat down thinking that there were no limits to the impudence of an impudent man. *She* blushed, and Jane blushed; but the cheeks of the two who caused their blushes did not change color.

There was no want of talk. The bride and her mother could

neither of them talk fast enough, and Wickham, who happened to sit near Elizabeth, began asking about affairs in that neighborhood with good-humored ease. They seemed each of them to have the happiest memories in the world.

"Only think of its being three months," Lydia cried, "since I went away. It seems but a fortnight, I declare. And yet there have been things enough happened in the time. Good gracious! when I went away, I am sure I had no idea of being married till I came back again! Oh mama, do the people hereabout know I am married? I was afraid they might not. We overtook William Goulding in his carriage, so I let down the side glass next to him, and took off my glove, and let my hand rest upon the window-frame so that he might see the ring, and then I bowed and smiled like anything."

Elizabeth could bear it no longer. She got up and ran out of the room, and returned no more till she heard them passing through the hall to the dining-parlor. She then joined them soon enough to see Lydia walk up to her mother's right hand, and hear her say, "Ah, Jane, I take your place now, and you must go lower, because I am a married woman."

Her ease and good spirits grew. She longed to see Mrs. Philips, the Lucases, and all their other neighbors, and to hear herself called "Mrs. Wickham" by each of them. In the meantime she went, after dinner, to show her ring, and boast of being married, to Mrs. Hill and the two housemaids.

"Well, mama," she said, when they were all returned to the breakfast-room, "and what do you think of my husband? Is he not a charming man? I am sure my sisters must all envy me. They must all go to Brighton. That is the place to get husbands. What a pity it is we did not all go."

"Very true. And if I had my will, we should. But I don't at all like your going such a way off. Must it be so?"

"Oh, Lord, yes. There is nothing in that. You and papa, and my sisters, must all come and see us. We shall be at Newcastle all the winter and I dare say there will be some balls, and I will take care to get good partners for them all. And when you go away, you may leave one or two of my sisters behind you; I dare say I shall get husbands for them before the winter is over."

"I should like it beyond anything!" said her mother.

Their visitors were not to remain longer than ten days with them; Mr. Wickham was to join his regiment at the end of that time. No one but Mrs. Bennet regretted that their stay would be so short. She made the most of the time by visiting about with her daughter and having very frequent parties at home. The parties were agreeable to all; at least they helped to avoid a family circle.

Wickham's affection for Lydia was just what Elizabeth had expected to find it, not equal to Lydia's for him. She might have wondered why, without greatly caring for Lydia, he had eloped with her at all, but she felt certain his flight was made necessary by pressing debts, and he was not the young man to resist the chance of having a companion. Lydia was very fond of him. He was her dear Wickham; he did everything best in the world; she was sure he would kill more birds on the first of September than would anybody else in the country.

One morning soon after their arrival, as she was sitting with her two elder sisters, she said to Elizabeth:

"Lizzy, I never gave *you* an account of my wedding, I believe. You were not by when I told mama and the others all about it. Don't you want to hear about it?"

"No, really," said Elizabeth, "I think there cannot be too little said on the subject."

"La! You are so strange! But I must tell you how it went off. We were married, you know, at St. Clement's, because Wickham's lodgings were in that parish. We were all to be there by eleven o'clock. My uncle and aunt and I were to go together, and the others were to meet us at the church. Well, Monday morning came, and I was in such a fuss! I was so afraid, you know, that something would happen to put it off, and then I should have gone quite distracted. And there was my aunt, all the time I was dressing, preaching and talking away just as if she was reading a sermon. However, I did not hear more than one word in ten, for

I was thinking, you may suppose, of my dear Wickham. I longed to know whether he would be married in his blue coat. Well, and so we had breakfast at ten as usual; I thought it would never be over—for, by the by, you are to understand that my uncle and aunt were horrid unpleasant all the time I was with them. If you'll believe me, I did not once put my foot out of doors, though I was there two weeks. Not one party, or anything. Well, and so just as the carriage came to the door, my uncle was called away upon business to that horrid man Mr. Stone. Well, I was so frightened I did not know what to do, for my uncle was to give me away. Then I remembered that if he should be late, the wedding need not be put off, for Mr. Darcy might have done as well."

"Mr. Darcy!" cried Elizabeth in utter amazement.

"Oh, yes! He was to come there with Wickham, you know. But, gracious me! I quite forgot! I ought not to have said a word about it. I promised them so faithfully! What will Wickham say? It was to be such a secret!"

"If it was to be secret," said Jane, "say not another word on the subject."

"Oh, certainly," said Elizabeth, though burning with curiosity. "We will ask you no questions."

"Thank you," said Lydia, "for if you did, I should certainly tell you all, and then Wickham would be angry."

On such an invitation to ask, Elizabeth was forced to put it out of her power by running away.

Mr. Darcy had been at Lydia's wedding! It was exactly a scene, and exactly among people, where he would have no wish to go. Guesses as to the meaning of it, rapid and wild, hurried into her brain, but she was satisfied with none. Hastily she wrote a short letter to her aunt Gardiner, asking an explanation of what Lydia had chanced to tell.

"You may readily understand," she added, "how I long to know why a stranger to our family should have been among you at such a time. Pray write at once and let me understand it—unless it is to remain secret, as Lydia seemed to think."

Jane's sense of honor would not allow her to speak to Elizabeth privately of what Lydia had let fall, and Elizabeth was glad of it; until she herself could have a better understanding of the affair, she had rather not speak of it, even to Jane.

Chapter Forty

Mrs. Gardiner's Letter

Mrs. Gardiner replied to Elizabeth's letter at once. Elizabeth, when she received it, hurried into the little grove, where she could be alone. She sat down on one of the benches and prepared to be happy, for the length of the letter told her that it carried the news she asked for.

Gracechurch Street, Sept. 6

My dear Niece,

I must say that I am surprised that *you* asked what I have to tell you. I did not expect it from *you,* for I supposed you would not need to ask. Your uncle is as much surprised as I am. Nothing but the belief of your being a party concerned would have allowed him to act as he has done. But if you really do not know, I must be more plain.

On the very day of my coming home from Longbourn, your uncle had a most unexpected visitor. Mr. Darcy called, and was shut up with him several hours. He came to say that he had found out where Lydia and Mr. Wickham were, and that he had talked with them both, with Wickham several times, with Lydia once. From what I can learn, he left Pemberley only one day after we left, and came to town to hunt for them. He said that he blamed himself that Wickham's character had not been so well known that no young woman would trust him. He generously

charged the whole to his mistaken pride. He confessed that he
had thought it beneath him to lay his private actions open to the
world; his own character was to speak for itself. He called it,
therefore, his duty to step forward and try to remedy an evil
which had been brought on by himself. If he *had another* motive, I am sure it would never disgrace him. He had been some
days in town before he was able to discover them. But he had
something to direct his search, which was more than *we* had, and
knowing this was another reason for his deciding to follow us
and take up the search. There is a Mrs. Younge, who was some
time ago governess to Miss Darcy and was dismissed for some
cause; he did not say what. This Mrs. Younge, he knew, was a
friend of Wickham's, and he went to her for news of him. But it
was two or three days before he could get from her what he
wanted. She would not betray her trust, I suppose, without brib-
ery, for she really did know where he was to be found.

In his first talk with Wickham he easily learned that he was
obliged to give up his commission and leave the regiment on
account of some gambling debts which were very pressing.
Wickham laid all the blame of Lydia's eloping on her own folly
alone.

He then saw Lydia, but she was determined to remain where
she was. She wanted no help of his; she would be married some
time or other, and it did not much matter when.

Wickham meant to give up his commission and go somewhere,
but he did not know where, and he knew he should have nothing
to live on. He was therefore in a position to be bought off. They
met several times; Wickham of course wanted more than he
could get, but at length agreed to be reasonable. Everything was
settled between *them*. Mr. Darcy's next step was to let your
uncle know of it, and he first called to see him on the very day I
came home. Your uncle and he had a great deal of talk together.
They met again next day, and it was not all settled before Monday. As soon as it was, the letter was sent off to Longbourn.

But Mr. Darcy was very stubborn. I fancy, Lizzy, that this is
the real defect of his character. Nothing was to be done that he

did not do himself, though your uncle would most willingly have settled the whole. They battled it together for a long time. But at last your uncle was forced to yield and put up with only having the credit of buying over Wickham, which went sorely against the grain. I really believe your letter this morning gave him great pleasure, because this explanation will relieve him of his borrowed feathers and give the praise where it is due. But, Lizzy, this must go no further than yourself, or Jane at most. You know pretty well, I suppose, what has been done for the young people. His debts are to be paid, amounting to much more than a thousand pounds, another thousand in addition to her own was to be settled upon *her*, and his commission purchased. But you may be sure that your uncle would never have yielded if we had not thought Mr. Darcy had *another interest* in the affair.

When all this was settled, he returned to Pemberley. But it was agreed that he should be in London once more when the wedding took place, and all money matters were then to receive the last finish. Lydia came to us. Mr. Darcy, as Lydia told you, was at the wedding. He dined with us the next day, and was to leave town again on Wednesday or Thursday. Will you be very angry with me, my dear Lizzy, if I say how much I like him? He lacks nothing but a little more liveliness, and *that*, if he marries *properly*, his wife may teach him. I thought him very sly; he hardly ever spoke your name. But slyness seems the fashion. Pray forgive me if I have said too much, or at least do not punish me so far as to exclude me from P. I shall never be quite happy till I have been all round the park. A low carriage with a nice little pair of ponies would be the very thing. But I must write no more. The children have been wanting me this half-hour.

Yours very sincerely,

M. Gardiner.

This letter threw Elizabeth into a flutter of spirits in which it was hard to know whether pleasure or pain bore the greatest share. He had followed them to town; he had taken on himself such a search. He had been reduced to meet, frequently meet, reason with, persuade, and finally bribe the man whom he always most wished to avoid, and whose very name was punishment for him to speak. Her heart did whisper that he had done it for her. But it was a hope shortly checked. For a woman who had already refused him! Brother-in-law of Wickham! Every kind of pride must revolt from the connection. He had done much. She was ashamed to think how much. But he had given a reason for it—he felt he had been wrong in not exposing Wickham's true character. Oh, how heartily she grieved over every saucy speech she had ever directed toward him. For herself, she was humbled; but she was proud of him. She read over her aunt's praise of him again and again. It was hardly enough, but it pleased her. She even felt some pleasure, though mixed with regret, in finding how steadfastly both her aunt and uncle had been led to believe that bonds of affection and confidence existed between Mr. Darcy and herself.

The day for Wickham and Lydia to leave soon came. Mrs. Bennet was forced to submit to the separation, as her husband by no means entered into her idea of their all going to Newcastle.

"My dear Lydia," she cried, "when shall we meet again?"

"Oh, Lord! I don't know. Not these two or three years, perhaps."

"Write to me very often, my dear."

"As often as I can. But you know married women never have much time for writing. My sisters may write to *me*. They will have nothing else to do."

Mr. Wickham smiled, looked handsome, and said many pretty things, in taking leave.

"He is as fine a fellow," said Mr. Bennet, as soon as they were out of the house, "as ever I saw. He simpers, and smirks, and makes love to us all. I am very proud of him. I defy even Sir William Lucas to produce a more valuable son-in-law."

The loss of her daughter made Mrs. Bennet very dull for several days. "I often think," she said, "that there is nothing so bad as parting with one's friends. One seems so forlorn without them."

"This is what happens when a daughter marries," said Elizabeth. "It must make you better satisfied that your other four are single."

"It is no such thing. Lydia does not leave me because she is married, but only because her husband's regiment happens to be so far off. If that had been nearer, she would not have gone so soon."

Chapter Forty-One

Mr. Bingley and Mr. Darcy Come Again to Netherfield

Mrs. Bennet's low spirits, brought on by Lydia's leaving, soon brightened. Her mind opened again to hope by news brought by Mrs. Philips. The housekeeper at Netherfield, Mrs. Nicholls, had had word that her master was coming down in a day or two, to shoot there for several weeks. Mrs. Bennet was quite in the fidgets. She looked at Jane, and smiled, and shook her head by turns.

"Well, well, and so Mr. Bingley is coming down, sister. So much the better. Not that I care about it, though. He is nothing to us, you know, and I am sure I never want to see him again. But he is welcome to come to Netherfield, if he likes it. And who knows what may happen? And so, is it quite certain he is coming?"

"You may depend on it," replied Mrs. Philips. "Mrs. Nicholls was in Meryton last night. I saw her passing by and went out on purpose to hear the truth of it. She told me that it was certainly true. He comes down on Thursday at the latest, very likely on Wednesday. She was going to the butcher's, she told me, to order some meat for Wednesday, and she has got three couple of ducks just fit to be killed."

Jane had not been able to hear of his coming without changing color. It was many months since she had mentioned his name to Elizabeth, but now as soon as they were alone together, she said:

"I saw you look at me, Lizzy, when my aunt told us the news, and I know I looked distressed. But I was only confused for the moment because I felt that I *should* be looked at. The news does not affect me either with pleasure or pain. I am glad of one thing, that he comes without his sisters, because we shall see the less of him. Not that I am afraid of *myself,* but I dread other people's remarks."

Elizabeth did not know what to make of the news. She still thought him partial to Jane, and she wondered whether he was bold enough to come there against Darcy's wishes. "Yet it is hard," she thought, "that this poor man cannot come to a house which he has legally rented without raising all this wonder! I *will* leave him to himself."

The subject which had been so warmly argued between Mr. and Mrs. Bennet about a year ago was now brought forward again.

"As soon as ever Mr. Bingley comes, my dear," said Mrs. Bennet to her husband, "you will visit him, of course."

"No, no. You forced me into visiting him last year and promised, if I went to see him, he should marry one of my daughters. But it ended in nothing, and I will not be sent on a fool's errand again. If he wants our society, he knows where we live. I will not spend *my* hours in running after my neighbors every time they go away and come back again."

"Well, all I know is that it will be very rude if you do not visit him. But, however, that shall not prevent my asking him to dine here. We must have Mrs. Long and the Gouldings soon. That will make thirteen with ourselves, so there will be just room at table for him."

As the day of his arrival drew near, Jane said to Elizabeth, "I begin to be sorry that he comes at all. It would be nothing, but I can hardly bear to hear it always talked of. My mother means well, but she does not know, no one can know how much I suffer from what she says. Happy shall I be when his stay at Netherfield is over!"

Mr. Bingley arrived. Mrs. Bennet, through the aid of servants, had the earliest tidings of it. She counted the days until the invitation to dinner could be sent, hopeless of seeing him before. But on the third morning after his arrival, she saw him from her window riding toward the house. She joyfully called the news to her daughters. Jane calmly kept her place at the table, but Elizabeth, to satisfy her mother, went to the window. She looked, she saw Mr. Darcy with him, and sat down again by her sister.

"There is a gentleman with him, mama," said Kitty. "Who can it be?"

"Some friend or other, my dear, I suppose. I am sure I do not know."

"La!" cried Kitty, "it looks just like that man that used to be with him before. Mr. what's-his-name. That tall, proud man."

"Good gracious! Mr. Darcy! And so it does, I vow. Well, any friend of Mr. Bingley's will always be welcome here, though I must say I hate the very sight of him."

Jane looked at Elizabeth with surprise. She knew but little of their meeting at Pemberley, and therefore felt sorry for the awkwardness which her sister must feel in seeing him almost for the first time after his letter to her. Elizabeth had not yet had the courage to show Mrs. Gardiner's letter to Jane, or to tell of her own change of feeling toward Darcy. To Jane, he could be only a man whom she had refused and whose merit she had undervalued. But to herself, he was the person to whom the whole family owed so much. The color which had been driven from her face returned with an added glow, and a smile of delight added luster to her eyes, as she thought that his affection must still be unshaken. But she would not be sure.

Jane looked a little paler than usual, but more sedate than

Elizabeth had expected. Her color deepened, yet she received the visitors with tolerable ease. Elizabeth said little to either and sat down again to her work. Darcy looked serious as usual and, she thought, more as he had been used to look when she first knew him than as she had seen him at Pemberley. But perhaps he could not in her mother's presence be what he was before her uncle and aunt. Bingley was looking both pleased and confused. He was welcomed by Mrs. Bennet with a warmth that made Elizabeth ashamed, especially when contrasted with the cold politeness of her manner to Darcy, who said scarcely anything. He was not seated by her; perhaps that was the reason for his silence. But it had not been so at Pemberley. There he had talked to her friends when he could not talk to herself. But now several minutes passed without bringing the sound of his voice, and he looked at Jane as often as at herself, and often at no object but the floor. He was more thoughtful and less anxious to please than when they last met. She was disappointed, and angry with herself for being so.

"Could I expect it to be otherwise!" she thought. "Yet why did he come?"

"It is a long time, Mr. Bingley, since you went away," said Mrs. Bennet.

He readily agreed to it.

"I began to be afraid you would never come back again. People *did* say you meant to quit the place entirely, but I hope it is not true. A great many changes have happened in the neighborhood since you went away. Miss Lucas is married and settled. And one of my own daughters. I suppose you have heard of it. Indeed, you must have seen it in the papers. It was in the *Times* and the *Courier,* I know; though it was not put in as it ought to be. It only said, 'Lately, George Wickham, Esq. to Miss Lydia Bennet.' Not a word of her father, or the place where she lived, or anything. It was my brother Gardiner's report, too, and I wonder how he came to make such a failure of it. Did you see it?"

Bingley replied that he did, and spoke his good wishes. Eliza-

beth dared not lift up her eyes. How Mr. Darcy looked, therefore, she could not tell.

"It is a delightful thing, to be sure, to have a daughter well
married," said Mrs. Bennet; "but at the same time, Mr. Bingley,
it is very hard to have her taken such a long way from me. They
are gone to Newcastle to stay I do not know how long. His regiment is there. Thank heaven he has *some* friends, though perhaps not so many as he deserves."

Elizabeth, who knew this to be levelled at Mr. Darcy, was in
such misery of shame that she could hardly keep her seat. Her
confusion drove her to speak; she asked Bingley whether he
meant to make any stay in the country at present. A few weeks,
he believed.

"When you have killed all your own birds, Mr. Bingley," said
Mrs. Bennet, "I beg you will come here and shoot as many as you
please on Mr. Bennet's manor. I am sure he will be happy to
have you and will save all the best of the coveys for you."

Elizabeth's misery increased at such excess of attention. Were
the same fair prospects to arise as had flattered them a year ago,
everything, she felt sure, would be hastening to the same vexing
failure. At this moment she felt that years of happiness could not
make Jane or herself amends for moments of such painful confusion. "The first wish of my heart," she said to herself, "is never
more to be in company with either of them. Let me never see
either one or the other again!"

Yet the misery, for which years of happiness could offer no
amends, soon afterwards received relief from seeing how the
beauty of Jane was rekindling the admiration of Bingley. When
he first came in, he had spoken to her very little, but every five
minutes seemed to be giving her more of his attention. He found
her as handsome as she had been last year, as good-natured and
as natural, though not quite so chatty. Jane was anxious that no
difference should appear in her, and believed that she talked as
much as ever, but her mind was so disturbed that she did not
always know when she was silent.

When the young men rose to go away, Mrs. Bennet invited them to dine at Longbourn. "You are quite a visit in my debt, Mr. Bingley," she added. "When you went to town last winter, you promised to take a family dinner with us as soon as you returned. I have not forgotten, you see. I was very much disappointed that you did not come back and keep your engagement."

Bingley looked a little silly at this and said something of having been prevented by business. They then went away.

Mrs. Bennet had been strongly inclined to ask them to stay and dine there, that day. But though she always kept a very good table, she did not think anything less than two courses could be good enough for a man upon whom she had such anxious designs, or would satisfy the appetite and pride of a man who had ten thousand a year.

As soon as they were gone, Elizabeth walked out to recover her spirits. Mr. Darcy's change of manner vexed her. "Why, if he came only to be silent and grave, did he come at all? He could be still pleasing to my uncle and aunt when he was in town. And why not to me? If he fears me, why come here? If he no longer cares for me, why silent? I will think no more about him."

Jane joined her with a cheerful look, which showed her better pleased with her visitors than Elizabeth. "Now that the first meeting is over," she said, "I feel perfectly easy. I am glad he dines here on Tuesday. It will then be publicly seen that on both sides we meet only as friends."

"Yes," said Elizabeth laughing. "Oh, Jane, take care."

"My dear Lizzy, you cannot think me so weak as to be in danger now."

"I think you are in very great danger of making him as much in love with you as ever."

Chapter Forty-Two

Jane Bennet Is Engaged

On Tuesday a large party gathered at Longbourn. When they passed to the dining-room, Elizabeth eagerly watched to see whether Bingley would take the place which in all their former parties had belonged to him, by the side of Jane. On entering the room, he paused doubtfully, but Jane happened to look round and happened to smile; it was decided. He placed himself by her. Elizabeth looked toward Darcy. He bore it with noble indifference, and she would have thought Bingley had Darcy's permission to be happy, had she not seen Bingley's eyes turn toward him with a look of half-laughing alarm.

Mr. Darcy was almost as far from her as the table could divide them. He was on one side of her mother. She could see how seldom they spoke to each other and how formal and cold was their manner whenever they did. She would at times have given anything to tell him that his kindness was not unknown and unfelt by the whole of the family. She had hopes that later in the evening she would have a chance to talk with him. But alas! the ladies crowded so close round the table where Jane was making tea and Elizabeth pouring out the coffee that there was not a single vacancy near her. Darcy had walked away to another part of the room. She followed him with her eyes, envied everyone to whom he spoke, had scarcely patience enough to help anybody to coffee, and was enraged against herself for being so silly! "A man who has once been refused!" she thought. "How could I ever be foolish enough to expect that any man would make a second proposal to the same woman!" She was a little revived, however, by his bringing back his coffee cup himself, and took the chance to say a few words. When she could think of nothing more to say, he stood by her for some minutes in silence, and at last walked away.

When the tea-things were removed and the cardtables placed, Elizabeth hoped to be joined by him. But he fell a victim to her mother's need for whist-players, and they were held for the evening at different tables.

"Well, girls," said Mrs. Bennet, as soon as they were left to themselves, "I think everything has passed off uncommonly well. The dinner was as well dressed as any I ever saw. The soup was fifty times better than what we had at the Lucases' last week. Even Mr. Darcy said the partridges were well done, and I suppose he has two or three French cooks at least. And, my dear Jane, I never saw you look lovelier. Mrs. Long said so too, for I asked her whether you did not. And what do you think she said besides? 'Ah! Mrs. Bennet, we shall have her at Netherfield at last.' She did indeed. I do think Mrs. Long is as good a creature as ever lived—and her nieces are very well behaved girls, and not at all handsome. I like them very much."

Mrs. Bennet, in short, was in very great spirits. She had seen enough of Bingley's behavior to Jane to feel sure that she would get him at last.

"It has been a very agreeable day," said Jane later, to Elizabeth. "You must not smile. I assure you that I have learned to enjoy him as an agreeable young man, without having a wish beyond it. I am perfectly satisfied from what his manners now are that he never had any idea of winning my affection. It is only that he is blessed with greater sweetness of manner and a stronger wish to please than any other man."

"You are very cruel," said Elizabeth. "You will not let me smile and you provoke me to it every moment."

"How hard it is in some cases to be believed!"

"And how impossible in others!"

A few days after this visit, Mr. Bingley called again, and alone. Darcy had left him that morning for London but was to return in ten days. He sat with them more than an hour and was in very good spirits. Mrs. Bennet invited him to dine with them. "Can you come tomorrow?" Yes, he had no engagement at all for tomorrow, and her invitation was accepted at once.

He came, and in such very good time that the ladies were none of them dressed. In ran Mrs. Bennet to her daughter's room, in her dressing gown and with her hair half-finished, crying out:

"My dear Jane, make haste and hurry down. He is come—Mr. Bingley is come. Make haste, make haste. Here, Sarah, come and help Miss Bennet on with her gown. Never mind Miss Lizzy's hair. Come, be quick, be quick! Where is your sash, my dear?"

But when her mother was gone, Jane would not go down without one of her sisters. The same anxiety to get them by themselves was visible again in the evening. After tea, Mr. Bennet went to the library, as was his custom, and Mary went upstairs to her music. Mrs. Bennet sat looking and winking at Elizabeth and Kitty. Elizabeth would not notice her; and when at last Kitty did, she very innocently said, "What is the matter mama? What do you keep winking at me for? What am I to do?"

"Nothing, child, nothing. I did not wink at you." She sat still five minutes longer, then suddenly got up and saying to Kitty, "Come here, my love, I want to speak to you," took her out of the room. Jane gave a look at Elizabeth which spoke her distress and her wish that *she* would not give in. Mrs. Bennet, in a few minutes, half-opened the door and called out:

"Lizzy, my dear, I want to speak with you," and Elizabeth was forced to go.

"We may as well leave them by themselves, you know," said her mother, as soon as she was in the hall. "Kitty and I are going upstairs to sit in my dressing-room."

Elizabeth made no attempt to reason with her mother but remained quietly in the hall till she and Kitty were out of sight, then returned into the drawing-room.

Bingley scarcely needed an invitation to stay to supper. And before he went away, an engagement was formed, chiefly through his own and Mrs. Bennet's means, for his coming next morning to shoot with her husband.

After this day, Jane said no more of her indifference. Not a word passed between the sisters concerning Bingley, but Elizabeth was happy in the belief that all must be speedily settled, unless Mr. Darcy returned early. And she had begun to feel that all this had taken place with that gentleman's approval.

Bingley and Mr. Bennet spent the morning together. Mr. Bennet was much more agreeable than Bingley expected. There was nothing in Bingley to provoke his scorn or disgust, and he was more talkative and less odd than Bingley had ever seen him. Bingley of course returned with him to dinner, and in the evening Mrs. Bennet was again at work to get everybody away from him and Jane. Elizabeth went into the breakfast-room to write a letter soon after tea. She thought, as all the others were going to sit down to cards, Jane would not need her to defeat her mother's schemes.

But on returning to the drawing-room when her letter was finished, Elizabeth saw, to her great surprise, that her mother had won. As she opened the door, she saw Jane and Bingley standing together over the hearth as if in earnest talk. The faces of both as they hastily turned round and moved away from each other told it all. Elizabeth was on the point of going away again, when Bingley whispered a few words to Jane and left the room.

Jane could keep nothing from Elizabeth that would give her pleasure. Embracing her, she declared with emotion that she was the happiest creature in the world. "It's too much," she added, "by far too much. I do not deserve it. Oh, why isn't everybody as happy!"

Elizabeth's warm delight could be only poorly expressed in words, but every sentence of kindness was a fresh source of happiness to Jane, who would not allow herself to stay with her sister or say half that remained to be said, for the present.

"I must go to my mother," she cried. "I would not wish her to hear it from anyone but myself. He is gone to my father already. Oh, Lizzy, how shall I bear so much happiness!"

She then hastened away to her mother, who had purposely broken up the card party and was sitting upstairs with Kitty.

In a few minutes Elizabeth was joined by Bingley, whose talk with her father had been short and to the point. "Where is your sister?" said he hastily, as she opened the door.

"With my mother upstairs. She will be down in a moment, I dare say."

He then shut the door and, coming up to her, claimed the good wishes and affection of a sister. They shook hands with great good will; and then until her sister came down, she listened to all he had to say of his own happiness, and of Jane's perfections.

It was an evening of delight to them all. Jane's happiness caused her to look handsomer than ever. Kitty simpered and smiled, and hoped her turn was coming soon. Mrs. Bennet could not give her consent in words warm enough to satisfy her feelings, though she talked to Bingley of nothing else for half an hour. And when Mr. Bennet joined them at supper, his voice and manner plainly showed how really happy he was. Not a word, however, passed his lips about it till Bingley was gone. Then he turned to Jane and said:

"Jane, I congratulate you. You will be a very happy woman."

Jane went to him immediately, kissed him, and thanked him for his goodness.

"You are a good girl, and I have great pleasure in thinking you will be so happily settled. I have not a doubt of your doing very well together. Your tempers are by no means unlike. You are each of you so yielding that nothing will ever be decided on, so easy that every servant will cheat you, and so generous that you will always exceed your income."

"Exceed their income! My dear Mr. Bennet," cried his wife, "what are you talking of? Why, he has four or five thousand a year, and very likely more." Then turning to her daughter, "Oh, my dear, dear Jane, I am so happy! I am sure I shall not get a wink of sleep all night." Wickham, Lydia, were all forgotten; Jane was now her favorite child.

Bingley was from this time of course a daily visitor at Longbourn, coming often before breakfast and always staying till after supper—unless some barbarous neighbor, who could not be enough detested, had given him an invitation to dinner which he could not refuse.

"He has made me so happy," said Jane one evening to Elizabeth, "by telling me that he did not know of my being in town last spring!"

"I thought as much," replied Elizabeth. "But how did he explain it?"

"It must have been his sisters' doing, which I cannot wonder at, since he might have married so much better in many ways. But when his sister sees that he is happy with me, we shall be on good terms again, though we can never be what we once were to each other."

"That is the most unforgiving speech I ever heard you utter. Good girl! It would vex me, indeed, to see you again the dupe of Caroline Bingley's pretended regard."

"Would you believe it, Lizzy, that when he went to town last November, he really loved me, but he thought I did not care for him! That is why he did not come again!"

"He made a little mistake, to be sure, but it is to the credit of his modesty."

Elizabeth was pleased to find that he had not betrayed the part Darcy had played, for, though Jane had the most forgiving heart in the world, it must prejudice her against him.

"I am certainly the most fortunate creature that ever lived!" cried Jane. "Oh, Lizzy, if I could but see *you* as happy! If only there *were* such another man for you!"

"Till I have your nature and goodness, I never can have your happiness. But if I have very good luck, I may meet with another Mr. Collins in time."

The affairs of the Longbourn family could not be long a secret. Mrs. Bennet was privileged to whisper the news of Jane's engagement to Mrs. Philips, and *she* ventured without any permission to do the same by all her neighbors in Meryton. The Bennets were speedily pronounced the luckiest family in the world, though only a few weeks before, when Lydia had first run away, they were generally declared to be marked out for misfortune.

Chapter Forty-Three

Lady Catherine de Bourgh Visits Elizabeth Bennet

One morning, about a week after Jane's engagement to Bingley, the family were sitting together in the drawing-room when a carriage and four came driving up the lawn. It was certain that somebody was coming, and Bingley at once begged Jane to avoid company by walking with him in the shrubbery.

When the door was thrown open, Lady Catherine de Bourgh entered. She wore an air more than usually ungracious, made no other reply to Elizabeth's greeting than a slight bow, and sat down without saying a word. Mrs. Bennet, all amazement, though flattered by having a guest of such high rank, received her with the utmost politeness.

Lady Catherine, after sitting for a moment in silence, said very stiffly, "You have a very small park here."

"It is nothing compared to Rosings, my lady," said Mrs. Bennet, "but it is much larger than Sir William Lucas's."

"This must be a most uncomfortable sitting-room for the evening, in summer; the windows are full west."

Mrs. Bennet assured her that they never sat there after dinner, and then added, "May I ask your ladyship whether you left Mr. and Mrs. Collins well?"

"Yes, very well. I saw them the night before last."

Mrs. Bennet begged her ladyship to take some refreshment, but Lady Catherine very firmly, and not very politely, refused. Then rising, she said to Elizabeth:

"Miss Bennet, there seemed to be a prettyish kind of little

wilderness on one side of your lawn. I should be glad to take a turn in it, if you will favor me with your company."

"Go, my dear," cried her mother, "and show her ladyship about the different walks. I think she will be pleased with them."

Elizabeth, after running into her own room for her parasol, led her noble guest through the hall. As they passed the dining-room door, Lady Catherine looked in and after a short view said it was a decent-looking room, and walked on. They went in silence along the gravel walk that led to the grove. Elizabeth would make no effort to speak with a woman who was now more than usually insolent and disagreeable. "How could I ever think her like her nephew?" she thought as she looked in her face.

As soon as they entered the grove, Lady Catherine began in the following manner:—

"You can be at no loss, Miss Bennet, to know the reason of my journey here."

Elizabeth looked with sincere surprise. "Indeed, you are mistaken, madam. I have not been at all able to account for the honor of seeing you here."

"Miss Bennet," replied her ladyship in an angry tone, "you ought to know that I am not to be trifled with. However insincere *you* may choose to be, you shall not find *me* so. I am known for being sincere and frank, and in a cause such as this, I shall certainly be so. A most alarming report reached me two days ago. I was told that your sister was on the point of making a very wealthy match, and that *you*, Miss Elizabeth Bennet, would be likely to wed my nephew, my own nephew, Mr. Darcy. I would not injure him so much as to believe the report, but I set off at once for this place that I might make my feelings known to you."

"If you believed the report false," said Elizabeth, coloring with anger, "why did you take the trouble of coming so far?"

"I came to insist upon having such a report denied."

"Your coming to Longbourn to see me and my family," said Elizabeth coolly, "will be rather like a proof of it, if, indeed, there is such a report."

"If! Do you then pretend not to know of it? Has it not been started by yourselves? Do you not know that such a report is spread abroad?"

"I never heard that it was."

"And can you declare that there is no *foundation* for it?"

"I do not pretend to be as frank as your ladyship. *You* may ask questions which *I* shall not choose to answer."

"This is not to be borne. Miss Bennet, I insist on being answered. Has he, has my nephew, made you an offer of marriage?"

"Your ladyship has declared it to be impossible."

"It ought to be so; it must be so, while he has the use of his reason. But *your* arts may, in a moment of weakness, have made him forget what he owes to himself and to all his family. You may have drawn him in."

"If I have, I shall be the last person to confess it."

"Miss Bennet, do you know who I am? I have not been used to such language as this. I am almost the nearest relation he has in the world, and am entitled to know all that concerns him."

"But you are not entitled to know all that concerns *me*."

"Let me be clearly understood. This match for which you dare to hope can never take place. No, never. Mr. Darcy is engaged to *my daughter*. Now, what have you to say?"

"Only this; that if he is, you can have no reason to think he will make an offer to me."

Lady Catherine hesitated for a moment and then replied:

"The engagement between them is of an unusual kind. From their infancy they have been intended for each other. It was the wish of *his* mother as well as of hers. While they were in their cradles, we planned the union. And now, to have it prevented by a young woman of inferior birth, of no rank in the world, and wholly unconnected with the family! Are you lost to every feeling of what is proper? Have you not heard me say that from his childhood he was intended for his cousin?"

"Yes, and I had heard it before. But what is that to me? If there is no other objection to my marrying your nephew, I shall certainly not be kept from it by knowing that his mother and aunt wished him to marry Miss de Bourgh. You both did as much as you could, in planning the marriage. Its outcome depended on others. If Mr. Darcy is not bound by honor or desire to his cousin, why may he not make another choice? And if I am that choice, why may I not accept him?"

"Because honor, and a sense of what is right and proper forbid it, as well as your own interest. Yes, Miss Bennet, your own interest; for do not expect to be noticed by his family or friends if you wilfully act against the wishes of all. You will be blamed, slighted, and despised by everyone connected with him. Your name will never even be mentioned by any of us."

"These are heavy misfortunes," replied Elizabeth, "but the wife of Mr. Darcy would have a station which, upon the whole, would enable her to hold up under them."

"Obstinate, headstrong girl! I am ashamed of you! Is this your thanks for my attentions to you last spring? Is nothing due to me on that score? Let us sit down. You are to understand, Miss Bennet, that I came here to carry out my purpose, and I will not be turned from it. I have not been used to bend to any person's whims."

"*That* will make your ladyship's disappointment the greater, but it will have no effect on *me*."

"I will not be interrupted! Hear me in silence. My daughter and my nephew are formed for each other. They come of the same noble line. Their fortunes are each splendid. That they are to be united is the voice of every member of their two houses. And what is to divide them? An upstart young woman without family or fortune. This must not, shall not be! If you know your own good, you would not wish to quit the rank in which you have been brought up."

"In marrying your nephew, I should not be quitting that rank. He is a gentleman; I am a gentleman's daughter; so far we are equal."

"True. You *are* a gentleman's daughter. But who was your mother? Who are your uncles and aunts?"

"If your nephew does not object to them, they can be nothing to *you*."

"Tell me once for all, are you engaged to him?"

Though Elizabeth would not have answered the question to merely please Lady Catherine, she could not but say, after a moment's thought, "I am not."

Lady Catherine seemed pleased. "And will you promise me never to enter into such an engagement?"

"I will make no promise of the kind."

"Miss Bennet, I am shocked and astonished. I expected to find a more reasonable young woman. I shall not go away till you have given me your promise."

"And I certainly *never* shall give it. How far your nephew might approve of your entering into *his* affairs I cannot tell. But you have certainly no right to concern yourself with mine. I must beg you, therefore, to say no more of this."

"Not so hasty, if you please. I have by no means done. I have still another objection to add. I am no stranger to your youngest sister's elopement. I know it all; that the young man's marrying her was a patched-up business at the expense of your father and uncle. And is *such* a girl to be my nephew's sister? Is *her* husband—is the son of his father's steward to be his brother-in-law? Heaven and earth! What are you thinking of? Are the shades of Pemberley to be thus polluted?"

"You can *now* have nothing further to say. You have insulted me in every possible way. I must return to the house."

And she rose as she spoke. Lady Catherine rose also, and they turned back. Her ladyship was very angry.

"You have no regard, then, for the honor and credit of my nephew! Unfeeling, selfish girl! Do you not know that marriage with you must disgrace him in the eyes of everybody?"

"Lady Catherine, I have nothing further to say."

"You are, then, bent on marrying him?"

"I have said no such thing. But I shall take such steps as will in my own opinion lead toward my happiness, without reference to *you* or to any person so wholly unconnected with me."

"Very well. I shall now know how to act. Do not think, Miss Bennet, that you will ever marry my nephew. I came to try you. I hoped to find you reasonable, but depend upon it I will carry my point."

In this manner Lady Catherine talked on until they were at the door of the carriage, when turning round, she added, "I take no leave of you, Miss Bennet. You do not deserve such attention. I am greatly displeased."

Elizabeth made no answer, and without asking her ladyship to return into the house, walked quietly into it herself. She heard the carriage drive away as she went upstairs. Her mother met her at the door of her room to ask why Lady Catherine would not come in again and rest herself.

"She did not wish to," said her daughter; "she would go."

"She is a very fine looking woman! She only came, I suppose, to tell us the Collinses were well. She is on her road somewhere, I dare say, and so, passing through Meryton, thought she might as well call on you. Her doing so was very kind. I suppose she had nothing particular to say to you, Lizzy?"

Elizabeth was forced to give into a little falsehood here, for to tell what she had really come for was impossible.

Chapter Forty-Four

Mr. Collins Writes a Letter of Warning

For many hours Elizabeth thought of nothing but this visit. Lady Catherine had actually taken the trouble of this journey from Rosings for the sole purpose of breaking off her supposed engagement with Mr. Darcy! What started the report of their engagement she could not imagine, till she thought that *his* being the friend of Bingley and *her* being the sister of Jane was enough to supply the idea. The Lucases would have reported to Charlotte Collins the engagement of Jane and Bingley.

If Darcy had been wavering before as to what he should do, which had often seemed likely, the advice of Lady Catherine might settle every doubt. In that case, he would return to Netherfield no more. Lady Catherine might see him on her way through town.

"If an excuse comes to Bingley for his not returning to Netherfield," she thought, "I shall know how to understand it. And I shall soon cease to regret him at all."

The next morning, as she was going downstairs, she was met by her father, who came out of his library with a letter in his hand. "Lizzy," he said, "I was going to look for you. Come into my room."

As she followed him, it suddenly struck her that the letter might be from Lady Catherine. She followed her father to the fireplace, and they both sat down. He then said:

"I have received this letter this morning that has surprised me greatly. As it concerns you, you ought to know of it. I did not know before that I had *two* daughters on the brink of matrimony. Let me congratulate you on a very important conquest."

The color now rushed into Elizabeth's cheeks in the belief that the letter was from the nephew instead of the aunt.

"You look knowing. Young ladies are very keen in such matters as these, but I think not even *you* could guess the name of your admirer. This letter is from Mr. Collins."

"From Mr. Collins! What can *he* have to say?"

"Something very much to the purpose, of course. He begins with good wishes for the coming marriage of Jane, of which it seems he has been told by some of the good-natured, gossiping Lucases. What concerns you is as follows:

" 'Your daughter Elizabeth, I hear, has chosen as partner of her fate, one of the most illustrious persons in this land—'

"Can you possibly guess, Lizzy, who is meant by this? But let me go on:

" 'This young gentleman is blessed with everything the heart of mortal can desire—splendid property, noble kindred. Yet in spite of all this, let me warn my cousin Elizabeth and yourself of what evils you may bring on by accepting this gentleman's proposals, which, of course, you will be inclined to do at once—'

"Have you any idea, Lizzy, who this gentleman is? But now it comes out:

"'We have reason to think that his aunt, Lady Catherine de Bourgh, does not look on the match with a friendly eye—'

"*Mr. Darcy,* you see, is the man! Now, Lizzy, I think I *have* surprised you. Could he or the Lucases have pitched on a more unlikely man? Mr. Darcy probably never looked at you in his life!"

Elizabeth could only force a faint smile. "Pray read on."

"That is enough. Much of the rest of his letter is about his dear Charlotte's situation and his expectation of a young olive-branch. But, Lizzy, you look as if you did not enjoy the gossip."

"Oh!" cried Elizabeth, "it is so strange!"

"Yes, *that* is what makes it amusing. Had they fixed on any other man it would have been nothing. But *his* perfect indifference, and *your* dislike make it very amusing. And, Lizzy, what did Lady Catherine say about this report? Did she call to refuse her consent?"

Elizabeth replied only with a laugh, and as he had asked the question without the least thought, he did not repeat it.

Never had she been more at a loss to make her feelings appear what they were not. She must laugh when she would rather have cried. Her father had most cruelly hurt her by what he said of Mr. Darcy's indifference. She wondered at his lack of insight, then feared that perhaps instead of his seeing too *little*, she had fancied too *much*.

Chapter Forty-Five

A Very Different Proposal from Mr. Darcy

But Mr. Bingley was able to bring Darcy with him to Longbourn before many days had passed after Lady Catherine's visit. They arrived early, and before Mrs. Bennet had time to tell Mr. Darcy of having seen his aunt (of which Elizabeth sat in dread), Bingley, who wanted to be alone with Jane, proposed their all walking out. It was agreed to. Mrs. Bennet was not in the habit of walking. Mary could never spare time, but the remaining five set off together. Bingley and Jane soon lagged behind, while Elizabeth, Kitty, and Darcy went on together. Very little was said; Kitty was too much afraid of him to talk. Elizabeth was thinking of what she had hoped to have courage to say to him, and perhaps he might be doing the same.

They walked toward the Lucases, because Kitty wished to call upon Maria. When Kitty left them, and while her courage was high, Elizabeth said:

"Mr. Darcy, I am a very selfish creature, and for the sake of giving relief to my own feelings, care not how much I may be wounding yours. I can no longer help thanking you for your kindness to my poor sister. Ever since I have known it, I have been most anxious to tell you how grateful I am. If it were known to the rest of my family, I should have more than my own thanks to speak."

"I am sorry, very sorry," replied Darcy in a tone of surprise and emotion, "that you have ever been told of what may, in a mistaken light, have given you uneasiness. I did not think Mrs. Gardiner was so little to be trusted."

"You must not blame my aunt. Lydia first mentioned that you

had been at the wedding. And of course I could not rest till I knew all. Let me thank you again and again, in the name of all my family, for all you did."

"If you *will* thank me," he replied, "let it be for yourself alone. Your *family* owe me nothing. I believe I thought only of *you*." After a short pause, he added, "You are too generous to trifle with me. If your feelings are still what they were last April, tell me so at once. *My* affections and wishes are unchanged. But one word from you will silence me on this subject forever."

Elizabeth, feeling all the more-than-common awkwardness and anxiety of his situation, at once gave him to understand that her feelings were so changed as to make her hear him with gratitude and pleasure. Had Elizabeth been able to meet his eyes, she might have seen how well the look of heart-felt delight, which spread over his face, became him. He spoke then as warmly as a man violently in love can be supposed to do. She soon learned that they owed their present good understanding to his aunt, who *did* call on him in her return through London. She had told him of her journey to Longbourn, of her talk with Elizabeth, and that she had refused to promise not to marry him. But unluckily for her ladyship, her story had an effect contrary to her wishes.

"It taught me to hope, as I had scarcely dared to hope before," he said. "I knew you well enough to be certain that had you been decided against me, you would have said so to Lady Catherine, frankly and openly."

Elizabeth colored and laughed as she replied, "Yes, you know enough of my *frankness* to believe me capable of *that*. After abusing you so to your face, I would not mind abusing you to all your relations."

"What did you say of me that I did not deserve? My behavior to you was unpardonable. I cannot think of it without horror."

"We will not quarrel for the greater share of blame," said Elizabeth. "Since then, we have both, I hope, improved in manners."

"I cannot so easily forgive myself. To think of what I then said is, even now, after many months, very painful to me. But it was some time, I confess, before I was willing to allow your words their justice. You thought me lacking in every proper feeling, I am sure you did. For you said that I could not have made an offer of my hand in any way that would induce you to accept me."

"Oh! do not repeat what I then said. This will not do at all. I have long been most heartily ashamed of it."

Darcy mentioned his letter. "Did it," he said, "did it *soon* make you think better of me? Did you on reading it believe me at once?"

She explained what its effect on her had been, and how gradually all her former prejudices had been removed.

"I knew," he said, "that what I wrote must give you pain, but it was necessary. I hope you have destroyed the letter. There was one part which I should dread to have you read again. It might justly make you hate me."

"The letter shall certainly be burnt if you believe it could alter my regard. But, though we have reason to know that my opinions of you can change, they are not quite so easily changed as that."

"When I wrote that letter," said Darcy, "I believed myself perfectly calm and cool, but I now know that I wrote it in a dreadful bitterness of spirit."

"The letter perhaps began in bitterness, but it did not end so. But think no more of the letter. Our feelings are now so widely different from what they were then that it ought to be forgotten."

"I have been a selfish being all my life, in practice though not in principle. As a child I was taught what was *right* but not taught to correct my temper. I was given good principles but left to follow them in pride and conceit. Unfortunately (for many years an only child) I was spoiled by my parents. I was selfish, overbearing, cared for none beyond my own family circle, and thought—or wished to think—meanly of all the rest of the world. Such I was from eight to twenty-eight. And such I might still have been but for you, dearest Elizabeth! You taught me a hard lesson. By you I was properly humbled."

"How you must have hated me after *that* evening!"

"Hate you! I was angry, perhaps, at first, but my anger soon began to take a proper direction, against myself."

"I am almost afraid of asking what you thought of me when we met at Pemberley. You blamed me for coming?"

"No, indeed, I felt nothing but surprise."

"Your surprise could not be greater than *mine* in being noticed by you. I knew I deserved no unusual politeness and I did not expect to receive *more* than my due."

"My object *then*," replied Darcy, "was to show you by every courtesy in my power that I was not so mean as to resent the past. I hoped to gain your forgiveness, to lessen your ill-opinion, by letting you see that you had taught me a lesson. How soon any other wishes arose, I can hardly tell, but I believe in about half an hour after I had seen you."

He then told her of Georgiana's delight in knowing her, and of her disappointment when she left Lambton so suddenly. She soon learned that he had decided to go to London to look for her sister before he had left her at the inn, and that his gravity and thoughtfulness there had been expressions of concern with his purpose.

After walking several miles in a leisurely manner and too busy to know anything about it, they found at last, on looking at their watches, that it was time to be at home.

"What could have become of Bingley and Jane!" was a wonder which started them to speaking of that couple. Darcy was delighted with their engagement, which he had heard almost at once from Bingley himself.

"Were you surprised?" said Elizabeth.

"Not at all. When I went away, I felt that it would soon happen."

"That is to say you had given your permission. I guessed as much." And though he exclaimed at the word "permission," she found that it had been pretty much the case.

"On the evening before going to London," he said, "I made a confession to him. I told him of all that I had done to separate them. His surprise was great. I told him, too, that I believed I had been mistaken in supposing that Jane did not care for him. It was plain that he was still attached to her. I felt no doubt of their happiness together."

Elizabeth could not help smiling at his easy manner of directing his friend. She longed to remark that Mr. Bingley had been a most delightful friend, so easily guided, but she checked herself. She remembered that he had yet to learn to be laughed at, and it was rather too early to begin. He continued to speak of the happiness of Bingley, which was, of course, to be inferior only to his own, till they reached the house. In the hall they parted.

Chapter Forty-Six

Mrs. Bennet's Cup of Happiness Overflows

"My dear Lizzy, where can you have been walking to?" was a question which Elizabeth had from Jane as soon as she entered the room, and from all the others when they sat down to table. She could only say in reply that they had wandered about until she was almost lost. She colored as she spoke, but neither that, nor anything else, awoke a thought of the truth.

The evening passed quietly. The known lovers talked and laughed; the unknown were silent. Darcy was not one in whom happiness overflows in mirth, and Elizabeth rather *knew* she was happy than *felt* herself to be. There were troubles before her. She knew that no one liked him but Jane, and even feared that with the others it was a *dislike* which not all his fortune and rank might do away. At night she opened her heart to Jane. Though trustfulness was Jane's general habit, she was completely disbelieving in this case.

"You are joking, Lizzy. This cannot be! Engaged to Mr. Darcy! No, no, you shall not deceive me. It is impossible."

"This is a wretched beginning indeed! My sole dependence was on you. I am sure nobody else will believe me, if you do not. Yet indeed I am in earnest. I speak nothing but the truth. He still loves me, and we are engaged."

Jane looked at her doubtingly. "Oh, Lizzy! it cannot be. I know how much you dislike him."

"You know nothing of the matter. *That* is all to be forgotten. Perhaps I did not always love him so well as I do now. But this is the last time I shall ever remember it."

Jane still looked all amazement. Elizabeth again and more seriously assured her of its truth.

"Good heaven! can it be really so! Yet now I must believe you," cried Jane. "My dear, dear Lizzy, I would—I do wish you joy—but are you certain? Forgive the question—are you quite certain that you can be happy with him?"

"There can be no doubt of that. It is settled between us already that we are to be the happiest couple in the world. But are you pleased, Jane? Shall you like to have such a brother?"

"Very, very much. Nothing could give either Bingley or myself more delight. But we talked of it as impossible. And do you really love him quite well enough? Oh, Lizzy! do anything rather than marry without affection. Are you quite sure you feel what you ought to do?"

"Oh, yes! You will only think I feel *more* than I ought when I tell you all."

"What do you mean?"

"Why, I must confess that I love him better than I do Bingley. I am afraid you will be angry."

"Now *be* serious, my dearest sister. I want to talk very seriously. Let me know everything that I am to know at once. Will you tell me how long you have loved him?"

"It has been coming on so gradually that I hardly know when it began. But I believe I must date it from my first seeing his beautiful grounds at Pemberley."

Jane again begged that she would be serious, and she soon

satisfied Jane by a solemn assurance of her real devotion. Once finally convinced on that point, Jane had nothing more to wish.

"Now I am entirely happy," said Jane, "for you will be as happy as myself. As Bingley's friend and your husband, there can be only Bingley and yourself more dear to me! But, Lizzy, you have been very sly with me. How little did you tell me of what passed at Pemberley and Lambton! Everything I know I learned from another, not from you."

Elizabeth explained the reasons for her secrecy. She had been unwilling to mention Bingley, and the unsettled state of her own feelings had made her avoid naming Darcy. But now she would no longer conceal from Jane his share in Lydia's marriage. All was told, and half the night was spent in talk.

"Good gracious!" cried Mrs. Bennet as she stood at a window the next morning, "if that disagreeable Mr. Darcy is not coming here again with our dear Bingley! What can he mean, to be always coming here to disturb us with his company? What shall we do with him? Lizzy, you must walk out with him again, that he may not be in Bingley's way."

Elizabeth could hardly help laughing at such a lucky proposal, yet she was really vexed that her mother should always speak of him as disagreeable.

As soon as they entered, Bingley looked at her so meaningly and shook hands with such warmth as left no doubt that he had been told the good news. And he soon afterwards said, "Mrs. Bennet, have you no more lanes hereabouts in which Lizzy may lose her way again today?"

"I advise Mr. Darcy and Lizzy and Kitty," said Mrs. Bennet, "to walk to Oakham Mount this morning. It is a nice long walk, and Mr. Darcy has never seen the view."

"It may do very well for the others," replied Mr. Bingley, "but I am sure it will be too much for Kitty. Won't it, Kitty?"

Kitty owned that she had rather stay at home. Darcy professed a great desire to see the view from the Mount, and Elizabeth silently agreed to go. As she went upstairs to get ready, Mrs. Bennet said:

"I am sorry, Lizzy, that you should be forced to have that disagreeable man all to yourself. But I hope you will not mind it. It is all for Jane's sake, you know, and there is no need to talk to him, except just now and then. So do not put yourself out."

During their walk, it was decided that Mr. Bennet should be told, and his consent asked, in the course of the evening. Elizabeth kept to herself the duty of telling her mother. She could not be sure how her mother would take it, sometimes doubting whether all his wealth and rank would be enough to overcome her dislike. And she could not bear that Mr. Darcy should hear the first raptures of her joy, if she were delighted with the match.

In the evening, soon after Mr. Bennet withdrew to the library, she saw Mr. Darcy rise and follow him, and her emotion on seeing it was extreme. She did not fear her father's objection, but he was going to be made unhappy and *she,* his favorite daughter, would be distressing him by her choice. She sat in misery till Mr. Darcy appeared again, when, looking at him, she was a little relieved by his smile. In a few minutes he came to the table where she was sitting with Kitty, and said in a whisper, "Go to your father; he wants you in the library." She was gone directly.

Her father was walking about the room, looking grave and anxious. "Lizzy," he said, "what are you doing? Are you out of your senses to be accepting this man? Have you not always hated him? He is rich, to be sure, and you may have more fine clothes and fine carriages than Jane. But will they make you happy?"

"Have you any other objection," said Elizabeth, "than your belief that I do not care for him?"

"None at all. We all know him to be a proud, unpleasant sort of man. But this would be nothing if you really liked him."

"I do, I do like him," she replied with tears in her eyes. "I love him. Indeed he has no improper pride. He is very amiable. You do not know what he really is; do not pain me by speaking of him so."

"Lizzy," said her father, "I have given him my consent. He is the kind of man, indeed, to whom I should never dare refuse anything he cared to ask. I now give it to *you* if you are bent on having him. But let me advise you to think better of it. I know you, Lizzy. I know that you could not be happy unless you truly esteemed your husband. My child, let me not have the grief of seeing *you* unable to respect your partner in life. You do not know what you are about."

Elizabeth was earnest and solemn in her reply that Mr. Darcy was really her choice. By explaining the gradual change which her opinion of him had undergone, relating her certainty that his affection was not the work of a day, but had stood the test of many months, she did overcome her father's objection to the match. She named with energy all his good qualities, and when she ceased speaking, he said:

"Well, my dear, I have no more to say. If this be the case, he deserves you. I could not have parted with you, my Lizzy, to anyone less worthy."

To complete the good opinion, she then told him what Mr. Darcy had voluntarily done for Lydia. He heard her with amazement.

"This is an evening of wonders, indeed! And so Darcy did everything, made up the match, gave the money, paid the fellow's debts, and got him his commission! So much the better. It will save me a world of trouble and economy. Had it been your uncle's doing, I must and *would* have paid him. But these violent young lovers carry everything their own way. I shall offer to pay him tomorrow; he will rant and storm about his love for you, and there will be an end of the matter."

He then recalled her confusion a few days before when he read to her Mr. Collins's letter. After laughing at her, he allowed her to go—saying, as she left the room, "If any young men come for Mary or Kitty, send them in, for I am quite at leisure."

Elizabeth's mind was now relieved from a very heavy weight. Though everything was too recent for gaiety, the evening passed happily away. There was no longer anything to be dreaded, and the comfort of ease would come in time.

When her mother went up to her dressing-room at night, she followed her and told the great news. On first hearing it, Mrs.

Bennet sat quite still, unable to utter a word. She began at length to recover, to fidget about in her chair, get up, sit down again, wonder, and bless herself.

"Good gracious! Lord bless me! Only think—dear me! Mr. Darcy! Who would have thought it! And is it really true? Oh! my sweetest Lizzy! how rich and how great you will be! What pin-money, what jewels, what carriages you will have! Jane's is nothing to it—nothing at all. I am so pleased—so happy! Such a charming man! so handsome! so tall! Oh, my dear Lizzy! pray apologize for my having disliked him so much before. I hope he will overlook it. Dear, dear Lizzy! A house in town! Everything that is charming! Three daughters married! Ten thousand a year! Oh, Lord! What will become of me? I shall go distracted."

This was enough to show that she approved; and Elizabeth, rejoicing that such an outbreak was heard only by herself, soon went away. But before she had been three minutes in her own room, her mother followed her.

"My dearest child," she cried, "I can think of nothing else! Ten thousand a year, and very likely more! 'Tis as good as a lord! But my dearest love, tell me what dish Mr. Darcy is particularly fond of, that I may have it tomorrow."

This was a sad omen of what her mother's behavior toward him might be. But the morrow passed off much better than she expected, for Mrs. Bennet luckily stood in such awe of her intended son-in-law that she did not venture to speak to him, except to offer him some attention or to defer to his opinion.

Elizabeth had the pleasure of seeing her father taking pains to get to know him, and he soon assured her that Mr. Darcy was rising every hour in his esteem. "I admire all my three sons-in-law highly," said he. "Wickham, perhaps, is my favorite, but I shall like *your* husband quite as well as Jane's."

Chapter Forty-Seven

A Happy Ending

Elizabeth's spirits soon rising to playfulness again, she wanted Mr. Darcy to account for his ever having fallen in love with her. "How could you begin?" she said. "I can understand your going on well enough, when you had once made a beginning, but what set you off in the first place?"

"I cannot fix on the hour, or the spot, or the look, or the words, which laid the foundation. It is too long ago. I was in the middle before I knew that I *had* begun."

"My manners—my behavior to *you* was at least always bordering on the uncivil. I never spoke to you without rather wishing to give you pain. Now be sincere; did you admire me for my impertinence?"

"For the liveliness of your mind I did."

"You may as well call it impertinence at once. It was very little less. The fact is that you were sick of women who were always speaking and looking and thinking for *your* approval alone. I roused and interested you because I was so unlike *them.* There —I have saved you the trouble of accounting for it. And really I begin to think it perfectly reasonable. To be sure, you knew no actual good of me—but nobody thinks of *that* when they fall in love. But what made you so unwilling to come to the point at last? What made you so shy of me when you first called and afterwards dined here? Why, when you called, did you look as if you did not care about me?"

"Because you were grave and silent, and gave me no encouragement."

"But I was embarrassed."

"And so was I."

"You might have talked to me more when you came to dinner."

"A man who had felt less might."

"But tell me, what did you come down to Netherfield for? Was it merely to ride to Longbourn and be embarrassed, or had you intended anything more serious?"

"My purpose was to see *you* and to judge, if I could, whether I might ever hope to make you love me."

"Shall you ever have courage to tell Lady Catherine what is to befall her?"

"I am more likely to want time than courage, Elizabeth. But it ought to be done, and if you will give me a sheet of paper, it shall be done at once."

"And I have an aunt, too, who must not be longer neglected." She was almost ashamed to find that her uncle and aunt Gardiner had already lost three days of happiness, and she at once sat down and wrote:

I would have thanked you before, my dear aunt, as I ought to have done, for your long, kind letter of explanation; but to say the truth, I was too cross to write. You supposed more than really existed. But *now* suppose as much as you choose; indulge your imagination in every possible flight, and unless you believe me actually married, you cannot greatly err. You must write again very soon, and praise him a great deal more than you did in your last letter. I thank you, again and again, for not going to the Lakes. How could I have been so silly as to wish it! Your idea of the ponies is delightful. We will go round the park every day. I am the happiest creature in the world. Perhaps other people have said so before, but not one with such justice. I am happier even than Jane; she only smiles, I laugh. Mr. Darcy sends you all the love in the world that he can spare from me. You are all to come to Pemberley at Christmas. Yours, etc.

Still another letter was written. It was from the pen of Mr. Bennet and was sent to Mr. Collins, in reply to his last:

Dear sir,

I must trouble you once more for congratulations. Elizabeth will soon be the wife of Mr. Darcy. Console Lady Catherine as well as you can. But, if I were you, I would stand by the nephew. He has more to give. Yours sincerely, etc.

Before an answer could arrive from Mr. Collins or any good wishes to Elizabeth from Charlotte, the Collinses were themselves at Lucas Lodge. Lady Catherine had been made so angry by her nephew's letter that Charlotte, really rejoicing in the match, wished to get away till the storm blew over. The arrival of Charlotte was a sincere pleasure to Elizabeth, though in the course of their meetings she must sometimes think the pleasure dearly bought when she saw Mr. Darcy exposed to all the parading civility of Mr. Collins. He bore it, however, with calmness. He could even listen to Sir William Lucas's long, stilted speeches. If he did shrug his shoulders, it was not till Sir William was out of sight.

Mrs. Philips was another tax on his forbearance. Though she, like Mrs. Bennet, stood in too much awe of him to speak freely, yet whenever she *did* speak, she must be vulgar. Elizabeth did all she could to shield him from the notice of either. And the uncomfortable feelings arising from all this took from the season of courtship much of its pleasure.

Caroline Bingley's letter to her brother on his coming marriage was all affection and all insincere. She wrote even to Jane to express her delight and repeat all her former words of regard. Jane was not deceived, and though feeling no reliance on her, wrote her a much kinder answer than she knew she deserved.

The joy of Georgiana Darcy on receiving news of her brother's coming marriage was so sincere that four sides of paper were not enough to contain all her delight and all her earnest desire of being loved by her sister.

Happy for Mrs. Bennet was the day on which she got rid of her two most deserving daughters. With what delighted pride

she afterward visited Mrs. Bingley, and talked of Mrs. Darcy, may be guessed. I wish I could say, for the sake of her family, that her happiness turned her into a sensible, good-humored, well-informed woman for the rest of her life. But she was still often nervous and always silly.

Mr. Bennet missed his second daughter greatly. A visit to her drew him oftener from home than anything else could do. He delighted in going to Pemberley, especially when he was least expected.

Mr. Bingley and Jane remained at Netherfield only twelve months. The nearness to her mother and Meryton relations was not desirable even to *his* easy temper or *her* affectionate heart. He bought an estate within thirty miles of Pemberley, and Jane and Elizabeth, in addition to every other source of happiness, had the joy of living near each other.

Kitty, to her great advantage, spent most of her time with her two elder sisters. Her improvement was great, and she was kept removed from Lydia's society. Though Mrs. Wickham often invited her to come and stay with her, with the promise of balls and young men, her father would never consent to her going.

Mary, the only daughter left at home, was obliged to mix more with the world, but she could still moralize over every morning visit. And as she no longer suffered by comparison between her sisters' beauty and her own, it was believed by her father that she was pleased with the change.

As for Wickham and Lydia, their characters did not change. They were always moving from place to place, and always spending more than they ought. Whenever they changed their quarters either Jane or Elizabeth was sure to be asked for some little help toward paying their bills. And in spite of everything, Wickham was never wholly without hope that Darcy might yet be persuaded to make his fortune. Though Darcy could never receive *him* at Pemberley, yet for Elizabeth's sake he assisted him farther in his profession. Lydia was sometimes a visitor there when her husband was gone to enjoy himself in London or Bath. With the Bingleys they both often stayed so long that even Bingley's good humor was overcome, and he went so far as to *talk* of giving them a hint to be gone.

Caroline Bingley was very deeply mortified by Darcy's marriage. But as she wished to keep the right to visit at Pemberley, she forgot all her anger, was fonder than ever of Georgiana, almost as attentive to Darcy as before, and very civil to Elizabeth.

Pemberley was now Georgiana's home, and the attachment of the sisters became exactly what Darcy had hoped to see. Georgiana had the highest opinion in the world of Elizabeth, though at first she often listened with surprise bordering on alarm at her lively, sportive manner of talking to Darcy. She began to see that a woman may take liberties with a husband which a brother will not allow in a sister more than ten years younger than himself.

Lady Catherine was so indignant on the marriage of her nephew that she gave way to all the genuine frankness of her nature. She sent him a letter so very abusive, especially of Elizabeth, that for some time all communication between them was at an end. But at length, by Elizabeth's persuasion, he agreed to overlook the offence. And after a little further resistance, Lady Catherine gave way and consented to visit them at Pemberley, in spite of that pollution which its woods had received, both from the presence of such a mistress and the visits of her uncle and aunt from the city.

With the Gardiners, they were always on the most intimate terms. Darcy, as well as Elizabeth, really loved them, and felt the warmest gratitude for the part they played in bringing them together.